Gone
Too
Soon

Dani Atkins

Gone Too Soon

bookouture

Published by Bookouture in 2021

An imprint of Storyfire Ltd.
Carmelite House
50 Victoria Embankment
London EC4Y 0DZ

www.bookouture.com

ISBN: 978-1-80019-513-4
eBook ISBN: 978-1-80019-512-7

To my son, Luke
Who I love to the moon and back

CHAPTER ONE

Alex

He'd have done everything differently, if he'd known. He'd have held her tighter, kissed her longer or simply wound his arms around her and refused to let her go. If he'd known.

But Alex's lips had brushed against hers in their sun-drenched kitchen as though there'd be a thousand more kisses in the decades to come. As though they'd still be doing this when her hair was threaded with grey and his own hair was thinner and his waistline thicker.

He'd been bent down, attempting to mop up the glass of orange juice Connor had just sent flying with his elbow, when Lisa entered the kitchen. She scoped the room, taking in the dripping of Del Monte's finest onto the checkerboard tiles and her son's tears that were also threatening to spill. Connor's lower lip was trembling.

'No one is cross with you, big man. It was an accident.' Alex's eyes went to his wife's, conveying his unspoken message. *This is what I mean about him being too sensitive.*

Her cornflower-blue ones flashed back her reply. *He's only six, and he hates being in trouble. Just let it go.*

'Here. Let me do that,' Lisa had said, reaching out to relieve Alex of the cloth as the puddle of juice continued to expand rather than diminish.

Alex had looked up at her, his eyes travelling from the red-soled stilettos, which would be pinching her toes uncomfortably by the end of the day, to the wheat-coloured shift dress. It was the perfect outfit for a speaker at an exhibition in London, but less perfect for sticky kitchen duties.

'Nah. I've got this, hon.' He glanced at his watch, wasting a few more precious seconds that he could have spent looking at his wife's face. 'You'd better hurry or you're going to miss your train.'

He was right, and yet, even so, she'd hesitated. Had she felt it then, the moment when the sand in the hourglass had started to trickle out?

'You're on the 7.48, right?'

Lisa had nodded, picking up her laptop bag and her car keys in a single swoop.

'I wish I could go with you, Mummy. I want to see the models of the planets and the moon.'

Lisa paused to crouch down beside Connor's chair. Alex loved how she unfailingly did that. She would always hunker down to speak to him on his level, both figuratively and literally. It was a trait he kept meaning to adopt, yet he always seemed to forget.

'I know you do, kiddo. But I'm going to be so busy giving that boring old talk, we wouldn't have had any time to explore all the cool exhibits together. Next year,' she whispered, leaning over and kissing her son's shaggy strawberry-blond hair. 'Next year you and I will go to the Astronomy Fair together. We'll go on the train and spend all day looking at every single stand. Just you and me.' Lisa swiped a pink-tipped fingernail across her heart. 'It's a promise.'

Alex's face was turned, to hide his smile, because he knew only too well how excited his thirty-three-year-old wife was to be giving that *boring old talk*. She'd been practising it every night, the laptop propped up on the bed between them as she spoke of black holes, supernovas and lunar seas with a passion that made his heart swell with pride that this bright and beautiful woman was his.

He knew her speech almost as well as she did by now. 'You're going to knock it clean out of the park,' he'd told her the night before, leaning across and carefully shutting the lid on her laptop.

'But I still need to—' she began on a protest that died on her lips as his mouth covered hers. 'Oh well,' she continued with a happy sigh, as she slid her hands beneath the hem of his T-shirt and allowed them to explore the muscles of his back, 'I can always wing it.'

'Wish me luck,' Lisa said now, rising smoothly on her skyscraper heels that narrowed the difference in their height to only a few inches. She moved in for a hug, enveloping Alex in a cloud of the perfume she only wore on special occasions. And this *was* a special day for her; he knew that from the nervous excitement glittering in her eyes.

He pulled her against him, his heart contracting weirdly as her familiar curves moulded against him, like a yin and yang symbol. He released her with a reluctance he couldn't explain.

'Break a leg – break both legs,' he said, claiming one last kiss before she left.

The sound of her laughter followed her down the hallway as she headed for the front door. Those were the last words he said to her that morning.

Connor was obviously enjoying the novelty of being left in the care of Parent Number Two, a clearly inferior candidate for the job who took twice as long as his mum to get him ready for school. That said, Alex felt he scored bonus points for dealing with Connor's claims that his toothbrush 'tasted funny' and for successfully locating the missing school shoe that mysteriously was found buried beneath his pillow.

Despite the fact that they should have already been in the car and on their way, Alex took his time lacing up the shiny black shoe on his son's swinging foot.

'Everything all right, big guy? Nothing bothering you about school, is there?'

Connor's scissoring feet stilled and Alex felt a frisson of panic. His son was a quiet, intelligent boy, the kind who teachers adored and other kids kept at arm's length. He had a few school friends, but both Alex and Lisa had also seen him standing all alone at the edge of the playground, waiting to be collected.

Alex briefly wished Lisa hadn't had to catch that early train, because she was way better at this kind of thing than he was. From the moment the midwife had placed their newborn son into her arms, there'd been an unbreakable bond between his wife and child. He'd never felt excluded, and yet he knew that Connor's need for his mum far exceeded his need for Alex. 'That'll all change when he has to learn how to shave, or parallel park, or ask a girl out on a date,' Lisa had predicted. 'That's when you'll come into your own, babe.'

As none of those things were imminent, Alex still felt like there was a gigantic L-plate pinned on his back; Lisa, meanwhile, was acing the parenting test.

'My tummy feels kind of funny,' Connor admitted, rubbing his hand against his stomach.

'Like you're going to be sick?'

'No. It just feels like I've eaten something squirmy.'

His words perfectly described the weird sensation Alex himself had felt in the kitchen. He laid an inexperienced hand against Connor's forehead, the way he'd seen Lisa do a hundred times before. As far as he could tell, his son's temperature was normal.

'Why don't we tell Mrs Anderson about it when we get to school, and then if you still don't feel well later, I can always come and fetch you? I'm going to be working from home today.'

Even while Alex was busy double-checking Connor's seatbelt was secure, he was wondering whether he should phone Lisa and run his decision past her. Was it the right call, to send Connor in? He glanced at the clock on the dashboard as he buckled himself into the driver's seat. The chances were she was already on the station platform by now, but if he told her that Connor was feeling ill, he knew she'd abandon the exhibition in a heartbeat and come back home to be with him. Alex shook his head determinedly. Lisa had worked too long and too hard for this kind of recognition, and he wasn't going to rob her of her big moment because of something as trivial as a 'squirmy' stomach – either his or Connor's. They could cope without her for a single day.

'Of course we'll keep an eye on him. But these things often miraculously disappear once they're here with their little friends.'

Alex's eyes flew to Connor, who was sitting alone at a low table and reaching for an overflowing pot of crayons and a sheet of paper. Quite a few of the children were running around the classroom like miniature escapees from an asylum; others were delving into boxes of construction toys, books and dressing-up clothes. His was the only child sitting down.

'He's a very good little boy,' Mrs Anderson confirmed warmly. She paused to separate two children who looked like obvious candidates for future ASBOs. 'I could do with a few more like Connor in this class, Mr Stevens, to be perfectly honest,' she confided with a laugh.

Alex experienced his usual giant-in-Lilliput feeling as he threaded his way past chairs as low as milking stools and tables that came up only to his knees to say goodbye to his son. Connor's head was bent low over his drawing, his hair a tousled mess. Had Alex remembered to comb it before they'd left the house? From the look of it, possibly not.

Luckily Alex did remember that goodbye kisses were only permissible in the privacy of the car, so he settled instead for a quick ruffle of Connor's already scruffy hair. 'I'm going now, big man.'

Connor lifted his head from the sheet of paper he'd covered with fat waxy crayon strokes. It was a drawing Alex had seen countless times before. Versions of it covered the walls of his son's bedroom, and others were fixed by magnets to their fridge door, beside Lisa's scribbled shopping list. Once again, Connor had captured the moon in an inky black sky, but not in the way usually depicted by a child his age. This was no glowing crescent a cow could happily jump over or even a cheesy ball with a smiling face; it was the real deal, with shadows, volcanoes and realistic-looking craters.

More than the fullness of her mouth or her impossibly long eyelashes, Connor had inherited his mother's love of astronomy. Suddenly the mysterious stomach squirminess made sense. Connor was obviously feeling upset that he'd not been allowed to go to the Astronomy Fair with Lisa.

Alex's car was the last one left in The Meadows Primary School car park. He ran lightly across the tarmac towards it, only just managing to dodge the first fat raindrops that had turned the sky a threatening shade of pewter. He'd spent far longer talking to Connor's class teacher than he'd realised, for the nine o'clock news bulletin had already finished when the car radio sprang into life. He switched on the windscreen wipers as the announcer predicted possible heavy showers later that morning.

'No kidding,' he said with a grimace as he drove through puddles deep enough to drench any unlucky pedestrian walking past. At least Lisa would have missed the worst of the rain, he thought; she should be warm and dry on the train right now.

Probably running through her speech for the hundredth time, he guessed with a smile.

After all these weeks of planning for the exhibition, he wondered if she'd find it an anti-climax going back to the children's book on astronomy she'd spent the last eight months working on. Once again he smiled, knowing Lisa was as passionate about that project as she was about everything she ever touched.

Although the book was still several chapters from being finished, he'd accidentally stumbled across the dedication page when he'd been looking for something on her desk the other day. There was a time he'd have felt embarrassed that tears had sprung to his eyes when he'd read: *To Alex and Connor, who I love to the moon and back.* But that was the old him; a hardened, trying-to-be-macho sort of bloke who Lisa had seen through in a heartbeat. Somehow she'd always known that hiding beneath that supposedly tough exterior was a man she could fall in love with. And thank God she had, because his life before her had been as colourless as a sepia photograph compared to the multi-coloured version he now enjoyed.

We should be celebrating tonight, Alex suddenly realised, annoyed that he'd not thought of this earlier. If the roles had been reversed, Lisa would no doubt have planned him a big surprise party *and* invited all their friends. It was too late to pull off anything like that, but at least he could take the three of them out to dinner; they could go to that Italian place she loved so much.

He just needed to know what time she'd be home, but despite scrolling back in his mind through recent conversations, he couldn't remember her telling him. No problem, he'd phone her on some pretext or other and casually slip the question into the conversation. He was already shaking his head as he flicked the button on the steering wheel to engage hands-free dialling. Lisa would see straight through whatever lie he told, she always did, but she'd pretend that she hadn't, letting him believe he'd surprised her anyway. They knew each other so well, it was as though at some point in the last nine years they'd stopped being two individuals and had somehow merged into a single entity.

'Phone Lisa,' he told his mobile, checking the clock as he did. She should still be on the train, so she'd be able to talk. Except that she wasn't.

'Hello.' Her voice filled the car, surrounding him from every speaker.

'Hey, babe, it's me. I was just wondering if—'

'I'm sorry, as you've probably guessed, I can't take this call right now. So you know what to do. I'll get back to you very soon.'

Alex felt oddly crushed that he'd not been able to speak to her, which was crazy as he'd only seen her about ninety minutes ago. He glanced down at the ring of platinum on his wedding finger and gave a rueful grin. *You got me good, babe*, he acknowledged with another shake of his head.

'Just wanted to wish you luck one last time, wife. Hope everything goes well today. Call me when you get a free moment.' He was on the point of pressing the button to disconnect the call when an unexpected feeling ran like a trespasser down every one of his vertebrae. 'I love you, Lisa,' he added in a rush.

CHAPTER TWO

Molly

'Once upon a time…'

I paused, though not for dramatic effect, which I knew from experience was largely redundant when your audience was a roomful of six-year-olds. I paused for the same reasons I had to stop halfway up every flight of stairs I climbed, why running for a bus was just a distant memory and why my bathroom cabinet was filled with medication rather than toiletries. If I'd been looking for one last confirmation that this was the right decision, there it was in my inability to complete even a four-word sentence without having to stop to catch my breath.

Twenty-four pairs of eyes looked up at me. For once no one was fidgeting, jostling their neighbour or even talking when they shouldn't have been. They sat cross-legged on the mat, waiting patiently for me to begin the story. It would be my last task as their class teacher and the importance of this day wasn't lost on them. They were young – too young to pronounce, much less *understand* cardiomyopathy – and yet they were dealing with my departure far better than most of my colleagues.

'Are you going to die, miss?' It was a question the children hadn't been afraid to ask, even if my fellow teachers at Green Hills Primary were too scared to do so. But I'd seen how my colleagues had watched with concern as my once rosy complexion had paled to the colour of parchment and my lips had taken on a bluish hue that no amount of pink lipstick could disguise.

Like most people in their early thirties, I'd never given much thought to my own mortality until, eighteen months ago, a virus changed the path of my future. A virus; it sounded so trivial and innocuous. People got them all the time, shook them off and thought nothing of it. But this one had its own agenda and now my carefully mapped-out five-year plan was being rewritten by my own body.

My family had always called me obstinate and they were probably right because I spent months quietly disregarding the doctors' advice that it might now be time to give up work. It took a fallen child in the playground, with bloodied knees and a sprained wrist, a child who I couldn't physically pick up, to make me finally realise the truth. The people who were suffering from my refusal to accept my limitations were the ones I cared about the most: the children.

'And they all lived happily ever after.' With perfect timing my words coincided with the ringing of the school bell.

Home time for a class of six-year-olds was usually a cross between a Colditz escape and the first day of the January sales. But surprisingly today no one was racing madly for the door. Instead, they formed an orderly line – something I'd never been able to make them do before. Every single child in my class patiently waited for their turn to hug me goodbye. No job reference on my CV would ever mean more to me than that. If this *was* to be my last moment as a primary school teacher, it was a pretty amazing one to go out on.

It had started with the boots. They were new. Gorgeous, butter-soft, caramel-coloured leather that hugged my calves like a glove. Every time I zipped them up, I conveniently managed to forget their horrendous price tag. They cheered me up. Low of heel but still stylish, they had been my go-to choice of footwear for work.

But one morning the zip on the right leg had felt tight and sticky. I remember frowning as I tried to jiggle it up. Boots this expensive were meant to last a whole lot longer than just a couple of weeks. I eventually managed to persuade the zip to slide up, only to have the same thing happen with the other leg. I forgot all about it – at least for ten hours.

I'd come home from work that evening and slumped against the front door as I shut it behind me, racked by another cough. I caught a glimpse of my face in the hallway mirror. I looked dreadful and sounded even worse. Like someone who'd never read the warning sign on their packet of cigarettes – yet I'd never smoked in my life.

It wasn't surprising that I'd come down with a bug. Practically everyone I knew had something or other. Usually my immune system was pretty effective at shaking off the infections small children liked to spread with unthinking generosity, but this cough was proving impossible to shift. My ribs were starting to ache from the nightly hacking that was making it difficult to sleep. Lying flat made it worse, but even using the now redundant pillows on Tom's side of the bed didn't help.

All I'd wanted to do was pull on my joggers and crash out on the sofa. Climbing the stairs felt like I was scaling a mountain, and although there were only thirteen treads, I still had to stop halfway up as I gave my lungs another good workout.

I stepped out of my dress, leaving it in a pool on the bedroom carpet because I'd run out of energy to carry it to the laundry basket. Tom would not have approved, but for the last six months I hadn't had to concern myself about that.

I flopped down on the edge of the bed and bent to unzip the boots. They wouldn't budge. The zips that had been reluctant to slide up that morning were even more resolute in their determination not to go back down. Five minutes of stubborn tugging and neither was more than halfway down my calves. The effort was not improving my cough, and by the time I straightened up, a thin film of perspiration was coating my forehead.

I yanked at the zips with so much force, I was surprised they didn't break. But the alternative would have been to cut the boots off. I wriggled my feet once they were free, stuck out both legs and examined them. All that pulling had made my ankles look puffy and kind of chubby. 'Sorry,' I apologised to my squishy-looking flesh, 'I'll wear flats tomorrow.'

That was how it started – with the boots.

By the following morning my ankles looked only marginally better and the cough was starting to make my chest feel tight every time I breathed in. The internet (which I'd consulted in the middle of the night, when sleep had been impossible) advised me that any cough that persisted beyond three weeks required a visit to the doctor. I looked at my reflection in the steamy bathroom mirror, aware I was leaning a little heavily on the basin for support. 'One more week,' I promised my washed-out reflection, 'then we'll nuke this cough with antibiotics.' I had no idea when I spoke those words that the clock was already ticking.

Before slipping my dressing gown back on I stepped onto the bathroom scales and then did a slightly horrified double-take at the numbers on the digital read-out. Seven pounds? I'd put on half a stone in less than a week? How was that even possible? I could practically feel a dark cloud of annoyance gathering above me as I headed back to the bedroom to get dressed. Admittedly since Tom had left I'd cooked from scratch far less than I'd once done, so, yes, the odd takeaway or two had now become a fairly regular fixture, but surely I hadn't eaten *so* badly to warrant that much of a gain?

On autopilot I reached for a couple of slices of bread to pop into the toaster before changing my mind and plucking some fruit and a yoghurt from the fridge instead. Not that I'd had much of an appetite over the last couple of weeks, which made my weight increase even more galling.

A time-check on the radio reminded me I needed to get going. I gathered up my things, staring through the fine morning drizzle down the road. I hadn't been able to snag a space near my house, so my car was parked several hundred yards away. The tote bag slung over my shoulder felt as though it was loaded with gold bullion. I had to stop twice; once to reposition the bag, the second time – worryingly – because I couldn't catch my breath. By the time I reached my car I was forced to admit that something was very wrong. Every inhalation felt as though I was slowly drowning.

With fingers that trembled as they dialled the numbers, I made two phone calls: one to the headteacher of Green Hills Primary School, the other to my GP surgery. Luck was with me on the second call. A patient had just telephoned to cancel their appointment; if I could get there in ten minutes, a doctor would be able to see me straight away. *Perhaps I'll still be able to go into work after my appointment*, I thought as I wove through the early-morning traffic.

The doctor was new, Polish and very thorough. Her accent made it hard to decipher everything she said, but there was no mistaking her expression as I shuffled into her office like someone fifty years older than the screen in front of her indicated. After she'd completed her examination, she spoke slowly and carefully, which helped with the accent, but nothing about what she said was even remotely comprehensible.

'I would like you to go to the hospital.'

'Do you mean you're referring me?' I asked, wondering why she was shaking her head.

'No. I mean today. Straight away. Is there anyone with you in the waiting room or someone who can take you?'

My chest felt so tight I was surprised there was any room inside it to register fear, but somehow it still slithered in, like a determined snake.

'No. I… I drove myself here. Can't I just drive to the hospital?'

She was already reaching for the telephone on her desk. 'I'm afraid I don't think that's advisable, Miss Kendall – er… Molly. I think it's best if I call an ambulance for you.'

Probably pneumonia. It's probably pneumonia. The GP's words ran like a silent mantra in my head throughout the journey to the hospital. Pneumonia was bad, I acknowledged that, but I was young and healthy. With antibiotics and rest I should be able to get over it fairly quickly.

They rushed me through triage, and I was still naive enough to think that was a *good* thing. It was only when the A & E doctor told me I was being admitted to the Acute Cardiac Unit that I began to realise I was in serious trouble. My thoughts were reeling; it felt like a horrible nightmare that surely I would wake up from at any moment. But it just kept getting worse. The truth of it didn't fully sink in until I made that first terrified phone call to my mother.

'Hey, Mum, it's me.'

'Molly?' she queried, sounding incredulous. It wasn't like she needed clarification – there was no one else in the world who called her 'Mum'; it was just that I should have been teaching a classroom full of lively six-year-olds at that precise moment.

A single tear ran down my cheek as I wondered when or even if I'd be able to do that again.

'Mum, don't panic, but I'm in the hospital.'

I imagined the colour washing from her face and her hand gripping the receiver so tightly it was probably turning her fingers white.

'What is it? What's wrong?'

'They say…' I swallowed convulsively several times as the tang of salty tears trickled into my mouth. 'They say I have heart failure.'

For the final time I tidied up the classroom. From tomorrow this room would belong to the supply teacher who was taking over for the rest of the term, and it was hard not to feel a tinge of jealousy that someone else would complete the journey I'd begun with these children seven months earlier.

When everything was put away, I straightened slowly and breathed in the familiar smells of the classroom one last time, trying to bottle and capture them in my memory. One aroma I wasn't going to miss was the one that lingered permanently in the back corner of the room.

'I guess this is goodbye, for now,' I solemnly told Gerald the gerbil. The class mascot looked up briefly from the never-ending marathon he was running on his wheel. In gerbil years, Gerald was definitely a senior citizen, and I'd spent far too much time worrying about how it would affect the class if he didn't make it to the end of the year. The irony wasn't lost on me that the lifespan I ought to have been worrying about wasn't Gerald's but mine.

'Maybe you'll still be here when I come back,' I said, sliding a farewell carrot stick through the bars. '*If* I come back,' I added softly.

'Of course you're coming back.'

I smiled and turned to face the owner of the voice with the unmistakable Aussie twang.

'This place wouldn't be the same without you.'

Kyra Davies, Class Six teacher, more friend than colleague, covered the distance of the classroom in considerably fewer strides than it would have taken me. With her long tousled hair and toned, sun-bronzed limbs, she looked like she ought to have been jogging along a beach somewhere with a surfboard tucked under her arm. Physically we were polar opposites: I was auburn to her blonde, shorter and curvier and with an English complexion that stubbornly refused to tan. But the major difference was that Kyra glowed with health.

Without a word, she crossed to my desk, where two cardboard boxes packed to the brim with farewell gifts from staff and students were waiting. 'Are these for your car?' she asked, picking them up with the sort of ease I'd once taken for granted.

I nodded gratefully as she balanced a box on each hip.

I paused at the classroom doorway before switching off the overhead lights. Leaving, when I didn't want to go, was turning out to be a great deal more painful than I'd expected.

'You've made a difference,' Kyra said softly. 'These kids aren't ever going to forget you.'

I was about to refute her words, to say that wasn't why I was sad, but the denial got stuck somewhere between my throat and my conscience. Because being forgotten, leaving no trace that I had ever been here, *was* the fear that gripped me tightly in the middle-of-the-night hours. It scared me far more than my heart condition ever could. I thought those fears were buried in a place my family and friends would never find. But it seemed those close to me could see them anyway.

CHAPTER THREE

Alex

Alex and Lisa shared an office on the second floor of their modern, executive-style home. It was the fourth bedroom, earmarked for Baby Number Two, whenever that family member should decide to put in an appearance. The gap between Connor and a new arrival had, admittedly, grown larger than either of them had wanted.

'Do you think perhaps it's time we considered seeing someone?' Lisa had asked, treading carefully as she tiptoed around Alex's aversion to medical intervention. It was more than just a passing dislike of doctors, it was a real irrational white-coat phobia that by the age of thirty-five he should have long since outgrown or dealt with. But dealing with it would have meant admitting to some doctor that he had a problem, and being in that kind of environment was the very thing he was uncomfortable with. The source of his problem was a mystery, and one he couldn't trace back to any incident in his childhood. 'You've always been weird about hospitals,' his older brother Todd said. 'Even when you were a little kid.' Perhaps, Alex acknowledged, it was finally time for him to address the issue.

He checked his phone as he sat at his desk, waiting for the document he'd summoned to appear on his laptop screen. There was no message from Lisa, and it was too late now to try her again. She was sure to be busy at the exhibition, catching up with former colleagues and getting set up for her speech.

He sent her a quick WhatsApp message instead, and then determinedly put his phone to one side and got lost in his own work. The PR company he'd set up eight years earlier was finally beginning to earn the kind of industry recognition he'd been dreaming of, and the pitch he was currently working on could be the contract that took them to an entirely different level.

Two hours later the muscles at the back of his neck were bunched and complaining from his lack of movement. He pushed himself away from the desk, deciding a coffee break was most definitely in order. Lisa's desk, in the opposite corner of the room, was far more cluttered than his, strewn with models of planets, framed photos of him and Connor, and a pile of papers that constantly teetered on the edge of becoming unmanageable. One good gust of wind and she'd have to spend weeks separating the next chapter of her book from printouts of downloaded recipes and a score of ancient to-do lists. He smiled because his wife was there in every haphazard item, from the half-eaten packet of jelly babies to the latest papier-mâché model she'd made with Connor.

Alex ran down the wooden staircase, remembering to take his phone with him in case the school called, although he was hopeful that whatever had been troubling his son that morning had already passed. As he waited for the coffee to brew, he called the Italian restaurant and booked a table for that evening. It would be late for Connor on a school night, but this was an important day in the Stevens household, and it deserved to be marked as such.

He watched the drip of the coffee, which for a moment looked uncomfortably like an IV as it plopped into the waiting jug. The house seemed uncommonly quiet without its two liveliest occupants and, more for a distraction than anything else, Alex reached for the TV remote. At this hour it would probably be yet another property programme or a commercial asking if he'd made adequate provision for his loved ones in his will. He grinned when he saw he'd guessed correctly; that was exactly what was being advertised during the break. He muted the sound, turned back to the worktop as the coffee machine buzzed, and filled his mug the way he always did, right up to the brim, making a spillage almost inevitable.

He had his coffee in one hand and the TV remote in the other and was about to switch off the set when he caught sight of a red 'Breaking News' banner in the top right-hand corner of the screen. The kitchen was warm, the efficient underfloor heating saw to that, but Alex suddenly felt as though he'd fallen through the icy crust of a frozen lake. The picture on the screen was grainy, the footage taken from a helicopter perhaps, or maybe a drone. But it was still easy to make out the scene of devastation. The train tracks were surrounded by emergency vehicles of every description. Only two carriages remained upright; the rest had been dislodged from the track and were lying on their sides in a confusion of twisted wreckage. It looked like a toy trainset that had been cast aside by the sweep of a gigantic hand.

Alex's fingers were slow and clumsy; he hit the wrong button three times before he finally found the one to un-mute the television. The crash could be anywhere in the country, he told himself as his eyes frantically flicked across the screen, trying to work out where the disaster had occurred. The sound from the TV blared into the kitchen as Alex read a tickertape update scrolling beneath the live images. He thought he might be physically sick. *Authorities now confirm at least four fatalities.* There was nothing on the screen for him to identify the location; all he could see were fields littered with train debris.

His eyes were starting to sting, but he wouldn't allow them to blink in case he missed a vital clue, something – anything – that would let him know this terrible tragedy had touched the lives of other families but not his. It was a selfish thought, he knew that, but he was helpless to stop it as his ears strained to hear the words of the announcer above the roaring rush of blood that was filling them.

'Once again we are seeing the scene of this morning's tragic train crash. As yet, details are sketchy, but we do know there are multiple injuries and that many passengers are still trapped in the wreckage. The 7.48 from Norwich was travelling towards—'

The mug slipped from Alex's fingers, shattering on the checkerboard tiles he'd cleaned of Connor's spilt juice only hours earlier. His feet crunched over the broken shards, some piercing the rubber soles of his trainers, which he never even felt. He could hear a low keening moan, which at first he thought was coming from the news footage. It was harrowing to realise that actually he was the source of the sound.

With his eyes still fixed on the screen, Alex snatched up his phone. His fingers jabbed at his list of contacts until Lisa's mobile began to ring. Her voice gave him a brief moment of respite from the nightmare before he realised, for the second time that day, that it was just a recording.

'Lisa,' he began, in a voice that even his wife would have struggled to recognise as his. 'Lisa, are you all right? I've just seen on the news that there's been an accident. Please tell me you're okay. Ring me. Oh, baby, please ring me.'

He hung up.

He didn't let go of his phone, just gripped it tightly within his sweat-slickened palm, and yet still it remained stubbornly silent. A number had flashed up across the TV screen, the kind he'd seen on numerous other incidents, the kind everyone hopes they'll never have to call. *For information about family or friends who may have been travelling on the train this morning, please call the emergency helpline number on the screen.*

Alex's fingers trembled uncontrollably as he scrabbled through the kitchen drawer for an elusive pen, coming up only with one of Connor's wax crayons. Terrified of tearing his eyes from the TV for even a single moment, he yanked a sheet of paper from the fridge door, sending its magnet flying across the kitchen. Defiling his son's drawing with the phone number felt wrong, but then so did everything else that had happened in the last five minutes.

His first attempt at dialling the number ended in failure, as did his second. It was as though all his motor skills had shut down. In contrast his brain was racing; scenarios and images were flashing through it at lightning speed, with a horrible degree of clarity he could only pray wasn't real.

It took seven rings before they answered him and he died a little bit inside with every one of them. The voice on the end of the line was calm and professional, but his panic was now an inferno that nothing could extinguish.

'Slow down, sir,' the man said gently. Alex tried, but within him everything was racing: his heart, his imagination, and his terror. 'You believe your wife was a passenger on the train that crashed this morning?'

Alex almost swore in frustration. Of course he believed that. Why the hell else would he be calling this number? 'Yes. Yes,' he said, interrupting the man before he could speak again. 'Lisa Stevens. She was definitely travelling to London on the 7.48. Do you know if she's okay?'

There was a pause and everything in the kitchen seemed to stop. This was the frozen moment in time he knew he would remember for the rest of his life.

'I'm sorry, Mr Stevens. She's not on our list.'

'What does that mean? That she's not been hurt? That she's okay?'

Beneath the professionalism, Alex could hear the sympathy in the man's voice. 'It means that the list of passengers we've been given by the transport police does not include her name, but as I am sure you can appreciate, the situation is changing minute by minute. We are continually being updated with details of further passengers.'

'So what do I do now?' Alex asked desperately. There were tears coursing down his cheeks and he made no attempt to hide the fact that he was crying.

'Have you tried reaching her on a mobile, if she has one?'

'It was the first thing I did,' he half sobbed, half yelled into the phone. 'I… I'm sorry. I left her a message earlier, but it's not been marked as read, and she's not picking up the phone or replying to her voicemail. If she was okay, she'd have got in touch straight away. She wouldn't want to leave me worrying like this.'

'I understand how concerned you must be. I'm going to give you the names and phone numbers of the three hospitals where the casualties are being taken for treatment. You'll be able to check directly with them to see if she has been admitted to one of them. And please don't assume the worst because she's not answering her phone. Possessions often get separated from their owners at times like this. We have your contact details now, so if we receive any news of your wife, we'll call you straight back.'

Alex made it to the downstairs cloakroom with only seconds to spare. The last time he'd been that sick he'd blamed it on Lisa's heavy hand with the tequila when she'd mixed a jug of margaritas. He'd staggered out of the cloakroom just the way he was doing right now, only this time he wasn't drunk and Lisa wasn't waiting for him in the kitchen with a smiling apology and a cool cloth for his forehead. She was… She was… He didn't know where the hell she was, and for a terrible moment he thought he was going to have to race back to the downstairs WC. But throwing up in terror was an indulgence he couldn't allow himself. He had phone calls to make.

Typically, each of the hospitals kept him on hold for an excruciatingly long time. And when eventually they came back to him, they all had the same response. No patient had been admitted with his wife's name. Alex stood swaying in the kitchen after ending the final phone call. Was this good news or bad? The switchboard operators had made it clear that the situation was ongoing and that ambulances were still arriving in a continuous stream to their A & E departments. 'What should I do?' he'd asked. 'Keep phoning back,' he was told.

The television was still playing, its volume turned down to a whisper. 'Wait,' they all said, every time he phoned back. Were they joking? How could he possibly do that when the woman who was his entire world was lost in their system, possibly hurt, possibly… No, he wouldn't let his mind go there, even though he'd staggered as though punched when the tickertape on the screen was updated with the dreadful news that the number of confirmed fatalities had now risen to eight.

'Hey, Alex, what are you doing calling us in the middle of the day?'

He liked Dee, his sister-in-law; he had done from the moment Todd had introduced them, but right now he had no desire to talk to her.

'Is Todd there?'

How she could tell from just those three words that something awful had happened, he had no idea, but clearly she was way more perceptive than he'd realised.

'What's wrong?'

The words were stuck in his throat. He didn't think he could get them out more than once. 'Dee, please, put Todd on the phone.'

The phone clattered in his ear and he heard voices, followed quickly by the sound of feet pounding down their hallway towards the phone.

'Alex?' Concern was in his older brother's voice, and perhaps that was what made the tears he'd hoped to hold back begin to fall once more.

'It's Lisa,' Alex said in a hoarse whisper. 'There's been an accident.'

'What? At the exhibition?'

Todd was confused, and suddenly Alex knew he couldn't say the words that were lodged in his throat, in danger of choking him. 'Turn on the news channel,' he said weakly, propping himself up against the wall as he heard his brother relay that message to Dee.

He heard his sister-in-law's cry and then a muffled sound, the kind people make when they're biting down hard on a clenched fist to stifle a sob.

'Oh Christ,' breathed Todd on a shaky sigh.

'I can't get any information out of the authorities. She might have been taken to any one of three hospitals, or she could still be trapped in the wreckage, or she... or she...' There was no way he was ever going to be able to finish that sentence.

'What can we do?'

This was why he'd made this call. Because Todd had always been the one who thought things through, who instinctively knew the right course of action. Alex, by his own admission, had been a hothead when they were younger. It had taken the arrival of a certain beautiful young woman with a love of astronomy, books and him to change him into the man he was today.

'I know you're off work for a few days, so do you think you could collect Connor from school this afternoon? I need to get there.'

'Get where?'

'To the hospitals. To where the train crashed. I don't know... I just need to find her.'

'Whoa. Slow down, mate. Take a breath.'

'I can't. Not till I know she's okay.'

The phone went muffled and Alex knew the handset was being held tightly against his brother's body as he spoke to Dee.

'Okay, this is what's going to happen. Dee will go to Connor's school and pick him up and bring him here. He can play with

Maisie until you get back – until you and Lisa get back,' he corrected rapidly. The slip didn't go unnoticed.

Todd continued in a voice that brooked no argument. 'No way am I letting you go off in a car on this search by yourself. You hang on twenty minutes and I'll pick you up. We'll go together.'

Alex didn't feel his knees give way, he just knew they must have done because he'd slid down to the bottom of the wall.

'Thank you, thank you, thank you.'

'Stay strong, little brother. I'm on my way.'

CHAPTER FOUR

Alex

Todd was as good as his word. They lived far enough apart for twenty minutes to have been an optimistic ETA, and yet Todd was there in seventeen.

Alex had spent most of that time pacing the confines of his kitchen, terrified of watching the news but powerless to tear his eyes from it. There was nothing new to report, on the TV or online, yet he scanned the same piece of footage over and over again, straining his eyes to find his wife's face among the casualties being helped from the wreckage. Each time he failed to find her, his panic went up another notch.

A flurry of gravel flew up on the drive as Todd swung his car in at speed, bringing it to a halt beside Alex's. Through the window Alex saw him leap out and run towards the front door, at a pace he'd never seen him use on the squash courts. Alex had the door open before he had a chance to lift the polished brass knocker.

They fell like magnets against each other, embracing in a way they hadn't done since their father's funeral four years earlier. 'It's going to be okay, Alex. I'm sure of it.'

It took a brother to know from the gruffness of Todd's voice that he was in fact far from sure about anything. When they were boys, Alex had idolised his older brother, believing everything he ever told him. He longed to do the same now, but the evidence was pointing to an entirely different outcome.

'You ready to go?'

Alex nodded and pulled the door to a close behind him, not even bothering to go back in to switch off the television or make sure the doors were locked. His disregard for home security would have appalled Lisa, who routinely double-checked everything. Why had he always found that trait so irritating? Alex wondered as he climbed into the passenger seat. He promised himself he'd never be annoyed by it again. This was the first of many bargains he struck with himself during the two-and-a-half-hour drive to London. Lisa would scarcely recognise the paragon of virtue he planned to morph into, he thought. His mouth twisted into a spasm that was the closest he'd be able to get to a smile until he saw her again.

Todd had always been a careful driver, a law-abiding individual, which had nothing to do with his profession as a lawyer, it was just the way he was wired. If Alex hadn't been so distracted, he'd have been shocked to see how his brother quickly reached the speed limit on every road and then pressed his foot down a little harder on the accelerator. But while Todd was busy gathering potential speeding fines, Alex was preoccupied with his phone. He contacted the hospitals in turn, allowing himself only a ten-minute respite between each round of calls before doing it all over again.

Todd said nothing, but his hands tightened on the wheel after every abortive call. They were still twenty miles outside London when Alex finally received the news he'd been waiting for.

'Lisa Stevens? Yes. She's just been admitted to St Mark's Hospital.'

The relief hit Alex like a punch, making him gasp as though winded. 'She's there? Oh, thank God. How is she? Can you tell me if she's been hurt?'

Todd briefly took his eyes from the motorway and flashed a look of relief Alex's way.

There was a pause, too long to be comfortable, before the operator came back on the line. 'I'm very sorry, but I don't have any further information on her condition. But the notes show that she's about to be moved to the ICU.'

Alex's hopes of minor cuts and bruises or even a broken limb or two were whipped away like confetti in a tornado, leaving a new level of concern in their place.

'It's got to be bad if they're taking her to Intensive Care.'

Todd's eyes were on the road and the speedometer showed that they were now doing eighty miles an hour. 'Not necessarily,' he replied carefully. 'It could be that they need to keep a closer eye on her, to assess her better.'

As they reached the outer suburbs of London, the inevitable snarl-ups slowed them down to a maddening stop-start crawl.

'Do you think I should phone them again?' Alex asked, his eyes flitting worriedly from the traffic to his watch. There was practically nothing left of Alex the confident husband and father, a man used to making decisions without the need to confer. The events of the morning had stripped him raw, leaving him with little capacity to process information, let alone think clearly. He hoped he wouldn't be asked to make any important decisions today, because he very much doubted he'd be capable of doing so.

'According to Google Maps we're only twelve minutes away. Let's hang tight and see what the situation is when we get there.'

Even before the tyres had come to a complete stop outside the main doors of St Mark's, Alex had leapt from the car and was racing towards the entrance.

'I'll park in the multi-storey and be right behind you,' Todd said, lifting his voice to be heard above the sound of sirens that seemed to be coming from every direction. But Alex was already sprinting through the hospital's revolving doors.

If there was orderliness in the foyer, Alex couldn't see it. All he could see was chaos and clusters of people standing helplessly around, most wearing expressions very similar to his own. Some of them were clutching photographs of their loved ones, desperately showing them to anyone who passed by in the hope that they had seen them. Others were huddled together in groups, quietly weeping.

A separate enquiry desk had been set up, with a handwritten sign stuck crookedly on the wall behind it for anyone enquiring about passengers on the train. Alex's heart thundered like a jack-hammer as he crossed the foyer. There were two people manning the desk and they looked like they were having one of the worst days of their working lives.

An elderly couple were already at the desk, their arms wound tightly around each other, making it impossible to tell who was holding who up.

'Our son, he was on the train,' Alex heard the man say brokenly. 'No one has been able to tell us where he is. Can you help us?'

The receptionist checked her computer screen and then picked up one of several clipboards on the desk. The list of names was shockingly long. Alex glanced sideways and locked eyes with the desperate couple, who looked far too old and frail to withstand bad news. He shuddered, imagining how he'd feel if it was Connor and not Lisa he was looking for. He thought he'd plumbed the depths of this waking nightmare and was surprised to discover it actually had a whole other level.

The second receptionist beckoned him to approach and the words were already tumbling from him before he reached her. She reached for her keyboard in response, her fingers moving nowhere near as fast as Alex would have liked. It had taken him so many hours to get here, and now he was only minutes away from seeing Lisa, being separated from her felt like an act of torture.

'Ah, yes, here she is.' The receptionist lifted the phone on her desk. 'Let me call the unit and ask someone to come down and take you up to her.'

'Don't worry. Just tell me which floor she's on. I'll make my own way there.'

The receptionist looked troubled, but Alex didn't give a toss that he was probably breaking hospital regulations. He couldn't wait a moment longer. The elderly man gave him a small nod of approval before turning back to his quietly weeping wife.

'It's on the fifth floor, but really you should—'

Alex had already turned from the desk, his eyes scoping the foyer for the lifts or a staircase. He paused for a second to address the elderly couple. 'I hope it's good news for you.'

The man with the sparse white hair and the fear-filled eyes nodded sympathetically. 'For you too, son.'

There was a crowd at the bank of lifts. Visitors with bunches of flowers waited patiently beside staff going about their everyday duties, as though this wasn't the day when the world changed. No one seemed the slightest bit bothered that every lift was still at least ten floors away from the foyer. But Alex minded. He minded a lot.

He turned away and barrelled through a pair of swing doors that led to the stairwell. After hours of impotence in the car, it felt good to push himself as he bounded up the steel-edged treads, taking the stairs two or even three at a time. He was running to her, finally closing the distance between them, and when he reached her side he had absolutely no intention of ever leaving it.

The ward was harder to infiltrate than Alcatraz. There were two sets of doors that required buzzed-in entry, and when he'd passed through them Alex was almost immediately stopped by a nurse whose bulging forearms said 'nightclub bouncer' more than 'healthcare professional'. Alex had a sudden vision of ducking past him and running down the corridor calling out Lisa's name. He wondered if it was possible for a person to actually go crazy from anxiety.

'Mr Stevens?' the nurse asked.

'I… Yes, I'm Alex Stevens. You have my wife here.'

That the receptionist had phoned ahead to forestall his arrival was a minor irritation which only gained significance much later. For now, Alex's sole concern was reaching Lisa without a further second of delay.

'Yes, we do. Let me take you to her.'

These were the words Alex had been waiting all morning to hear, and yet his footsteps dragged inexplicably as he followed the nurse down the squeaky, linoleum-floored corridor.

'How is she? How badly is she hurt?'

The nurse slowed his pace and placed one hand – which was roughly the size of a bear's paw – on Alex's shoulder. 'The doctors will need to explain the full extent of your wife's injuries,' he said, his eyes unconsciously flicking left and right along the empty corridor, as though hoping someone better equipped to answer Alex's questions might miraculously appear.

'Lisa has sustained multiple injuries,' the man began, speaking slowly, as if he already knew that Alex would struggle to comprehend his words. 'We understand she was in one of the front carriages, which were the worst affected by the impact.'

The newsreel looped through Alex's mind and he saw again the crushed and broken carriages beside the train tracks. Unable to cope with the sympathy on the nurse's face, his eyes dropped to the man's bench-press-sculpted chest and focused on the nametag pinned there. *Declan O'Keefe*, he read, realising he hadn't even noticed his thick Irish accent. He heard it now as he continued to speak.

'The reason your wife has been transferred to this ward is because of the injuries to her head.'

Alex swayed, and the nurse's hand was now needed more for support than for comfort. Head injuries? Suddenly they were in a whole new nightmare.

'Before I take you to her, I need to prepare you for the machinery and monitors she's hooked up to currently. People can get a little freaked out if they're not expecting it and—'

'But she's going to be okay, isn't she? She's going to get better?' Alex's interruption bordered on angry accusation, but Declan's shoulders were broad and experienced enough to take it. Alex suspected he'd been here a great many times before.

'Lisa's doctors are the ones you need to talk to next. As soon as I've taken you to her, I'll see if I can get someone to come and see you.' His face wore a rueful apology. 'As you can imagine, things have been a little crazy around here today.'

Alex's teeth were gritted, probably forcefully enough to damage the enamel. Through them he managed to beg. 'Please, can you just take me to her. She must be so scared being here all alone.'

He'd been warned. Declan had done his best to prepare him, and yet even words like 'head injury', and 'monitors' hadn't equipped Alex for the stomach-lurching terror he felt when he was ushered into the small side room where his wife lay waiting for him. He faltered at the doorway, and when he did manage to step forward, it was as though he'd stepped into a lift shaft only to find there was no carriage waiting inside it.

He turned to Declan. 'She's not breathing by herself? She's on a ventilator?'

Declan nodded slowly.

On legs that had never felt less able to support him, Alex crossed to the bed, where the only woman he had ever loved lay immobile. It was the stillness of her that shook him the most. Lisa was never still; even in sleep she was an irrepressible stealer of the duvet and hogger of the pillows. Seeing her now, looking like a waxwork model of herself, felt beyond unreal. There was an ugly dark bruise along her jaw, but far more shocking was the plastic breathing tube protruding from between the lips he'd kissed only hours earlier. With mounting concern he allowed his gaze to travel up to the enormous bandage swathing her head. It was so thick it gave her head a strangely misshapen look.

'Lisa, baby, I'm here. It's me, Alex.' He bent down to kiss her cheek, his gaze fixed on her closed eyelids, which were as still as a porcelain doll's. He reached for her hand, weaving his own past the snaking wires and tubes that attached her to God only knew how many machines and monitors. Lisa would probably have been able to tell him what each one was called. She was an avid viewer of TV hospital dramas, but Alex had never cared for them. He was completely ill-equipped, in every way imaginable, for finding himself dropped right into the middle of one.

Lisa's hand was still as he threaded his fingers between hers, and even when he tightened his grip, there was no familiar responding squeeze. Tentatively, with fingers that were visibly trembling, he reached to touch the smooth skin of her cheek.

'Can she… Can she hear me? Has she been conscious at all since she got here?'

Declan looked torn, unwilling to lie but equally reluctant to sever the strands of hope that Alex was clinging to like a man drowning. 'She's been like this since she was brought here,' he replied, each word carefully chosen. 'But you should definitely keep talking to her.'

With a magician's dexterity, he swept up a plastic chair and positioned it behind Alex's knees. 'Sit down,' he urged, pressing Alex gently onto the chair. 'I'll be back as soon as I can.'

Alex dragged the chair even closer to the head of the bed, as though those precious extra inches would make all the difference.

'Hey, baby. It's time to wake up now.' The words he roused Lisa with each morning felt wrong; they belonged to the quiet haven of their bed, whispered beneath the duvet, not in a hospital room, against a background of beeping machines. But maybe they were the key to the door behind which his wife was trapped. 'Please, hon. Open your eyes now. Let me know you're all right, that everything's going to be okay.'

His tears splashed down on their joined hands. He tasted the salt of them on her wrist when he buried his face against the pulse point there and took comfort in the steady throb beating rhythmically against his lips.

The sound of hurried footsteps jolted him upright and he jerked around, uncaring about the tears staining his cheeks. His body thrummed with tension as he braced himself for the sight of a white coat in the doorway, but the only thing white about the man who entered the room was his face. It was the colour of bleached bone.

'Jesus Christ. Oh fuck.' Todd was neither religious nor given to profanity, so his gasped exclamation confirmed that things looked every bit as bad as Alex had feared.

Todd approached the bed with hesitant steps, his eyes flashing between his sister-in-law and his brother, who appeared to have aged twenty years in the time it had taken him to park the car. 'How is she?'

The fear had lodged in Alex's throat, choking his airway and allowing only a helpless, inarticulate sound to escape. It took three attempts before he found his voice. 'I've not seen a doctor yet. They said someone's coming to talk to me.'

Todd nodded and came to stand beside him, his eyes taking in the machines, the unconscious woman in the bed, and the lack of medical activity. He was a logical man, as befitted someone in his profession, but now he found himself praying that he'd misinterpreted what he was looking at.

CHAPTER FIVE

Molly

There were three texts from her on my phone. They were all incredibly long, which meant they must have taken her ages to write. For some reason my mother had never managed to master the art of using her thumbs when texting. Maybe it was a generation thing. The messages were perfectly punctuated, with paragraphs, indents and even a semi-colon or two – all used correctly. Once a librarian, always a librarian, I thought with a smile.

I took the phone out to my postage-stamp of a garden, where the reception was better. The wooden bench, positioned in a corner suntrap, felt comfortingly warm against my back as I waited for her to pick up.

'Molly.' I had no idea how it was possible to infuse that much concern into simply saying my name, but my mum managed to do it anyway. 'Why are you using your phone to call me?'

'Because that's why the nice people at Apple invented them?' I replied. Going for humour had always been my default setting. Sometimes I forgot Mum didn't always appreciate it.

She made a 'tsk' sound, the kind I imagined Victorian dowagers used to favour. 'You know perfectly well what I mean. You should be messaging so that other calls – like important calls from the hospital – can still get through.'

'Mum, I'm sure if anyone needs to get hold of me that urgently, they won't just give up if I'm on another call.'

'There's no point taking unnecessary chances.'

I sighed softly. It was futile to disagree with her. There was no use telling her to calm down, and not to worry about me. 'I'm your mother; it's my job to worry.' She'd repeated those words so often, they were starting to sound like a mission statement. She was certainly devoting all her energy to the task, and had been doing so for the last eighteen months, ever since my diagnosis.

At seventy years of age, she should have been out trouncing her pals at bridge and whist, or playing bowls or finally taking that cruise she'd been promising herself. Instead, she'd been thrust back about twenty years in time, to a period when her priority was to look after her little girl. The fact that the 'little girl' had recently celebrated her thirty-first birthday appeared to be completely irrelevant.

'How was your last day?'

'Sad, touching and emotional.' A lump I hadn't been expecting had formed in my throat. 'It was harder than I thought it would be, Mum.'

'I'm sure it was, sweetheart.' I'd opened a door, so I couldn't really blame her for trying to squeeze through it. 'Perhaps it's time I came to stay with you – just for a little while, to keep your spirits up.'

I smiled wryly. By now I should have been better at avoiding the conversational landmines, but I'd walked right into that one 'We've been over this a hundred times, Mum. I don't want you putting your whole life on hold because of me.'

'My life won't mean much to me if you're not in it any more.'

I hadn't seen that one coming. Just when I thought I'd got everything sorted in my head, when I'd made peace with the hand I'd been dealt, an unseen dagger slipped straight through my ribs and found my heart. My failing heart.

'Come on now, Mum. We agreed – we've got to stay positive. Everything's going to be fine. And I don't need anyone to
look after me.' *At least not yet*, I added silently. 'Besides, what
would Bertie do if you came to stay with me?' I wasn't playing
fair, but I knew how much she loved her little West Highland
terrier. After my father's death five years ago, I'd bought her the
feisty little dog for companionship, never imagining that he'd
become the new love of her life. It was no secret that nothing
Bertie ate came from the pet-food aisle in the supermarket and
that he slept on top of the duvet, on what was once Dad's half
of the bed. Not that I could blame her for that. I knew from
experience how that vacant half of a double bed could take a
while to get used to.

'Well, I've got my suitcase all packed and ready. Just to be on
the safe side.'

I thought of my own bag, also packed and waiting at the
bottom of the coat cupboard. Statistically it was likely to gather
a whole lot of dust before I ever needed to pull it out of there.

'It could be years, Mum,' I reminded her gently. We'd read
the same literature; she knew this as well as I did.

'Or it could be five minutes,' she batted right back.

I opened the freezer door and stared with tepid interest at the
array of ready meals stacked neatly on its shelves. It was hard
to summon up enthusiasm for something I would struggle to
identify after it came out of the microwave. There was a time,
not that long ago, when cooking had been my favourite pastime.
I'd spend hours poring over recipe books and enjoyed the whole
process of planning, shopping, and then preparing and cooking.

'You do know you're gradually turning into a fifties housewife,'
Kyra had teasingly observed as she'd watched me snip recipes from
a magazine in the school staffroom.

'I find it really satisfying making something home-cooked and wholesome from scratch. And besides, Tom really appreciates it.'

'I bet he does. He's definitely struck gold with you, my friend. If that man has got even half a brain, he'll never let you go.'

But in the end he had. Or I'd let him go. I was never quite sure which.

My desire to cook had disappeared right along with my appetite and my flagging energy. The plus side was that my waist had never been so small. The downside – there was no longer an arm sliding around it to notice.

CHAPTER SIX

Alex

To Alex, it seemed like several hours before anyone came to talk to them. But Todd knew that it was actually fifty-six minutes before the doctor arrived. He'd watched every single one of them jerk forward on the clock face on the wall.

'Mr Stevens.'

Both men turned at the sound of their name. The doctor was tall, with dark hair and thick eyebrows that joined above his nose. There was a covering of bristle on his jawline that was several hours past a five o'clock shadow. He looked like a man who hadn't seen his own bed for a worryingly long time.

From the degree of despair on their faces, it must have been easy for him to work out which Mr Stevens was married to the woman in the bed. The doctor crossed to Alex, extending his hand in a formal greeting.

'Mr Stevens. I'm Dr Lloyd-Gordon, the physician leading the team who've been caring for your wife today.'

Alex bit down on the retort that apart from Declan, who'd been in and out of the hospital room several times, there had been no one attending to Lisa.

'I'm sorry we've kept you waiting for so long. I realise how anxious you must be.'

Alex's aversion to the medical profession tended to manifest itself in a variety of ways, including through anger. 'Why aren't they doing something for her?' he'd fumed to Todd earlier as they'd waited for someone to come and speak to them. 'Shouldn't she be in surgery or getting treatment?'

'I don't know, mate,' Todd had replied, as much out of his depth as his brother. 'Maybe they have to wait for her condition to stabilise or something?' They were using vocabulary from a language that neither of them spoke, and the frustration of not knowing had fermented toxically during the long wait.

'Can I suggest we go somewhere a little quieter to talk?' Dr Lloyd-Gordon asked, glancing up with a brief nod of recognition as Declan once again slipped into the room.

'No,' Alex said, his voice low, like the growl of a cornered animal. He swallowed and dug deep to find his composure. 'I really don't want to leave Lisa alone.' He looked at his unnaturally silent wife, the woman who was never still, never quiet. It seemed unlikely she'd even realise if he left the room, but still he didn't want to go. Alex already knew what kind of news got delivered in rooms that were 'a little bit quieter'. He was nowhere near ready to go there. 'Can we please just talk in here?'

The doctor responded with a single nod. His eyes went to Declan, who quietly closed the door. For a long moment the four men looked at each other. Dr Lloyd-Gordon cleared his throat, but Alex surprised himself by being the first to speak.

'It's bad news, isn't it?'

Dr Lloyd-Gordon sighed softly. Alex wondered if anyone else heard the thread of relief running through it. 'Yes, Mr Stevens, I'm afraid it is. Your wife's situation is extremely grave. I realise this is a lot for you to take in and—'

'How bad?' Alex interrupted. Whatever the doctor had to tell him, it surely couldn't be worse than the torment of not knowing. Only it was.

'In layman's terms, Lisa sustained an acute and catastrophic trauma to her skull in the train crash.'

Catastrophic. The word belonged in news reports about cyclones, earthquakes or tsunamis. It had no place being used in the context of a young wife and mother who'd been anticipating one of the best days of her professional life. How had they ended up here? How had this happened to them?

'But you can fix her, can't you?' Alex asked, perfectly aware his desperation made it sound as if he was asking a mechanic to mend his car rather than restore the woman he loved to full health.

'Lisa's head injuries are extremely serious.' The doctor paused as his words found the darkest place in Alex's heart and settled there. 'The paramedics and doctors on the scene worked to stabilise her condition and after being transferred here she was placed on a ventilator, which is now effectively breathing for her.'

'And she can stay on that until she starts breathing for herself again?'

'I'm so sorry, but you need to understand that Lisa will not recover from her injuries.'

The world split open, pitching Alex into a bottomless crevasse with unscalable sides. 'But there has to be something you can do? You can't just give up on her.' Despair and fear were rising in Alex's throat, threatening to choke him. 'We have a little boy. His name is Connor.' Ridiculously, he could feel himself patting his pockets for his wallet, as though showing the doctor a photograph of their son would somehow change everything. 'He's only six. He still needs his mum,' Alex added brokenly. 'We both do.'

He could hear crying, but when he swiped the back of his hand across his cheek, Alex was surprised to find it dry. More than anything the doctor had said, more than the evidence of his own eyes, it was the sound of Todd quietly weeping that made everything horribly real.

'When Lisa arrived on the unit this morning, a senior colleague and myself performed a series of tests on her; tests that are designed to determine the level of her brain function.'

Alex had no need to ask what the results were; his brilliant wife, who'd never failed a test in her entire life, had clearly failed this one.

'We'd like to perform those tests again to confirm our findings.'

The room they were shown to was small and impersonal. It seemed like an eternity and yet also far too soon before a respectful knock on the door heralded the return of Dr Lloyd-Gordon, Declan and a woman they'd not seen before. No one needed to say the words; their body language spoke for them, exuding the truth like an airborne poison.

'No, no, no.' Alex's head was shaking in denial. 'But she's still warm. She's still breathing. I could feel her pulse.'

'It's just the machines,' the doctor explained. His voice was different now: firm, allowing hope no foothold. 'I'm very sorry to have to confirm that the tests we have carried out are conclusive. Lisa is dead. Her loss of brain function is irreversible. It can never come back.'

His words were like jagged pieces of glass tearing the fabric of Alex's world apart.

'We need some time,' Todd insisted, taking command in a way that Alex was no longer capable of.

'You knew, didn't you?' Alex asked hoarsely as they walked on leaden feet down the corridor, back to Lisa's room.

If he lived to be a hundred, Alex would never forget the way Todd turned slowly to face him, his eyes full of pain. 'You did too, didn't you?'

Alex nodded as he stumbled blindly towards the bed. Todd backed awkwardly out of the room, mumbling something about having to 'sort things out'. Alex didn't even look up.

'I'm back, sweetheart,' he said, his voice cracking as he realised he'd never again call out those words to her as he unlocked their front door. Never again would he hear the sound of her laughter filling the house or look into her beautiful blue eyes and see his love for her reflected back at him. There were thousands of *I love yous* he'd never get the chance to say, and the weight of a future without her made his legs buckle.

Ignoring the chair beside the bed, he somehow managed to perch on the edge of the mattress and slide his arms beneath his motionless wife. Very carefully he pulled her towards him, into her favourite sleeping position with her cheek resting against his chest.

The rain was still falling; tears pouring down the window pane. He watched it cascading down the glass as her chest rose and fell against him, the very last time he would hold her like this.

'It's raining,' he whispered to the precious, silent shell in his arms. She would leave him today, in the rain. Which perhaps was how it was always meant to be, because that was how they'd met – in the rain…

If Alex hadn't been such a piss-poor excuse for a boyfriend, he would never have met Lisa. He'd been seeing Anna for a month or so, having met her through work, and seven dates in he'd thought they were both on the same page. But apparently they'd been reading entirely different books. Alex's relationship manual hadn't made it clear he was supposed to be putting in way more effort by this point. It was probably a valid criticism. He did have a habit of forgetting to phone when he said he would or turning up late for their dates.

In an effort to prove he wasn't a total loser, he'd decided to surprise Anna that night. He'd bought a tartan picnic blanket, a bottle of overpriced red wine and two tickets for an open-air performance of *Romeo and Juliet*.

He'd texted her the details that afternoon, and fifteen minutes before anyone had the chance to tell them what had been going on recently in Fair Verona, Anna had texted him back. Dumping him. It was probably deserved, although he could have done without the bonus information that she was now sleeping with her flatmate who she'd secretly fancied all along.

The actors were about to go on and it was too late to disrupt nearby members of the audience by gathering up his belongings, so Alex popped the cork on the wine, lay back down on the blanket and did his best to look as though he was interested in the play. He'd leave after the first half, he promised himself. But by the second act he'd made the surprising discovery that he rather liked Shakespeare after all. Who knew?

The rain had come hard and fast, startling both the audience and the actors. This was no light summer shower; it was a downpour of biblical proportions. Juliet was still gamely up on her balcony when the stage manager came on to announce they were going to have to stop the performance.

People were running in every direction, like they'd never seen rain before. Abandoning his sodden picnic blanket, Alex picked up the bottle of wine and ran for shelter beneath the boughs of a tall oak tree. He shook himself like a dog and was still wiping water from his eyes when he was joined by another equally drenched audience member.

'May I?' she asked, indicating the dry spot beneath the branches, as though he had exclusive rights to the space.

Alex shrugged. 'Feel free.'

She smiled at him, pushing her saturated hair back from her face. It was shoulder length and probably blond when dry. They stood side by side and watched the rain. She was tall, almost the same height as him, and she had that toned look that meant she probably knew what the inside of a gym looked like. She was one hundred per cent not his type. Alex always went for short, curvy brunettes – like Anna, he thought with a wry twist of his lips.

'Do you think it will stop soon?'

He leant forward beyond the cover of the foliage. If anything, it was coming down even harder now.

'I don't think so. It looks like it's set in for the rest of the evening.'

'Damn,' she said, and then flushed charmingly as though she'd said something really filthy. Was that when he looked at her, properly looked at her, for the first time and realised he liked what he saw?

She was wearing a long filmy skirt that the rain had plastered to her thighs and a strappy T-shirt that made it pretty obvious she hadn't bothered putting on a bra beneath it. With an effort, Alex forced his attention to stray no further south than her chin.

'Are you cold?' he asked, which was a pretty unnecessary question as her teeth were chattering away like a set of maracas. Not giving her a chance to answer, he slipped off his denim jacket and draped it around her shoulders.

She smiled gratefully up at him and his insides did a very curious flip. All at once he really didn't want it to stop raining; he wanted it to keep on pouring down so they'd have to stay beneath this tree for the rest of the night.

'So, is the tale of star-crossed lovers one of your favourites?' he asked, aware he sounded like an idiot but unable to help himself. He just wanted to keep her there, talking to him.

She was kind enough not to laugh at his clumsy attempt to chat her up. 'Anything to do with stars is okay with me,' she had said intriguingly. 'I study astronomy.'

'Ahh. Interesting. I'm a Virgo, by the way.' Was it too soon to be that flirty, Alex wondered. He didn't care. There was something about this girl.

'Astronomy, not astrology,' she corrected, her lips only just managing not to break into a smile.

'I knew that.'

Their eyes met and it was far harder than it should have been to look away.

'I'm Alex.'

'Lisa.'

He looked up at the sky, which was still wonderfully full of rain.

'Do you fancy making a run for it? There's a pub on the other side of the common, where we could get dry… and maybe have a drink?' His heart was thumping nervously like it was the first time he'd ever asked anyone out.

She didn't hesitate – which wasn't like her at all, she confided later.

The ground was wet and dangerously slippery, and to keep her from falling he held out his hand to her and she took it. By the time they reached the pub, Alex already knew he never wanted to let it go.

'They want to talk to us again,' Todd said gently, his hand on Alex's arm.

'Why? What else is there for them to say?'

Todd's hold was firm but insistent. He was in full coping mode, and Alex imagined he felt better for having something to do. He had phoned everyone who needed to be told and then spent a long time in the corridor, speaking on his mobile to Dee. Alex knew he was being given time to say goodbye. If it had been decades, it still wouldn't have been long enough.

When Todd returned with red-rimmed eyes, he was at least able to reassure his brother that Connor was playing happily with his cousin Maisie. The young boy had been told nothing about the accident.

'How am I going to break it to him?' Alex asked, his voice cracking on every word. 'How do you explain something like this to a child?'

'One step at a time,' Todd said wisely. 'Let's get the hospital formalities done first.'

'You knew nothing about this, Mr Stevens? Lisa never mentioned it?'

Alex shook his head dumbly, his thoughts in freefall. The conversation had blindsided him. The woman with Dr Lloyd-Gordon was a specialist nurse, whose softly spoken words had pierced him like javelins. 'You were unaware that your wife had signed up to the Organ Donor Register?'

Alex's horrified glance had darted to his brother.

'She never discussed her wishes with you?' Gillian, the specialist nurse, probed.

'No, never.' Alex's answer was emphatic.

What he hadn't expected was the quiet contradiction from his older brother. 'Actually, that's not strictly true. There was that time a year or so ago, round at our place, when the subject came up.'

Snippets of that long-forgotten conversation floated like flotsam through Alex's memory. Lisa had been talking about something on the news to do with a new opt-out system. He shook his head again, trying to shake the years off the throwaway remarks. He could recall her saying, 'If anything ever happened to me—' before he'd quickly interrupted her, hating even the thought of a world without Lisa in it. 'Well, I doubt anyone will have much use for *my* liver, not once I've finished with it.' It was a feeble joke, and the fear in his voice had given away his true feelings.

'Why wouldn't she have told me she'd signed up to be an organ donor? How come I had to hear about it from a specialist nurse?'

Todd was quiet for a moment. 'I imagine Lisa didn't say anything to you because she knew how weird you get about medical shit.'

Alex looked down, examining his hands, which were clenched into fists on his knees.

'What if I object? What if I say I don't want her put through all that?'

Todd sighed. 'I'll support you whatever you decide. But do you really want to go against something Lisa felt so passionate about that she signed up in secret rather than upset you? Even if we do try to legally oppose it – which I'm not sure we can – do you want to stop her from helping people when that's what she did all her life? It was how she was with everyone. Lisa had the biggest and most generous heart—'

Todd bit his lip at his unfortunate choice of words and fell abruptly silent. But when he looked up, there was something new on Alex's face, something that looked very much like pride.

'Yes, she did,' he agreed softly.

CHAPTER SEVEN

Molly

It felt strange going to bed that night without having to set the alarm for a six o'clock start. The future stretched ahead of me like an unmarked road, and it wasn't a journey I was particularly looking forward to. I glanced over at the empty side of the bed, and for the first time in a very long while I found myself missing the man who used to lie there.

Tom and I had been uni housemates who'd become an item in our final year and moved in together after graduation, without ever pausing to question if we should. University relationships are a bit like holiday romances, some manage to last in the real world, and some don't. We had six years together, but by the last two all that was left between us was friendship. We separated amicably, vowing that we'd keep in touch. Of course, we didn't. But perhaps that was just as well, because six months later I fell sick. Tom was one of the good guys, and if he'd still been in my life when I'd received my diagnosis, he would never have gone. And that would have been bad for both of us.

Bizarrely, even if *you're* the sickest person in your entire family, when the phone rings in the middle of the night you automatically start cataloguing your elderly relatives, wondering which one of them you might have lost. *Not Mum, please don't let it be Mum*, I prayed silently as I threw back the duvet and rushed out into the hallway. 'I'm coming! I'm coming!' I told the phone as I hurried as fast as I could towards the staircase. For someone who never ran anywhere any more, I made surprisingly good time as I pushed my body faster than it wanted to go. Even so, I got there one ring too late and stared in dismay at the now silent handset. But before I could punch in the code to see if I recognised the number, I heard Nina Simone's distinctive voice filtering down from my bedroom, declaring, as ever, that she was 'feeling good'. It had been my father's favourite song, and whenever my mobile's ringtone sounded, it made him feel that little bit closer.

I hurried back up the stairs and just managed to snatch up the phone from where it was charging on my bedside table. I was wheezing badly, and fear had turned my voice into an inarticulate gasp. Fortunately, the caller spoke first.

'Is that Molly? Molly Kendall?'

Stupidly I nodded, before remembering I needed to attempt some kind of verbal response. We ended up speaking at exactly the same time, so I caught only the tail end of the woman's sentence.

'… get to the hospital.'

There *had* been an accident. There must have been. Had Mum had a fall, or maybe in a cruel twist of irony, *she'd* had a heart attack? She was the right age after all, and God knows she was permanently stressed. *About me*, a guilty voice silently reminded me. *It's not meant to be you, Mum*, I thought, as I sank down shakily onto the bed.

'Sorry. Can you say that again?'

'This is Mount Crescent Hospital, Molly. We need you to get here as soon as possible. We have a potential donor heart.'

*

The cab was there within twenty minutes. Just enough time for me to reach into my wardrobe and pull out the first thing my searching fingers fastened upon. My chest felt tight, but for once I wasn't panicked by the sensation. It had been so long since I'd felt this kind of excitement, I almost didn't recognise the emotion.

Having previously shot down my mother's hopeful prediction that the call could be just minutes away, I reached now for my mobile, fully prepared to eat a large slice of humble pie. Figuratively speaking, that is, because from this moment on I was nil-by-mouth. If my leaping around the room days hadn't been long gone, I would definitely have been doing a happy dance right there in my bedroom.

Mum answered her phone on the first ring, due to either insomnia or being permanently on high alert for bad news. Neither was good for her health. Perhaps after this we'd both have a chance to get well again. She made me repeat my news three times, and I truly don't think it sank in until the final telling. 'I can't believe it! I thought we'd have to wait… Are you sure that's what they said, Molly?'

My laugh sounded fragile, like glass breaking in a nearby room. I could feel how easily it might get away from me. I took a deep breath and tightened my grip on myself. 'I don't think it's the kind of thing they prank you about, Mum, not when you already have a dodgy heart.'

Her voice was suddenly thick with the tears she was struggling to hold back. 'It's so soon. They've only just put you on the list. Can it really be happening tonight?'

Something cold gushed like a geyser from my stomach all the way up to the back of my throat. 'Yes, it can.'

There was a pause as the enormity of the moment travelled the distance of the phone line between us. Mum was the first to break it. If my default setting was humour, hers was always practicality.

'How are you getting to the hospital? You're not planning on driving yourself, are you?'

'No. I've called for a taxi; it'll be here in a few minutes.'

'Then I'll meet you at the hospital, sweetheart.'

It was two thirty in the morning, and while the sensible part of me knew I should be telling my seventy-year-old mother to stay in her own home and wait for news, there was another part of me that didn't want to do this without her. Apparently thirty-one isn't too old to discover that you still need your mum by your side after all.

'Would you mind carrying my case to the car for me? I'm sorry, but I can't manage it myself.'

The driver bent down and swung up my bag with such ease I wondered if I'd mistakenly forgotten to pack anything inside it. He paused in the yellow pool of light from a nearby streetlamp and studied me. I could practically see the equation forming in his eyes. Young woman; clearly nervously excited; calling for a cab to take her to the hospital in the middle of the night.

'If you don't mind me asking, you're not about to have a baby, are you? Because I've had someone give birth in the back of my cab once, and, no disrespect, but I'd prefer not to go through that ever again.'

Even as I reassured my driver that I wasn't about to turn him into a reluctant midwife, I was mentally consigning the baggy top I was wearing to the charity shop. 'I'm definitely not having a baby,' I told him. There was something in my voice that didn't sound quite right. It wasn't just nerves or suppressed excitement, it was something else hiding behind those emotions, elusively just out of reach. 'Although in a way it *is* almost like being born again,' I continued. 'You see, I'm getting a new heart tonight.'

The driver didn't look like the kind of man who was often lost for words, but my reply made his mouth drop open and it took several seconds before he remembered how to close it. He took a step back, looking at me in the way I imagine a bomb squad might survey an unexploded device.

'Should I carry *you* to the car too?' His eyes darted around and beyond me, presumably hoping to spot a previously unseen companion who'd be accompanying us to the hospital.

Sorry, my friend, it's just you and me. 'I'm fine to walk.'

It was the first time I'd ever had a cabbie triple-check I was safely buckled up before he drove off. He was still muttering to himself as he checked his rear-view mirror twice before pulling out into the totally deserted street. He drove like an eighty-year-old on a driving test or a man transporting nitro-glycerine. This was one fare I didn't imagine he'd forget in a hurry, and I could almost hear him regaling the story to his cab driver friends over something artery-damaging in a greasy-spoon cafe come breakfast-time.

Even though I didn't need it, he insisted on taking my elbow and supporting me all the way into the cardiology department. He was so invested in my care that I actually had to remind him that I still owed him money for the ride. In a sappy film he'd have told me to forget it, but real life isn't like a Hollywood script. Paying him felt delightfully normal, in a night that was anything but.

Like a well-organised team of commandos, the hospital staff swung into action. A wheelchair was waiting for me, which I insisted I didn't need but was gently led to anyway. I'd been in and out of hospital so often since my illness, I was surprised by how alien everything felt. Even though I recognised the faces of several members of the cardiac team, tonight there was a serious-ness and intensity in them I'd never seen before.

I'd read up extensively on what would happen on this day, still never quite believing it would ever come. I was prepared for the blood tests, the X-rays and the ECG, as well as the many questions about my current state of health. What I hadn't been expecting was the feeling of niggling disquiet, the one that had been lingering just out of reach since the hospital's phone call. In a quiet moment between the tests and before my mother arrived, it surfaced suddenly like submerged wreckage rising from the ocean floor.

Someone had died.

On this night, when my life was about to be given back to me, someone else had lost theirs. The end of their story was the beginning of mine, and the weight of that responsibility felt suddenly overwhelming.

'Do you know whose heart it is I'm getting? Do you know what happened to them?'

With tears rolling down my cheeks, I listened solemnly as they gave me my answer. My donor was a woman; she'd been in her thirties and had been involved in an accident.

There were gaps, cavernous ones, which they weren't allowed to fill. But I asked the questions anyway. 'What happened to her? What kind of accident? Was she married? Did she have a family?' They answered me with a gentle shake of the head. In the world of organ donation, patient anonymity was more than just a byword, it was a sacred oath.

'How can you accept something this precious without thanking the people who gave it to you?'

The transplant coordinator took hold of my hands. Hers felt warm, while mine hardly ever were these days. *That will change*, I thought. *After tonight, when the donor's heart replaces mine, my hands and feet will be warm again; my body will grow stronger. It'll be like turning back time as everything I've lost will be returned to me, given by a woman I'll never be able to thank.*

'You'll be able to write to the donor family – afterwards,' the coordinator told me gently. 'It will help both you and them.'

She left me with thoughts of half-drafted letters that would never be able to adequately express the gratitude in my heart. *Her heart*, I silently corrected.

*

'Am I in time? Is she still here?'

The starchy pillowcase felt scratchy behind my neck as I twisted my head towards the billowing cubicle curtains. In their gap stood my mother, white-faced and wide-eyed with concern.

'Molly! Thank God,' she said. The escaping tension seemed to instantly deflate her. Her eyes looked wet and were filled with a mix of hope, love and fear as they fell on me. We hugged, getting tangled up in the wires that connected me to a variety of monitors.

'The cab took so long to get here and then I couldn't find the ward and I was petrified you'd already have been taken up to the operating theatre—'

She was as close to panicking as I had ever seen her and it was a weird reversal of the roles we'd played all our lives to suddenly be the one calming her.

'Everything's okay, Mum. Breathe.' The sedative they'd given me had slowed my speech, but my new-found serenity wasn't due to the drugs. A feeling of peace I hadn't been expecting had settled over me, as comforting as a thick, downy fleece. My fate was no longer in my own hands, and, oddly for someone who liked to be in control, I was perfectly okay with that.

'They're still waiting for the heart to get here. It shouldn't be long now.'

Mum gulped noisily and her head bobbed up and down like a nodding-dog mascot on a car's parcel shelf. 'How do you feel, Molly?'

I smiled into the face I'd loved for thirty-one years. Never before had I seen it look this terrified.

'Like I've had one too many glasses of Prosecco,' I said, my voice slurred from the medication.

She went for a laugh, but it broke halfway through. She reached out and brushed the hair back from my forehead, the way she'd done through countless childhood fevers.

'My brave, beautiful daughter,' she murmured, as quietly as a prayer.

I took her trembling hand in mine and laced my fingers through hers. We both turned with a start when the cubicle curtains parted with a parrot-like screech. In the opening stood a nurse I didn't recognise and an orderly.

It was time.

'Please try not to worry, Mum,' I urged as they began uncoupling my bed from the bay. She still had hold of my hand as they began to wheel me away, our palms gradually sliding apart until only our fingertips were touching.

I knew how long the operation would take, and I really didn't want her waiting around for another five or six hours, but there would have been little point in telling her not to stay. She would be there at my bedside until I opened my eyes. Hers would be the first face I saw – as long as everything went well. And if her greatest fear was realised and things went badly, then the face I would see would be my father's.

Either way, someone I loved would be waiting for me.

CHAPTER EIGHT

Alex

Alex's recollections of leaving the hospital would always be a series of distorted images; out-of-focus, jagged-edged memories that were too painful to either remember or forget.

He recalled the porter wheeling Lisa's bed from her hospital room and how, in a mark of respect that almost destroyed him, every nurse and doctor, and even passing orderlies, had stopped whatever they were doing to stand back against the walls of the corridor, bowing their heads in silence as Lisa made her final journey to the operating theatre. It was a guard of honour, and it ripped what was left of Alex's heart to shreds.

He sobbed unashamedly in the lift, as though the steel box was a confessional booth. Todd reached out blindly, pulling his distraught brother towards him. Neither was aware of the passengers that joined and left the lift on its descent, although Alex would always remember the gentle squeeze of a stranger's hand on his shoulder and the gruffly spoken words of the heavily tattooed man who had the courage to speak when others did not. 'Really sorry for whatever's happened to you today, mate,' he said before walking away.

In the car Alex was numb. 'He was practically catatonic,' Todd told Dee later. 'It felt like we'd lost both of them. He just stared out the windscreen for the whole two-hour drive. He only snapped out of it when he realised we were back home and that Connor was waiting.'

Alex followed Todd down the path to the front door on legs that felt as detached as the rest of him. 'Dee's not told Connor anything?' he asked as Todd fished in his pocket for his door key.

Todd shook his head and Alex noticed how pale his usually ruddy-complexioned brother looked. All colour had been leached from his skin. Was that how *he* looked too, he wondered. He slapped his cheeks hard enough to hurt as he crossed the threshold into the house. The physical pain was a welcome momentary distraction from the all-consuming emotional pain.

Dee hurried into the hallway to greet them, her hand fleetingly grasping her husband's as she swept past him to reach Alex. It was late in the evening, every light in the house was lit and yet she was wearing sunglasses. She pulled them off before enfolding her brother-in-law in her arms. The reason for the Ray-Bans became clear; the red of her eyes matched the colour of her hair.

She held him close for a long moment, saying nothing, because words were redundant.

Gathering up his resolve, Alex gently extricated himself from her embrace. 'Where is he?'

'Watching TV with Maisie.'

He nodded dumbly.

'I think… I think he knows something's wrong,' Dee said, her voice dropping to a whisper as the door of the lounge swung open and Connor hurtled through it. His glance took in the adults in the hallway. The realisation in his eyes was impossible to ignore. Three instead of four. Someone was missing.

'Would you like us to stay?' Dee asked softly, her eyes already going to her own daughter, who was standing hesitantly in the doorway her cousin had just raced through.

Alex shook his head, his gaze fixed on his son's confused face. 'Where's Mummy?'

Connor peered around his father, as though Lisa was playing a really effective game of hide-and-seek. The quiet click of the lounge door confirmed to Alex they were alone.

'Where's Mummy?' Connor asked again, and his voice was different this time, higher and more babyish than Alex had heard in years.

'Come over here,' Alex said, sitting down on one of the lower treads of the stairs and patting the vacant space beside him.

Connor stared suspiciously at the step and then looked back at the front door. He shook his head.

'Is Mummy still at the Astronomy Fair? She said she'd be back in time for my bedtime story, but it's so late now.'

The gaping wound in Alex's chest was growing larger with every second. The last thing in the world he wanted was to inflict this pain on his own child, but that was exactly what he was about to do.

'Connor, please sit down,' Alex urged, and something in his father's tone got through to the young boy. His lower lip began to tremble as he shakily did as he was asked.

'Am I in trouble?' he said, his voice wobbling now as much as his lip. 'Is it about the juice this morning?'

Alex stared at him blankly. As though it had happened to an entirely different Alex and Connor, he remembered the incident in the kitchen. It existed in a world where Lisa was there to make everything right. A world he'd never live in again.

'No, Connor. It's nothing to do with that.'

He wrapped one arm around his son and drew him gently against his side. His bones felt fragile. *Make this not be real*, Alex silently pleaded to a God he had never believed in. *Please make this go away and I'll do anything you want.* He closed his eyes, but when he opened them again all he could see were Lisa's eyes staring worriedly up at him from Connor's terrified face.

'I have something very sad to tell you.'

The lower lip was trembling so much, Alex was surprised his little boy could still speak.

'I don't want to hear anything sad. I want Mummy.'

Me too, Alex thought, his own tears beginning to fall.

'You know that Mummy went to the Astronomy Fair today?'

'On the train,' said Connor, looking scared when Alex winced as the words stabbed at him.

'Yes. Well, a terrible thing happened. The train had an accident and a lot of people were hurt.'

Connor made the connection almost instantly. 'Was Mummy hurt?'

Alex's throat had tightened. No words could squeeze through it, so he just looked into Connor's eyes and nodded slowly.

'But we can give her some Calpol and she'll get all better,' Connor said, his small fingers digging deeply into the flesh of Alex's arm.

Alex pulled Connor even closer, but it felt as though he was cuddling a small marble statue. *He knows*, Alex thought. *Somehow, he already knows.*

'Mummy hit her head in the train and the doctors tried very hard to make her all better, but they couldn't fix it.' Alex swallowed. He was almost there. Just one more sentence and this torture would become an entirely new kind of agony.

'A really bad thing has happened to Mummy, Connor. She has died.'

'No. No. No. No. No.'

The word rang through the house like a tolling bell. Connor wriggled violently out of Alex's hold and marched towards the front door as though to leave this evil place where grown-ups told lies that couldn't possibly be true.

He turned around and faced his father, who was getting shakily to his own feet and reaching out for him.

'No. I don't want you. I want Mummy. Please, Daddy, make her come home. Make her come home *right now*. She promised. She promised me she'd come back.'

CHAPTER NINE

Molly

Six months later

'Honestly, Mol, it hardly shows at all.'

I paused halfway through dusting another layer of powder onto the concealer I'd applied to the scar, which rose like an antenna from the V of my jumper. I sighed and leant a little closer towards the age-flecked mirror in the staff toilets. The light was always harsh in here, making everyone appear to be in need of an extended period of sick leave, even if – like me – you'd just had one. Under the ghostly white fluorescent glare, the vivid cerise of my scar refused to be hidden.

'I don't know why you're worried about it. It's a victory badge; you should wear it with pride.'

Kyra was right, and I certainly wasn't ashamed of my scar, but it did invite comment – even from total strangers, who'd boldly ask how I got it. It was a topic I still found difficult to discuss. But short of spending the rest of my life in polo necks, it was a hurdle I was going to have to get over. Perhaps it was something I should mention at my next counselling session?

I zipped up my make-up bag and turned to my friend and colleague, who I doubted had suffered a single moment of insecurity about her appearance. Kyra had a face that made magazine models look ugly and risked giving men whiplash when she walked past them in the street. But perhaps that was just as uncomfortable as having people stare at your post-op scar.

'I just don't want to draw the children's attention to it,' I said. 'I wouldn't want it to scare them.'

Kyra gave an inelegant snort, making her sound like an Antipodean Miss Piggy. 'You're joking, right? Half the kids in my class are convinced you're related to Iron Man. Your street-cred rating is through the roof.'

I laughed and turned back to the mirror, running my finger down the line in the centre of my breastbone. It was less puckered now than it had been, but it was still raised, like a brand seared onto my chest.

Beneath my fingertips I could feel the strong steady beat of my new heart. If the school boiler hadn't been noisily chuntering away on the other side of the plasterboard wall, I might even have been able to hear it. Transplanted hearts beat faster and louder than the ones we are born with. In the middle-of-the-night hours, in the quiet of my bedroom, it resonated with a rhythm I still couldn't decipher. Was it protesting about its new location or beating out a tattoo to signal that it lived on?

'And I wouldn't go wasting a single second worrying about what any future boyfriend will think of it,' added Kyra, jumping lithely down from the narrow window ledge she was perched on.

If my eyebrows had risen any higher, they'd have disappeared into my hairline. 'I truly can't think of anything less likely to have crossed my mind.'

'Good,' Kyra said, throwing an arm around my shoulders and giving me a comforting squeeze. 'Because, believe me, with assets like yours, the last thing any guy in that region will be looking at is your scar.'

A wave of pink flooded my cheeks, which even the draining fluorescent lights couldn't wash away.

We walked together down the corridor towards our respective classrooms. The novelty of being easily able to keep up with Kyra's long-legged stride still hadn't worn off. It was just one of the many changes I was getting used to. These days there were sportswear outfits hanging up beside the vintage dresses in my wardrobe, and they weren't just there as a fashion statement. Tom, who'd begged me for years to join his gym, would have barely recognised the new me. At times, when I looked in the mirror and saw the healthy glowing complexion – no hint of grey in it now – I didn't either.

'Whoa. You've certainly rung the changes in here this term,' Kyra exclaimed, coming to an abrupt halt by the open doorway of my Year One classroom. 'Where's the woodland frieze with the cute foxes and bunnies you always put up at this time of year?'

I followed her gaze to the back wall, which this year was covered in a wide swathe of black sugar paper rather than the forest green she'd clearly been expecting to see. She was right; in place of the trees, tractors and farm animals was a galaxy of stars and planets.

I gave what I hoped was an inconsequential shrug, while trying to ignore the prick of disquiet that pierced my conscience like a needle, because this new fascination was a mystery to me too. 'I don't know. No reason, really. I just fancied doing something a bit different with the class this year.'

Kyra looked at me curiously, before sending a broad grin my way. 'Well, good on you for doing something different,' she replied, her accent suddenly much more pronounced. 'I bet the kids will love it.' She glanced once more at the display I'd worked on for hours after school the day before, and then with a shrug turned towards her own classroom. I wondered if she even realised she was quietly humming the *Star Wars* theme tune as she went.

*

I parked in my favourite spot in the hospital car park. It was tucked away in the furthest corner, half hidden beneath the boughs of an elder tree. By June, when I'd finally been given the all-clear to drive, I used to come out from the latest of my frequent appointments to find my car half buried in confetti-like blossom.

I marked the passage of time not via the pages of the calendar but from the foliage by my car. The end of summer had seen the ground covered in leaves which crunched like cornflakes beneath my feet. But now, as October took hold, the tarmac was a minefield of spiky green husks from a horse chestnut tree that towered over the elder like an elderly guardian.

'No problems with any of your anti-rejection medication, Molly?'

'None.' The drugs I would need to take for the rest of my life were a small price to pay for still being here.

'And are you sleeping better now?'

'Yes. Much better, thanks.'

The doctor paused to scratch a tick against the form in front of him and moved on to his next question. You weren't meant to lie to your physicians, but I did so instinctively. Perhaps I didn't want a single negative to mar my progress. Because from the moment I'd woken up in the ICU ward, my recovery had read like a page from a medical textbook. 'You're like the poster girl for organ donation,' my cardiologist had declared happily. And yet the biopsies, ECGs and blood test results that swelled my medical file only told half the story.

It was hard to pinpoint exactly when the dreams had begun or why they continued to tug me from my sleep at least twice a week. They were unlike any I'd experienced before, but I couldn't have said how or why, because the second I woke up, I couldn't remember a thing about them. There were images, colours and sounds that danced enticingly just out of reach as my eyes snapped open, but they instantly disappeared behind a veil my waking mind couldn't seem to penetrate.

They'd been worse in the summer, so intense that they'd frequently dragged me from my bed, breathless and covered in a film of sweat. Quietly, so as not to disturb my mother, who'd invariably be snoring rhythmically in the spare room, I'd tiptoe like a burglar through the house and let myself out into the garden. It was only when the cool night air caressed my skin that the dream would slowly unshackle itself from my head. In all the heart-transplant accounts I'd read – and I'd read a lot – I couldn't find a single patient who'd experienced such dreams.

Even a small city garden like mine wore a different face at night from its daytime persona. It had felt exotic and oddly alien as I sat on the wooden bench, staring up at a star-strewn sky. It made me feel a connection with something – nature, maybe – that I'd never known before.

My nocturnal forays had stopped when the weather got too cold for middle-of-the-night stargazing, but the dreams had persisted.

The sodium lamps that illuminated the hospital car park had not yet come on as I made my way back to the car, avoiding the potholes and puddles and pulling my coat a little tighter around me to keep out the damp chill. It had rained while I'd been in the hospital and a windfall of spiky seed pods from the horse chestnut were now scattered across the roof and bonnet of my car. I went to sweep them off but at the last moment changed my mind. There were loads of them, almost enough for every child in my class to have one, and they'd make a great display for the nature table.

After a brief and fruitless rummage in my car for a carrier bag, I scooped up the hem of my dress to form a makeshift pouch and began lobbing in the husks. I was four short of my target, so I ducked into the shadows behind my car to make up the numbers. Disappointingly, there were none there, but there were at least half a dozen behind the car parked next to mine. I dropped to a crouch and was scooping them up when I was suddenly dazzled by the glare of brilliant white lights just inches from my nose. There was only a split second to register they were reversing lights. The heart so newly transplanted in my chest gave a leap as though struggling to get out. To have survived transplant surgery only to get run over in a car park while collecting conkers seemed beyond ludicrous.

I jerked to my feet, scattering the seed pods in every direction as I thumped on the rear panel of the car with enough force to hurt my hands. The white lights immediately turned to red. I heard the screech of a handbrake being applied, moments before the driver's door was flung open.

'Jesus. Are you okay?'

He was tall, but in the dimming light that was all I could make out.

'I very nearly wasn't,' I said, stepping out from behind his car, my new heart still pounding at its very first encounter with danger. Well, its first encounter while it was in *my* care, that is.

'What kind of person hides behind parked cars in a poorly lit car park?'

His attitude was as spiky as the horse chestnut casings I'd just dropped.

'What kind of person reverses without looking?' I shot back.

'I looked.'

'Well, apparently not very carefully,' I said, striding towards my own driver's door just as the car park lights finally flickered on.

The man had been impossible to age from his voice, but I could see now he was probably in his mid-thirties. Anything else was hard to discern as his eyes were hidden behind a pair of sunglasses. *Who on earth wears dark glasses on a winter's afternoon,* I thought testily as I fumbled for my door handle.

'What were you doing back there, anyway?'

Perhaps it was the close call that had brought that edge into his voice. Or perhaps he was always like that. It was impossible to tell.

'Conkers. I was collecting conkers.'

He stared at me for a long moment as though I was genuinely crazy; at least that's what I assumed he was doing. Then, when I'd decided he might very possibly be the most disagreeable person I'd ever met, he surprised me by asking once again, 'Are you sure you're all right?'

'Perfectly, thank you.'

Both of our voices had become more clipped, in a terribly British and unnatural way. We sounded like we'd walked straight off the set of a period drama.

He nodded curtly and then slipped back into the driver's seat, shaking his head as though bemused. He muttered a single word before shutting his door with a definitive clunk; I couldn't tell for sure, but it sounded an awful lot more like 'bonkers' than 'conkers'.

I was still bristling as I pulled the seatbelt across my body and slotted it home. The fault here was largely mine, but if he hadn't been wearing those idiotic Ray-Bans when it was twilight… My thoughts trailed away as my headlamps caught the sign outside the nearest outpatient department, the one I must surely have seen a dozen times on my previous visits but had never really noticed. *Ophthalmic Unit.*

The man's tail lights had disappeared into the distance, so there was no opportunity to offer him an apology, but perhaps those glasses *had* been something more than just a fashion statement after all.

CHAPTER TEN

Alex

It was the pronouns that always tripped him up. He still said *us* instead of *me*, and *ours* instead of *mine*. He'd done it again just now and couldn't decide which was worse: to correct the mistake or let it go and hope no one had noticed.

Todd was scrutinising the vegetables on the board in front of him before starting to chop them at a speed that made Alex fear for his fingertips. Dee, meanwhile, sprang to her feet and began topping up their practically full wine glasses. They'd noticed.

The kitchen smelt fragrantly of the meat roasting in the oven. Alex already knew Dee would pile his plate up like a miniature Mount Everest in an effort to put back some of the ten pounds he'd lost over the last six months. He didn't have the heart to tell her to stop, that there wasn't enough food in the world to fill the aching void inside him.

There were five stages of grief, or so Alex had read, but it felt as if he'd uncovered at least a hundred more. He carouselled between most of them on an almost daily basis. If it hadn't been for Connor, who was the thread binding his life together, Alex had no doubt he'd have unravelled completely long ago.

Thoughts of his son drew him off the shiny chrome breakfast bar stool, and he padded across his brother's kitchen to the open doorway of the family room. The two young cousins were sitting cross-legged on the floor, amidst a sea of Lego bricks. They had their backs to the door, so Alex could watch unobserved as seven-year-old Maisie gamely attempted to entice Connor into her game.

'If you like, we could make it a space station for Barbie instead of a house. She's always wanted to live on the moon.'

Maisie was like a playful puppy who never once stopped looking for the Connor she used to know in the quiet, withdrawn boy who'd taken his place. The smallest things could crack an already broken heart, and watching his son's shoulders lift in a dispirited shrug did so for Alex. But maybe his young niece was onto something, because without saying a word, Connor leant forward, grabbed a handful of colourful bricks and began snapping them together.

Feeling a little relieved, Alex backed quietly away from the door and re-joined Todd and Dee in the kitchen. It took three mouthfuls of chilled Sauvignon Blanc before he found the courage to speak.

'That thing I was talking about the other day…' He glanced towards the family room door and lowered his voice a decibel or two. 'I've decided to go ahead and do it. I'm going to invite them.'

Todd's eyes found Dee's and Alex followed the look of concern that flashed between them like a distress flare. Todd cleared his throat as though to rid it of all the words of disapproval he knew he shouldn't be using right now.

'I see.' As hard as Todd had tried, 'politely interested' had still come out as 'seriously concerned'.

'I know what you both think,' Alex said, jumping in before further objections could be raised. 'And I know you're both worried about me and Connor – and I love you for that – but this is something I want to do. That I *have* to do,' he quietly corrected.

Todd nodded slowly, though Alex knew better than to mistake that for approval. 'And when do you think you might… When were you thinking of asking—'

'It's already done. I posted the letters yesterday.'

'Who to?'

'To all of them.'

The subject wasn't raised again until Alex and Connor were shrugging on their coats and getting ready to leave. Dee had bustled down the hallway from the kitchen and pressed a warm, foil-wrapped bundle into his hands.

'It's the rest of the beef. It should make another dinner for both of you.'

'Dee, you don't have to—' Alex began, but he was silenced by her hand on his arm and the look in her eyes.

'We're here for you, Alex. Todd and me, and Maisie, we just want to help you through this.'

They had, he wanted to say. They'd been walking invisibly beside him for the last six months; picking him up when he stumbled, taking his elbow to guide him when he was so lost in missing Lisa he didn't know how to go on. He couldn't have got through this without them.

'Whatever you need from us, you only have to ask, remember that.'

It was obvious no one was talking about leftover Sunday roast any more. Alex was under no illusions; he knew Todd and Dee weren't exactly on board with this plan, but he hoped they'd support him regardless.

'You'll still come, won't you? Both of you?'

Dee glanced towards Todd, who was just far enough away not to be able to hear what they were talking about.

'It's to celebrate Lisa's birthday. Of course we'll be there,' she promised.

*

'You okay back there, champ? You were a bit quiet at Uncle Todd's today.' It was the understatement of the century, thought Alex as his hands tightened unconsciously on the steering wheel.

He met Connor's eyes in the rear-view mirror. Where once there'd been laughter and mischief in their blue depths, all he could see now was sadness and loss. It was the same expression Alex saw in his own bathroom mirror every morning.

'It looked like you and Maisie were having fun building a moon station,' he coaxed.

Connor looked down, his fingers twiddling with the zipper tag on his jacket. 'You can't live on the moon. Mummy says it's not possible.'

Alex forced his mouth into a smile of agreement. If pronouns were *his* downfall, then with Connor the struggle was with tenses. He only spoke of Lisa in the present, never in the past. The bereavement counsellor Connor had been seeing for the last four months said this was perfectly normal. That in time he would adjust his language to his new reality.

It was now six months since Alex had held his sobbing child in his arms after brokenly explaining through his own tears that Mummy wasn't coming back home again. In truth, Alex couldn't see that Connor was any closer to accepting what had happened. And how could he blame him for that when neither was he.

'That's all for tonight. We'll finish the story tomorrow,' Alex promised, easing himself off the single bed and drawing the duvet up snugly beneath Connor's chin. As he replaced the book on the brightly painted shelving unit (the one Lisa had stencilled with stars) and bent to retrieve a rogue sock that had missed the laundry basket, he could feel his son's eyes following him. Locked behind their cerulean depths – the colour he'd inherited from his mum – were feelings Connor wouldn't, or couldn't, share with anyone. Not even his father. It didn't matter that Alex was doing all the right things, keeping to the familiar routines and following Lisa's blueprint of parenthood to the letter. Somehow he was still managing to screw it all up.

He turned off the overhead light and flicked a switch by the plug, looking upwards as the ceiling became a revolving carousel of stars. It was an infant's night light, one which Connor had outgrown several years earlier. But just days after the train crash his son had dragged it out from the back of the toy cupboard and refused to sleep without it. The image of Lisa lying beside Connor and pointing out each of the planets as they travelled from one ceiling cornice to the other burnt brightly in Alex's memory every time he switched it on. In Connor's too, he suspected.

'We're going to have the only kid in the nursery who's better acquainted with Galileo than Peppa Pig,' he'd teased, wrapping his arms around Lisa and feeling the weight of her relax against his body as they'd stood in Connor's bedroom doorway, watching the planets spiral their little boy into sleep.

'And that's wrong, how?' she'd asked, twisting in his arms and tilting up her face for his kiss. It was an invitation he'd never been able to refuse.

The memory sliced like a stiletto through his ribs, and Alex fought to keep it from his face as he bent to kiss Connor's forehead.

'Goodnight, big man. Sleep tight. I love you.'

Connor tore his gaze away from Ursa Major, or Minor – Alex never had been able to figure out which was which – and gave his dad a smile; it was all lips and no eyes. 'Me too.'

Alex had stopped waiting for more. Connor loved him, he knew that, but for now the words were locked away behind a wall of grief.

He left the room, his bare feet soundless on the bedroom carpet, but out of sight in the hallway he stopped and waited for the wound to be ripped open all over again. Connor's voice, which was barely more than a whisper in the darkened room, still travelled straight to Alex's heart.

'I love you, Mummy. To the moon and back.'

It was their refrain, Lisa and Connor's. She'd said it to him ever since he was a tiny baby. Those words had accompanied her goodnight kiss every single night. Only now it was Connor who said them, as softly as a prayer in the quiet of his room.

The night sky was their secret place, Connor and Lisa's, so of course his son would look for his mum there. How could he not? Alex felt the tug of a memory pulling at his heart, to a night seven years earlier when he and Lisa had stood beneath a sky full of stars...

'I want to walk.'

'Well, that's not happening right now,' Alex said, reaching for another scoop of ice chips from the wine cooler bucket beside him. 'Here, suck on this,' he said, holding them out to her.

Amazingly, Lisa laughed. 'That's the kind of offer that gets people into exactly this sort of situation.'

Alex's cheeks grew hot as the midwife crouched on the floor behind him tried very hard to suppress a laugh. 'I'm sorry,' he apologised over his shoulder. 'She's not normally like that.' To be fair, the woman didn't seem the least bit fazed by his wife's out-of-character remark.

'That's okay. You get to hear all kinds of things when they're in transition.'

Alex nodded, having absolutely no idea what she was talking about. In truth, he had no idea about anything that was happening that night. He'd politely declined all suggestions he might want to read some of the many books Lisa had devoured during her pregnancy or watch the childbirth DVDs she'd come home with from her antenatal classes. It had stung a little that she'd chosen to take Dee with her to those sessions, rather than him. 'They'd only freak you out even more than you already are,' she'd told him, softening her words with a gentle kiss. 'You know how you get about this kind of thing.'

He did know, but that didn't mean he wasn't going to be right there beside her for the birth of their first child. 'It'll be far better for you if you just wing it on the day,' Lisa had assured him, letting him off the hook in a way he'd been grateful for back then but was now beginning to regret.

'I really do want to walk somewhere,' Lisa repeated, a little more firmly this time.

'That's a good idea, actually,' chimed in the midwife before Alex had a chance to reply. 'It often makes things happen much quicker.'

Quicker was good, Alex thought, trying to disguise the fact that he was so far out of his depth now, he was starting to panic. The sooner this was over and Lisa's body was no longer being racked by wave after wave of pain, the better.

'Where do you want to walk?' he asked, getting to his feet and offering her a helping hand up from the nest of blankets and cushions they'd created on the floor of their lounge.

'The garden,' she said on a gasp, as another contraction took hold of her.

While he waited for it to pass, Alex turned to the midwife, who he still thought looked far too young to be in charge of the night's events. She nodded her approval, and when Lisa was ready, he gave her his arm and took her weight as they headed outside.

The newspaper headlines that had predicted an almost tropical heatwave hadn't been wrong. It was well past midnight, and yet the air was still muggy; the temperature had barely dropped from its barometer-rocking heights of the day. The French windows leading onto the patio were cracked open – enough for air but not enough for a moth to gain entry, which was the last thing Lisa needed right now. Alex flung them wide and led his labouring wife into the quiet stillness of the garden.

Wearing nothing except one of Alex's oversized university T-shirts, now gossamer thin with age, Lisa still looked uncomfortably hot as they headed towards the lawn. Beneath a waxy yellow moon Alex could see the tiny rivulets of sweat running down her body, joining together like tributaries as they passed her now impressively large breasts and the even more impressive swell of her belly. Her face was glistening with perspiration and her hair was damp against her forehead. Alex didn't think she had ever looked more beautiful.

'You'd better not be thinking of giving birth out here by the flowerbeds, because I'm telling you right now, I'm vetoing any plant names for our child. No Pansy, Lily or Rose. Okay?' He was desperate to say something to make her smile, and he succeeded.

'I'm okay with that, especially as I'm convinced it's going to be a boy anyway.'

Alex ran his free hand over the dome of her stomach, realising this might be one of the last times he'd be able to do that. They'd both agreed they didn't want to know the sex of their baby, but there seemed to be an awful lot of blue baby clothes in the collection of newborn garments Lisa had bought.

'Maybe we could name him after a planet,' she suggested after yet another contraction had shuddered through her.

'If we call him Pluto, people are just going to think of the Disney dog,' Alex reasoned, 'and don't get me started on the teasing he'll have to endure if you name him Uranus.'

Lisa's laughter was snatched away by a gasp that sounded urgent. 'You know what, maybe we should go back inside.'

Fifteen minutes later, beside the open French windows through which the stars were still visible, their son had slipped quietly into the world.

'I'd like to call him Connor,' Lisa had whispered, the baby wet and slippery against her naked chest.

Alex's heart had been so full, words were almost impossible. He'd looked down at the two people who were now his entire universe and nodded happily while the tears ran freely down his cheeks.

CHAPTER ELEVEN

Alex

These days, Alex worked from home far more than he'd done before, his workday frequently extending late into the night until exhaustion finally forced him to switch off his laptop before he made careless mistakes. Ironically, while the rest of his life felt as though it was quietly disintegrating, his business was actually thriving. Which was more than could be said for his social life, which comprised only time spent with Todd and Dee. It was all he'd been capable of coping with. Until now.

Alex slipped the foil-wrapped parcel of meat Dee had given him into the fridge and then reached into the back of a tall kitchen cupboard and drew down a half-empty bottle of whisky and a tumbler. Without Connor to consider, it might have been all too easy to have developed an unhealthy relationship with Messrs Bean and Daniels. But Alex strictly rationed his intake to a single glass each night. *To help me sleep*, or so he told himself. Although, in fairness, falling asleep wasn't a problem for him. His body was more than eager to relinquish consciousness at the end of each day. It was staying asleep that he struggled with.

The ice cubes rattled in the glass like dice on a gaming table until he drowned them in several fingers of alcohol. He took the drink with him as he padded back up the stairs to the office he and Lisa had shared. Her desk looked the same. He couldn't bring himself to either touch or clear it. It was the same story in the bathroom, where shower gels he would never use sat beside hair products he had no need of. He had no idea if keeping so much of Lisa around them was making it easier or harder for him and Connor. All he knew was that he was unable to contemplate a time when he'd open the wardrobe doors and see a line of empty hangers swinging there instead of his wife's clothes.

Whisky in hand, he entered the office and settled himself at his desk. But the file he reached for didn't bear the name of a client or have anything to do with his PR company. The edges of the portfolio were gently curled, like a much-borrowed library book or a well-thumbed bestseller. But this was neither of those. Alex took a fortifying mouthful of his nightcap before opening the folder. Within it was a collection of coloured plastic sleeves, but he pushed those to one side to reach the document he'd first clipped into the file two weeks after Lisa died.

It was a letter he could have recited in his sleep. He knew the position of every comma, every full stop. He'd read it a thousand times, and yet it still hit him like a punch in the solar plexus. He skipped over the opening paragraph, and allowed his eyes a brief rest stop on the sentence that always caught him like a tripwire:

I am pleased to tell you that at the time of writing this letter, four people have received an organ transplant following Lisa's donation.

Almost unconsciously, Alex's gaze flashed to the four coloured plastic sleeves. Was there ever a time this letter would be easy to read? The lump in his throat told him probably not. He drew the letter further into the pool of light from the desk lamp before reading on.

A young man in his twenties who had been on the recipient waiting list for over one year received a double lung transplant. A gentleman in his thirties received a double cornea transplant. A woman in her seventies who had been on the recipient waiting list for over five years received a kidney transplant. And a young lady in her thirties received a lifesaving heart transplant.

Four strangers. Four recipients of a priceless gift Alex would never stop wishing *he'd* given instead of *her*. These were the four lives Lisa had changed when her own had been lost.

In flashback he could visualise himself in that small sterile room at St Mark's, as Gillian, the specialist nurse, passed him the consent form to sign. There'd been a roaring in his head as his blood pumped too hard and too fast through his veins, just because it could. It had felt like an insult to Lisa. Through the roaring, Alex had vaguely heard Todd talking; asking the nurse some question, he guessed. Their words were hazy and indistinct, sharpening only as he set the pen to the dotted line and signed his name.

A hand was laid on his arm, too light and soft to be his brother's. 'If you're willing,' the nurse said, 'we'd like to write to you within fifteen days to tell you how Lisa's donation has been used. Donor families often find this a great comfort. And in time, some of those recipients might want to contact you themselves, to thank you directly. But you don't have to decide right now if you'd like to receive those messages. And please don't feel you're under any obligation to say yes, Alex. Not tonight, nor anytime in the future.'

His head had shot up, and even though nothing was making sense in his life any more, even though the world as he knew it had ceased to turn, about this one thing he was completely certain.

'Of course "yes". Absolutely. I want to know who Lisa has helped. I want to know everything you can tell me about them.'

Perhaps Gillian had warned him at the time that the information he'd receive would be limited. He really couldn't remember.

But she'd definitely emphasised it several times since that day. Alex hadn't known the care from the donor-family service would be ongoing, but it had been an unexpected and tremendous support. Not quite so helpful were their strict rules which prevented him from being given any further information about the people Lisa had helped.

'Some patients take months or even years before they're ready to contact their donor family. Some are never ready,' Gillian had warned him. Alex already understood that any message he received would be vetted before it reached his hands. And he was okay with that. But as the weeks slipped into months and still he'd heard nothing, a new despondency took up residence. What if he never knew? What if no one ever reached out to him and Connor? It would be like losing Lisa all over again. Four times over.

He was pinning too much on hearing from the recipients – a quiet, sane, part of his mind realised that. But knowing that, somewhere, a piece of the woman he loved lived on was all he could think about.

The nights were the worst. He'd wake after only a few hours' sleep to find his arm searching for her on the empty half of their double bed. He'd glance across at her pillows, smooth and forever un-dented, and the loneliness he managed to keep at bay during the day would threaten to swallow him whole.

The summer had been long and hot, the nights sultry and uncomfortable, and even though Alex now slept with the windows wide open – something Lisa's moth phobia had never allowed – there never seemed to be enough air for him to breathe freely. Not anywhere.

It was only in the garden, under a canopy of stars, that he felt a small measure of relief. Luckily they weren't overlooked, so Alex was free to pace its confines at night, with chest and feet bare. Sometimes he'd lie down on the cool damp grass, letting it tickle the space between his shoulder blades like a caress against skin that would probably never be touched again. With arms folded behind his neck, he'd look for answers in the stars, the place where Lisa would surely leave them for him. For this had been her world, this was the passion that came second only to Connor and him. This was where she lived. It was the closest Alex could get to her, but as he stared up at the Milky Way there was only one question he could ever think to ask. Why? Why Lisa? Why her?

The peace of mind, heart and soul he'd so casually taken for granted in the years they'd shared was starting to fade. What if Lisa faded too? Alex was terrified of the day when he wouldn't be able to remember the smell of her, or how her nose wrinkled when she laughed or the way her body fitted so perfectly against his, as though they'd been cast from one mould. How could a love they swore would last forever – 'with every beat of my heart', she used to tell him – be gone in an instant? Snatched away in a moment of senseless tragedy.

'Just give me a sign that you're still here, that you're not gone,' Alex implored the velvet-black sky. 'Show me how to find you again, baby, please,' he begged, searching the constellation above him for a shooting star until his eyes watered from the effort. Eventually, feeling ridiculous, he'd got to his feet and padded back through the silent house to their empty bed.

The first letter had arrived the next morning.

The whisky in his glass was gone, although he had no recollection of drinking it. He reached out to the four plastic sleeves fanned out like a poker hand on the desk before him. As ever, he felt an almost magnetic pull towards the red one. It was the one that held the letters from Molly, the woman who'd received Lisa's heart. He slid the collection from the sleeve, surprised by how thick the bundle of handwritten letters had grown over the last four months.

Her first letter had been both the best and the worst thing he'd ever received. It had made him want to howl like an animal in pain as he read it with knuckles pressed against his lips to muffle the sound of his sobs. Her words were beautiful, but, like poetry carved with a razor blade, they sliced into his soul.

Dear Family,

This is the hardest letter I know I'll ever write, and I'm sure it will be equally difficult for you to read. Before thanking you, please know how deeply sorry I am for your loss and how nervous I am about saying the wrong thing and causing you even more pain. That is truly the last thing I'd ever want to do.

My name is Molly and your wife saved my life when she decided to be an organ donor. Eighteen months ago my heart was attacked by a virus and, despite the doctors' best efforts, the only chance I had of living beyond my early thirties was if someone, someone I'd never know, were to give me a gift I could never repay.

There is so much I want to tell you about me, to reassure you that I'll spend the rest of my days trying to be a worthy custodian of this heart. But there are rules I must follow. What I can tell you is that my life immediately before my transplant was very different to how it is now. When I got sick I was forced to give up my job as a primary school teacher, even though it was all I'd ever wanted to do. I watched my elderly mother live in fear that she'd outlast her only child, which broke my already failing heart.

But because of you, because of your wife's gift, I have the chance to rewrite my future. It's not just a heart I've received, it's hope, and that was something I didn't dare have for a very long time.

In the years you've granted me, I hope that I'll be lucky enough one day to find someone to share the rest of my life with, perhaps even to have a family of my own. And if there are children in my future, please know that I'll tell them about the woman who allowed me to be their mummy.

I grieve for the person you lost, because even though we never met, I already know she was incredible. Anyone who donates so willingly to a total stranger belongs in a league of heroes.

I will honour this heart and carry it with pride for the rest of my days.

Thank you,
Molly x

Alex wondered how many versions of the letter there'd been before Molly had found the words he must have read over a hundred times. For him, one of the best things was learning that Molly was as a primary school teacher. That had felt absolutely right. Lisa had always loved children, so it felt good knowing her heart would still be surrounded by them.

'There's no need to reply to the letters,' Gillian had told him. 'Sometimes the best gift they bestow is that of closure.' Perhaps that was what some families were looking for, but not Alex. He had replied the very next day. And Molly had written back to him a week later. And so it had begun.

Over the following months, their letters became more relaxed and natural. From them, Alex learnt that Molly loved many of the things that Lisa had also enjoyed. They even liked the same food! Instinctively he knew that if the two women had ever met, they'd have liked each other, maybe even have become good friends. But fate had made sure that would never happen.

Almost as though Molly had opened an invisible floodgate, the letters from the other transplant recipients had followed in quick succession. Despite being vetted by the authorities, the letters still revealed clues that jumped off the page, or at least they did to Alex, who spent more hours than he probably should have reading and rereading them. Todd, who was already worried about the continued correspondence, would have worried even more if he knew just how many hours they were talking about.

Molly's letters were handwritten on thick, cream-coloured writing paper that looked expensive and carried a vague scent he could never quite place. The two male transplant recipients both sent their letters electronically, although Alex had printed them out because words on a screen weren't a close enough connection. He needed something more tangible to anchor him to these last pieces of Lisa.

Alex would have been able to figure out the age of the young man who'd received Lisa's lungs even if Jamie hadn't revealed it. His emails were peppered with text and messaging abbreviations and even the occasional GIF. There was an untamed exuberance in the way Jamie wrote that reminded Alex of himself at that age. Traces of a daredevil nature fluttered like red flags as Jamie wrote about all the things he planned to do and the places he was going to visit as soon as he was fully recovered. Either he was extremely well off or a big dreamer. Whichever it was, it didn't really matter, because Alex liked the sound of him.

The image Alex had of Barbara, the elderly woman who'd received one of Lisa's kidneys, was so vivid, he felt sure he could have picked her out of a line-up. She wrote to him on notelets covered with images of cats. He learnt from her first message that she'd been widowed ten years ago and had never been blessed with children. Reading between the lines – which looked so straight, they must surely have been ruled – Alex guessed there were no close family members in her life. Well, no *human* family. There was regular mention of a great many names, but Alex suspected these were her pet cats. He liked to think that his writing back to Barbara made her world a little less lonely than it had been before her transplant.

The person Alex felt he knew least about was Mac, the man whose sight had been restored after receiving Lisa's corneas. His folder was far sparser than any of the others. His first communication had started with him expressing his heartfelt condolences to Alex for his loss, before going on to say how grateful he was for Lisa's generous donation. But after that, the emails had dried up. Alex was pleased that this thirty-six-year-old man could now return to his profession as an architect, that he'd be able to drive a car again, travel and do all the things his blindness had stolen from him, and he told himself he didn't mind that Mac didn't elaborate on how he had felt at each of those milestone moments. Alex reluctantly accepted Gillian's cautionary warning that not all recipients felt comfortable sharing personal details with their donor family.

'This is not something we recommend, Alex. It's... It's pretty irregular,' Gillian had told him after she realised Alex and the transplant recipients intended to keep writing to each other. Alex got the impression his lack of conformity sat uncomfortably with all of the Donor Family Care Team, but perhaps with Gillian most of all.

He liked to think she had a soft spot for him and Connor. She checked in on them far more regularly than he suspected her job spec required. And those phone calls weren't just to alert him when they'd received another letter. She really seemed to care about them.

Alex had thought he'd left his old rule-breaker self firmly in his past, so it was quite surprising to find that facet of his personality re-emerging now. He briefly wondered whether Lisa would disapprove. Given the circumstances, he thought not.

'I understand why you'd prefer to keep acting as a conduit for the letters,' he'd said, picking his words carefully so as not to cause offence or appear ungrateful. 'But if both sides want to communicate without going through your offices, what harm can it do?'

'Plenty. These people are fragile, Alex. *You're* fragile.'

Alex had bristled slightly but had said nothing. If this conversation had been taking place face to face instead of over the telephone, Gillian might have been daunted by the steel in his eyes. As it wasn't, the specialist nurse pushed her point home.

'I know how tempting it is to draw these people into your life, Alex. They're your tangible connection to Lisa. I realise that. We all realise that. But having the letters go through us is for everyone's protection.'

Alex sighed softly. Her reaction wasn't unexpected, but she was measuring what was happening here against their normal working practices, and even she had to admit that their case was far from typical.

'You said yourself that everything about this has been unusual. That it's extremely rare for *all* the recipients to make contact, much less for everyone to want to continue writing to each other.'

'You're right. It is highly unusual,' Gillian agreed.

'So perhaps in this instance you need to let all of us decide to go forward by ourselves from now. What's the worst that could happen? What is it that you're so worried about?'

For a long time he thought her silence meant she wasn't going to answer him. In the end, he almost wished she hadn't.

'I'm concerned that sooner or later someone is going to suggest taking things to the next level. You have to understand that meetings between recipients and donor families are very sensitive situations. These people might disappoint you; *you* might disappoint them. What if you feel they're not worthy of having received Lisa's donation? What then? Please, Alex, think about this very carefully, for your sake and Connor's. You think you know these people, you think you're ready to meet them, but I'm not sure if you realise how much this might hurt you both. At least promise me you'll think about it.'

That at least had been an easy promise to make. Since Molly's first letter he had thought of nothing else. For she was the one he wanted – no, needed – to meet more than any of the others.

And now he was going to.

CHAPTER TWELVE

Molly

It was there on the mat when I got home from work, nestled between an electricity bill and a flier from the local Chinese takeaway. I bent to gather up the rest of the post, keeping the one I most wanted to read on the top of the pile.

I launched my coat in the direction of the banister rail and kicked off my shoes in the hallway, before making my way to the kitchen. It was a small rebellion that I took uncommon pleasure in. Tom had been a compulsive neat freak and my habit of leaving a trail of belongings through the house used to drive him crazy.

The kettle seemed to be taking an incredibly long time to boil, but finally I pulled out a chair at the kitchen table and drew the stack of post towards me, my lips curved in a smile of anticipation. I couldn't believe how much I enjoyed this little ritual: pacing myself so that I didn't dive straight in to read the message. The front was an eye-catching vibrant blue, the domes of Santorini's iconic churches perfectly matching the colour of the sky. She would have taken ages picking out just the right postcard to send; it was the same with any greeting card. I'd truly never seen anyone deliberate longer over a Hallmark purchase than my mother.

I read it through twice, my smile growing broader as her excitement and enthusiasm radiated off the card like glare on the ocean. Mum was having the most amazing time. She'd made friends on board the cruise ship and being a solo traveller didn't seem to be worrying her at all. With every postcard – and there had been many over the last few weeks – I quietly congratulated myself that I'd persuaded her to book an extended voyage. After months of looking after me while I recuperated, she had definitely earned this holiday.

I flicked through the rest of the mail, refusing to lose my happy glow by opening anything in a brown envelope. Afterwards I wondered what would have happened if I'd thrown away the junk mail without looking at it properly. It would have been so easy to have lobbed it into the bin without noticing the handwritten white envelope that had somehow slipped inside a leaflet from a plumbing company. It fell out onto the table, right side up, and I instantly recognised the bold lettering. Was he as decisive in real life as his handwriting appeared to be?

Alex's letters had become something I looked forward to perhaps a little too eagerly. Whenever I received one, this new heart of mine would flutter, almost as though it recognised his writing. It was an unsettling thought and one I did my best to ignore. His letters were genial and comfortable to read; hygge on Basildon Bond paper. He had a relaxed, chatty style, and he unfailingly began each one by asking about my health, paying more than just lip service to the question 'How are you?'

Sometimes I wondered if we were crossing a line here. How easy would it be for polite interest to spill over into censure if he felt I wasn't taking good enough care of his late wife's heart? I shook the feeling off, because I didn't want to think anything bad of this man – or his son. It had been upsetting to learn that my donor had been a mother, and I'd cried the first time Alex had revealed how difficult his little boy was finding life without his mum. I must have drafted half a dozen replies to that letter, but in the end I hadn't found anything to say that could comfort a young child who was pining for his lost parent. Connor was the same age as the kids in my class, and I witnessed on a daily basis how their mums were the sun they orbited around. You could see it in the way they ran towards them at the end of the day, and in the hugs that were waiting for them. My heart – Lisa's heart – ached to think of her little boy never knowing that moment again.

I'm not sure what I was expecting from Alex's letter that day. More of the same newsy chatter we'd been exchanging over the last month or so, I guess. Our language had become freer now that it was no longer scrutinised by the Donor Records Department. Alex had told me that he was also in contact with several other transplant recipients, and in unguarded moments I found myself wondering if his correspondence with them was as natural and friendly as ours. A small stab of something that surely couldn't have been jealousy jabbed uncomfortably at my conscience.

'Oh.' The word sounded strange in the silence of my kitchen. I wasn't in the habit of talking to myself, but here I was, shaking my head and once again speaking out loud to absolutely no one. 'Ooh, no. I'm not sure about that.'

'Christ on a bike!'

Kyra's profanity jarred slightly, possibly because I'd spent most of the afternoon rehearsing the end-of-term Nativity play with Class One.

'Please tell me you said no,' she continued, sliding the invitation back across the wine bar table towards me.

I lifted it like it was a playing card, my eyes troubled as I read it again before dropping it back into my handbag. It wasn't yet six o'clock and the bar was still virtually empty. Even so, I drew my chair a little closer towards hers and lowered my voice before replying.

'I've not said anything yet.'

Kyra's perfectly threaded brows drew together. The frown brought temporary lines to her forehead that nature wouldn't be leaving there for at least another fifteen years. 'But you're going to turn him down, Mols, aren't you? I mean, you're not seriously thinking of going?'

I reached for my glass, really wishing it was filled with rioja like Kyra's, instead of Diet Coke. Although I was allowed to drink on my medication, in moderation, this was the kind of conversation where it was best to stay sharp. Besides, it was so long since I'd drunk anything, I was bound to be a complete lightweight.

'Lots of transplant recipients meet their donor families. You see it all the time on YouTube and the *Six O'Clock News*.'

'I tell you what else you see on the news, stories about women who go missing after meeting up with some crazy person they've been "innocently" communicating with.' She unnecessarily air-quoted the word 'innocently' for emphasis.

I shook my head and focused on the flames curling lazily around the pile of logs in the bar's open fireplace. 'I'm not sure how you've got hold of the idea that Alex is unstable.'

Kyra's mouth opened and closed as she searched for the words that would convince me I was making a mistake here. 'I'm not saying he's a nutter or anything like that. But you have to admit that *this*' – she pointed an accusatory finger towards the invitation now tucked inside my leather tote – '*this* is not exactly normal.' She took a large mouthful of red wine before continuing. 'The man is grieving, I get that, and it's not that I don't feel sorry for him, because I do, but I simply can't see how this is going to help either of you.' Like a heron diving for a fish, her hand swooped into my bag and plucked Alex's invitation back out. 'He's inviting you to a gathering of his friends and family to celebrate his late wife's birthday. Doesn't that sound a bit odd and creepy to you? Am I the only one who can hear the *Twilight Zone* theme tune playing in the background here?'

My lips twisted into a reluctant smile. 'I admit it *is* a little strange.' Kyra's eyes widened meaningfully. 'Okay, very strange. But he's not suggesting we meet at his home – which would definitely be weird. He's holding this party, for want of a better word, at a planetarium. Apparently it was one of his wife's favourite places, and it'll be a great opportunity to look round it after hours. And besides, I'm not the only recipient he's asked. He's invited all of us.'

'And since when were you interested in astronomy?' Kyra challenged.

'I'm not… especially.' It was the truth, yet it felt strangely like a lie. Had last summer's insomnia and the middle-of-the-night stargazing brought about this new interest? Was that why Class Six had a frieze of the galaxy on their wall instead of one with fields and farm animals?

'I'm sorry, Molly, I know you don't want to hear this, but it all sounds a little too Mary Shelley for my liking.'

It took a moment or two for me to follow her train of thought, and when I got it, it was hard to suppress my shudder. 'That's not what he's doing.'

'He's gathering all of you together. You've gotta admit, it's kind of weird.'

I glanced around the room, trying to avoid her laser-sharp gaze. This wasn't the reaction I'd expected from her. Given how many internet dating sites Kyra was signed up to, and the number of blind dates she happily went on, this degree of caution seemed misplaced and extreme.

In the early days, when I'd been worried about saying the wrong thing, I'd shared several of Alex's letters and my replies with her. Out of all my friends, Kyra was the one person I'd been certain would understand my conflicted feelings about meeting him. Was she massively overreacting to Alex's invitation or actually seeing something dangerous here that I couldn't?

'I've not made my mind up yet, either way,' I said, anxious not to ruin either the evening or, worse than that, our friendship.

She met my eyes. 'Yes, you have.'

It could have been an awkward moment, but Kyra averted it by leaning over and squeezing my hand affectionately. 'Just be careful, Mols, that's all.'

She got to her feet in a single graceful move that I was sure had drawn the attention of every red-blooded man in the room. 'Another round?' I nodded as she turned towards the bar. 'And when I get back you can hear all about my latest disastrous blind date. If there are any good men left out there, I sure as hell don't know where they're hiding.'

It was an effort not to glance back down at Alex's invitation, but somehow I managed to resist.

'Ugh.' I sighed with frustration as I yanked down the zip of yet another dress. I threw it onto the pile scattered across my bed, which was starting to resemble a jumble sale stall. There were very few things left hanging in my wardrobe to try on, and the taxi I'd booked was now only twenty minutes away.

I'd finally decided to accept Alex's invitation several days ago, so there'd been plenty of time to find something suitable to wear. Why had I left it to the last minute? *Because subconsciously you always intended to cancel?* suggested a knowing voice in my head. I ignored it and returned to the depleted rail in my wardrobe. There were only two dresses remaining. I immediately discarded the red one, whose plunging neckline had always been a little too daring. That left me with the dove grey woollen dress with the cowl neck, totally different from the vintage fifties-style dresses I usually went for. I stepped into it, enjoying the feel of its soft cashmere against my skin. I'd only worn it a couple of times, and as I fastened the button behind my neck I remembered how

Tom's eyebrows had shot up appreciatively at the way it clung to my curves. I turned back to the mirror in alarm. Sexy was definitely not the look I was aiming for this evening, but at least the high neckline hid my scar. The last thing Alex would want to see was a visible reminder that his wife's heart now lived in my chest instead of hers.

'Interesting place. Brought my kid here last summer,' commented the cabbie as he pulled up outside the planetarium. I paused in the act of extracting a twenty-pound note from my purse and looked towards the enticingly lit frontage.

Buttery yellow lights gleamed invitingly through glass double doors and the short flight of stone steps seemed to beckon me in. Even so, I lingered on the forecourt in the bitingly cold October wind long after the cab was just tail lights disappearing into the night. Several people were forced to weave around me on their way inside, and every time someone passed me I stole a glance at their face, wondering if there was an invitation from Alex in their coat pocket or handbag too.

Pull yourself together, I told myself sternly, stamping my cold feet on the gravel drive when my toes began to protest at my flimsy footwear. I straightened up and tightened my grip on the bouquet in my hand. The white lilies looked almost too perfect to be real under the glow of the planetarium's floodlights. They had called out to me from a metal trough in the florist's earlier that day. Arriving empty-handed to something that was technically supposed to be a party had felt wrong. Even if the person whose birthday we were honouring wasn't going to be there themselves – for obvious reasons.

I'd had every intention of buying a potted plant and had actually picked out a gorgeous pink orchid when my eye had fallen on the lilies. Before I knew it, the orchid was back on the shelf and I was carrying the bouquet of lilies to the till. It was only now, seeing them against the black of my coat, that my brain made the too-late-to-be-useful connection between white lilies and funerals. These were flowers for dead people and I couldn't believe how insensitive I'd been, thinking they were a suitable gift for Alex. I looked around for a bin to chuck them into, but of course there wasn't one. I was still deliberating about what to do when the chimes from a distant church announced the half hour. Punctuality had always been a thing with me, and I definitely didn't want the head-turning attention of being the last to arrive. I decided I'd just have to leave the flowers with my coat and dispose of them later.

'I'm meeting some… people… here, for a private event,' I explained to the smartly dressed woman on the reception desk. I stopped myself at the last moment from saying 'friends', which would have been just as wrong as admitting the truth: *Hi, I'm meeting a group of strangers, and the only thing we have in common is the dead woman whose birthday we're here to celebrate.*

The woman unfolded and extended her arm as though directing me towards an emergency exit on a plane. I glanced to my right and saw a small printed sign with Alex's name and an arrow pointing upwards. 'The Stevens reception is being held in our Stargazer Room. First floor, last door on the right,' she confirmed.

'Is there a cloakroom or somewhere I can leave my coat?'

'You'll be able to leave it upstairs.'

I was okay as my heels clipped across the marble-floored foyer, but when I got to the foot of the stairs the trepidation set in. It slowed my feet and made my pulse race. The staircase was steep and I hesitated at the bottom tread for such a long time that a young man behind me grew impatient and with a pointed 'Excuse me' squeezed past and ran on up.

I was being ridiculous, I knew that. I'd made the decision to come tonight and could hardly bottle out now. But after vacillating for days between accepting and declining Alex's invitation, why was it only now occurring to me that Kyra might have been right all along? This *was* a weird thing to be doing. And I didn't even want to consider what my transplant coordinator would have said if he could have seen me now. One thing was certain: this wasn't the normal way for anyone to meet their donor family for the first time.

By the time I was halfway up the stairs, my heart was thumping so heavily I wondered if the staples holding my breastbone together were up to the job of containing it. Oddly, although I was terrified about the forthcoming meeting, it didn't feel like it was fear that was making my heart race; it felt more like excitement.

I found the door and came to a stop before it. Through the polished oak I could hear the muted hum of voices. There was no laughter, no music, none of the usual soundtrack that accompanies a party. This truly was going to be one of the strangest experiences of my life. Was I supposed to knock or walk straight in? I raised my arm, knuckles poised, when suddenly the door opened. A waitress clad in black, carrying two empty platters, stood before me, and behind her, half hidden in the shadows, was a tall man with sandy-coloured hair. His eyes widened at exactly the same moment as the breath caught in my throat.

'Molly,' he cried, as though he already knew it was me. Which was odd, for we'd never exchanged photographs, and I had no Facebook account for him to have stalked.

'Alex,' I replied with equal certainty.

The room behind him appeared full, although every guest had fallen silent at the opening of the door. Like a convention of tango dancers, they all turned my way with perfect synchronicity. This was hardly the inconspicuous entrance I'd been hoping for.

'I'm so glad you could make it,' Alex said, the warmth in his voice unlocking the frozen room behind him. Conversations resumed, but heads were still turned my way. I felt like the new girl in class on the first day of school.

'Come on in,' he urged, reaching behind me to close the door. As I stepped forward, his hand brushed my back. Every hair on my arms stood up as though statically charged.

'Can I take your coat?' he asked, one hand already outstretched in readiness. It was too late to say, *Actually, I don't think I can stay*, even though the words were screaming in my head. This whole situation felt wrong – except that it didn't. And that was what was confusing me. I didn't like the way I was responding to him; it didn't feel like me.

I spent longer than necessary unwinding my scarf and trying to persuade coat buttons to go back through holes that now seemed to have mysteriously shrunk. Even my class of six-year-olds had better motor skills than this. Alex was still patiently waiting, his face wearing the mask of a polite host. But it slipped and then dissolved when he saw the bunch of flowers I'd been trying to keep out of sight beneath my arm.

'You brought flowers.' It was somewhere between a question and a statement.

I searched for a reply that wouldn't involve me having to apologise for my thoughtless choice. On every trawl, I came up empty.

'Er, yes,' I began, the apology already in my voice.

The hand that had been waiting for my coat took the bouquet instead. His eyes were fixed on the perfect waxy petals and when he lifted them to meet my gaze, they looked suspiciously bright, but perhaps that was just a trick of the light. The first thing I'd noticed about the room was its spectacular domed skylight, designed to showcase the night sky. The wall lights were low wattage and unobtrusive, making the Stargazer Room a place where emotions could easily be hidden.

'Lilies. How did you know?'

This wasn't the moment to say 'Huh?' and all at once I didn't need to. I shivered, and it wasn't because the room was cold.

'I… I, er…'

He nodded just once and the shiver made a final pass down my spine before letting me be. Lilies had been his wife's favourite flowers. He didn't need to say the words because I knew this was true, with a frankly disturbing certainty.

'Hello, I'm Dee,' said a woman with striking red hair cut into a sharply angled bob. She was slicing through the roomful of guests and heading towards us like a coastguard on a rescue mission. It wasn't a bad analogy. Her hand was small, but the grip of her handshake was surprisingly firm.

'Molly,' I supplied, my voice hesitant as though for a moment I'd actually forgotten who I was.

'You must be one of the people Lisa helped,' she said gently.

Of its own volition, I could feel my hand going to my chest, checking that my dress was covering my scar.

Dee's eyes dropped and then came back up, full of understanding. 'Let me get you something to drink,' she said with a smile. The hand that hadn't yet released mine moved up to my elbow and was gently guiding me towards a buffet table set up against the back wall.

'We have red or white, or something non-alcoholic?'

'Lemonade would be great, if you have it,' I said, my voice scratchy. I had a feeling no amount of fizzy drink was going to alter that.

I glanced back to the other side of the reception room, where Alex was still staring at the lilies as though I'd brought a bomb to the party.

Dee followed my gaze and laid her hand briefly on my forearm. 'He'll be fine. He just needs a moment. Every now and then things hit him hard.'

I'd seen death up close on a number of occasions during my hospital stays, but I'd never witnessed the raw devastation of someone grieving for a life lost decades before its time. This was totally different to how Mum and I had been when Dad passed away, and I realised suddenly how out of my depth I was here. I had no comfort to offer this man. His wife had died, and in her place I lived. How could that ever seem fair to him?

'So,' said Dee, placing an icy-cold tumbler in my hand. 'Would you like me to introduce you around?'

What I really wanted was to head for the exit as fast as I could, but that was out of the question, so I nodded and took a gulp of my drink.

'Well, over there, the guy in the blue shirt who's practically inhaling canapés, is Todd—'

'Alex's brother,' I said involuntarily.

Dee looked briefly startled. 'I keep forgetting that Alex has been writing to all of you for so long, that you know all about us.'

'Just your names,' I said, although that wasn't strictly true. Intentionally or otherwise, Alex had revealed enough about his family for them to no longer feel like strangers, even though we'd never met.

I knew of his genuine affection for his sister-in-law Dee, a natural overspill of the love he had for his brother. I knew they had a daughter who was almost the same age as Alex's son. My glance flitted across the reception room to a velvet banquette whose cushioned seat was incongruously scattered with toys.

'Alex's little boy is here tonight?'

For the first time a look I couldn't quite read flickered behind Dee's olive-green eyes. 'He wanted Connor to be here.' She paused and looked up, her gaze lingering on the crystal-clear night sky, clearly visible through the skylight. 'This was a special place for my sister-in-law. She used to bring Connor here all the time when he was little – Maisie too, sometimes. They'd booked this room for her birthday party almost a year ago… long before… before everything happened. Alex couldn't bring himself to cancel the party and said it would be wrong to mark Lisa's birthday without

Connor being here. So I brought Maisie along, to make things seem more... normal.'

My eyebrows rose and Dee's unconscious frown filled in the gaps.

'But you tried to talk him out of inviting the four of us tonight, didn't you?' I almost gasped at my own boldness.

Her smile seemed both sad and weary. 'Todd did. Many times. He didn't think this was the appropriate place for you all to meet. But you know Alex...' Her voice trailed away as we both realised that of course I didn't know him, not at all.

And yet why did it feel very much as though I did?

'Oh good, Dee's got you a drink,' Alex said, coming up and resting a hand on his sister-in-law's shoulder.

She looked up at him and smiled, and a small knot of worry slowly unravelled inside me. He had people who cared. Even though he'd lost the woman he loved, he still had family who cared about him. That made me happy in ways I couldn't explain.

'Everything okay?' Dee asked.

I was staring into my glass of lemonade, and yet I swear I felt the moment when his eyes rested on me.

'Yeah, everything's fine.'

'In that case, if you'll excuse me, I'll go and investigate what Maisie and Connor are getting up to in the bathroom. They've been gone a while.'

There was only so long I could keep staring into my glass as though expecting my ice cubes to do something scintillating, but it felt way safer than looking at Alex.

'This is an amazing venue. I'm embarrassed to admit I've never been to a planetarium before.'

'Neither had I – until I met Lisa,' Alex said, his mouth managing a smile that his eyes couldn't quite replicate.

I groped frantically for something to say. I wasn't usually socially awkward, but this was such a bizarre situation.

'Your… your wife was certainly passionate about astronomy.' I groaned inwardly at my lame attempt. Why was it so easy to talk to him in the letters we'd exchanged and so difficult when he was standing right there in front of me?

'Lisa was passionate about everything she did. That's just how she was. And it's okay to say her name, Molly,' he added softly, intuitively sensing my discomfort. 'After all, she's the reason you're here.'

For a second I thought he was referring to my transplant, before realising he meant the birthday party.

'Lisa *is* the reason I'm here,' I confirmed boldly. 'Not just tonight; I mean, she's the reason I'm still here in the world.'

Following an instinct that took me by surprise, I reached for his hand, positioning my grip as though we were about to formally shake on a deal but so that his index finger was directly over my pulse point. His eyes were the colour of sticky toffee. They widened as they met mine and he realised what I was doing. His throat tightened and he had to swallow several times. The pad of his fingertip moved gently over the sensitive skin of my wrist. It wasn't a caress, or if it was, it wasn't intended for me.

It seemed to take him a long time before he could speak again.

'That's the closest I've been to her in six months. Thank you.'

His eyes glistened once again as he excused himself and made his way out of the room. It wasn't hard to work out why.

CHAPTER THIRTEEN

Alex

Alex needed air. There was none in the Stargazer Room, nor in the corridor outside. He took the steep stairs three at a time, miraculously managing to avoid losing his balance and tumbling to the unforgiving marble floor below. The foyer was deserted now except for a lone security guard who barely even glanced up as Alex pushed his way through the planetarium's double doors and out into the night.

The cold October air was like a slap to his face, the kind people administer in films when someone starts to become hysterical. It had the same effect on Alex. It slowed him down, putting the brakes on his need to put distance between himself and whatever it was he was fleeing from. He was sure it wasn't Molly, or any of the other transplant recipients come to that, not when he'd spent so long hoping they'd all come tonight. Frankly, he was still amazed that every one of them had accepted his invitation.

Something was happening here. Alex could feel it stirring beneath the surface of the life he was meant to be putting back together. It was more than just grief, although that was the one-size-fits-all label his brother kept trying to slap on it.

'It's more than that,' Alex reiterated, startling himself by saying the words out loud. Not that there was anyone around to hear him. Anyone with any sense was inside in the warm, not pacing the forecourt in near freezing temperatures, their breath pluming before them like dragon smoke.

He knew he ought to go back inside, that he wasn't being fair to Todd and Dee. Or to Connor. But then nothing he did was right for Connor any more. Trying to be the parent Connor needed felt like walking a tightrope where one careless misstep could send him plummeting to the bottom of a crevasse. His failures came on a daily basis. Tonight had been no different...

'Are you ready to go, big man?' Alex had asked, popping his head around Connor's bedroom door. It was a relief to see his son had changed into the clothes he'd left out on the bed, although he still hadn't put his shoes on.

'Come on, Connor. I don't want us to be late. Get your shoes on.'

Like an obedient automaton, Connor reached for the pair of black school shoes that Lisa had bought for him at the beginning of the year. Alex was anxious to avoid the rush hour traffic and the urge to step in and take over the tying of the laces was hard to resist, but he managed to stop himself. *Be patient*, he imagined Lisa whispering in his ear. *He needs to do things for himself.*

'It will be nice to visit the planetarium again, won't it?' Alex had asked. Even to his ears, his voice had sounded falsely jolly.

Connor looked up from what appeared to be a struggle with his left shoe and something flickered in his eyes, a memory perhaps of the last time he'd visited the place with Lisa.

'Is Mummy going to be there?'

Alex's sigh hurt all the way up from his diaphragm to his larynx.

'No, pal, we've talked about this, remember? This is a party to celebrate the day when Mummy was born.'

'But if it's her birthday party, she'll come too, won't she?'

There was a flash of pain on his face, which Alex was slow to realise was caused by more than just crushed hopes. Connor wiggled his foot into the shoe and winced.

'Is something wrong with your foot?' Alex asked, crossing the expanse of carpet and dropping to a crouch before his son.

Connor shrugged.

'Sit down, let me have a look,' Alex instructed, all thoughts of the mounting rush hour traffic now forgotten. It was immediately apparent even before he'd whipped off Connor's sock. It was obvious from the degree of force he'd needed to pluck the shoe from his son's left foot. The right was just as bad.

Beneath the cartoon character socks, Connor's toes looked red and there were twin blisters on both of the little ones.

'Are your shoes too tight?' Alex asked, staring in dismay at his son's damaged feet.

'A bit,' Connor mumbled.

'Why didn't you tell me they were hurting you? Why didn't you let me know you needed new ones?'

Connor's blue eyes looked impossibly huge as he stared down at his father. *Why didn't you know yourself? This is your job*, they silently accused.

'I'm so sorry,' Alex said, hearing the catch in his own voice. 'I should have known you needed new ones. Mummy always used to buy you new shoes in the summer,' Alex said, his voice dull with blame.

'I was going to tell her tonight,' Connor confided on a wobbly whisper. 'About the shoes, I mean.'

Alex pulled Connor into his arms. He didn't exactly relax into the hug, but at least he didn't pull away.

'I'm sorry. I'm so sorry,' Alex murmured into his son's strawberry-blond hair.

*

Maybe after tonight things would begin to change, Alex thought. He had no reason to think this, but it felt true in a way he couldn't explain.

Despite a few scudding clouds, it was a crisp, clear night with a generous scattering of stars. It was the kind of night Lisa wouldn't have allowed them to ignore; there'd have been no hurrying straight to the car and turning on the heater. She'd have wanted to linger, pointing out the stars, trying to share her passion for astronomy with the man she loved.

Alex's face was tipped up to the inky black sky when the first raindrops fell, mingling inconspicuously with the tears he hadn't known he was crying. Rain – it hadn't been forecast, but of course it would fall tonight. Some couples had a song that was uniquely theirs. But for Alex and Lisa, it had always been the rain.

CHAPTER FOURTEEN

Molly

After Alex's hasty exit, I wandered over to the buffet table. It was laden with food that looked absolutely delicious but which I doubted many guests had the appetite to eat. I jumped when a hand came to rest on my shoulder. Spinning around, I found myself face to face with the young man who'd bustled past me on the stairs earlier. He was only about twenty; his hair was a little too long, and he was probably one day beyond needing a shave. He was wearing a worn leather jacket and ripped skinny jeans, which I assumed were a fashion statement.

'Hi. I'm Jamie,' he said, holding out a hand with nails that were bitten so brutally short I almost winced.

There was something about the warmth of his handshake that made me study his face more closely. He too had a puzzled look in his pale grey eyes. He was leaning in, encroaching on my personal space in a way I should have found uncomfortable, and yet I didn't. I'd been expecting to catch the smell of alcohol or tobacco, but all I got was a whiff of toothpaste and shower gel. Even before he said another word, I knew who he was.

'So, I'm lungs. And you're…?'

His grin was irrepressibly engaging, and I got the impression he rather liked shocking people.

'Heart,' I whispered back, as though sharing a secret.

His eyes went to my chest, but not in the way that men's usually did.

'You doing okay?'

In just three words he'd encapsulated everything that needed to be asked. Few people were able to do that.

'Really well. You?'

In reply he drew in an enormous lungful of air, his chest swelling as though he was about to dive into a pool. 'Couldn't do that before. Not even close. So I'm doing pretty fuckin' good, all things considered.'

His eyes twinkled, so I knew the profanity had been deliberately placed to see if I would take the bait. I'd had classrooms full of kids just like him. All talk, no malice. I smiled, feeling like I'd just found a golden ticket in my chocolate bar.

'Are any of the others like us here yet?'

Jamie placed his hands on my shoulders and swivelled me slightly, turning me towards the furthest corner of the room, where an elderly lady was seated on a leather Chesterfield, talking animatedly to Todd. She bent down and pulled something from a voluminous bag by her feet. I was so used to people sharing photos on their phones, it was quite unusual to see an old-fashioned wallet of photographs.

'Maybe I'll go over and introduce myself,' I said. Jamie nodded, his hand already reaching out and scooping up half a dozen canapés in a single swipe. 'I forgot to say, I'm Molly by the way.'

His eyebrows lifted as though I'd just said something incredibly stupid. 'I know. We *all* know that. He's mentioned you more than once in his letters.'

I could feel the blush beginning right where the cowl neck of my dress met my skin. It rose like mercury in a barometer. 'Oh. He... He never... I mean, I don't think...'

Jamie shrugged before turning back to the buffet table. 'It is what it is. You should go and say hi to Barbara. She's sort of cool in an old-lady kind of way.'

Alex's brother was chatting to Barbara on the dark leather settee, but when I crossed the room and apologised for interrupting them, he immediately sprang to his feet. From the expression in his eyes I suspected he didn't mind the intrusion.

'You must be Molly,' he said. I nodded, slightly thrown by the fact that every stranger here knew my name and I knew theirs. 'Please sit down,' he urged. 'You're still recuperating and you must be feeling tired.'

My lips parted to reassure him I was more than capable of standing, but then I saw the desperation in his eyes. It was hard to suppress my smile, but I just about managed it. The look of gratitude he flashed my way told me I'd just made a friend for life.

'Would you like me to get you a plate of food from the buffet?' he asked Barbara, his eyes going to the ivory-handled walking stick she'd propped up against the settee.

'That's very kind of you. Yes, please,' she replied. When Todd was safely out of earshot, she turned to me. 'I don't think the poor man knows what to say to any of us.'

'It *is* a very unusual situation,' I agreed, which had to be the understatement of the century.

'I'm pleased to see you looking so well, my dear,' Barbara said, as though we were old friends catching up. 'So young to have needed a heart transplant,' she added in that unfiltered way the elderly sometimes have.

'I am,' I agreed. 'Although of course it's not always about age.'

'That's true,' Barbara said, her wrinkled, liver-spotted hands fiddling unconsciously with the packet of photographs on her lap. I guessed she'd been about to show them to Todd. No wonder he had the look of a man who'd just dodged a bullet.

'I was as fit as a fiddle in my sixties, then just two years after losing my Archie, there I was, suddenly hooked up to dialysis machines, thinking that would be how I'd spend the rest of my life. And now look at me. Look at all of us.'

My eyes travelled the private reception room and its occupants. Four of Lisa's recipients had been invited this evening, but it was impossible to pick us out from the other guests. Before our surgeries we'd have been easy to spot. But because of Lisa and what she'd given each of us, we blended in undetectably.

'My heart breaks for Alex and his little boy,' Barbara went on, her gaze settling on our host, who'd just come back in, looking slightly distracted as he spoke into his mobile phone. He strode to the edge of the room by the buffet table, the phone pressed against his ear to block out the background noise. 'Their devastation is the flipside of our good fortune. And I'm not sure if we should be seeing it up close like this.'

Barbara might have looked like a quintessential old lady, with her candyfloss-white hair and accordion folds of wrinkles, but those faded-watercolour-blue eyes obviously didn't miss much.

'Do you have children, my dear?' she asked me unexpectedly.

I turned towards her, surprised at how reluctant my eyes were to leave the other side of the room. 'I do. Thirty-two of them, actually.'

She grinned, displaying teeth that were too white and straight to be her own. 'You're a teacher.'

'I am. Green Hills Primary. But to answer your question properly, no, I don't have any children of my own.'

'Plenty of time for that, my dear,' she said kindly, covering my hand with her wrinkled one. 'Now that you're well again.'

She was right. What had once been a total impossibility was now something I could consider, one day, if the right man ever came into my life. Feeling a change of subject was in order, I nodded towards the envelope of photographs clasped in her hands. 'Are those photos of *your* family?'

Her face lit up with a grandmother's joy. 'They are. My babies… and their babies. Would you like to see them?'

'I'd love to.'

It took only a few photographs before I realised the truth. As she proudly shared the names and ages of each subject, I swallowed hard at the lump that had unexpectedly formed in my throat. They were cats. Every one of them. I didn't need to ask if she'd ever had children of her own. The answer was there in the bundle of photos. Despite being more of a dog person, I was pleased with how I managed to find something complimentary to say about every single furry member of Barbara's family.

An oblong of light fell into the room and I looked up to see Dee standing in the open doorway, flanked on either side by a child. The girl was the spitting image of her mother, with hair the exact same shade of red, only hers was worn in two long plaits and not a bob. As cute as she was, my eyes lingered only briefly on her before focusing on the other child, the one who was hanging back, slightly hidden behind his aunt. I'd seen that manoeuvre a great many times before, although usually only on the first day of school and in children a few years younger than Connor.

The urge to get out of my seat and rush to him was as shocking as it was inappropriate. The poor kid would have been scared to death. But almost as though he'd read my thoughts, the little boy raised his head and looked straight at me. My heart began to race in a way the medication I was taking was supposed to prevent. Did everything really go quiet in the room for a moment or was that simply my imagination?

The spell was broken when Alex, who'd now finished on the phone, joined his son by the door. Barbara was saying something, but my attention was split between her and the family on the other side of the room.

'Poor little mite. His daddy says he's taking it very hard.'

Even if Alex hadn't already told me that, I would have known it was true. When Dee directed the two youngsters back to their seat, I stopped trying to fight the inevitable and got to my feet. I perceived a glimmer of understanding in Barbara's eyes when I excused myself, and maybe even a tiny nod of approval.

The little girl had picked up an electronic toy I recognised and was happily jabbing away at its buttons, but Connor had climbed onto the chair and was sitting too still and too straight, his hands folded unnaturally in his lap. I couldn't remember a single child in my class ever sitting that quietly.

I bent to an easy crouch before them. 'Hello there, guys. My name's Molly. And you must be Maisie and Connor.'

Maisie's eyes widened as though I'd performed an amazing feat of telepathy, but from Connor there was nothing except a long, careful stare. I swallowed and brought every ounce of my experience to the fore.

'That's a great game,' I said, pointing to the electronic device in Maisie's hands. 'Except I can never beat the timer.'

'You know how to play this?'

I suspected I'd just gone up even higher in Maisie's estimation, but with Connor it was impossible to tell. His attention was now directed at his knees.

'In the school where I teach, Friday is toy day, and lots of my class bring this one in.' I smiled widely at both of them. Only Maisie smiled back. 'Do you have a favourite toy?'

Maisie started rattling off half the items in the Argos catalogue, and although I was smiling and nodding as I listened, my attention kept being drawn back to Connor's face. It was impassive, but at least he was looking at me now. Quite intently, in fact. Perhaps if I'd had longer, I'd have broken through his defensive wall, but his gaze shifted suddenly and travelled beyond me as his father and uncle approached.

'So, was that him on the phone?' I heard Todd ask.

I was still crouched down before their offspring and very much in their way.

'Yes, that was Mac. Looks like he's going to be late – if he makes it at all. He apologised, said something urgent had come up at work. It sounded a bit like an excuse to me.'

My legs were starting to cramp. I needed to stand up, but doing so without bumping into either of the men behind me was going to be tricky. With a complete lack of grace, I wobbled on my unaccustomed heels. Both of the Stevens brothers reached out to grab me, but it was Alex's hand that caught my elbow to steady me. Connor's head shot up, his eyes like miniature lasers boring into the spot where his father's hand was touching me. I immediately disengaged myself with a mumbled word of thanks.

'Auntie Dee is going to take you guys home in a minute. So why don't you start gathering up your stuff?'

Maisie gave a token bleat of complaint, but Connor simply slithered off his chair and silently began dropping items into a bag. As I stepped discreetly aside, I caught the worried expression on Alex's face as he looked down on his son's bent head.

Not your business, I told myself. This family were scarcely more than strangers to me. Walking away from them shouldn't have felt this hard – so why did it?

It was an evening of surprises, and perhaps the biggest one of all was that I ended up having an enjoyable time. I just had to stop myself from dwelling on the fact that we were there to mark the birthday of someone who would never celebrate another one herself.

Once Dee had left with the children, Alex's guests seemed far more comfortable talking openly about Lisa. I lost count of the times someone told me how much I would have liked her. Every clustered group had their favourite Lisa story to tell, and it was clear how well liked and loved she'd been.

Welcoming though Lisa's friends and former colleagues were, I spent most of my time chatting to Barbara and Jamie, aware that to outside eyes we must have appeared a very peculiar trio. By unspoken agreement, none of us talked about our surgeries, which should have left us with nothing in common, but it didn't feel that way at all. I had no friends of Jamie's or Barbara's age, and yet as the evening wore on, I realised that I'd been missing out. In their individual and completely different ways, they were both great company.

Even so, it was still a surprise when Jamie was the one to suggest, 'You know, we ought to swap numbers and meet up again sometime. Maybe we could go out for a pint or something?'

I tried and failed to visualise Barbara in the kind of pub I imagined Jamie liked to visit.

'Or afternoon tea,' Barbara quickly countered. 'I do love a cream tea,' she said, with obvious longing in her voice.

Jamie delicately nibbling on cucumber sandwiches was an equally hard stretch.

'I'm sure we can find something we could all do together,' I said. 'I think it's a great idea.' And it really felt as though it was.

'Right then,' said Jamie, his attention now on the buffet table, which had just been replenished. 'I might just go and see what else they've brought out.'

He cut an incongruous figure as he loped a pathway between Lisa's family and friends. Barbara waited until he was at a safe distance before leaning closer and saying something that I didn't quite catch. It was either 'He's a really lovely boy' or 'He's a really lonely boy'. Either could have been true. I looked at Barbara and felt a sudden and inexplicable connection to both her and Jamie that was more than a little unsettling.

Alex had been busy circulating, spending a little time with every group. I sensed he was leaving ours until last. On more than one occasion I had the feeling that if I were to turn around, I would find his eyes on me. I'd never considered myself particularly sensitive, but it was as though I could feel his presence whenever he walked past or stopped to talk to people nearby. I was pretty certain Barbara and Jamie felt it too. Was it because we were the outsiders here, or was something drawing us together like an invisible thread?

I shook my head at the fanciful notion as I made my way back to the buffet table to investigate the desserts that had just been brought in. Apparently they'd all been Lisa's favourites, and it was uncanny how her taste in confectionary was practically identical to mine. I was weighing up the merits of cheesecake versus something sinfully chocolatey, when the final dish was set down on the table. It was a pyramid of golden-brown profiteroles held together by gossamer strands of spun sugar. Plate and fork in hand, I approached the miniature mountain, trying to work out what it reminded me of. The answer came in a blinding flash. The tiny choux buns looked just like conkers, and all at once I was back in the hospital car park staring up at a tall man wearing sunglasses and an irritated expression. Which meant that when I looked up and saw that same man standing right there in front of me, I was shocked enough for the plate to slip from my fingers and embarrassingly shatter all over the floor.

'Is it just me or are you a really awful juggler?'

If anyone else had made that comment, I would probably have laughed, but there was something about this man that made my hackles rise. Besides, I was bent low, busily picking the shards from the floor before someone accidentally stood on them.

Like a swooping angel, one of the catering team suddenly appeared beside me, wielding a dustpan and brush and politely urging me to step aside. I took my time straightening up, aware from their heat that my cheeks were still flushed pink.

The man standing before me dropped his own handful of broken crockery into the dustpan before speaking.

'Are you okay?'

I nodded. 'You seem to have an unfortunate habit of surprising me.'

'Ah, yes, I can see how my standing here might easily have startled you.'

There was more than enough humour in his voice to defuse the sarcasm, but I still felt wrong-footed and awkward. Was it suddenly several degrees hotter in there, I wondered. Trickles of perspiration had begun moving in convoy down my spine. The cashmere dress was starting to seem like a huge mistake, and I lifted a hand to pull the cowl neckline away from my skin.

'Careful!' the man cried out as his hand shot forward, cobra fast, to capture my wrist and immobilise it.

'What the—?'

'You're bleeding,' he explained, turning my hand over to reveal a pearl-sized drop of blood on the tip of my index finger. 'You must have cut it on one of the fragments. You were about to get it all over your dress.'

I hadn't felt or even noticed it, but somehow he had, despite the dimly lit room and the fact that he was once again wearing dark glasses.

'Oh, I see,' I said awkwardly. 'Well, thank you, then.'

The moment stretched on, and just before it got really awkward he suddenly remembered he still had hold of my wrist. As soon as he released it, I lifted the finger to my mouth and sucked it in an automatic reflex. Were his eyes on me as I did this? In the reflective glare of the polarised lenses, all I could see was my own face.

'Molly, did you cut yourself? Are you okay?'

Alex must have covered the distance in quick long strides, and there was a look of concern on his face that was making me quite uncomfortable.

'Despite being terminally clumsy, I'm fine,' I assured him. The words froze on my lips a split second too late to recall them. What was the very worst thing you could say to a recently bereaved widower? Referring to yourself as being 'terminal' surely had to be up there in the top five. There was no chance that he hadn't noticed. Having to project my voice above a classroom of excitable six-year-olds had made me pretty good at being heard – even when I wished I hadn't been.

Surprisingly, it was the man in the dark glasses who salvaged the situation. Taking a step forward, he extended his hand in Alex's direction.

'You must be Alex. It's nice to finally meet you. I'm Mac, by the way.'

Their handshake went on for what seemed like a very long time. It flew easily past a polite business introduction and then just kept on going, leaving a normal social greeting far behind. It was only then that the pieces fell into place: the hospital car park; the ophthalmology department; the coincidence of finding this man had also been invited to this curious birthday party. Mac was the missing transplant recipient. The eyes that were now turned towards me had come from the same person whose heart was beating a little too fast in my chest.

'Is this… Are you… Are you Molly?'

My gaze flashed to Alex, who had the grace to look chastened. He'd told all of the others about me, and yet he and I had never discussed any of them in our letters. It set me apart from the rest of them in a way I didn't understand or like.

'That's me,' I said, aiming for chirpy and failing by quite a few degrees.

Mac's hand went to his dark glasses and very deliberately he took them off, sliding them into the top pocket of his shirt. I tried not to stare at his eyes, mindful of how self-conscious I was whenever anyone directed their attention to my own transplant site. His eyes were an incredibly vivid blue, and I knew their colour would have been his before the transplant. The only thing he'd have received from Lisa were the corneas, but even so, it felt as though the gaze of more than one person was on me now, as he gave a nod of recognition. 'It's nice to see you again.'

Alex's head jerked sharply towards Mac, as though shocked to discover we'd already met. I braced myself, feeling certain he'd ask one of us to explain, but he didn't. It was a relief because I wasn't entirely sure what Mac had meant. Was he referring to our encounter in the hospital car park? I hoped so, because, quite honestly, any other interpretation was just too creepy to consider.

CHAPTER FIFTEEN

Alex

The speech Alex gave wasn't great. Even he knew that. For a man who could hold the attention of a boardroom full of executives while pitching for a contract, there were far too many 'er's and 'um's in his disconnected ramblings. It was only marginally better than the one he'd given at Lisa's funeral – at least he didn't break down this time. But it was a world away from the joyous one he'd given on their wedding day, when he'd been unable to stop smiling or take his eyes off the amazing woman sitting beside him in the lacy white dress.

Almost everyone in the Stargazer Room that night had also been there on those previous occasions. All except the group of four individuals in the far corner, who had gravitated towards each other like iron filings on a magnet.

Lisa had always been a collector of people. Anyone lucky enough to become her friend kept that title for life. She never neglected a friendship or let it carelessly slip away. It was one of the countless things Alex loved about her. There were people there tonight whom she'd known since childhood, ex-neighbours who now lived hundreds of miles away, as well as colleagues from every job she'd ever had.

She had a knack of holding on tightly to the important people in her life. So how could she have left Connor, and him, to flounder helplessly without her? She just wouldn't have done that; would never have abandoned the two of them. Which was why Alex found it so hard to accept.

'I want to thank you all for coming tonight. I know how much it would have meant to Lisa to see you all here.' He paused, his eyes drawn to the far corner of the room. 'Even those of you she never got to meet.'

The words were catching in his throat, and all around the room tissues were being surreptitiously tugged from pockets and handbags. It was time for him to stop.

After a hesitant pause, a small ripple of applause travelled the room like an uncertain Mexican wave. As Alex wove through the clusters of people, he was buoyed by the comforting hands patting his shoulder or squeezing his arm. It carried him across the room to the one group he hadn't spent enough time with that evening – the ones who could only be here because his late wife could not.

But when he reached them, he saw with dismay that Barbara was already putting on her coat. Molly was holding her walking stick and had her own black coat draped over her arm. Alex had left it too late, he'd taken too long worrying about finding the right words to say to them, and now they were about to leave with so much still left unsaid.

'That was a really good speech,' Mac said. Alex smiled tightly, recognising a lie when he heard one.

He looked at each of them in turn, hoping the desperation he was suddenly feeling wouldn't be heard in his voice. 'You're going? Already?'

Guilt jumped from one face to the next.

'It's past my bedtime,' Barbara explained, reaching out to capture one of Alex's hands between both of hers. 'And my cats start to fret when I'm away too long.'

'Of course,' he said, trying but failing to stop his eyes from settling on Molly as he asked, 'Do you all have to go now?' He noted their hesitation and pushed harder than he should have. 'I'm sorry. Perhaps tonight wasn't the best time to meet all of you. I feel like I still haven't got to know you properly.'

'You already know us, mate, from our letters. And we can carry on writing, if you like?'

Alex nodded at Jamie's suggestion, like a drowning man being thrown a life ring he already knew wouldn't keep him afloat.

'And maybe we *could* meet up again, sometime in the future,' Molly offered, looking a little taken aback at her own suggestion, as though someone else had made it for her.

Alex turned to her, and the gratitude on his face wiped the uncertainty from hers. 'Yes. I'd really like that.'

'Well, we've all exchanged numbers tonight,' Mac revealed, 'so fixing something up shouldn't be too difficult.'

Alex forced himself to accept their need to leave right now. He was surprised they'd swapped numbers, for it was hard to imagine a more unlikely quartet of friends. But of course they had something very unique in common. Did they feel it too, he wondered, that connection that ran so deep and defied all logical explanation?

'Thank you all for coming. I really hope we see each other again soon.'

Alex entered a cloud of lily of the valley when he bent down to brush his lips against Barbara's cheek. He felt the rise of a flush on her skin and wondered if there were still people in her life to kiss her hello and goodbye. He really hoped so, because she was too nice a lady to have no one but a family of cats to lavish her love on.

For the second time that night he shook Mac's hand, which felt staid and middle-aged compared to the complicated handshake routine Jamie instigated. This involved slapping, fist-bumping and several other moves Alex couldn't keep up with. *You're not very street, my love*, he heard Lisa laughingly observe in his head.

Alex hesitated as he turned to Molly. He was still deliberating between a kiss and a handshake when she took the decision from him. Very lightly placing her hands on his shoulders, she reached up and pressed her lips against the bristle on his cheek. The softness of her breath scorched him like fire, but he schooled his features to remain impassive.

'Goodnight, Alex. You did a really nice thing for your wife tonight,' she whispered into his ear, as though confiding a secret.

Alex watched all four of them slip silently from the room, already knowing that Molly's parting words would stay with him for a very long time.

CHAPTER SIXTEEN

Molly

'Are you sure I can't offer anyone a lift?'

I paused in the hunt for my collapsible umbrella. This was the first question Mac had directed my way since he'd discovered who I was. I wasn't usually over-sensitive, but it was glaringly obvious that although he'd been perfectly happy chatting away to Barbara and Jamie all night, he'd barely said two words to me.

'Oh, that's so sweet of you, Mac,' said Barbara, answering before I had a chance to. 'But my next-door neighbour is coming to pick me up. Oh, I think that's him parked over there,' she said, sounding suddenly flustered.

It was hard not to admire the way Mac immediately took her elbow and stepped out from beneath the planetarium's canopy into the pouring rain. He saw Barbara safely across the forecourt to the waiting car before trotting back, weaving past the deep puddles that had pooled in potholes. He was looking considerably less polished by the time he re-joined us. His hair and face were dripping wet, as though he'd just taken part in an enthusiastic round of apple bobbing, although I couldn't imagine anyone less likely to play that particular Halloween game.

'How about you, Jamie? Can I drop you somewhere?' The youngest member of our group had mentioned earlier that he hadn't received the all-clear to drive yet. 'Which is a bloody waste when I've got a practically new Beemer sitting waiting for me in the garage,' he'd grumbled. I'd been so busy explaining to Barbara what a Beemer was, I hadn't stopped to wonder how someone as young as Jamie could afford to own such a vehicle. It had taken me several years of teaching before I'd been able to upgrade my own car from a tired old jalopy.

'I'm gonna pass, if you don't mind, Mac. I've arranged to meet up with some mates at a pub not far from here.' Jamie gave a wink that managed to look both devilish and endearing. 'There's still plenty of life left in the night, if you know what I mean.'

Mac nodded as though he understood perfectly, while all I could think about was a hot cup of tea and finally slipping off the toe-pinching sandals that had seemed such a good idea a few hours ago. Perhaps Kyra was right and I was more than halfway to becoming a bona fide shut-in, which strangely didn't worry me nearly as much as it should have.

Finally, with no one left to ask, Mac turned to me.

'Thanks, but I'm good. I've booked a cab to pick me up,' I assured him as I fumbled with the button on the telescopic umbrella that I'd finally unearthed from the bottom of my bag. With an unexpected whoosh, the umbrella shot open, its spokes coming perilously close to his eyes. I felt genuinely sick at the near miss and the way he'd been forced to take an instinctive step backwards. There was an unreadable expression on Mac's face as he looked at me, but if I had to take a guess, it would be something like: *You really are a disaster waiting to happen, a total liability.*

'I'm so sorry,' I gasped.

And although Mac politely dismissed it as nothing, I couldn't help noticing that he reached for his dark glasses and slipped them back on.

Apparently unaware of any tension in the air, Jamie headed off into the rain with a cheerful 'See ya,' leaving Mac and me alone beneath the planetarium canopy, which was proving to be not quite as waterproof as it had first appeared. Mac turned up the collar of his coat as a few enterprising raindrops found gaps in the canvas and trickled down the back of his neck. *Why doesn't he just go to his car*, I thought, knowing this was the point where I probably ought to be inviting him to share my umbrella, and yet I was reluctant to invite him into my personal space.

'Look, you really don't need to wait here with me,' I said, which sounded every bit as ungrateful as I'd feared it would. I tried again. 'What I mean is that there's no point both of us getting wet, and I'm perfectly okay about waiting alone.' The dark glasses made it impossible to see his eyes, but I was pretty sure they were narrowed as he looked at me. 'I'll probably go back inside until my taxi gets here,' I added, glancing over my shoulder at the invitingly dry foyer.

'Well, if you're absolutely sure,' Mac said, giving a very eloquent 'it's up to you' shrug before delving into his pocket for his keys.

'I am. So, goodnight then,' I said in a rush, juggling handbag and umbrella to free my hand and extend it towards him.

His fingers were warm, and his grip lingered a second or two longer than I was expecting. Then without a word he turned and headed off into the torrential downpour.

Ten very long and wet minutes later, with still no cab in sight, I finally had to admit that my taxi was a no-show. I was thoroughly cold and wet, and annoyed with myself for having rejected Mac's offer of a lift for no good reason. He'd done nothing to deserve the prickly way I seemed to act in his company, and I truly couldn't work out what it was about him that bothered me so much. 'Bothered' wasn't quite the right word, but it was the closest I could manage.

I doubt I'll ever see him again, so it's hardly worth worrying about, I told myself as I turned back towards the planetarium's entrance. It looked as though I was going to have to call for a new taxi, and there was little point standing out in the rain while I did so. But before I could take a step towards the door, I saw that the entrance lobby had filled with several departing guests. Standing among them, bidding people farewell, were Alex and Todd.

My stomach flipped in a way that was surely physically impossible, but it was enough to stop me in my tracks. Had they looked up, the Stevens brothers would have spotted me staring in at them through the window, but they were deeply absorbed in conversation. Alex said something and gave a sad shrug, which crazily made me want to abandon all good sense and dash straight back in to join them. It was an idiotic impulse, but I couldn't deny there was an almost magnetic pull tugging me towards these virtual strangers that left me confused and unsettled. What the hell was the matter with me tonight?

From the forecourt behind me I heard the crunch of gravel and a car's engine slowing down from a roar to a purr. The planetarium's window reflected the outline of a low sedan that had just pulled up alongside the stone steps. Through the steadily drumming rain came the unmistakable whirr of an electric window sliding down.

'Molly?'

Mac called out to me at the exact same moment that Alex looked up and noticed me. Through the glass I saw his lips form my name. For what seemed like an age, I hesitated, but something in Alex's eyes scared me. It made me want to run, and I didn't know if that was towards or away from him. With no conscious thought, I spun around and dashed through the rain towards the passenger side of Mac's car. Without saying a word, I climbed in.

'And then what happened?' Kyra asked, leaning so far forward on the uncomfortable plastic chair, she looked in danger of falling off.

'Shhh…' hissed a woman in the row in front of ours, twisting around to give us a particularly pointed glare.

'Sorry,' Kyra mouthed, pulling an irreverent face as soon as the woman had turned back to face the stage.

The next guest speaker was already at the lectern, shuffling her notes while colliding them clumsily against the microphone. A screech of feedback ricocheted around the school hall. Everyone winced. I had a feeling it was going to be a very long morning. Consortium training days were a necessary evil in our job, but I'd yet to meet a teacher who genuinely enjoyed attending them. Except, perhaps, the woman sitting in front of us.

As the speaker introduced herself to the room full of teachers, Kyra reached for the notepad balanced on her knees. *Well??!!* she scribbled in bold strokes across the top of the page. There were an excessive amount of question and exclamation marks following the word.

With a wry smile I reached for my own pad to reply. We were a cliché, the two disruptive kids at the back of the classroom passing notes to each other instead of paying attention.

Nothing happened, I scribbled back, and because she was a self-confessed stickybeak, I added for extra emphasis, *Nothing at all. Mac drove me home. End of story.*

Except, of course, it wasn't.

Mac's car had the kind of leather seats that probably didn't come as standard. I only hoped the upgraded spec also meant they were water-resistant, because I appeared to be depositing an awful lot of raindrops on them. The car even smelt expensive, in comparison to mine, which exuded a permanent odour of forgotten damp gym towels and well-worn trainers.

I was still clicking the seatbelt into place when Mac spotted a gap in the flow of traffic and pulled swiftly and wordlessly onto the road.

'Thank you for this,' I said.

His attention was on the traffic, so perhaps that explained the single nod he gave in reply. Not everyone appreciates chatty passengers when they're concentrating on their driving, so I kept quiet, waiting for him to ask why I'd changed my mind or even what had happened to my taxi. But he was either the least curious person on the planet or simply not interested enough to enquire. I had a feeling it might be the latter.

Although I usually enjoyed sitting in silence, as many people who spend their entire day in the company of six-year-olds tend to, this one was stretching uncomfortably. It was as though we were playing a game of chicken to see which of us would break it first.

He won.

'This is really kind of you, Mac, but I must be taking you out of your way.'

'Actually, until you tell me where you live, that's hard to say for sure.'

There it was again, that dry, teasing humour that was clearly his trademark. We were stopped at a junction, allowing him to swivel in his seat as he waited for directions. The dark glasses were off again and even in the ambient glow of the dashboard lights, the colour of his eyes was arresting. I blinked a couple of times, not quite a rabbit in the headlights, but more dazzled than I had reason to be.

I tore my gaze away to look out the passenger window. 'Look, it's quite a drive from here, so why don't you just pull over and I'll call an Uber.'

'Absolutely not,' Mac said emphatically. His foot pressed down a little harder on the accelerator, further blurring my view from the passenger window. But even with the rain and the poorly lit streets, I glimpsed a figure I was sure I recognised studying a timetable beneath the canopy of a bus stop. I cupped my hands against the glass to form a pair of makeshift binoculars, but we'd already left the bus stop far behind us. Common sense told me it couldn't possibly have been Jamie, who'd set off in the opposite direction to meet up with his friends almost half an hour earlier. It was just someone wearing the same kind of clothes. But even so, the resemblance had been uncanny.

'Is something wrong?' Mac asked, his foot already moving to cover the brake.

'No. Nothing,' I replied, turning away from the side streets to study the man who seemed determined to take me home, regardless of whether I wanted him to or not.

'I like driving,' he admitted, after I'd finally conceded defeat and told him where I lived. 'The novelty of being able to do it again hasn't worn off yet.'

I smiled, suddenly understanding him a little better. Perhaps this wasn't such an imposition after all.

'Whenever I can't sleep at night – which is pretty often these days – I grab my car keys and just drive around. Sometimes for hours.'

I almost shared that I was also a new member of the insomniacs' club, but then thought better of it. 'So where do you go when you're driving for hours in the middle of the night?'

Illuminated by the headlights of an oncoming car, I saw a slightly embarrassed look flicker over his face. 'Anywhere. Nowhere. Although I seem to end up at the coast more times than I can count. And I've no idea why. It's like something keeps pulling me there.'

'Well, that's not creepy. That's not creepy at all.'

Mac's laughter seemed to catch him by surprise, as though he hadn't known I could be funny. Which of course he hadn't. It was weird how I kept forgetting that everyone I'd met that evening was a complete stranger.

'I guess I must have really missed driving,' Mac confessed.

'What else did you miss? Were there other things?' I was suddenly curious about his life before he'd been ill. All I knew of him was his age – thirty-six – and that until he'd lost his sight he'd been a successful architect.

'There were other things too. Obviously.' His voice was tight, as though he'd pulled down an invisible shutter on his previous life.

I hadn't just stepped on a nerve, I'd practically annihilated it. I got the impression Mac didn't talk about his condition very often, which made me even more curious. 'Always trying to fix everyone,' Tom used to say – lovingly in the early days, and then with a bite of irritation by the time we started to fall apart. Ironically, by then the only thing that was truly beyond fixing was us.

But this wasn't simply interfering. Mac's life had been dramatically altered, just as mine had. Once by disease, and then by the woman who'd given us both a second chance. It led us naturally to finally mention the elephant in the car, the one who'd followed us all the way back from the planetarium.

'It was kind of weird tonight, wasn't it? I mean, I think I understand why Alex wanted us all there, but the only reason we *were* there was because his wife couldn't be.'

'We're not responsible for the train crash, Molly,' Mac said gently, so in tune with my thoughts, it was a little scary.

'I know that. But it's still so odd to feel this guilty and grateful at the same time. Do you think the guilt ever goes away?'

Mac made a soft whistling sound. 'God, I hope so. I'd hate to think it would always feel like this.'

He took his eyes off the road briefly and an understanding I hadn't been expecting travelled between us.

'I wasn't sure about coming tonight,' he admitted.

This time it was my turn to sigh. 'Me neither.'

'I'm glad I went though. I'm glad I've finally met Alex. Although I can't help wondering if he feels the same way now he's met all of us. I hope it's given him whatever he needs to allow him and his little boy move on.'

Something twisted inside me, like a knife in my gut, when he mentioned the boy with the bowed shoulders and the saddest eyes I'd ever seen. For some people it's puppies and kittens, but for me it had only ever been children. It had made my choice of career an absolute no-brainer.

'And I'm also glad to have met you – and Barbara and Jamie, of course,' Mac added hastily, hammering home that there was nothing remotely inappropriate in his remark.

To be honest, I'd been out of the game for so long, I doubted I'd have even recognised 'flirty' any more, much less remembered how to respond to it. Even so, it seemed safer to stare out through the windscreen rather than at his face, and when I did I saw with surprise that Google Maps had already led us to my road.

'That's mine just up ahead. The one by the streetlight.'

Mac pulled up directly outside, the engine idling as he appraised my house. It always looked a lot better in dim light than it did in the daytime.

'Nice place,' he commented, his architect's eye running approvingly over the contours of the building. 'You don't come across many of that age that still have a lot of the original features. You were lucky to find this one.'

'It wasn't me,' I said, bending down and retrieving my dripping umbrella from the footwell. 'My boyfriend was the one who spotted it on Rightmove and insisted we buy it.'

'Ahh.' Mac smiled stiffly, paused, and then seemed to relax in a way he hadn't before in my company. He had the look of a man whose very painful tooth had just been extracted. All at once I wanted nothing more than to hurry back into the home I no longer shared with Tom.

I was wondering if we'd once again shake hands or if I should just say goodnight and get out of his car, which in hindsight would have been preferable to what did happen. Mac leant across and towards me, and I met him halfway and pressed a kiss on his cheek, which to be fair was right there in front of me. All of which would have been fine, if I hadn't realised too late that he'd actually been leaning over to courteously open the door for me.

I scrabbled out of the car so fast, you'd have thought my seat had been electrified. In the amber glow of the streetlight it was impossible to tell if Mac was smiling, but I suspected that he was. I can't recall whether my manners held out long enough for me to thank him for the lift home, as, quite honestly, the seconds between exiting the car and collapsing in an embarrassed heap against my front door were rather a blur.

'So, on a scale of one to ten, how boring was the last speaker?' Kyra asked as we shuffled like sheep towards the school canteen and the promise of coffee.

'Please don't tell me you slept through it,' I said, only half joking. I'd thought her bent head had meant she was deep in thought. Who would have known that behind that curtain of long blond hair my friend had actually been snoozing?

'I'm pleading the fifth,' she said, with mischief dancing in her eyes. 'Much as I believe you've been doing about last night.'

'There really isn't anything more to tell. I went to the planetarium, I met Alex and his family, and then spent most of the evening chatting with the three other transplant recipients. They seemed like nice people. I think you'd particularly like Mac.'

We were almost at the head of the queue for the coffee urns, and I grabbed two mugs off the stacked pile.

'And why's that?'

'Well, he's tall – like you.'

Kyra gave a snort of laughter. 'Are you so desperate to find me an English boyfriend that all we need to have in common now is our height?'

'I just don't want you to go disappearing back to Australia any time soon. That's all.' From out of nowhere I felt unexpectedly emotional. 'I'd miss you too much.'

Kyra pulled a silly face, but I could see my words had touched her. 'Well, seeing as you love me so much, how about buying me one of those cakes to go with our coffees. I've left my bag back in the hall.'

'Sure,' I said, handing her my mug as I delved into my large tote bag for my purse. My fingers groped around among the usual detritus, passing over something unfamiliar and then hesitantly returning to it.

I drew it from my handbag like a surprised magician.

'Who are you phoning?' Kyra asked.

I was still looking at the slim device in the palm of my hand like I'd never seen one of its kind before.

'No one. It's not my phone.'

'Then what's it doing in your handbag?'

'I have absolutely no idea.'

CHAPTER SEVENTEEN

Alex

He looked in all the logical places first, before moving on to the downright ridiculous ones. Having checked the pockets of his shirt and trousers and come up empty, Alex padded barefoot down the stairs through the empty house and frisked his coat, which was draped over the banister post where he'd thrown it. Nothing.

He stood in the hallway rewinding his movements of earlier in the evening. He could remember speaking to Mac on his phone and then switching it off so that it wouldn't ring during his speech. But when he tried to visualise slipping it back into his pocket, his mind was a complete blank.

He plucked up his car keys and with a grimace ran through the rain to where he'd parked on the drive. His mood was growing as dark as the night sky as he crouched beside the driver's door and groped beneath the seats while the rain plastered his shirt against his back. The gravel chips were digging painfully into the sensitive skin of his bare soles. Why the hell hadn't he stopped to at least pull on some shoes?

His thoughts had been chasing themselves like a dog after its tail ever since he'd left the planetarium. He'd gone ahead with the party to celebrate the day Lisa had entered the world as though it might act as an antidote to the last occasion when everyone had gathered, to mark her exit. But had he been lying to everyone, including himself? Had it all just been an excuse to invite four total strangers who shared a closer connection to him and Connor than anyone else in the world? What kind of fucked-up logic was that?

With a grunt, Alex got to his feet, giving up his hunt for the missing phone, at least for now. He shut the front door a few degrees short of a slam, as though that might stop his troublesome thoughts from entering, but they knew all the cracks in the frame and squeezed through anyway.

Tonight was meant to have been a one-off; that was what he'd promised himself. It was only natural that he'd been curious about the people Lisa had helped, but once he'd met them, seen they were well – thriving, even – he believed he'd finally find the closure everyone had told him would come.

But meeting them in person hadn't closed that door in the way he'd thought it would; instead, it had blown it off its hinges. Who were they, these people? There were over six thousand patients in the UK on the transplant waiting list – he knew, because he'd looked it up. Why had these four been chosen to receive Lisa's organs over all the others? Why them?

Alex climbed the stairs wearily, as though he'd aged twenty years in a single night. His feet stopped automatically outside Connor's room. The curtains were open and a beam of moonlight illuminated the empty bed, with its smoothly plumped pillow. It was a house full of empty beds, and suddenly Alex regretted having Connor spend the night with Todd, Dee and Maisie. He instinctively reached into his pocket for his phone, wondering if it was too late to go round and bring him home. His laugh sounded unnatural when he remembered his phone was every bit as absent as his son.

To confirm he really had looked everywhere, Alex dropped to a crouch beside his own bed and peered beneath the wooden frame. There were a few prairie-sized dust bunnies that would never have been there six months ago, and also something else glinting in the dark, something small and shiny. There was no reason for his fingers to tremble as he grazed them against the floorboards trying to reach the elusive object, and yet they did. *It'll just be a coin that's fallen from my pocket*, he told himself, not believing the lie as his fingers fastened over it and drew it out.

It was strange how a delicate twist of silver could bring a six-foot-two-inch man to his knees. But it did. Alex gently blew the dust off the solitary earring from the pair he'd bought Lisa for their ninth anniversary – their last anniversary, as it turned out. He stared at it in the palm of his hand for a long time. Had Lisa known it was missing and been too scared to tell him she'd lost it? The stupid things you worry about, he thought, when you are blissfully ignorant that there's so much worse that can happen than losing a piece of jewellery.

For the first time he understood why some people moved house so soon after a bereavement. Your home became a mine-field of memories, and sometimes it was just too damn hard to walk through it without injury. It had taken months before he'd stopped finding strands of long blond hair everywhere. And the realisation that one day he would unknowingly vacuum up the last one had left him with an aching sense of loss.

When he got to his feet, the dust bunny skittered across the floor as though it really was alive. Maybe he should be more bothered about the state of the floor beneath their bed, he thought; about what Lisa would have said if she could see it.

He fell asleep on top of the covers, as he often did these days. You needed a peaceful mind to achieve a good night's sleep, and Alex could no longer remember what one of those felt like.

'Did you try ringing it?'

Alex gave his sister-in-law a Homer-Simpson-worthy 'Doh!' look.

Dee laughed. 'Yes, of course you did. Sorry, stupid question.'

Alex shrugged and reached for the mug of coffee that she was sliding across the breakfast bar towards him. 'It was a waste of time anyway, because I definitely remember switching it off yesterday evening.'

'Oh, so that "Find My Phone" thingy won't work either, will it? Maybe one of the planetarium staff will find it today.'

'They didn't sound hopeful earlier, as it hasn't been handed in.'

Alex stared morosely into the swirling brown Americano in his mug. 'There were photos on there I hadn't backed up anywhere else.'

Dee nodded sympathetically. There was no need for her to ask who was in those photos.

'So, was Connor okay staying here last night?'

He saw Dee hesitate as though torn between which might hurt him more, the truth or a lie. She went for the truth. 'He woke up in the night, calling out for Lisa.'

It felt like a punch to the pit of his stomach, and the mouthful of coffee Alex had just swallowed gurgled unpleasantly in protest.

'Damn. He's not done that for a couple of months. I'd hoped we'd got past that.'

'To be fair, he was more asleep than awake, and he settled back down very quickly. I just stroked his hair for a while until he dropped back off—' Her voice was hoarse and Alex's head shot up to see that a single tear was trickling down Dee's cheek. 'He thought I was her.'

Alex bit down so hard, he could taste blood on his tongue. He would *not* cry here, in his sister-in-law's cheery kitchen, with its bright red fridge and matching oven. He simply wouldn't.

The click of the front door opening had them both wiping their hands beneath their eyes. Todd strode into the room, his cheeks bright red from the cold.

'How was the park?' asked his wife in an overly jolly voice.

Todd's eyes flashed between the two people he loved, but wisely he didn't ask what he'd just interrupted. 'It's real brass-monkey weather out there, but at least the kids had the swings to themselves.'

Alex made a move to climb off his stool and follow the elephantine footsteps that had just pounded up the stairs, but Dee's hand reached out to stop him. 'Hang on. I've just remembered something. I think I know where your phone is.'

'Huh?'

'I think Connor might have taken it. Last night, when I was tucking him in, he slipped something under his pillow. I didn't think anything of it at the time, and it was too dark to see properly, but now I think about it, it did look like a phone.'

Alex's smile was sad as he told her, 'It is a phone. But it's not mine. It's Lisa's. I gave it to him.'

Todd turned around from the sink, where he was filling the kettle, a look of surprise on his face. 'Isn't seven a bit young to have an iPhone?'

Alex briefly bristled at the implied criticism, then realised his brother was probably only worrying that Maisie would want one too, if she knew.

'The phone's locked, and he only has it for one reason.'

The tears Dee had successfully stopped looked in danger of returning as she nodded slowly in understanding. 'He uses it to speak to Lisa, doesn't he?'

Alex nodded, and Todd's face went red again, and this time it was nothing to do with the cold.

Dee left a long enough pause for them all to recalibrate before saying, 'Connor was telling me the two of you have big plans for Saturday.'

'We do?'

'He said you were doing something with ginger men.'

Like a character in a sitcom, Alex slapped his forehead in dismay. 'Shit. I forgot about that. Bugger it.'

Two pairs of raised eyebrows waited expectantly for an explanation.

'It's for the school fete. Each kid is meant to bring in something homemade to sell for charity. We've been told to make two dozen gingerbread men.' There was a look of genuine despair in his eyes.

Dee laughed. 'Ah, that makes more sense. I thought the two of you were off to an Ed Sheeran concert or something.'

Todd was laughing as he crossed the kitchen and lovingly squeezed his wife's shoulder. For a moment Alex felt excluded. He missed those small moments of intimacy – the silly ones, the ones that reminded you why you'd fallen in love with the person you'd married. Why you still loved them all these years later.

'So you're doing a Paul Hollywood, are you? *That* I'd pay good money to see. Why don't you just fake it and buy them?'

Alex clenched his jaw. 'Because all the other kids are going to be bringing in stuff they've helped to bake at home, and Connor doesn't need another reason to not fit in with the rest of them.'

Dee once again reached across the breakfast bar, this time to capture his hand and press it gently. 'You don't have to do this, Alex.'

'Yeah, I do. The fete is next—'

'I'm not talking about the bloody biscuits.' The profanity had the desired effect. It was one of only a few times that Alex had ever heard his sister-in-law swear. She drew in a deep breath as though to clear her palate of the dirty word. 'I'm going to say something now you probably don't want to hear.'

Alex briefly considered interjecting with a 'Don't say it then,' but he could tell by Dee's face that she meant business.

'This is what they call tough love, Alex. And you have to understand that it comes straight from the heart. Because you know how much Todd and I love you, don't you?'

Something hard and uncomfortable had lodged in Alex's throat, making any type of verbal response suddenly impossible. He nodded.

Dee took another breath, glanced at her husband as though for approval, and then dived in. 'Your whole life has been torpedoed, and the ship you were happily sailing in went down. But it's been six months now, and it's time for you to stop flailing about in the water and swim back to the shore. Do you get what I'm saying here?'

'That I'm slowly drowning?'

He'd meant it to sound jocular, but from the sadness in Dee's eyes he realised that was exactly what she'd meant.

'You're never going to be able to be a mother to that wonderful little boy of yours. The shoes you're trying to fill are simply too big. The harder you try, the more it's just going to keep hurting both of you. And it's breaking our hearts watching it happen. There's nothing you can do, Alex, to give Connor his mummy back.' Dee bit her lip and then delivered what Alex had to admit was a powerful closing argument. 'But you *can* give him his daddy back.'

It was almost a relief when the herd of elephants chose that moment to descend the stairs again. Maisie barrelled into the kitchen like a Chinese acrobat, with Connor a few sedate steps behind her.

Dee reverted seamlessly to their former topic as though they hadn't just been swimming in waters too deep and dark to navigate. 'Would you like me to bake those gingerbread men for you? I could drop them round sometime tomorrow.'

Alex could feel Connor's eyes on him, as though he was waiting for his father to let him down again. How many times had he done that since Lisa had been taken from them? And how bad was it that Alex didn't know the answer to that question?

'No. We're good. Connor and I will figure it out together. How hard can it be to bake a batch of gingerbread men anyway?'

CHAPTER EIGHTEEN

Molly

Before the start of the afternoon session, I asked the organisers to make an announcement about the mysterious mobile. This prompted a flurry of delving into handbags and pockets, but no one claimed it. And though I taped up my contact details in the hall on my way out, I was no longer convinced the phone belonged to a fellow teacher after all.

When I got home I set the phone down on my kitchen table, where my glance kept returning to it as I chopped the vegetables for a healthy stir-fry dinner. This was my antidote to a day of mindless snacking, which Kyra had solemnly declared was 'the only way to survive a CPD day'.

As my dinner sizzled in the pan, I picked up the phone, turning it over in my palm as though the answer to how it had come to be in my bag was at the end of a thread I had to unravel. The sensation came so unexpectedly, I thought it was an electric shock. It almost made me drop the phone on the quarry-tiled floor, which would have rendered the question of returning it a moot point. I didn't believe in psychometry, or anything remotely 'woo-woo', as Tom used to laughingly call it, and yet when I'd held the phone there'd been… something. Something I couldn't explain. It was a feeling of connection or familiarity, for want of a better word.

I eyed the phone with caution, then took a deep breath, tightened my grip around it and waited for the inexplicable feeling to hit me once more. But this time there was nothing. It was just a phone, two models up the scale from mine, but with nothing more intriguing about it then a passcode I couldn't crack.

Later that evening I was curled up on the settee in a pair of very unsexy pyjamas – a description that applied to all my sleepwear in those days – with the latest bestselling thriller everyone was talking about in my hands. I was two chapters in when something happened that shook me far more than the author's edge-of-the-seat storyline had.

Propped up on the settee cushion beside me were the two mobiles: mine and its mystery counterpart. I'd keyed in a quick message to my mum on mine, because she still had a tendency to panic if she didn't hear from me every day, but before returning to my book I picked up the other phone. I pressed the home button, shaking my head at the screen when it told me once again to enter my passcode. I'd tried a few random sequences earlier, in the vague hope that its owner had thought 1-2-3-4 or 1-1-1-1 was a good choice. They hadn't.

'Where on earth did you come from?' I asked the device in my hands. Admittedly, talking to inanimate objects was a little worrying, but nowhere near as disturbing as what happened moments later as my fingers drummed absently on the touch-screen, forming themselves into a pattern as if they had a mind of their own. With no idea how I'd done it, the phone came to life. My gasp of shock wasn't because I'd somehow tapped in the correct passcode – although that was freaky enough. It was because, half hidden by the icons on the screen, I could see a face I recognised, cuddled up beside one I didn't.

In all the letters Alex and I had exchanged, I'd never once asked to see a photograph of Lisa, and he'd never volunteered one. I'd always imagined that one day I'd see the face of the woman whose heart had saved my life. I just never expected this would happen because I'd accidentally hacked into her husband's mobile.

It was the first frost of the season, and the view from my bedroom window wouldn't have looked out of place on the front of a Christmas card. There was a charm to the thick rime coating the roofs, branches and leaves that didn't quite extend to the car's windscreen. After a fruitless search for a scraper I had to resort to a credit card, which did the job but left me with fingers the kind of blue I hadn't seen since before my operation.

I left the engine running as I studied the route to Alex's house. Google assured me it would take only thirty-eight minutes to get there. I hadn't realised he lived that close, and as I sat in the gradually warming car, it occurred to me how unusual it must be that all of Lisa's transplant recipients came from roughly the same region. I'd done my research when I'd been placed on the list, so I knew that organs could be transported from anywhere in the UK, or even abroad. And yet Lisa Stevens's had gone to four people who lived in the same part of the country as she had. The more I thought about it, the more bizarre it seemed, until eventually I heeded the voice in my head, the one which was calmly advising me to accept it as a coincidence and move on. It was just 'one of those things'. Although there did seem to have been quite a few of 'those things' recently.

As I pulled away from the kerb, I thought back to the call I'd made to Kyra late the night before.

'You all right?' she'd asked, sounding breathless with concern at seeing my name flash up on her phone screen.

I felt a pang of remorse that I'd not bothered to check how late it was. Before I had the chance to answer her, I heard a low male voice saying something in the background, and suddenly I realised there was probably a whole other reason why Kyra was out of breath. In the dim light of my living room I blushed at what I'd interrupted.

'No worries,' Kyra assured me, sounding more Aussie than ever. Given that her Friday night was clearly far more interesting than mine, she was surprisingly intrigued by what I'd called to say.

'You hacked into his phone?'

'Only accidentally,' I emphasised.

'How on earth did you do it?'

'I've absolutely no idea.'

'Crikey, do you know what the odds are against you just randomly guessing the right code?'

'Ten thousand to one. I checked online.'

Kyra gave a low whistle, like a plumber preparing to give someone a hefty estimate, before asking a question I hadn't yet considered.

'Why do you think Alex put his phone in your bag?'

I shivered in the warmth of my cosy lounge. 'I... I don't know that he did. Not deliberately.'

I heard a rustling of sheets and imagined Kyra had now swung out of bed and was pacing the room. It was what she did when teaching or trying to get a point across. At least it would give her companion something interesting to look at while he waited.

'Where did you keep your bag when you were at the planetarium the other night?'

'It was under my coat, in a pile with everyone else's.'

'Zipped up, I assume? You're always pretty vigilant about that.'

'I... I guess so.'

'Then someone had to have *put* the phone in there. Perhaps someone who wanted to make sure you'd meet up with them again?'

'You're making this all sound vaguely sinister and premeditated.'

Kyra remained silent, letting my own observation find a place to land.

'I just don't see why he'd do something like that.'

'Maybe Alex was worried that after last night you might not agree to meet with him again. Which, incidentally, I happen to think would be a very good decision. There's something really wonky about this whole thing, if you ask me.'

'I just don't see why anyone would willingly pretend to lose their phone. It's too much of an inconvenience being without it. And besides, he didn't know I'd be able to unlock it and work out it was his. For all he knows, I could have already handed it in to my local police station.'

'Hmm,' agreed Kyra, before murmuring something placatory to whoever was currently sharing her bed.

'Look, I'm really sorry to have bothered you tonight. Just go back to… whatever it was you were doing, and I'll figure out what to do with the phone.'

'Just don't do anything stupid like dashing round to his house in the middle of the night. I don't want the next time I see your face to be on a missing persons poster somewhere.'

I laughed, nervously.

'How did you figure out the phone belonged to Alex? Did you read his messages or something?'

'Of course not,' I said, in a tone that was a great deal more shocked-Sunday-school-teacher than I'd intended. Probably because I didn't want Kyra to know how tempted I'd been to do exactly that. 'I didn't need to anyway. There was a picture of Connor and his mum on the home screen. He looks just like her,' I added softly as my eyes dropped to the phone in my hands.

CHAPTER NINETEEN

Molly

I would have called to let Alex know I was coming, but his landline was ex-directory, so all I could do was hope my unannounced arrival wouldn't feel like an intrusion – or, worse, an ambush.

The Saturday morning traffic was heavier than I'd been expecting and I was glad because it forced me to concentrate on my driving rather than on the moment when I would knock on Alex's front door. I'd always thought the first meeting between a recipient and their donor family would be really emotional, but strangely the birthday party in the planetarium hadn't felt that way. Perhaps because there'd been so many other people present. But as the map counted down each mile to my destination, I realised that today might feel more like a first meeting. Was Alex ready for this so soon after the party? Was I?

The home Alex and Lisa had shared was on the edge of a quiet estate, not quite a gated community but pretty exclusive nonetheless. Each house was slightly different from its neighbour, but the one thing they all had in common was an abundance of windows, most of which were currently catching and reflecting the low October sun like a row of miniature flares. I slowed my car to walking speed, but it was still impossible to make out the house numbers through the glare, so I pulled into a parking bay to allow the butterflies in my stomach to rest their wings.

Alex's phone was on the passenger seat beside me and I slipped it into the pocket of my quilted jacket before climbing out of the car. The early-morning ice had long since melted, so I wasn't able to blame my wobbly legs on a slippery pavement. Number 7 Woodview Gardens, the address I'd written on numerous envelopes over the past few months, was tucked away at the far end of the road. Beyond its back garden a copse of tall poplar trees cast long, eerie shadows on the gravel driveway as I crunched slowly along it towards the front door.

The traffic sounds from the nearby main road and the twitter of the birds in the trees began fading out as though a dial was being turned. The sound of my heartbeat filled the void. Had I ever heard it this loud before? I truly didn't think so. The drum crescendo got steadily louder the closer I got to the door, as if my heart recognised this place. It knew it was home.

I shook my head to dislodge the ridiculous idea, pressed the shiny brass doorbell and unconsciously began counting the seconds. I'd got to seven before the front door was flung open. A loud, high-pitched beeping filled the air.

'Molly!' Alex cried, a look of consternation on his face. I couldn't tell whether it signalled annoyance, surprise or even relief.

'Hi, I—'

'Sorry, I think the kitchen's on fire. Come in.'

Strangely, I didn't even hesitate. Alex had already spun around and was running down the hallway towards a closed door which was shimmering as though through a heat haze.

'Daddy?' came a tremulous voice from the top of the staircase. I glanced up and saw a very worried-looking Connor about to make his way down.

'Stay up there,' Alex commanded fiercely, reaching for the kitchen-door handle. He barrelled into the room before I had a chance to call out a warning. I'd seen enough disaster movies to know he definitely shouldn't have done that. In the film version, flames would have belched through the open doorway, engulfing him, but in reality it was just a thick fog that smelt of burning and also curiously of ginger.

'Shit!' Alex exclaimed, flinging open the oven door and releasing yet more smoke. I coughed and he whirled around, looking momentarily surprised to see me standing there. 'You should get out of here. This smoke probably isn't good for you.'

I doubted the cremated remains of whatever he'd been attempting to cook represented any risk to my health, but given whose heart it was, I simply nodded and backed away. The last thing I saw before closing the kitchen door was Alex thrusting open a set of French doors and lobbing a charcoal-encrusted baking tray into the garden.

Connor was a small white-faced statue sitting on the top step. His eyes looked enormous and his lower lip was trembling. I began slowly climbing up to reach him, approaching him as cautiously as if he were the rabbit with a broken leg I'd found in my garden last summer.

'Hi Connor. It's Molly. Do you remember me?'

I was halfway up the staircase, but Connor hadn't even glanced my way. His attention was fixed on the closed kitchen door. He was visibly shaking and it was all I could do not to run up the last few treads and enfold him tightly in my arms.

'Is my daddy all right? Is he hurt?'

Sod it. There was no way to stop my feet from running towards him. I closed the distance between us in four strides.

'He's fine, sweetie. He's just opening all the windows and the doors to let the smell out of the kitchen.'

Connor turned his head very slowly towards me, as though on rusty hinges, a blank look on his face. Then a tiny spark of recognition flared in his deep blue eyes.

'I know you.'

Hearts don't really leap into throats, and I knew for a fact that mine was firmly stitched into place, but it certainly felt as though it had broken free at Connor's words.

'You're the teacher lady from the party.'

My crashing disappointment at this response made absolutely no sense. I mustered up a smile. 'That's right. I'm Molly. I met you and your cousin Maisie the other night.'

Connor couldn't quite manage his own smile yet, but at least the trembling had stopped. His eyes went back to the closed door. There was no sound from within the kitchen, and even though I knew there hadn't been an actual fire or any real danger, a tiny frisson of apprehension tiptoed down my spine.

I was hunkered down on the step below Connor and, working purely on instinct, I held out my hand to him. Aeons passed; trees blossomed and then lost their leaves; fruit withered on branches in the time it took Connor to decide to place his hand in mine. Or so it seemed.

I held the hands of children his age every day, but this felt very different.

'Shall we go and see what your daddy is up to?'

He nodded mutely up at me and allowed me to pull him to his feet.

I knocked lightly on the kitchen door, keeping Connor slightly behind me in case I'd seriously underestimated the situation. 'Hi, Alex. Can we come in?'

Alex opened the door, letting out a waft of reassuringly fresh air. Connor was a blur. Greyhound fast, he raced past me and hurled himself at his dad. His spindly arms were wound so tightly around Alex's waist that his clasped hands had turned white.

'I think Connor was a little concerned you were okay in here?' I kept my voice deliberately light, careful not to embarrass the boy, but my eyes filled in the blanks.

Alex looked momentarily lost, unsure how to react, then bent down and kissed the top of his son's head. 'I'm fine. Everything's fine.'

Connor shook his head fiercely, his face still buried in his dad's pale blue shirt.

'Everything except our gingerbread men, that is,' Alex joked.

Connor gave a sound that fell halfway between a laugh and a sob.

'Oh, is that what you were making?' I asked.

Alex directed his gaze towards the lawn and a smouldering baking tray. 'That was batch number three. I think maybe the universe is trying to tell us that we shouldn't go for lucky number four.'

'Not if you don't want to raze your home to the ground,' I said teasingly, breathing a silent sigh of relief as I saw Connor relax enough to release his bear-hug hold on Alex.

'I actually didn't incinerate the first two attempts, but they were still inedible,' Alex said. 'Somehow I don't think *Bake Off* are going to be knocking at my door anytime soon.' He turned to Connor. 'Your mum would be horrified if she saw what I've done to her baking tray.'

The light which had only just returned to Connor's eyes was gone in an instant, as if a switch had been flicked. I saw it. And his father did too. Alex bit his lip: one step forward and two steps back.

'Can I go back upstairs and play?' Connor asked, shutting down and shutting us out so effectively, I already knew this was something that happened more often than it should.

'Sure you can, champ,' Alex said, resorting to the kind of jollity I could have told him little kids always saw right through.

Left alone in the cold kitchen with the lingering smell of burnt biscuits, Alex turned to me with a look so helpless, it made my heart lurch just as it had with Connor on the stairs.

'I can't seem to get it right,' he said.

'It must be so hard.'

'It is.' Two words, but there was a whole world of pain in them.

There was a brief silence, and then Alex glanced at me and said, 'Not that I'm trying to be rude or anything, but what exactly are you doing here today, Molly?'

I blushed like a nervous teenager. 'Oh, sorry. I should have said. I found this.' I reached into my pocket for his phone.

His look of astonishment was almost comical. 'Oh my God. Where on earth did you find it?'

Kyra had been wrong about him. She had to have been. Surely no one was that good an actor? He seemed genuinely amazed.

'In my handbag, actually.'

'Huh? How did that happen? Did you mistake it for yours?'

There was a sound in the hallway, a kind of shuffling noise.

'No. I have a different model. But the weird thing is that my bag was tucked away all night, so it's hard to work out how your phone ended up in there. Unless…' My voice trailed off; there was no way I could say 'unless you put it in there' without creating the world's most awkward situation.

But in the end I didn't have to.

'Unless someone put it there,' Alex interjected, his eyes travelling beyond me to the hallway, where the shuffling footsteps suddenly picked up speed, changed direction and pounded up the stairs.

'Connor?' I said, surprised. 'What makes you think it was him?'

Alex's smile transformed his face from pleasant to really good-looking. 'You mean other than the guilty exit we just witnessed?'

A grin twitched at my lips.

'I think, Dr Watson, we might have found the culprit.'

Without missing a beat in our conversation, Alex's fingers had gone straight to the camera icon on his phone's home screen to check that whatever it was he was hoping to find was still there. How many times a day did he continue to do that, I wondered

– search for her face because he couldn't go a minute longer without seeing it again?

'I'm really grateful to you for bringing this back,' he said, slipping the phone into the back pocket of his jeans. 'I was actually on hold with my insurance company just now, trying to arrange for a replacement. That was how come I lost track of time – which would have been a really poor excuse if I'd burnt the house down.'

I made a sympathetic sound and wondered if it was time to make my excuses and go.

'Coffee?' Alex asked, lifting up the pot and waggling it enticingly in my direction.

'I'd love one,' I said, suddenly very glad that I didn't have to leave straight away, even though my business here was done.

Despite the cold breeze blowing in through the open windows, there was a warmth to the kitchen that had nothing to do with its physical temperature. Even with the film of flour coating the worktops and the pile of sticky mixing bowls in the sink, it was the kind of kitchen that magazines or TV adverts would feature to represent perfect family life. It was only when I looked a little closer that I noticed that the handwritten shopping list held by a magnet on the fridge door was yellowed and curling at the edges and that there was a light covering of dust on the shelf where the recipe books lived. This room was missing Lisa's touch.

Alex had his back to me as he pulled two matching mugs down from a cupboard. He filled them with coffee and then turned around with the milk carton in hand and a question in his eyes. I nodded.

'I hope Connor's not going to get in too much trouble about the phone thing?' I said, knowing it was none of my business, but asking anyway.

Alex sighed and gave a small shrug as he returned the milk to the fridge. Its doors were covered with colourful crayon drawings that reminded me very much of the mural of the galaxy in my classroom.

'I know I should probably tell him off. There's bound to be some speech I'm meant to give about respecting other people's belongings, but to tell you the truth, this is the first vaguely naughty thing he's done since... Well, in a long while. So part of me wants to embrace it. It's not as if—'

'Erm, sorry, I should have said,' I interrupted hastily, cutting him off. 'I don't take sugar.'

Alex looked down at the mug into which he'd just spooned a generous serving. There was no need to even bother asking. I already knew that must have been how Lisa had taken hers. He gave a small laugh, but it held almost no humour. 'It's been a while since I've poured coffee for two,' he said, sounding suddenly lost. 'I guess I was on autopilot.'

I had an awful feeling he might be about to cry, and if he did, there was a good chance I'd join in. So I summoned up my best jolly teacher voice, the one I used when knees were bloody or mothers disappeared out of the door on the first day of term.

'What prompted the great gingerbread men experiment today?'

It was terribly poignant watching Alex pour the coffee he'd made for Lisa down the sink and making a fresh one for me.

'"Experiment" is a good word for it. Do you know what happens when you think baking powder is the same thing as flour?'

I couldn't help the bubble of laughter that escaped me. 'Oh, no! You didn't...?'

'Batch one literally erupted. It was like a mini Vesuvius inside the oven. Batch two tasted foul, and batch three... Well, you saw what happened there. We might have to buy some to take to Connor's school fete this afternoon after all.'

The question was on my tongue, but there was a voice that sounded an awful lot like Kyra's in my head, screaming at me not to ask it. I loved my friend: her fierce loyalty, her support when

I'd been so sick, and her caring heart. But that didn't mean she was always right.

'I could help you and Connor make some more – if you like? If you don't think that would be too weird?'

Alex looked momentarily floored by my suggestion. 'I couldn't ask you to do that.'

'You didn't ask. I volunteered.'

'Well, that would be really great, as long as—'

I didn't wait to hear what his proviso was going to be but inserted my own instead. 'But only if you ask Connor first if he'd like me to help. I don't want him to think that I'm... butting in... where I'm not wanted.'

Alex shook his head. 'I think his little stunt with my phone should give you the answer to that one. Connor doesn't form new attachments easily, but he really does seem to have taken to you.'

And me to him, I thought silently as Alex left the room to ask his son if he'd like to help me in the kitchen.

He was gone for quite a while, so I used the time to tidy up and make some space on the worktop, marvelling that Lisa had kept so many of her utensils in the same cupboards that my own lived in at home. I threw the thought out before it could take root and multiply. Keeping your spoons in the same drawer did not constitute some kind of mystic connection, and if I was going to do more good than harm here, I needed to keep that kind of nonsense firmly out of my head.

'You cleaned up,' observed Alex guiltily, walking into the kitchen with the hand of a suddenly much shyer Connor in his.

'Only a bit,' I said, feeling my cheeks turning pink and hoping he'd think it was from my exertions rather than a flush of pleasure. It felt far safer, for all kinds of reasons, to direct my conversation solely towards Connor and pretend Alex wasn't even there. *Come on, Molly*, I told myself, *this is what you do. You're good with kids, you've got this.*

'Connor, your dad tells me you need some gingerbread men, which makes this your lucky day, because it just so happens they're the things I can bake better than anything else in the world.' That may have been a slight exaggeration, seeing as I'd only ever made them once before, but I'd found a recipe on my phone while Alex was coaxing Connor back downstairs, and I was fairly confident I could knock up a batch without anyone needing to summon the fire service.

Alex seemed content to take a back seat and took himself off to the far end of the kitchen table, drawing a nearby laptop towards him. At regular intervals he clattered noisily on the keyboard, presumably without realising that from the reflections in the French windows I could see it wasn't turned on. He was watching me closely with his son, and I was perfectly all right with that. If Connor had been mine, I'm sure I'd have been just as cautious – probably even more so.

'First we need to weigh out the flour,' I told my young assistant in a slightly unnatural TV chef voice. I tipped flour onto the scales, disappearing briefly behind a smokescreen of Homepride's finest. I hadn't dressed for this kind of activity, and my dark indigo jeans and black polo-neck jumper were already covered with white specks.

'There's an apron on the inside of the larder door, if you need one,' Alex volunteered.

'That might be an idea,' I said, opening the door and then catching the look of horror on Connor's face as I reached for the apron with *Mummy* emblazoned on the front. My stomach took a plummet and I shut the door so fast they'd have been forgiven for thinking the apron was planning to escape.

'You know what, I don't think I need one after all.'

With that hurdle behind us, Connor seemed to relax a little and for the next twenty minutes he spooned, stirred and rolled with a fierce concentration that told me a great deal. He was a conundrum: far brighter than most seven-year-olds, and yet far less confident than the children in my class. There was a watchfulness about him, and a fear of doing something wrong that made it difficult not to abandon the cooking and envelop him in an enormous hug. Had he been this way before he lost his mum or were these insecurities new? I tried to imagine how I might phrase that question to Alex, and then realised I had no business asking it.

While the gingerbread men were baking in the oven, I returned the ingredients to their various cupboards, correctly lucky-guessing where they'd come from so many times, I was inspired to buy a lottery ticket on my way home. Alex stepped into the garden to answer a phone call, and the second he left, I released a long breath I hadn't even realised I'd been holding.

'Did you enjoy baking today, Connor?' I ventured, pulling open the fridge and popping the butter back into its compartment.

'It was okay,' he murmured. He'd had fun, I knew he had, but he didn't want to admit it, as though it was somehow disloyal to do so. *This child isn't yours to fix*, a sensible voice in my head reminded me. But I refused to listen to it. Wasn't a child in pain *everyone's* responsibility?

'These are really excellent drawings,' I observed as I closed the double-fronted American-sized fridge. I stepped back as though studying paintings on a gallery wall. Although they were mainly drawings of the moon, there were a few that featured other recognisable planets.

'This must be Mercury,' I said, pointing to the small planet closest to a flaming ball of crimson Crayola, which had to be the sun. 'And the craters on this one of the moon are so realistic.'

For the first time the hesitant look left Connor's eyes and was replaced by one of amazement. 'You know about the planets?'

I suppressed a smile and nodded solemnly. 'Well, only a little bit. I still have lots to learn. I have a big mural of the solar system on the wall in my classroom, but to be honest your drawings are way better than mine.'

Connor took the compliment with a slow nod. 'My mummy knows all about the planets. When I grow up I'm going to be an astronomer, just like she is.'

From the corner of my eye I could see that Alex had returned in time to catch the end of our conversation. Was it Connor's use of the present tense when he spoke of his mum that had put that unbelievably sad expression on his dad's face?

'Well, that's a fine ambition to have. I bet you'll be a really marvellous one.'

The gingerbread men were cooling on a rack, ready for the fete that afternoon, and I'd politely declined Alex's invitation to stay for a second cup of coffee.

'Molly has things she has to do,' he told Connor, who'd looked flatteringly disappointed when I'd reached for my jacket. 'She doesn't want to hang around with us all day.'

I wondered which of the three of us would have been the most shocked if I'd confessed that actually that was exactly what I'd have liked to have done. The rest of my Saturday stretched ahead of me with boring predictability.

Connor was busily decapitating a gingerbread man with his front teeth as I waved a cheery goodbye from the doorway, having resisted a totally inappropriate urge to hug him goodbye. It was as if I'd never attended a single training day about boundaries, I thought to myself. Why was it suddenly so hard to stick to them with this lost little boy?

'Thank you again for returning my phone,' Alex began awkwardly as he stood with one hand on the Yale latch, 'and also for what you did today – for Connor.'

I smiled sadly. 'I didn't do anything. Not really.'

'He opened up. We got a glimpse of the boy he was before…'
Lisa died, we both completed silently.

'I noticed that when he spoke of her—' I started hesitantly.

Alex nodded. We were speaking in half sentences, as though this was a familiar shorthand between us.

'Yeah, I know. The counsellor has advised me not to correct him. But I'm not so sure.'

'He needs time.' I looked up. *You do too*, I wanted to add, but that would have been stepping so far over the boundary, I might never have found my way back.

With perfect timing, Connor came racing out of the kitchen just then, clutching something against his chest. He screeched to a stop in front of me and extended his arm. It was the drawing of the moon that I'd admired from the fridge door. A lump the size of a golf ball threatened to choke me as I took it from his outstretched hand.

'Well, this is going straight up on my fridge when I get back home,' I assured him, willing my voice not to crack.

Connor was now tugging Alex down to his level and hurriedly whispering something in his ear. Whatever it was, Alex's expression was unreadable when he straightened up to face me.

'Connor wanted to know if you'd like to come to the Bonfire Night party that Todd and Dee are holding at their place next week. It's a bit of a Stevens family tradition.'

I looked from father to son, indecision clouding my face.

'It would be really great to have a chance to talk to you properly. Today's been too chaotic, and it was impossible to speak to all of you at the planetarium the other night.'

'Oh, I see. So you'll be asking the others as well: Barbara, Jamie and…' I had no idea why I instinctively hesitated. It wasn't as if I'd forgotten his name or anything. 'And Mac,' I finally completed.

My suggestion had clearly thrown him. Inviting the other recipients obviously hadn't been his intention, but after taking a moment to think about it, I could see that he rather liked the idea.

'Yes, I will. If they'll come.'

'Then I will too.'

There was an unexpected lightness to my stride as I walked back to my car. I didn't know exactly what or who had put it there, but I liked the feel of it.

CHAPTER TWENTY

Alex

'All I'm saying is that it would have been nice if you'd checked with me first, that's all.'

Alex dived to one side, took an out-of-control swipe at the squash ball, and not surprisingly missed.

'Your point wins,' he muttered, bending to retrieve the ball.

'Do you mean in the game or our conversation?'

Alex straightened up, rubbing at the low, dull ache that was developing between his eyebrows. He forced himself to unclench his jaw. They played another couple of points, with the squash ball taking the brunt of both brothers' frustration. If they hit the damn thing any harder, it was likely to end up embedded in the wall, Alex thought as he peeled his sweat-soaked T-shirt away from his body. He usually looked forward to their weekly game, but today it was pretty obvious that neither of them was in the mood. Unspoken words were ricocheting silently around the court at a speed the ball could never have matched, and the air felt heavy with testosterone.

'Shall we just call it a day and go for a pint?' Todd suggested, fast-forwarding to the reward they'd scarcely earned after less than twenty minutes' play.

The pub around the corner from the gym was surprisingly busy for so early in the evening. Alex managed to snag a free table in the corner and watched as his brother slalomed through the crowds to the bar. The headache showed no sign of quitting anytime soon, and he doubted that alcohol would improve it. A few minutes later Todd emerged from the throng, holding aloft two pint glasses of craft beer.

Even a casual observer would have known they were related. They had the same build, the same sandy-coloured hair and caramel eyes, and a cleft chin they'd apparently inherited from a grandfather they'd never met. They were similar in a thousand ways and yet also very different.

Todd pushed a glass wordlessly towards his brother and then without preamble, as though there hadn't been a thirty-minute break during which they'd showered, changed and walked to the pub, he resumed their conversation as though releasing a pause button.

'I'm not trying to be a dick about this party thing,' he began. It was an unfortunate opening remark, and Alex's eyebrows eloquently replied that it might already be too late for that. 'And I'm not saying I don't like these people. They all seemed perfectly pleasant the other week. But I just assumed that this year, given everything that's happened, you'd want to make it purely a family thing.'

Two beats passed, then three. It was as though Alex kept missing his cue. 'Well, these people *are* kind of like family.'

Even worse than Todd's anger was the pity in his eyes as he looked across at his younger brother.

'No, Alex. They really aren't.'

Alex reached for his glass and swallowed deeply, hoping the emotions that were threatening to rise up would get washed back down. He loved his brother, and he truly didn't think he'd have got through the last six months without the support from him and Dee. But right now, the distance between them felt far greater than the width of a sticky-topped bar table; it felt as wide as the Grand Canyon.

Todd was wearing his patient 'I know what I'm talking about; I'm the sensible one here' expression. It was the one that used to make a teenaged Alex clench his fists in frustration. Apparently the thirty-five-year-old Alex felt much the same way.

'Well, I don't know what you want me to do about it now. I can hardly un-ask them. And don't forget it wasn't me who thought of inviting them, it was Connor.'

'Yes. And next week I'm letting Maisie do my tax return.'

Alex looked away, because deep down he knew Todd was right, but there was no way he could admit it. At the table beside them sat a young couple in their twenties. They were holding hands and staring so intently into each other's eyes, they were obviously somewhere far away from the pub, with its noisy jukebox and rowdy drinkers. Alex had a sudden burning desire to be there too.

'And don't think I don't know who it is you really want to come. It's *her*, isn't it?' Todd pressed.

'I take it you're not talking about Barbara?'

The twist of Todd's lips was the closest he was going to get to a smile. He drew in a long breath. 'She's not Lisa. You know that, don't you? Molly. Isn't. Lisa.'

'You think I don't realise that?' Alex's reply was so sharp, his words pierced the bubble around the couple at the adjacent table. They stared at him, wearing identical expressions of surprise. Alex smiled weakly and then turned back to his brother, his voice a lot lower now.

'I know that. But you should have seen the way she was with Connor, and the way he responded to her. I haven't been able to reach him like that since the accident, but she did it within seconds of walking through the door.'

'She's a schoolteacher, mate. It goes without saying that little kids respond to her. Don't go reading anything more into it than that.'

They'd reached the point in the conversation that Alex wasn't sure either of them was ready for; the question he'd been asking himself for months, usually in the middle of the night. He knew Todd would look at him differently once he'd voiced it.

'Why them, Todd? Why these four people?'

His brother looked completely mystified. 'What do you mean?'

'There are thousands of people waiting for transplants. Why were these four people chosen?'

Todd gave an uncomfortable shrug. 'It was their turn? They'd got to the top of their waiting list?'

Alex knew he was sounding more and more like a crazy conspiracy theorist, but it was impossible to rewind now he'd started. 'But that's just it. They hadn't. Molly had only just gone on the list. And neither she, nor Jamie nor even Barbara were critical at that point. They leapfrogged over God knows how many other people. And why were there no other matches? Why just four people? You were there that day when I signed the forms.' Todd reached out and squeezed his brother's hand. 'We both heard Gillian say that as many as twenty people could be saved by Lisa's donation. But in the end it was just these four. And every single one of them got in touch with me. They all felt compelled to make contact. Do you know how rare that is?'

Todd shook his head and Alex waited for his brother to subtly suggest that perhaps he ought to 'see someone' to discuss these feelings. But Todd stayed quiet, letting his silence do the talking.

'There has to be a reason behind all of this,' Alex continued. 'A reason why Lisa was taken when everyone else in her carriage survived. A reason why these people have been given a second chance. There's an answer here, and just because I haven't figured it out yet doesn't make it any less true.'

Alex knew it was the right house without even checking the number on the gate. It perfectly matched the image he had in his head. Perhaps she'd described it to him in one of her letters, he mused, or perhaps it was simply because it looked so very *her*. He switched off the car's engine, and yet even when it had cooled into silence he remained in the driver's seat, staring at the house. Much as he hated to admit it, Todd's misgivings had sown tiny seeds of doubt, and as fast as Alex plucked them out, they kept shooting up again.

He sighed and reached for the bouquet of flowers on the passenger seat. To linger any longer would probably cause curtains to twitch at one of the many windows sporting a Neighbourhood Watch sticker, so he drowned out Todd's annoyingly persistent voice with a tuneless whistle and climbed out of the car.

There was no bell to be seen, so he knocked lightly on the frosted glass panel on the door and composed his features into a smile as he waited. One minute stretched into two. *If it gets to three, I'll turn around and leave*, he promised himself. *I'll take it as a sign that I shouldn't have come here today.* He smiled wryly. He was doing a lot of looking for signs these days, for hidden messages from the universe or from—

The shadow behind the glass twisted and morphed into the shape of an approaching figure, and Alex fought the desire to run away, like a kid playing Knock, Knock, Ginger – a game his ten-year-old self had found hilariously addictive. There was the rattle of a latch and the door swung open, and suddenly all thoughts of running were gone as the surprised expression on her face dissolved into one of delight.

'Alex.' She turned his name into a greeting, and he smiled back. He briefly considered leaning in to kiss her cheek, but instinctively knew that was a step too far.

'Come in,' she urged, inviting him in with a wave of her arm.

'I'm sorry for just turning up unannounced like this,' he said, following her into the small but cosy lounge. 'Is it a good time for you?'

'Of course. Any time is a good time for me, and it's a lovely surprise to see you again so soon. My goodness, are those for me?'

Alex glowed with pleasure at the genuine delight on her face as the bouquet passed from his hand to hers. 'I don't think anyone has given me flowers since my sixtieth birthday.'

That was one of the saddest things Alex had heard in a while, and he made a mental note to be sure to bring her flowers whenever they met again in the future. *If* they met again, the annoying voice in his head chipped in.

'Please sit down,' Barbara said, gesturing to the settee behind him, which had already been claimed by several small furry bodies.

Alex felt a twitch in his nose and wondered if he might be allergic to cats; there really did seem to be quite a few of them in there.

'Can I make you some tea?' Barbara asked, sounding a little flustered as she added, 'If I'd known you were coming, I'd have baked us a little cake.'

Alex shook his head with a gentle smile. 'Tea would be lovely, thank you, Barbara. Can I help you?'

'No, no. You just sit and relax and make friends with my family.'

Alex made a small mental correction, because *that* was the saddest thing he'd heard in a while. He cast his mind back through the letters they'd exchanged and realised she'd never once mentioned a family – not a human one, at least.

Very gingerly he sat down on the edge of the faded chintz settee, careful not to disturb the very large black cat curled up on the cushion behind him.

'Just push old Lucifer out the way,' Barbara advised, already heading towards the door. 'He'll probably come back and sit on your lap in a minute.'

Alex smiled weakly. Frankly, anything with claws that long and the devil as a namesake could keep the cushion he was on; after all, he'd got there first.

As crockery clinked in the kitchen, Alex got to his feet and examined the framed photographs on the mantel above the small Victorian fireplace. Most showed a much younger Barbara alongside a barrel-chested man with a bushy moustache, presumably her late husband Archie. Their wedding photo, taken on the registry office steps, featured Barbara in an extremely short white dress and floppy-brimmed hat; Alex tried but failed to see the snowy-haired, wrinkly-skinned pensioner in the leggy, fresh-faced girl in the photo.

'The seventeenth of May 1965. The happiest day of my life,' Barbara said as she came in carrying a plate of custard creams that Alex knew he would eat, even though he wasn't in the least bit hungry.

She crossed to where he stood at the hearth, miraculously staying upright as one of her cats wove between her feet like a determined assassin. 'I always thought we'd go together, somehow,' she said sadly. 'I wasn't ready to spend my old age alone.' There were tears in her watercolour-blue eyes and she brushed them away with an angry swipe of her hand. 'Goodness, this isn't like me at all,' she said, absently bending down and scratching the head of a white cat at her feet. 'And of course, I'm not alone, not really.'

Her words resonated with Alex in a way that suddenly made his eyes feel hot and scratchy. He really must be allergic to cats, after all.

'How many of them do you have – cats, I mean?'

'Just the six at the moment,' Barbara said, her eyes going to a large crate in the corner of the room which Alex hadn't even spotted until then. Inside it was a very fat ginger-coloured cat.

'Has that one been exceptionally naughty? Is that why it's locked up?' he joked.

'No. That one is my Meg. She's a queen. She's due to give birth any time now.'

On that disturbing piece of information, Barbara once again left the room to continue preparing their tea. Alex's eyes went to the cat in the cage, and a prickle of sweat formed on his upper lip. The room was ridiculously hot, but perhaps that was because it was about to become a delivery suite. The ginger cat was pacing restlessly, her claws clicking like a metronome on the newspaper lining the crate as she completed circuit after circuit of the place where her kittens would be born.

Alex sat down as far from the cage as he could. He'd never been much of a pet person, but Lisa had spent quite a while quietly campaigning for them to get a dog. 'I think it would be really good for Connor,' she'd said, and Alex had begun to waver. But then… Well, things had changed, and a puppy was now the last thing on his mind.

'I hope English Breakfast is okay? I never could get on with those fancy foreign ones.'

Alex had been so lost in thought, he hadn't even heard Barbara come in, and it took a moment or two for him to return to the present. He leapt to his feet, taking the heavy tray from her hands, which were trembling under the weight of it.

'It's the only type we buy,' he replied, aware the pronoun landmine had tripped him up once again. He wondered if Barbara had noticed.

There was a family-sized teapot beneath a knitted cosy, and a matching milk jug and sugar bowl, complete with dainty miniature silver tongs. He was touched that she'd gone to so much effort and wondered how frequently this tea service came out of the cupboard. Not that often, he guessed.

'So, Alex,' Barbara said as she passed him a bone-china cup so delicate it was practically transparent, 'what exactly is it you've come here to ask me today?'

Forty-five minutes later, a slightly discomfited Alex put his car in gear and pulled away from Barbara's neat Victorian house. He'd achieved his objective – she'd agreed to join them at Todd's

Bonfire Night party – so why was there a lingering bitter taste on his tongue that even an entire plate of custard creams hadn't managed to erase?

Because you exerted your not inconsiderable charms to persuade a sweet old lady to spend a second night with a group of people she doesn't know, Lisa's voice chided softly. It was strange how his conscience had started to sound more and more like his late wife over the last six months.

She's lonely, he countered, in the confessional booth of his car. *It'll be good for her to spend time with real people instead of a bunch of cats.*

She loves those cats, his late wife reminded him gently. *That's why she was reluctant to accept. She's worried they'll be frightened by the fireworks.* Lisa's argument was so persuasive, he had to force himself not to turn to the passenger seat, where, had the dice been rolled differently, his wife would be sitting, gently taking him to task.

Not that Barbara had needed Lisa to be her champion. She was perfectly capable of asking her own hard questions. 'You say you want to get to know us better, Alex dear, but wasn't that what we were all doing the other evening?'

Alex had fidgeted uncomfortably as though under interrogation. 'I may have misjudged things by inviting everyone to Lisa's birthday celebration at the planetarium,' he admitted.

Barbara had demurred charmingly. 'Not at all. It was important for us to see how much Lisa was loved and is missed by her family and friends.'

Alex had smiled sadly. *This* was why he liked Barbara. She wasn't afraid of speaking Lisa's name. Having lost her own partner, she understood that the only thing more painful than talking about them was never hearing them talked about at all.

'I… I just want Connor to get to know the people his mum helped,' he'd said awkwardly, trying to drown out Lisa's hiss of disapproval in his head. *Not fair, Alex*, she chided. *You can't use our son as a bargaining tool here.* But he did.

Barbara's eyes might have been cloudy with incipient cataracts, but there was no mistaking the flash of sympathy in them. 'He still doesn't know who we are, does he?'

Alex shook his head. 'He knows that there were some people Lisa helped to get better before she... went away.' He'd always hated euphemisms; he'd always been a-spade-is-a-spade type of person, but that was before he'd discovered some things were just too painful to put into words. 'Connor refuses to believe his mum died. He's still positive that she's coming back for him.'

That was what had persuaded Barbara. 'Then of course I'll be there, Alex. How could I not come?'

CHAPTER TWENTY-ONE

Molly

The fog was dense, bouncing the car headlights back at me as I circled the station car park looking for a space. The one I found was far enough away from the main entrance to justify pulling on a bobble hat and winding a chunky scarf around my neck before leaving the car.

I glanced at my watch and forced myself to walk faster across the tarmac, praying I wouldn't twist an ankle in one of the potholes hidden by the swirling carpet of fog. I felt like a performer walking across a stage pumped with dry ice. And oddly that illusion continued when I entered the brightly lit station, where the tuneful sound of piano music rose above the hum of the crowd.

There were far more people on the concourse than I'd expected this late on a Saturday afternoon. I zigzagged past passengers talking hurriedly into their mobile phones, catching snatches of disgruntled conversations. When I eventually found a pocket of space to stand in and read the electronic board, the chaos began to make sense: *All trains delayed due to fog.*

The piano was still playing somewhere nearby, an upbeat tune I vaguely recognised, but it wasn't enough to lighten my spirits. Mum had been away for weeks on what had felt like the world's longest holiday, and I'd been really excited about seeing her today. I'd even wanted to drive down to the port where her ship had been due to dock, a proposal she'd immediately rejected. 'You shouldn't be driving halfway around the country,' she'd said. 'Not with your…' And then she'd laughed, almost embarrassed. Old habits died hard, and I could hardly blame her for forgetting that I was no longer incapable of driving for hours, or lifting heavy suitcases, or doing anything else a healthy woman in her early thirties might normally be expected to manage.

The crowd was starting to surge towards the food outlets and cafes at the perimeter of the station, and I bobbed along with everyone else. It was a shame I hadn't brought a book to read, but at least the piano music was a pleasant distraction. The two pianos had been donated to the station concourse six months ago. They were there for anyone to play, and I'd heard 'Chopsticks' crucified on them on many occasions, as well as a few concert-level classical performances. Today's pianist was way better than most, although obviously not a professional. It was their choice of easy-listening jazz that put a bounce in my step, a style of music that always reminded me of my dad.

I was humming – probably a little tunelessly – under my breath as the unseen pianist segued into their next song. My feet recognised the tune first, and faltered, then my heart skipped a beat as though trying to sync with the rhythm of the music. My ears were slow in identifying the song, when they should probably have been expecting it.

I couldn't remember the last time I'd heard 'Fly Me to the Moon', but here it was now, being played by some random person who'd jumped on the piano to while away the minutes. Ever since Connor had presented me with his drawing, I seemed to have been having encounters with the moon at every turn. It had been on the front of my mum's last postcard and on the fabric of a scarf I'd found in the street, and it had even featured as a topic at the top of a podcast chart when I'd been searching for something to listen to at the gym. But more than that, the moon had begun to infiltrate my dreams, vividly enough to jerk me from sleep. I'd woken on several occasions in the last week confused and disorientated, with thoughts of Alex's son bizarrely in my head. Could an obsession be contagious, I wondered, because it certainly felt like I was being stalked by something I'd given scarcely more than a passing thought to before.

The haunting melody filled the concourse. I committed the cardinal sin of coming to an abrupt stop in the fast-flowing crowd, causing people behind me to collide like falling dominoes. They swerved around me, cursing in irritation as I slowly pivoted in the direction of the music. *This is just a coincidence*, I told myself as my feet led me like a sleepwalker towards the unseen piano, though the odds of someone playing this particular song did seem extraordinarily high. Those odds became truly incalculable when a gap in the crowd gave me my first glimpse of the piano, or rather the person who was seated at the keyboard.

He hit two wrong notes when he saw me, before swiftly recovering. I came to a stop a few feet away from him, transfixed by his fingers as they flew skilfully over the keys. He was playing without sheet music or any trace of inhibition as far as I could tell. He seemed relaxed, as though this was his comfort zone; I, on the other hand, was completely thrown by the sight of him in this unexpected setting.

He said nothing until the final chords had dissipated, then turned to me with an easy smile as he reached for the dark glasses he'd left folded on the piano's lid.

'Hello, Molly.'

My mouth felt weirdly dry, making my voice sound scratchy as I replied. 'Hi, Mac.'

He slid smoothly off the piano stool, with a smile and a nod to the person who'd been patiently waiting to take their turn at the keyboard, and crossed to stand before me. I instantly regretted having opted for flat boots instead of heels. Mac made me feel small, like a child, a sensation I'd never experienced before with any of my taller friends.

'You play the piano,' I said idiotically, as though informing him of something he might somehow have failed to notice.

'I do,' Mac confirmed. There was a grin hovering on his lips which he seemed to be having trouble containing.

'Why that particular song, if you don't mind me asking? Why "Fly Me to the Moon"?'

The grin disappeared and Mac's dark brows drew closer together. I could hardly blame him; even I could hear it was a strange question to have asked.

'No reason, really. I was just playing whatever popped into my head. I probably heard it on the radio or somewhere recently.'

'You play really well,' I said, trying to ignore the frisson as he placed a guiding hand on my back to steer me through the crowd. Mac was surprisingly tactile. Was that a lingering trait from when he'd lost his sight or had he always been that way? I couldn't imagine a time when I'd know him well enough to ask that question.

'My mother would definitely thank you for the compliment. She was my piano teacher and I was without doubt her most reluctant and inept student.' He grinned and gave a what-are-you-going-to-do shrug that instantly shaved a decade off him.

'Are you here to catch a train?' I really did seem to have cornered the market in stupid comments. Mac had a knack of making me feel nervous and awkward, turning me into a bumbling fool.

'No, I'm not travelling anywhere,' he replied, his eyes flicking up to the arrivals board, which showed no update on its last message. 'I'm here to meet someone, but their train's been delayed.'

'Same.'

He looked down at me and I could practically see the suggestion pop into his head like a thought bubble. 'Do you fancy grabbing a coffee somewhere and keeping each other company while we wait?'

Say no. Say you have something else you need to do. Keep your distance, Molly Kendall. Your connection to this man is just too weird.

'Yes, I'd love to.'

The coffee bar was heaving. They were clearly reaping the rewards of the transport chaos. With no tables free, I followed Mac to the counter, where he placed our order. He saw me fumbling in my bag for my purse and those eloquent eyebrows of his rose once again.

'I'll get these.'

'Always split the bill,' Kyra had a fondness for saying. 'That way if the date's a complete write-off, you've nothing to feel guilty about.' Except this wasn't a date, I reminded myself. It wasn't even close.

Mac leant across the counter, speaking too low for me to hear what he'd said, and the barista immediately quadrupled our bill, even though we'd only ordered a couple of flat whites. She was smiling and thanking him, and I realised he must have put down some money for people who might come in but be unable to afford a hot drink. Warmth bloomed inside me as I realised I actually liked Mac much more than I'd first thought. I'd made some swift and sweeping assumptions about him when we'd met, but I wasn't too proud to admit that most of them were turning out to be wrong.

He spotted a booth near the window that had just become vacant and we hurried over to claim it.

'Whose train is it you're meeting?' he asked as he slid into the seat opposite me.

'My mother's,' I replied. 'She's coming back today after a really long cruise. It's the first holiday she's allowed herself in years.' Did he read the guilt on my face or simply hear it in my voice?

'Your illness must have been very hard on her.'

I nodded, knowing better than to trust my voice right then. I was usually reluctant to talk about my condition, especially with people I didn't know well. But Mac straddled every boundary wall I'd ever set up. Because of our unique link, because of Lisa, we were probably the most intimately connected strangers in the world.

'Are you an only child?' he asked.

'Yes. It's just Mum and me. We… We lost my dad a few years ago.' As I suspected, it was still way too soon to speak those words without my voice cracking.

The touch of his fingers against the back of my hand was so unexpected, I almost pulled it away. His fingertips travelled over my knuckles. *Blind people do this*, I told myself. *They touch, when they can't see.* I'd seen it in films, and on TV. And yes, Mac could see *now* – maybe every bit as well as I could – but perhaps it was a hard habit to lose?

'Well, I'm here today to meet my best mate from uni,' Mac continued, understanding I needed a moment or two to regain my composure. 'Andi's going to be staying with me for a while. There were eight of us who shared a student house in Edinburgh, and almost everyone else chose to stay up there after graduation.'

'But not you?'

'There were more job opportunities down here, and I had other… attachments at the time.'

He was closing down that topic, just when it was starting to get interesting, for it sounded like he'd come back for a girl. Were they still together, or was he single now? I was itching to ask, but for once I listened to the voice in my head reminding me it was none of my business.

'Can I ask *you* something? Why were you so curious before about the song I was playing?'

It was hardly a trick question, but it blindsided me. My hand jerked, spilling a sizeable amount of coffee onto the table as I set down my cup.

'Oh God, I'm so sorry,' I said, reaching for a wodge of serviettes to stem the encroaching tide of brown liquid heading his way. Mac was wearing a light-coloured jumper, the kind that would stain badly and would probably end up being pure cashmere if I had to replace it.

'I'll fetch you a fresh cup,' he said, getting to his feet before I had the chance to tell him it wasn't necessary.

While he queued at the counter, I finished swabbing the table and caught sight of my flushed reflection in the window. How would Mac react if I told him about the string of peculiar coincidences that had freaked me out, or the weird moon dreams? I could visualise him smiling politely before suddenly remembering there was somewhere else he had to be, *right now*. And who could blame him? No, far better to say nothing.

I nodded at my reflection, and the woman in the very unfashionable bobble hat nodded back. I gasped in embarrassment and pulled it from my head, horrified I hadn't remembered I was wearing it, and then even more horrified when it revealed a terrible case of hat hair.

I was still desperately trying to smooth it down with my hands when Mac returned carrying two more coffees and a couple of enormous muffins.

'I took a guess that you're a double-chocolate kind of girl,' he said with a smile, sliding one of the plates in my direction.

As I sank my teeth into the soft sponge, I wondered if what he really meant was with curves like mine I looked like someone who couldn't say no to anything related to a cocoa bean. I shrugged and gave myself permission to enjoy every last calorie. My illness had taught me well; life was too short to worry about stuff like that.

'Are you going to the thing on Friday night?' I asked, once all that was left of my muffin was a plateful of crumbs.

Mac looked back at me blankly, and I felt a sudden sinking sensation in the pit of my stomach, making the muffin stir unpleasantly. *Please don't say Alex hasn't invited him*, I willed. That would be beyond awkward – and also kind of deceitful of Alex, who I didn't want to think badly of, for reasons too complicated to fathom.

'What thing would that be?'

'Erm… the Bonfire Night thing at Alex's brother's house.'

I was so relieved to see the light dawn in his eyes. He did know what I was talking about.

'Ah, yes. Alex emailed me about it the other day.' His lips twisted tellingly. 'To be honest, I'm not sure if it's such a good idea.'

'You don't think we should meet up with Alex again?'

Mac's gaze was steady. The eyes that were now perfectly capable of boring into mine were doing so with unblinking intensity.

'Do you?'

I flinched but held our eye contact. 'I think Alex and Connor are both hurting and that, just maybe, seeing all of us might help them.'

'Or make it even harder for them,' Mac countered.

I'd considered that too, of course. 'Maybe he's looking to find some meaning in Lisa's death. Maybe *we're* that meaning.'

Mac shuddered. 'God, I hope not.'

Before the conversation could take an even darker turn, Mac's mobile began to vibrate on the table top. I thought I saw relief in his eyes as he read the message. 'Ah. My friend's train is about to get in.'

My own phone pinged too, with a similar message from my mum.

Someone else was playing the piano when we strode back out onto the main concourse. To my untrained ear, they weren't a patch on the tall man walking beside me.

'Is that something you do frequently?' I asked, nodding in the direction of the piano. 'Give impromptu recitals in public?'

He laughed, and I was glad that the tension of our last conversation seemed to have evaporated. 'Playing is something

I've only rediscovered fairly recently. For years I didn't even own a piano, but then…'

'You missed it?' I guessed.

He shook his head, and there was regret in his smile. 'It was one of the few things I still had left when my vision deteriorated. Some of the best pianists in the world are blind, you know.'

He'd meant for it to sound amusing, or maybe self-deprecating, and in a way it did. But it also sounded incredibly sad. For a moment I saw not the successful man the rest of the world undoubtedly saw when they looked at him but a man who'd come back after almost losing everything. It didn't seem to matter how much we fought it: Lisa and our individual illnesses were like a length of elastic that would always pull us back to a place and a time we'd never be able to leave behind.

Mac's height was an obvious advantage in a crowd, and over the heads of the mass of commuters he lifted an arm and waved as he spotted his friend. His face lit up with pleasure, and for a crazy moment I wondered what it would be like to be on the receiving end of that look.

'Thank you for keeping me company while we waited,' he said genially, coming to a stop in front of me.

Anxious to avoid another clumsy to-kiss-or-not-to-kiss moment, I took the initiative and thrust out my right hand. 'Thanks for the coffee and the muffin,' I replied, my eyes dropping meaningfully to my gloved fingers, which he appeared to be ignoring.

'It was my pleasure,' he said, his eyes crinkling into a smile as he finally took the hint and clasped my hand in his.

There are probably etiquette books describing how long a handshake is meant to last, but this one sailed right past an acceptable length. Mac's eyes were on mine, and I saw the moment when the amusement faded and confusion took its place. In hindsight, a kiss on the cheek would have been far less disturbing.

We severed the handshake as though coming out of trance.

'I should go,' he said dazedly.

'Me too.'

But neither of us moved.

'Goodbye, Molly Kendall,' he said, the use of my surname making it sound much more final than a casual farewell.

'Goodbye, Mac,' I replied, but he was already gone, swallowed up by the crowd that buffeted against me as I stood motionless in the middle of the station concourse, trying to work out what had just happened.

CHAPTER TWENTY-TWO

Alex

'You don't get many for your money, do you?'

Alex straightened up from where he was building a bonfire on the lawn. 'You say that every single year.'

'Do I?' Todd was peering into the box of fireworks in his arms with an expression that clearly said he felt the manufacturers had diddled him.

'I've got a couple of extra boxes of sparklers in the car. The kids always love them best, anyway.'

And just like a lingering sparkler trail, a memory scorched its way across Alex's thoughts. Only twelve months earlier, Lisa and Connor had stood side by side on this very spot, bundled up like polar explorers, drawing pictures with sparklers in the cold night air. While Connor was frantically trying to write the last letter of his name before the first one disappeared, Lisa had looked for Alex across the flames of the bonfire and daubed a message just for him. *I ♡ U*

'I love you too, babe,' Alex whispered to the memory.

'Sorry? Did you say something?' asked Todd, who was now busy transferring the fireworks into a sturdy metal toolbox.

'No, nothing.' Alex brushed tiny pieces of bark from his hands as he came to stand beside his brother.

Todd took fireworks safety very seriously, but Lisa had been the one to always insist on the bags of sand, the buckets of water and the emergency first-aid kit being present. It was overkill, and Todd had loved teasing her about it every year. When Alex had walked to the far end of the garden earlier to begin getting things ready, he'd stopped in his tracks at the sight in front of him. Beneath the table that would later hold the fireworks, there was a whole row of buckets neatly lined up, some filled with sand, others with water. It was Todd's quiet way of acknowledging Lisa, his way of saying he missed her and that she was still very much with them. It had taken a good few minutes before Alex's eyes were clear enough for him to see properly again.

'I think I'll go and ask if Connor wants to help me build the fire. What little kid doesn't like burning stuff?'

His little kid didn't, apparently. He found Connor sitting at one end of the kitchen table, his head bent over yet another drawing. Alex exchanged a meaningful look with Dee, who, with Maisie's questionable assistance, was preparing plates of snacks for the party.

'I did ask him if he'd like to help us,' Dee mouthed silently above her daughter's head. She shrugged and looked helpless, an expression she didn't wear often.

Alex nodded his understanding and came to stand beside his son. The bones of Connor's shoulder felt fragile beneath his hand, like a bird's, a tiny broken bird's.

'Watcha doin', big guy?' he asked in that faux jovial voice he somehow couldn't stop himself from using whenever he spoke to Connor.

Connor raised his head and absently wiped a crayon-smeared hand across his forehead, trying to brush his shaggy fringe from his eyes. Lisa would have had him at the hairdresser's long before it had got to this length. Alex was failing at every single parenting task, even the basic ones, and could not seem to get anything right.

'Drawing,' Connor replied. Monosyllabic was now his son's favourite method of communication. If there was a key that would release the chatty little boy he'd once been, Alex had no idea where to find it.

'Do you feel like helping me stack the wood for the bonfire?'

Two big blue eyes, so achingly like Lisa's, stared up at him for a long moment. 'No thank you,' he replied politely. 'I want to finish my picture.'

The smile Alex found felt totally out of place on his face. 'Oh, okay. Well, maybe later, then.'

Connor's head was already bent over his drawing again.

'I bet you two are really looking forward to the fireworks tonight?' Alex asked gamely.

Maisie squealed her confirmation, her hands actually clapping together in glee, but Connor just looked at him sadly.

Alex was halfway to the back door when an unexpected full sentence from his son stopped him. 'Mummy says the worst thing about Fireworks Night is that you can't see the stars properly.'

Alex ignored the mule kick to his stomach and tried to remember if he'd ever heard Lisa say that. Maybe. It certainly sounded like the kind of comment she might have made.

'You can remember her saying that?' he asked, hoping he'd injected just the right amount of nonchalance into his voice.

'She told me today,' Connor said.

From the other side of the kitchen a very freaked-out-looking Dee was pretending not to be listening. Alex tried to remember what the counsellor had advised him to say at times like this, but his mind was a complete blank.

'Did she?' was the best he could come up with.

'Yes,' said Connor, suddenly sounding a lot less certain as he became aware that the eyes of both adults were focused on him. 'She… She said it when I spoke to her on the phone.' He finished in the voice of a child who knew they'd been caught out in a fib.

Alex could practically hear Dee's sigh of relief. He glanced down at Lisa's old iPhone, which was sitting in the top of Connor's pencil case, among the crayons. If this was what his son needed, if this was the way Connor had found to cope, then Alex would rather cut off his own tongue than tell his grieving child that he didn't believe him.

'Well, if Mum said so, she's bound to be right,' he said solemnly. 'She knows about these things.'

This time, Alex was fully aware he'd used the wrong tense. It was deliberate. For the briefest of moments, he thought he saw something in Connor's face. It was too fleeting to catch, but it was enough to give him hope that one day they'd be able to find their way back to each other again. They just needed time.

'Oh, I do hope they taste better than they look,' Barbara said anxiously as she prised the lid off the cake tin she'd carefully cradled in the taxi from her house to Todd's. 'I'm not sure what happened to the icing, it's gone a rather strange colour.'

Alex employed all of his poker-playing skills as, along with Todd and Dee, he peered into the container. 'They look absolutely delicious,' he lied, deliberately not making eye contact with anyone as he surveyed the decidedly grey butterfly cakes.

'That's very sweet of you, Alex, my dear, but I do believe that's what my Archie would have called "horse poo".'

There was a moment of stunned silence when all three members of the Stevens family wondered if they'd heard correctly. It was finally broken by an embarrassed chortle from Barbara, whose cheeks were flushed. Alex's burst of laughter was quickly joined by his brother's, and he easily interpreted the look in Todd's eye. *Okay, this one I like, and I can see why you do too.*

'Oh, I hope the little ones didn't hear that,' Barbara said.

Alex patted her hand reassuringly, noting the fragility of the bones beneath the wrinkles.

As if on cue, Maisie trotted into the kitchen, with Connor a few subdued paces behind her. 'Ooh, cakes,' she exclaimed, clambering up onto a high chrome stool and peering into the tin. 'They look like tiny moths.'

This time it was Dee who blushed, as she hurriedly apologised to their guest for her daughter's words.

In the confusion, Alex was the only one who heard Connor's softly spoken comment. 'Mummy doesn't like moths.'

Molly and Jamie arrived within about a minute of each other, and Alex, who'd been trying not to compulsively check his watch for the last twenty minutes, felt the knot of anxiety in his stomach slowly unravel.

Jamie was buckling slightly under the weight of two six-packs and looked a little hesitant as he passed them to Alex. 'I wasn't sure what to bring. I didn't know what kind of party it was.'

Probably not the kind someone your age usually goes to, Alex thought as he greeted the young man with a hearty clap on the shoulder. Although to be fair, Jamie had sounded genuinely pleased to have been invited. Alex tried to imagine himself at twenty choosing to spend a Saturday night with a crowd of much older people he didn't know instead of hanging out with his mates; he couldn't picture it. But then twenty-year-old Alex hadn't been through the life-changing experience that Jamie had endured. That had to have left its mark.

If Alex had harboured any doubts about having invited these people to Todd and Dee's party, they dissipated as soon as Connor spotted Molly. Connor's face instantly lit up and he rushed across the room like a small Exocet missile. Molly was talking to Dee, but she broke off when a small hand eagerly took hold of hers, his face upturned. Dee's eyes widened in surprise.

'Well, hello there, Connor,' Molly said warmly.

Alex had to blink away his disbelief at the expression on Connor's face. That look of animation – no, more than that:

excitement – had been absent for so long, it took him a moment to even recognise it.

'So, do you have a favourite type of firework?' Molly asked, dropping down easily onto her haunches before him. 'Mine have always been Catherine wheels.'

Connor gave the question some serious consideration before announcing decisively, 'Rockets. Because they can go up to the stars.'

Before Molly could reply, Connor silenced her – silenced the whole room, really – with a solemn confession. 'I think that's where Mummy's waiting until it's time to come back for me.'

Molly rose from her crouch, but Alex noticed that her hand remained on Connor's shoulder, as though it belonged there. Her eyes met his over the little boy's head and there was a look of sympathy in them that made his throat tighten. Concerned glances ricocheted from face to face, and an uncomfortable silence descended on the kitchen. Surprisingly, the awkward moment was rescued by Jamie, who'd spotted something hanging on the far wall. He loped across the room to examine it.

'Who's the musician?' he asked, his gaze fixed admiringly on the gleaming electric guitar.

'Todd,' answered Alex, wondering why Molly had opened her mouth to reply and then snapped it shut again, as though she'd almost spilt a secret.

'I was in a band at university,' Todd confirmed, his chest puffing out a little.

Dee and Alex exchanged a glance that dared the other not to laugh.

Todd lifted the guitar from its hooks and placed it in Jamie's hands. 'Do you play?'

Jamie shook his head. 'Not really. Although I picked up a couple of chords when I was working as a roadie.'

This time it was Todd and Alex who shared a look. It seemed an unlikely career choice for someone with Jamie's slight physique.

The only roadies Alex had known were built like brick outhouses, with necks thicker than Jamie's waist.

'That must have been an interesting job,' Dee said, more trusting than her husband or brother-in-law. 'Did you work with anyone famous?'

It was only when Jamie casually named Coldplay and Muse as two of his roadie gigs that the whiff of rodent reached her nose too. Jamie, seemingly unaware that he'd been rumbled, was happily recounting a series of events Alex was pretty sure had never happened. He didn't blame the guy for embellishing his life. When you'd spent that long stuck in a hospital bed, waiting for a transplant that might never come, you'd earned the right to be a little creative with the truth.

He caught Molly's eye, and she flashed him a look so similar to the one he'd have expected from Lisa that for a second the room swam out of focus and he saw not the pretty young teacher but a taller blonde woman with dancing blue eyes and a heart that would always be his. A rush of nausea engulfed him, and his chest tightened as an overwhelming craving for fresh air forced him to his feet.

'I think I'll go and make a start on the bonfire,' he said, already heading towards the sliding glass doors leading out to the patio.

Dee hijacked him with a hand on his arm as he was shrugging on his wax jacket. 'Should I wait a bit longer before putting things in the oven, as Mac isn't here yet?'

From the corner of his eye, Alex thought he saw Molly lift her head, like a deer in the forest. Something bitter stirred unpleasantly in Alex's already queasy stomach, it felt a lot like jealousy. 'No. Don't bother waiting. He couldn't guarantee he'd be free this evening.' Alex gave an eloquent shrug. 'Which may or may not have been an excuse. Who knows?'

It was a real effort not to turn and see if his reply had any impact on Molly. But somehow he resisted the temptation.

*

The bonfire was beginning to crackle, tiny tendrils of smoke winding out from between the twigs and branches he'd carefully laid that afternoon. When he was certain it would take, Alex stepped away from the pyre and went to stand beside Todd, who was busily sorting through the fireworks in the metal box.

'I don't want you to take this the wrong way…' Todd began.

The box of matches Alex had been lightly tossing from one hand to the other stilled in his palm. Why did people always say that as a preamble to a comment they knew was going to piss the other person off? Two seconds' warning wasn't going to be long enough to make whatever Todd had to say any more palatable.

'If I was one of your guests, you would definitely be creeping me out tonight.'

'What do you mean?'

'You keep looking at them,' Todd replied, his lips a tight line of disapproval.

Alex bristled and his jaw tensed. Only Todd had this effect on him.

'Isn't that what you're meant to do when you're talking to someone?'

Todd sighed heavily. 'It's the way you're looking.' Alex was staring at him blankly. 'Maybe you don't even know you're doing it. But it's kind of like—' He brought his face closer to his brother's and adopted an intense, wide-eyed stare.

Alex took an instinctive step backwards, giving in to a snort of laughter. 'I've a horrible feeling that might be your sex face. If it is, Dee has my sympathy.'

When Todd didn't even crack a smile, Alex realised they'd somehow gone from nought to deadly serious in seconds.

'I'm not joking, mate.'

Alex shook his head. They were never going to agree on this one. 'I know you're not. But I'm not sure what you want me to say here. I genuinely like these people. They feel like friends now.'

Todd stared into the box of fireworks. 'Just answer me this. Before what happened to Lisa, could you ever have imagined becoming best mates with a little old lady, a young guy with a Walter Mitty thing going on, and a high-flying architect?'

He turned to Alex, holding his gaze like a prisoner. The silence stretched on and on, begging for one of them to break it. Finally Alex did.

'You forgot one.'

The curl of his brother's lips told Alex the omission had been deliberate.

'Yes, I did. And we both know why. Because she's the one this is really all about, isn't she?'

CHAPTER TWENTY-THREE

Molly

This isn't weird. It isn't weird at all. It didn't seem to matter how many times I tried to convince myself. Something peculiar was definitely happening here, and I had no idea how to stop it. More than that, I didn't even know if I wanted to stop it.

As I stood on Todd and Dee's lawn, ostensibly absorbed in the fireworks display, my thoughts were all over the place, shooting out like sparks from a Roman candle. Every now and then I would feel a small testing squeeze from the mittened hand gripping mine, as though Connor was making sure I was still there. He had hardly left my side all evening, which was immensely flattering and slightly worrying in equal measure.

I understood little children – or at least I hoped I did. As a primary school teacher, I was frequently a lap to climb onto or a hand to hold, and I'd been mistakenly called 'Mummy' on far too many occasions to find it strange any more. And yet with this one child, with Connor, I was feeling things I'd never experienced before.

The biological clock has a tendency to run a little slower in childless primary school teachers. I, for one, had never felt that burning desire to have a child of my own; it was always something Future Me would deal with one day. And then, for a long time, when it looked as though Future Me might not be around to make that kind of decision, all thoughts of babies and children faded, like a memory of something I'd never known. But suddenly all of that was changing. Tonight there was a pull, which felt almost physical, whenever I looked at Connor.

I gnawed on my lip, already numbed by the cold November air, as I forced myself to admit that there was another pull too, towards Connor's father, which was wrong on far too many levels. And none of that explained why I felt so drawn to every single person gathered around this bonfire in a stranger's garden. I kept telling myself that with Barbara and Jamie it was the things we had in common – our illnesses and surgeries – that made them feel so much more than newly made friends. But it was getting harder and harder to convince myself that this was the only reason.

All of this should have been scaring the life out of me. It should have made me want to get as far away as possible. And yet I knew I didn't want to pull away from these people. Not yet. What I didn't know was why.

Alex and Todd were working harmoniously together, with no trace of the tension I'd sensed between them when we'd all moved from kitchen to garden for the fireworks. Todd read out the instructions by torchlight, and Alex followed them to the letter. Touchpapers were lit with extreme caution, but that didn't stop my heart from racing as I watched Lisa's husband backlit by the flames of the bonfire. I wanted to call out for him to be careful so many times, I practically had to clamp my lips together to stop the words from escaping. It wasn't like me to be such a panicker. Perhaps the nervousness was contagious or perhaps I really was going a bit crazy, because the intensity I thought I saw in Alex's eyes when I lit Connor's sparkler made the hairs on the back of my neck stand up. Was that watchful look just a father's natural concern when I steadied Connor's arm as he swirled the wand through the air or was it something else?

When the last rocket trail had disappeared into the night sky, Dee herded everyone back into the kitchen like a sheepdog on a mission. Trays of sizzling sausages were pulled from the oven and my mouth was already watering as I added my outer clothes to the mountain piled up on a kitchen chair.

I loved the casual informality of the evening, the way no one worried about pedestrian things like cutlery, serviettes or sitting down to eat. Todd lifted Maisie and Connor to sit on one of the kitchen worktops, and for the first time Connor seemed to be acting more like a boy of seven than a sombre little old man trapped inside a child's body. His gaze was split equally between the night sky, visible through the open patio doors, and me. I told myself his interest was just the fascination of someone new, which was as good a lie as any to try to swallow.

Alex was doing the rounds of the room with a bottle of Merlot in hand. I rarely drank these days, but somehow the 'no' that was ready and waiting on my lips turned into a 'yes' before I even realised it. I could feel a flush on my cheeks as he steadied my hand with his before filling my glass with a measure far larger than any bar would serve. It must have been the alcohol in my veins that was making my pulse suddenly race faster, I told myself, as I thanked him with a smile.

'Did you enjoy the fireworks?' he asked.

'I did. I thought the whole evening was very...' The room was noisy, and there were several conversations going on around us. Jamie was laughing uproariously at something Todd had just said, while Dee was looking like she might be regretting asking Barbara about her family of cats. Alex took a step closer towards me, to better hear what I was saying, which was unfortunate, because his proximity derailed my train of thought so effectively that my sentence simply hung in the air between us.

He was waiting, and with every second my heart was racing a little bit faster. *It knows him. It knows what it's like to be this close to his body.* Ridiculous as it sounded, I couldn't shift the notion.

'Nice. It was nice,' I finished pathetically.

There was a slightly unflattering look of relief on his face when he stepped away from me. Dear God, was I was so rusty at this that I now actually repelled members of the opposite sex? For no reason at all a memory of Mac queue-jumped to the front of my thoughts. My eyes flew to the door, which was daft, because it was perfectly obvious by now that he wasn't coming. Maybe Mac was right though, maybe we *were* all making a huge mistake continuing this – whatever it was.

I was distracted, my thoughts scattered all over the place, which was the excuse I later went with for what happened next. I didn't see the moth's fluttering approach until the very last moment. It was heading straight towards my face, no doubt attracted by the large, vintage-style light bulb in the lamp beside me. One minute I was a slightly flustered party guest, and the next I'd turned into a raving lunatic as the huge silvery-winged insect landed on my arm.

It was an exceedingly large moth, almost the size of my palm, but that was no excuse for my overreaction. I shrieked – possibly for the first time in my life – and, even worse, I also threw my arm upwards, as though to protect myself from the poor, defenceless, light-dazzled moth. A shower of Merlot arced into the air like a red waterfall. Most of it, luckily, landed on me rather than the biscuit-coloured settee I was sitting on.

Not surprisingly, every head had turned at my cry. The bits of me that weren't red from the wine now turned ruby with embarrassment.

'What the…?' began Alex, his mouth dropping open into an O of surprise. For some reason the moth had decided its safest course of action was simply to hang on to my arm, for when I lowered it, it was still there.

'Hang on, don't panic,' Alex said, his voice uber calm as he began to walk carefully towards me, his hands outstretched.

Before he could reach me, I brought my free hand down over the moth, trapped it against my forearm and crossed as steadily as

I could towards the patio doors. When I was clear of the house and all artificial light, I shook my arm and released it into the night.

'I'm so sorry, I've made a dreadful mess,' I said as I re-entered the kitchen.

The Stevens family stared at me with a range of unfathomable expressions.

'That was the King Kong of moths,' declared Jamie. 'I haven't seen one that size since I was backpacking around Australia.'

It didn't seem the right moment to remind him that earlier in the evening he'd admitted he'd never visited the Antipodes.

'Have you got a cloth, so I can wipe this up before it stains?' I asked, gesturing towards the large puddle of wine on the floor, that I couldn't help thinking looked horribly like blood.

At this, everyone seemed to come alive again, as though simultaneously emerging from a hypnotist's trance.

'I'll get the mop,' said Todd, heading towards a tall kitchen cupboard.

Alex tore his eyes from me and went to Connor, whose face appeared several degrees paler than before.

Dee shook off whatever had held her temporarily immobile and said, 'Oh no. Your poor top.'

It was only then that I looked down at the stretchy white lace top I'd bought to dress up the dark skinny jeans I was wearing. One look at the red blotches told me it was probably the first and last time I'd be wearing it.

'Come upstairs, I'll find you something to change into,' said Dee, taking my arm and leading me towards the hallway. 'We're pretty much the same size.'

Could this night get any more peculiar? I wondered as I stood in my hostess's bedroom while she rummaged in the drawers of a dresser for something I could wear. It was probably going to be more of a challenge than she realised, because I was pretty sure I was a couple of cup sizes larger than her.

'If you whip off your stained one, I'll put it straight in to soak for you,' she offered kindly, unaware of my reluctance to get changed in front of her. She was waiting, hand outstretched, and the pause was growing more uncomfortable with every passing second. This was why I avoided communal changing rooms in department stores and made a beeline for the curtained cubicles at the gym. But Dee was oblivious to that, and short of asking her to turn around, which was too excruciating to contemplate, there was nothing I could do.

The wine-stained top came off over my head, and with a degree of self-control I didn't know I had, I managed to stop myself from crossing my hands protectively over my scar.

Her quiet gasp in the softly lit room contained a thousand emotions. Remorse and shock were probably uppermost. Too late, she finally understood my hesitation. She stared at the long vertical line that bisected my breasts, beneath which her late sister-in-law's heart was pounding away, like I'd just been to a spin class.

'Oh my God, Molly, I'm so sorry. That was really insensitive of me.'

'It's nothing,' I murmured, very glad she and Todd favoured subdued bedroom lighting, which just about hid the raging blush that was coursing over my cheeks.

'I should have realised; I can't believe I didn't even think of it.'

I plucked up one of the tops she'd set down on the edge of the bed for me, discarding it almost immediately when I saw its scooped neckline.

'Er... do you have anything that's not quite so low cut?' I asked awkwardly.

This time she was the one who blushed. 'Oh God, I'm such an idiot. I'm so sorry.' She reached for a dark blue long-sleeved top. 'Here, try this.'

I took it from her, already knowing it would do the job.

'It's just that I wouldn't want Connor to see this,' I said, my finger grazing the length of my scar. 'Or Alex.'

'No. No. I completely understand,' Dee said, looking just about as awkward as a person could look in their own bedroom. 'I'll just leave you to get yourself straightened up,' she said, turning hurriedly towards the door. 'I'll put this into some cold water for you.'

Her hand was already on the doorknob as she turned back to me once more. 'You know, Lisa would have really liked you. She'd have been pleased with who they chose.'

There was nothing I could think of to say to that, so I didn't even try.

It felt like I'd walked back into an entirely different party. The one I'd left had shocked-faced hosts, slightly uncomfortable-looking guests, and a huge puddle of red wine on the floor. The one I returned to had spotless kitchen tiles and a relaxed air. I could hear it in the laughter and casual banter as I descended the stairs wearing Dee's borrowed top.

As I'd suspected, the navy T-shirt was far more form-fitting on me than it probably was on her. The silhouette in their bedroom mirror had looked a little too Jessica Rabbit for my liking, with the top clinging to me in all the right – or wrong – places. I forced my shoulders back from an instinctive stoop, took a deep steadying breath, and returned to the kitchen.

In the ten seconds before anyone noticed me, I saw that the party dynamic had changed. Barbara had produced a pair of chunky wooden needles and a skein of wool from her bag and was guiding Maisie's small hands through what I imagined was her first knitting lesson. It ignited a flashback memory I hadn't visited in years, of my own grandmother doing exactly the same with me when I was around Maisie's age. Barbara's smile was beatific as she patiently guided the little girl's hands, picking up every dropped stitch along the way.

On the other side of the room, Jamie was showing Connor a game on his phone that from the sound of it might not have been entirely age appropriate. Which possibly explained why Connor appeared to be enjoying it so much.

But it was the far end of the kitchen that held the greatest surprise. Todd was leaning back against the cupboards, his arm looped casually around Dee's shoulders, and opposite them, laughing with an ease I'd not heard before, were Alex... and Mac.

Even though he had his back to me, Alex was the first person to register my return. He spun around, a big smile already in place as I stood in the doorway like a vampire seeking an invitation to enter.

'Molly. Are you okay now?'

It was a curious question, as though I'd been upset about something, when in reality the only thing that had been upset was my glass of wine.

'I'm fine.'

'Oh, that top looks great on you,' said Dee, inadvertently drawing every eye in the room to the skin-tight garment. 'Way better than it does on me, in fact.'

The kitchen felt suddenly warmer, but perhaps that was because someone had closed the patio doors in my absence.

'Molly had a bit of a mishap with a glass of wine,' Alex explained to Mac.

Mac's eyes went straight to mine, and it was impossible not to see the light of amusement dancing in their depths. 'How unusual,' he murmured, his voice gently teasing.

I probably deserved that, seeing as every time we'd met I'd either dropped, broken or spilt something.

'What can I say? Juggling-school dropout.'

That made him laugh, and I could sense the others were waiting for us to explain, but neither of us did. I quite liked having our own private joke – even if it was at my expense.

'What made you change your mind about coming tonight?' I asked quietly, as soon as the attention was focused away from us.

Mac looked momentarily uncomfortable, his glance travelling across the room to Alex, who was now talking to Jamie and Connor.

'The official version is that my house guest had other plans for the evening, so I was free to come. But in truth…' His voice trailed away, sounding a little lost. 'I don't really know. It just felt too… ungrateful not to come.' He winced, unhappy with his choice of words, but unable to find better ones. 'Does that make any sense at all?'

'More than you could imagine,' I said, my eyes lingering on Alex and Connor.

I leant in closer to Mac, with the intention of explaining further, but got immediately distracted by the head-whirling aromas of whatever he'd used in the shower, together with his own signature smell. For the second time that night, standing so close to a man had left me confused. With Alex, my heart had pounded at the familiarity, but my reaction to Mac was something altogether different. *I am not attracted to you. I will not go there*, I told myself, so firmly that for an awful moment I wondered if I'd actually said the words out loud.

Mac was still looking at me as though I was relatively sane, so I guessed I hadn't. Even so, it was a mantra I knew I would do well to repeat regularly.

'Mac was just telling us about the opening ceremony for a building he designed,' Todd said, filling me in on what I'd missed. 'It's that tall glass one in the centre of town; the one with all the fountains.'

My desire to play it cool around this man now faced another challenge. I knew the building in question; everyone in the area did. It was exceptionally beautiful and stood out like a jewel in a sea of concrete monoliths.

'You designed that?'

Mac blushed, a seemingly rare occurrence. 'Well, there was a whole team of very talented architects supporting me, but yes, I was the project leader.'

I liked his modest generosity. 'It's a really beautiful building. You have an incredible eye.'

There'd been many times in my life when I'd have given anything to press rewind and erase what I'd just said, and this was definitely another of them. The rest of the room had fallen silent at exactly the wrong moment, and it was obvious that everyone present was all too mindful of precisely whose eyes Mac was now seeing through.

Mac rescued the moment by drawing the conversation back to the building under discussion. 'I started work on it quite a few years ago.' And because it was now impossible for any of us to avoid the elephant in the room, he added, 'Actually, it was the last thing I finished before my sight got so bad I was forced to step down.' He looked across the room, his gaze finding Alex. 'I never thought I'd get to see the completed building. But thanks to Lisa, and the incredible thing she did, I can.'

Alex gave a tight nod of acknowledgement before his eyes darted worriedly over to Connor to make sure he'd neither heard nor understood Mac's words. Thankfully, he had not.

'And that's why I'd like you all to come as my guests to the opening ceremony,' Mac continued. 'It should be a fun night: black tie, champagne bar, that kind of thing.'

Without taking time to consider the invitation, Jamie jumped in with his response. 'Can I be absolutely honest—' he began.

To our credit, not one of us asked, *I don't know… can you?*

'—black tie isn't really my kind of thing. Would you mind terribly if I passed?'

'No, of course not,' Mac said graciously.

My own response was pure knee-jerk. 'Er, I'm not sure I can make it either.' I felt, rather than saw, Alex's eyes fix on me. Too late, I realised I should have waited until I knew the date of the event. 'It's just that I don't usually go out on a school night,' I added lamely, which was right up there with 'the dog ate my homework' as pathetic excuses went.

'Fortunately it's on a Friday night,' Mac said smoothly.

'Oh, well, I'm not sure I have the right kind of thing to wear to that type of event.' At least that one wasn't a lie.

'Is that important?' he asked, which said as much about the old Mars/Venus theory as it did about Mac's knowledge of women. 'What you have on right now looks great. Couldn't you just wear something like that?'

Once again, everyone's attention was drawn straight back to me. Dee flashed me a sympathetic look and thoughtfully swivelled the spotlight elsewhere.

'Well, *I'd* love an excuse to get all dressed up, but sadly I doubt we'll be able to get a babysitter for a Friday night.'

'I could do it,' said Barbara, who'd been following the conversation as though watching a very interesting play. There was a hesitancy in her eyes as they travelled from Alex to Dee. 'That's if you're happy to trust them with me.' Her forehead creased, creating even more lines. 'I don't have any references or anything. But it would be an honour to look after these two poppets and let you all have a night out together.'

Alex bent and pressed a kiss on her cheek. 'No references needed,' he said gently. Barbara went a little pink but seemed to grow in stature at the compliment. 'But Mac's invitation included you too,' he reminded her.

She glanced from Alex to Mac with an expression that would have moved even the stoniest of hearts. 'I'm not much of a party person any more, now that Archie's gone. It would be a joy to help out by looking after the little ones for a few hours.'

'That's decided then,' said Todd happily, pre-empting any further discussion or decision-making, which I suspected his wife might call him on later.

'Will you come, Molly?' Mac asked, turning to me once again, perfectly aware I was clean out of excuses.

I nodded slowly.

'I can pick you up, if you'd like,' suggested Alex. 'It doesn't make sense for all of us to drive or turn up in separate taxis.'

'Great,' Mac replied, irritatingly accepting Alex's offer on my behalf.

I tried to think of a way of extricating myself, but there was no way of doing so without sounding rude, or, worse, of making it obvious I was nervous of being alone with Alex.

I smiled at him as, deep within my chest, my traitorous heart thumped out a tattoo of approval.

CHAPTER TWENTY-FOUR

Alex

Alex's knees cracked like a rifle shot in the darkened room as he bent to lift up a sleeping Connor from his brother's couch. Connor stirred briefly in his arms, mumbling something indistinct before burying his face in the soft wool of Alex's jumper.

Alex turned to his brother and sister-in-law, who had tiptoed into the lounge to retrieve their own sleeping child. 'Thank you. Both of you,' he said quietly. 'For tonight, and for making them feel welcome. It meant a lot to me.'

'They're good people,' Dee said, sounding worried. 'I really like them, all of them.'

Todd's eyes went briefly to his wife's. Something passed between them in a code Alex couldn't crack.

'But—' began Todd.

Alex could have bet money on there being a 'but'.

'— have you thought about where any of this is going, Alex?'

'You can't plan that, you can't plan anything,' Alex said, unable to keep the bitterness from his words. 'You have to let things run their course. And that's what I'm doing here.'

'Just don't… Don't…'

'Don't what, Todd?' Alex asked, though he was pretty sure he knew where this was heading. Dee's dropped gaze confirmed his suspicion.

'Don't go reading things into this that aren't there. That thing tonight, with the moth… it didn't mean anything.'

Alex thought he saw a flicker of fear in Todd's eyes. All of this must be tearing his pragmatic solicitor's soul to shreds, he realised. 'You see it too,' Alex said. 'I know you do. You're just too scared to admit it.'

Their eyes locked. It was a game they used to play as kids. Back then, Todd always won, but there was a steely conviction in Alex's gaze tonight that made his victory inevitable. Todd was the first to look away.

'Do you remember what Lisa used to say?' Alex asked them both.

Todd looked to be just a blink or two away from crying; not for Lisa – his tears for her were all but spent – but for the man she'd left behind.

'She used to say she would always love us "with every beat of her heart".'

'And your point is?' asked Todd nervously.

'That heart is still beating.' Alex looked down at the sleeping child in his arms. 'It's not over yet.'

Was it Connor's mumbled words that had set him on this path, Alex wondered. It was gone two o'clock in the morning and his eyes felt hot and gritty, but he was unable to stop himself from clicking on just one more link. No – he couldn't and wouldn't blame his son for this journey he'd embarked on. He'd have got here himself sooner or later. All Connor had done was nudge him a little closer to the edge of the rabbit hole. It was Alex's decision to allow himself to tumble head first down into it.

Surprisingly, Connor hadn't stirred when Alex had unclipped the car's seatbelt and carried him into the house and up the stairs to his bedroom. The excitement of the evening must have wiped him out, because even tugging off his trainers and slipping off his clothes had scarcely roused him from his sleep.

He was as floppy as a rag doll as Alex eased him into his favourite *Star Wars* pyjamas and laid him gently on the bed. He bent to kiss the little boy's forehead as he tucked the duvet more securely around his slight body.

'Goodnight, son,' Alex whispered softly.

For just a moment, those impossibly long eyelashes fluttered, but Connor's bright blue eyes remained closed.

'Mummy?' he asked faintly, lost in a dream where the terrible last seven months had never happened.

'No, sweetheart, it's Dad,' Alex said. 'Mummy's not here.'

His son's lips curved into an unexpected smile. 'Yes, she is,' he corrected, still fast asleep. 'She came back.'

Too many geese to count strutted over Alex's grave. They were still doing it as he crept silently from his son's room.

His own clothes never made it to the laundry basket, and he stepped over them like landmines as he climbed onto his bed and reached for his MacBook. He piled up the pillows behind him and propped the open laptop on his bare legs. Even the subdued lighting from the bedside lamps was too bright for his tired eyes to cope with. But that was okay, because somehow this felt like the kind of search that ought to be conducted in the dark, with only the glow of the screen to light the room.

He hadn't even made a dent in the 85,700,000 hits Goggle had found for him before the laptop grew too hot for his skin to bear. In fact, it wasn't just his legs that were feeling the heat, his whole body seemed to be burning, as though an uncontrollable blaze was travelling through his capillaries. He got up, strode to the window and flung it open, his thoughts instantly returning to the incident in Todd's kitchen.

'Don't go there,' Todd had advised. But Alex was way ahead of him and had been since the moment he'd heard Molly's shriek as the moth landed on her arm. Her startled cry had seemed to surprise her, but it hadn't surprised Alex – he'd heard it many times over the years.

Cellular memory. This was more than just a phrase he'd stumbled across when reading about transplant patients: it was the key to a door he'd not felt quite ready to unlock. But now he was. The evidence was becoming too compelling to ignore.

By the time dawn had begun lightening the sky to a dull grey, Alex had half-filled a ruled pad with scribbled notes and citations. He'd highlighted some words and underlined others so vigorously his pen had gouged grooves into the pages he'd not yet turned. There were question marks beside some phrases: *Personality changes? Food cravings?* Others were circled in red – *the ones you want to believe in most,* said a voice he'd spent most of the night studiously ignoring. The one his eyes returned to time and time again was printed in defiant strokes and ringed in red on the first page of his notes: *Memories from the donor's life???*

In the two weeks that followed, Alex spent every free moment reading everything he could about cellular memory. His interest was in danger of tipping into an obsession; even he could see that. But like anyone with a compulsive condition, he was getting very good at hiding it.

He now had three notebooks filled with case histories. He found the accounts of patients who exhibited new interests and skills particularly fascinating. They ranged from the woman who was terrified of heights who'd taken up climbing after receiving the lungs of a mountaineer; the man who previously couldn't draw, and now could, after receiving an artist's organ; to the twenty-five-year-old man who'd received a woman's heart and now had an insatiable desire to go shopping. But there were darker tales too that haunted him in the middle of the night. Patients with recurring nightmares featuring the manner their donor had died and even a terrifying tale of a man who'd taken his own life in the same way his donor had done. Those Alex skipped over, hungry only for accounts where patients remembered people and places they had never been, but which their donor had known and loved.

His tuxedo felt loose. The collar of his dress shirt was roomy too, in a way he couldn't recall it being before. He attempted to cinch it tighter as he stared into the mirror, trying to remember how long it had been since he'd had to fasten his own bow tie. He missed the ritual of Lisa standing before him, dressed in something that would invariably take his breath away, instructing him to stay still while her long, slender fingers threaded and tied the length of black satin. It had taken him four attempts tonight, and yet it was nowhere near as neat as Lisa would have made it.

His suit smelt of her, or rather her perfume – the one she used to save for special occasions. A fragrant cloud of it had been released when he'd unzipped the suit bag, lingering on his jacket from a gala event they'd attended. He remembered holding her close on the dance floor beneath a twirling glitter ball that he'd told her looked like a constellation of stars.

'Says the man who can't even find the North Star,' she'd lovingly teased him.

'Don't need to,' he'd replied, burying his face in the fall of her long blond hair and lightly kissing her neck. 'You're my one true north. As long as I have you, I won't ever get lost.'

Only now he didn't have her. Or did he?

He pressed the lapel to his face, inhaling the remnants of her scent like an addict desperate for one last hit.

'Enough now. Enough,' he told himself sternly, slipping on the jacket and trying to outrun the memory as he jogged down the stairs.

*

The roads were sluggish with rush hour traffic. Alex briefly took his eyes from them to glance at his watch. He frowned. A crisis at work had delayed him at the office, but as long as he could be straight in and out collecting Connor from his after-school club, he might be able to recoup the lost time. He quickly realised that wasn't going to happen.

'We've looked everywhere for Connor's school bag,' the young teaching assistant told him. 'I suggest we give up for now and have another hunt for it on Monday.'

She was new. She didn't know Connor or what had happened to their family. Which might have explained her look of disapproval when a white-faced Connor insisted, 'We can't go without it. The phone is in my bag. What if Mummy wants to speak to me?'

'You know, Connor really shouldn't be bringing a mobile phone to school, it's not—' the assistant began, before a wild-eyed glare from her colleague silenced her.

Ignoring the staff, Alex crouched down before his son and laid a reassuring hand on his shoulder. 'Don't worry, big guy. We're not leaving here without Mummy's phone. *I'll* find it.'

And he had, buried beneath an avalanche of beanbags and footballs in the dusty cloakroom, but it had taken forty precious minutes of time he hadn't really had to spare.

It made him late for dropping Connor off at Todd's, where Barbara was to be babysitting the two young cousins that evening. And that was another thing that worried him. He was very fond of Barbara, she was a lovely lady, but she had far more experience looking after cats than people.

'Well, don't you look nice,' Dee had greeted him with at the door. 'Very 007.'

Alex smiled vaguely as he passed her Connor's overnight bag. 'You too,' he replied automatically, his eyes following his son as Maisie led him away down the hallway.

'Alex, this is my dressing gown,' Dee laughed, playfully slapping his shoulder, which at least made him take a second look at her floor-length blue satin robe. His laughter sounded like the canned variety they used in TV sitcoms.

The playfulness was gone from Dee's voice as she leant closer and reassuringly squeezed Alex's hand. 'Connor will be absolutely fine. We're only going to be gone for a couple of hours. And Barbara has all our numbers, as well as the one for the doctor, the emergency dentist and even the local police station.'

'It's just that I've not left him with anyone except you and Todd, since...' *Would it always be this hard to say the words*, he wondered.

'I know. And I understand. But he'll be okay, Alex. Barbara will probably spoil them both rotten. She's really psyched to be playing grandma for the evening.'

Alex nodded reluctantly. Dee had given him a gentle push away from her front door. 'Go and pick up Molly and we'll see you both in a little while.'

A near miss with a swerving taxi en route to Molly's house had set Alex's heart racing, and oddly even when the black cab was just a pair of red tail lights disappearing into the rain, his agitation remained. He was nervous, he realised, with a small jolt of surprise. Not for the first time he found himself thinking how life had been far easier before the four recipients had ever met. He'd orchestrated something when he'd invited them all to the planetarium, something that had slipped from his grasp and taken on a life of its own. They'd formed an instant connection with each other which he'd never expected, and which none of the articles he'd read on cellular memory had mentioned.

Alex's hands tightened on the steering wheel as a feeling he wasn't proud of elbowed its way to the front of his mind. Was he jealous? Did he begrudge them their individual friendships because they excluded him? In a series of snapshot memories he saw Molly running through the rain to jump into Mac's car at the planetarium, and the look in Mac's eyes when Molly had entered the kitchen on the night of the bonfire party. Alex knew that look, it was one he'd given Lisa a thousand times. Only now Mac was looking through Lisa's eyes, and sharing it with Molly.

Thirty minutes later, his phone's satnav led him to the address where the heart of the woman he loved now lived. He shook his head as his car headlights spliced the darkness of Molly's street. He had to stop thinking like that.

CHAPTER TWENTY-FIVE

Molly

He was late. And I was growing increasingly anxious, with no real idea why. Should I have insisted on making my own way there tonight? Surely that would have been easier for everyone, plus it would have allowed me to make an early escape whenever I wanted. Because there was something about this evening that was making me nervous. No, scratch that, there was a lot about this evening that was making me nervous. Not least of which was that I didn't have anything suitable to wear.

'I've a couple of dresses you could borrow,' Kyra had offered, which was sweet of her, but unless I suddenly grew a foot taller, I couldn't see how that would work.

'My only formal dress is cut down to here,' I told her, pointing to the middle of my ribcage. 'Even without my scar, I wouldn't be comfortable wearing something like that with these people. It seems kind of… disrespectful?'

Kyra gave an extremely laid-back Australian shrug. 'Well, it looks like you and me are going shopping then.'

She'd been on my doorstep ridiculously early on the first Saturday after payday. I was dressed but a good twenty minutes short of being ready.

'Sorry,' she said, handing me a cup of takeout coffee she'd picked up on the way. 'Doesn't seem to matter how long I've lived here, I can't shake the Aussie habit of rising early.'

'I won't be a minute,' I promised as she followed me into the kitchen.

My ceramic wall tiles threw up our reflections, and in them I caught the moment her steps faltered on seeing the row of medication lined up on my worktop beside a large glass of water. My hands went from packet to packet, releasing pills from their blister casings and popping them into my mouth.

She waited until the last one was gone before asking quietly, 'Will you always have to take that many?'

I swept up the boxes and put them back in the cupboard. They took up almost an entire shelf.

'Without them, my body would go into rejection,' I said, trying not to shudder. For transplant patients, mentioning the R-word is like invoking Voldemort. I gave a small shrug. 'So yes, this is me for the rest of my life.' I dropped my eyes to hide the unspoken tag end of that sentence. *For however long that might be.*

It was the elephant in every room. It was the topic my mother refused to discuss. My operation had been a success, my recovery practically textbook, but there were no guarantees with this kind of procedure. Every heart transplant patient knows and understands that. However carefully I looked after it, Lisa's heart might resist its new location and not give me the extra decades I was hoping for.

Despite the winter sun streaming in through the window, it suddenly felt as though a cloud had passed over my kitchen.

'Come on then,' Kyra urged, shaking off the dark mood and knocking back the last of her coffee. 'Let's go and spend a shitload of your money on a dress you'll probably only ever wear once.'

We found the dress in one of the more upmarket department stores in town, when I was only minutes away from abandoning my quest. There it was, waiting for me to discover it, hidden away at the end of a rail. *It won't be my size*, I thought as I lifted the hanger down. *Or it'll be another one with a plunging décolletage.*

But I was already smiling broadly. This was *my dress*. I spun around to show it to Kyra, who wolf-whistled impressively. I grinned at the black halter-neck gown with the high, jewel-encrusted collar and the back that was almost not there; it was as though I'd just found an old friend.

'I'm trying it on,' I said.

Sometime between slipping out of my jeans and boots and into the amazing dress, I appeared to forget I was a modestly paid primary school teacher with a big mortgage. Even sliding over my debit card at the till – quickly, in case I changed my mind – failed to remind me.

My phoned pinged with an incoming message, dragging my attention away from the woman in the mirror, the one who looked like she'd mistakenly wandered off a red carpet and somehow ended up in my bedroom. She was the glamorous and more sophisticated twin I'd never had. Although a stranger to me, I rather liked the beachy waves in her hair and the smoky shade of grey across her eyelids. Even the red gloss on her lips looked good, if she could only remember to stop biting them anxiously.

Sorry. Running late. Be with you in five. Alex

It was a relief to see no 'x' after his name. It drew a line in the sand that neither of us should think about crossing. *Ever.* I wasn't disappointed, not at all, I told myself resolutely as I slipped into my coat.

The pavements were slick with rain, and I was wearing the kind of heels that made anything faster than a sedate walk virtually impossible. As I approached his car, I saw him unbuckling his seatbelt. He stepped out of the car and reached my side when I was still several feet away from the passenger door.

'Molly,' he said, with what sounded like genuine pleasure. I could feel my pulse racing as he rested his hands lightly on my shoulders and leant in. His lips grazed my cheek for less than a second, and yet the warmth of his mouth lingered on my skin as he politely held the car door open for me.

'I'm sorry I'm late,' he said as he unspooled a length of seatbelt for me. I was afraid he intended fastening it around me, so I reached for the buckle, missed and ended up grasping his fingers instead. We both laughed awkwardly. Within my chest, Lisa's heart gave the customary little jump I'd almost come to expect whenever it got close to the man she'd loved. I willed it to be still, and thankfully, as we pulled away from the kerb, it began to quieten.

It turned out that Alex drove even faster than Mac did. That wasn't a criticism, just an observation, but I didn't share it with him. Drawing comparisons between the two men felt weirdly wrong – on any level. Despite having corresponded for months, this was the first time Alex and I had been completely alone, so perhaps it wasn't surprising that I felt anxious. We kept our conversation to fairly neutral topics: Connor; Alex's job and my job; and how we'd chosen our careers.

'It was always going to be something to do with children for me,' I said, relaxing back on the leather seat and basking in the warmth from his car's efficient heater.

'If how you are with Connor is anything to go by, you're a natural-born teacher.'

I gave an embarrassed laugh and turned towards the side window, surprised to discover we were almost at our destination. Before us was the elegant glass-walled tower designed by Mac. It blazed with lights from the ground floor foyer all the way up to its rooftop garden.

'It looks pretty impressive at night,' Alex observed, his eyes like mine travelling to the four enormous fountains that flanked the building. Discreetly positioned lasers illuminated the cascading water, turning them into moving sculptures of red, green and gold.

A cluster of dark-suited security officers were positioned by the door, carrying clipboards and muttering importantly into two-way radios. There was even a length of red carpet on the pavement leading up to the entrance, giving the scene a decidedly Oscar-like air.

Alex had taken my arm when we'd crossed the road and had somehow forgotten to release it again. I wondered how awkward it would be to tug it away and decided it was easier to leave it.

'Could I have your name, please, sir?'

'Stevens,' Alex supplied automatically. The guard ran his finger down the list on his clipboard, before eventually switching to the sheet reserved for VIP guests. Alex's eyes widened in amusement, and I only just managed to hide my own smile. Mac hadn't been kidding when he said it was a fancy event.

'Enjoy your evening, Mr and Mrs Stevens,' he said, summoning the lift that would carry us up to the penthouse floor. A spasm of pain flashed across Alex's face.

Neither of us mentioned the guard's mistake as we rode the mirror-walled lift. Whichever way I turned, I could see two elegantly dressed people who might look like a couple but who were really little more than strangers. What our reflections couldn't show was the unique and unbreakable bond that would forever tether my life to his. It would be there with every beat of this heart, I realised silently, as the doors slid open and spilt us out into the party.

Nervous tension thrummed through me as we stepped out onto the penthouse floor. It was certainly an incredible venue for a party. There had to have been more than two hundred people present, and yet it managed to feel spacious. Many of the women had chosen to wear black, and with the men in formal dress too, the room resembled a colony of penguins in an Attenborough documentary.

Breaking the unwritten colour code, the figure approaching us through the crowd was dressed in a vibrant emerald-green satin gown.

'You made it,' declared Dee, hugging first her brother-in-law and then, surprisingly, me too. It was only the third time we'd met, but it felt completely natural to hug her back.

'Have you had a chance yet to call…' Alex began, breaking off as I slipped off my coat. The look on his face made every penny I'd spent on the dress I couldn't afford worthwhile. '… erm… home?' he completed, with a shake of his head, as though his thoughts needed jiggling back into place.

Dee laughed lightly. 'Twice,' she admitted, with a self-deprecating grin.

'Twice? I thought you said you trusted Barbara?'

'Relax!' Dee leant forward and squeezed Alex's hand reassuringly. 'I have total faith in Barbara; it's Maisie who can't be trusted.'

Dee wore a look I recognised from practically every mother's eyes in the school playground. I'd never coveted that kind of love before, but lately I'd felt my emotions shifting.

'I keep hoping some of Connor's good behaviour will rub off onto his cousin,' she explained with a wry smile. 'But so far, no such luck.'

'Well I'd prefer it the other way around. I'd love Connor to do something outrageously naughty. He's so distant most of the time.'

Completely of its own volition, my hand reached out and settled on Alex's forearm. 'You have to give him time. It's still very raw for him. I'm sure he'll find his way back to you eventually.'

Three pairs of eyes looked down at where my hand was resting on the black silk of Alex's tuxedo. I'm pretty sure my own wore the most surprised expression. I was taken aback by my boldness.

'Champagne,' cried a very welcome voice, breaking the spell. Todd was weaving his way through the crowd, carrying a cluster of four champagne glasses in his hands.

'Has anyone seen Mac yet?' asked Alex, relieving his brother of one of the glasses with one hand and taking my coat from me with the other.

'Only from a distance,' Dee said. 'He's being monopolised by the owners of the building and a gaggle of businessmen.'

Todd laughed and slid an arm around his wife's waist. 'Did you just invent a new collective noun?'

Dee turned and smiled at her husband so brightly, I felt like my eyes needed Polaroid protection. In a moment of blinding insight, I realised that this was how the banter must have always been between the four of them: easy, loving and filled with laughter as they bounced off each other like practised performers. I felt suddenly like an intruder, trying to step into shoes that weren't even vacant, let alone my size.

'I think I'll just go over and say hello to him,' I said a little awkwardly. I caught a glimpse of what might have been a small frown as Alex disappeared in search of a cloakroom for my coat.

Even in a sea of black tuxedos, Mac was easy to spot, being one of the tallest men in the room. At least the heels I was wearing would make me feel less like a child alongside him, I thought as I carefully manoeuvred my way through the throng of partygoers.

My nerves failed me when I was almost upon him. He was busy listening to a man with a shock of grey hair, nodding occasionally at whatever was being said. I'd fled from the presence of Lisa, who seemed to have unexpectedly joined us at the party, and now I worried that disturbing Mac would make me feel just as uncomfortable. He was turned away from me, so I made a snap decision to melt back into the crowd unobserved. Unfortunately, I didn't stop to look where I was going – a trait that had become so routine lately, I was considering having it etched on my gravestone. I spun around sharply, completely blind to the waiter with the tray of canapés standing right behind me. The edge of the platter caught my shoulder, and several dark, sticky, caviar toasts flew into the air. A few stuck to the waiter's white jacket and the rest tumbled to the ground, followed seconds later by the silver platter. It clattered on the floor like a cymbal solo in an orchestra.

I closed my eyes and willed myself to be anywhere else in the world.

'Molly,' cried a voice immediately behind me.

I turned around, more slowly this time.

'I thought that had to be you.' His eyes dropped briefly to the waiter, who was hurriedly scooping up the remaining canapés before they got trodden into the bleached wooden floor. Mac had a broad smile on his lips. 'I recognised your calling card.'

There was no malice in his words, and I could hardly argue with him. I was batting one hundred in my bid to claim the title of world's clumsiest woman.

His eyes were warm as they looked at me, but he made no move to close the distance between us or kiss me hello. *He's probably keeping you at arm's length in case you break something else*, a voice in my head jibed wickedly. *I'm surprised he's willing to let you anywhere near his beautiful brand-new building*.

'Are the others here?' he asked, scanning the crowd for the rest of the Stevens family.

The *rest* of the Stevens family? I flinched at the ease with which my subconscious had made it seem as though I too was a member of that family.

'They're over on the other side, near the windows,' I said, which was hardly a reliable description, as the entire room was edged with floor-to-ceiling windows, many of them opening onto a floodlit deck and the rooftop garden.

Mac was scoping the room for them, but his search was derailed when he spotted someone approaching us. His smile grew immediately broader, and he raised a hand to beckon them over.

'Let me introduce you to my friend Andi,' he said.

'Ah, from university.' I nodded, pleased at how impressed he looked that I'd remembered his friend's name.

The Andi my imagination had conjured was tall, like Mac, and rugged. I saw them playing rugby together at uni and then sinking pints in the student bar afterwards. What I hadn't been expecting was an exceedingly pretty blonde, whose face had transformed into a beam every bit as wide as Mac's. The other thing I hadn't anticipated was that the beer-swilling, sports-loving Andi in my head would also turn out to be six months pregnant.

'Where did you get to?' Mac asked, his arm going around her shoulders.

'Loo trip,' she said succinctly, the Scottish burr in her voice immediately detectible. 'The baby's playing hopscotch on my bladder tonight.'

There was a softness on Mac's face that I hadn't seen before. He looked down at Andi's not inconsiderable bump with genuine affection. My unreliable imagination was rapidly rewriting their story and making up sums that for some reason I didn't particularly like. Two plus two doesn't always equal four – but more often than not, it does.

'Hello,' said Andi, thrusting out her right hand towards me. But it was the left one, with the absence of a ring on it, that caught my attention. Her shake was just this side of bone crushing. Perhaps the rugby-playing image hadn't been that far off the mark after all.

'I'd better introduce myself, as this big dolt seems to have forgotten his manners. I'm Andi.'

'Molly,' I supplied in return, summoning up a smile that I really hoped looked genuine.

Mac hadn't seemed to take offence at the jibe. He'd referred to Andi as his closest friend from university, and although those days were clearly more than a decade in the past, the affection between them appeared undiminished.

'Molly?' Andi queried, her voice and eyebrows rising in tandem. 'The heart girl?'

It wasn't the way I'd have chosen to be introduced, but I was too distracted to say anything as she turned her head swiftly to Mac.

'How come you never mentioned she was this pretty?'

It was probably a toss-up to see which of us looked the most embarrassed: Mac or me. I think I won by a whisker.

'Because that's not something you really notice about your friends,' he answered easily, his eyes travelling to me as though he'd just said something nice.

And maybe it was nice; I was too muddled to decipher it properly.

Mac was in the middle of explaining how Andi was a fellow architect who worked for a prestigious company in Edinburgh when he was stolen away by the man with the grey hair. 'There are some people here who'd like to meet you,' the man said, with only a cursory apology for having interrupted us.

'Away with you,' Andi said, wafting her hand at Mac when he seemed torn. There was a look in his eyes that must have carried a hidden message to his old friend, because she read it and looked slightly affronted. 'I'm not going to eat her. We'll just have a wee girlie chat.'

'That's what I was afraid of,' Mac said, sounding as though he was only half joking.

'He's worried I'll give you the third degree,' Andi said with a grin, swiping a glass of orange juice from the tray of a passing waiter.

'Why on earth would he think that?'

Her eyes were twinkling with amusement. 'I may have been guilty of grilling one or two of his potential girlfriends in the past.'

She didn't look in the least bit contrite. 'Well, more flambéed than grilled, if I'm being completely honest.'

She was forthright and feisty, and there was a lot about her that reminded me of Kyra. It's no bad thing to have a fiercely loyal friend who always has your back, and Andi clearly came into that category.

'Well, you don't have anything to worry about on that score. Mac and I are nothing more than friends.' If I was being strictly accurate, even that was an exaggeration.

Andi shrugged. 'You're his type,' she said, as though scoring a winning point.

I was too taken aback to reply. But whether Andi was right or wrong was actually immaterial, because a new relationship was the last thing on my mind at the moment. Besides, Mac was too successful, too worldly, and too much of a grown-up for me. We might only be a few years apart in age, but decades of life experiences separated us. I simply couldn't imagine myself fitting into his life, nor he into mine.

'And obviously, after the whole Carrie thing when his sight started to go...'

This should have been the time to point out I had absolutely no idea what Andi was talking about, but I had a feeling the more I stayed silent, the more I would learn.

'I swear to you, if I ever meet that woman in a dark alley...'

I nodded, as though I too harboured similarly murderous thoughts.

'He's better off without her,' Andi growled.

I wasn't sure how happy Mac would be if he knew we were discussing his personal life, and the topic was starting to make me uncomfortable, so I changed it. Fortunately, Andi was fiercely proud of her native city, so we were able to spend the next ten minutes discussing Edinburgh, a place I'd only visited once, for the festival, back in my student days.

'Well, if Mac decides to go for the senior position at my firm, you'll have an excuse to come up and visit again,' said Andi, unaware she'd just dropped a bombshell.

'Mac is thinking of moving back to Scotland?' I'd been aiming for a tone that suggested polite interest, but even I could hear I hadn't quite pulled it off.

'If I have any say in it, he will. It would be great to have him back up there before the bairn arrives.'

I tried out several questions in my head, all of which were thinly disguised versions of *and how exactly is Mac connected to your baby?* As I couldn't find a single one that was remotely acceptable, it seemed like a good time to make a polite excuse about needing to find my friends again.

'It's been nice meeting you, heart girl,' Andi said.

'And you,' I replied, not sure if that was entirely true or not.

After the conversational landmines with Andi, it felt wonderfully comfortable to be back in the company of Alex, Todd and Dee once more. I allowed myself one more glass of champagne and then applied the brakes. As delicious as the canapés were, they weren't substantial enough for someone who was no longer used to drinking. Dee was recounting an amusing story about some scrape Maisie and Connor had got into when they were younger, while behind me the conversation between Alex and his brother sounded a good deal more sombre. I caught random snatches and managed to piece together that Alex was having some issues concerning the lease on his business premises.

Todd clapped his brother on the shoulder. 'Just let me know if there's anything I can do, okay?'

I'm not sure what Alex was going to say in reply, because the room was suddenly filled with the screech of feedback from a PA system. Everyone winced as the man who'd earlier been talking to Mac tweaked something on the microphone stand before him. His speech was long and rambling. I found myself stifling several yawns, and I wasn't the only one.

'And now, in conclusion, I'd like to hand over to the man we have to thank for designing the magnificent building we're in tonight – Mac Derwent.'

My boredom evaporated in an instant as a reluctant-looking Mac stepped up to the microphone. Unlike his predecessor, Mac's speech was just about perfect: brief and amusing. I thought it had come to an end and was getting ready to applaud when he suddenly paused, as though weighing up something carefully. His eyes scanned the crowd, looking for someone. I thought it might be Andi, but they travelled straight past her, stopping only when they reached the four of us at the edge of the room.

He cleared his throat, and there was an entirely different emotion in his voice when he spoke again. 'For a very long time I didn't think I'd get to see the finished building I'd designed several years earlier. I won't go into the details, but those of you who know my story will understand what I'm talking about. That I'm here tonight, able to see it – to see all of you – is thanks to one very special person.'

Beside me, I felt Alex stiffen. Without even thinking about it, I reached for his hand and gripped it tightly.

'I can't dedicate this building to them, but I *will* dedicate the rest of my career to creating buildings that always please both the eye and the heart.'

Mac's eyes found mine and wouldn't let go. There was no glass in his hand, but he raised his hand anyway in a salute.

'To Lisa,' he said softly.

Her name, a stranger to all but four people in the room, was repeated by everyone.

CHAPTER TWENTY-SIX

Molly

'I'm glad we all decided to come tonight,' Alex confided as he passed the cloakroom attendant the token in exchange for my coat. 'To be honest, I wasn't sure how weird it might feel.'

I sighed with relief, glad to know I hadn't been the only one with reservations. The smile we shared felt comfortable and familiar.

It was raining hard as we exited the building, and we paused beneath its porticoed awning, watching as the downpour ricocheted off the road and passing cars.

'Do you want to wait until it eases off?' Alex asked.

I glanced up at the sky and then towards his car, which was parked a short distance down the street.

'We could make a run for it? It's just rain,' I said with a shrug.

He turned towards me, very, very, slowly, giving me plenty of time to worry that I'd somehow said the wrong thing. There was a moment when the air between us appeared to shimmer like a heat haze. Alex's eyes were on my face, but he seemed to be looking not just at me but also through and beyond me. The sensation was so strong, I almost turned around to see if someone was standing behind us. Before I could, he'd reached for my hand.

'Come on then,' he urged, pulling me out from under the canopy and into the deluge.

We were laughing for no reason at all as we tumbled like children into his blissfully dry car. He shook the raindrops from his hair and switched on the engine to clear the windows. The world outside had disappeared behind a cloak of condensation. We could have been anywhere at that moment – and wherever it was, it felt like I'd been there before.

We turned towards each other in the steamy car, and it took only a single glance to know I wasn't the only one experiencing this curious moment of déjà vu. We both spoke at once, as though the silence was a dangerous hole that had to be plugged.

'Do you want to put some music on while we wait?' he asked, flipping open a hidden cavity in the console and revealing a stash of old-school CD cases.

I glanced down at the collection, which was illuminated by a yellow pool of light from a nearby streetlamp. They all appeared to be country music, which wasn't my favourite genre; an instinct I was fast learning to trust told me it wasn't Alex's either.

'Why don't I find us something on the radio?' I suggested. For a split second he looked disappointed, as though I'd failed a test.

I twiddled the dials until I found a station playing soft, easy-listening jazz. He gave a small nod of approval as Etta James's soulful voice filled the car, telling us that at last her love 'had come along'. In hindsight, a song full of yee-haws might have been preferable.

After that slightly awkward start, Alex steered our conversation onto safer ground. His humour was dry and sharp, but never unkind. He was the sort of person who'd never forget or fluff the punchline of a joke, and I was laughing for most of the journey back to my house. By the time he pulled up outside, we'd happily regained the gentle banter that had made it so easy to continue writing to him all those months earlier. Perhaps that was why, instead of politely thanking him for the lift, I heard myself asking if he'd like to come in for coffee.

He hesitated, which made me wonder if it was too late to rescind the invitation. Was this a really bad idea?

'But maybe you need to pick up Connor?' I asked, knowing perfectly well that his son was spending the night at Dee's house. I'd given Alex a very easy escape route, but he chose not to take it.

'No. I'm not collecting him until the morning.' If there was a battle going on within him, it was very short-lived. 'I'd love a coffee, Molly.'

'Please excuse the mess,' I said, letting us into the hallway and quickly shoving aside a pair of trainers and a sports bag that I'd dumped at the foot of the stairs.

Alex followed me into the kitchen, smiling as I threw things willy-nilly into cupboards in an attempt to straighten up the room. Unlike Tom, Alex seemed to find my congenital untidiness curiously endearing.

'Do you think you'll remember you tossed the cornflakes packet into the broom cupboard when you're looking for it in the morning?' he teased, bringing the easy banter from the car right there into the kitchen with us.

'Probably not,' I replied with a grin, turning to fill the kettle.

Tom used to warn me that I'd live to regret my untidiness, but he couldn't have imagined it would be in quite this way. In a room with so many half-closed drawers and cupboards, it was Sod's Law that one of them would be the place where I kept my meds. Alex saw the collection of pill packets – I could tell from the clouding in his eyes and the spasm of emotion that crossed his face. I shut the cupboard door fast, but the ghost of Lisa had joined us.

She disappeared briefly when we moved into the lounge, which was thankfully tidy enough to look lived-in rather than messy. 'Make yourself comfortable,' I urged, kicking off my shoes and giving a sigh of relief that made him smile knowingly.

He ignored my invitation as he stood before my floor-to-ceiling bookcase. His eyes ran across the eclectic mix of titles, as though doing a forensic character assessment. I wished him luck with that. The shelves were packed so tightly, I now had books lying sideways on every row. I'd always loved to read, but books had become more than entertainment when I'd been too sick to live my own life; they'd become my passport into other lives, other places.

His hand reached for one of them, and, too late to stop him, my breath caught uncomfortably in my throat. There was a look of shocked recognition on his face as he stared down at the volume in his hands. Shit. What sort of an idiot was I? Why on earth had I left the astronomy book his wife had collaborated on where he could find it? *Because you never intended to ask him in?* my conscience offered forgivingly.

No. That wasn't good enough. It was as though I'd deliberately booby-trapped my bookcase with hidden weapons.

'I'm sorry, Alex. I should have put that one away.'

He shook his head, his fingertips running over the embossed name of the woman he'd loved as though greeting her in Braille.

He turned to me, his eyes seemed to shimmer in the dimly lit room. 'Why do you have this?'

'I… I was doing astronomy with my class. I thought I should learn a bit more about the subject.'

It was a lie so full of holes, I was surprised he didn't call me on it. There were hundreds, maybe even thousands of more age-appropriate books on the topic. I'd read several of them. But the one written by Lisa had found its way onto my bookshelves for a wholly different reason. Could it be called stalking when the person you were secretly following was dead? And was it better or worse that their heart was the reason you were still alive?

'She was writing one for kids, you know. She was only halfway through it when—'

His words drew me to my feet. Very gently I reached out, removed the book from his hand and slid it back onto the shelf.

There was a crack in his voice when he spoke. 'I miss her. Every single day, losing her gets worse instead of better.'

I bit my lip, wanting to comfort him, to give him something to hold onto as he crested the dreadful tsunami of grief. It was a wave he kept riding, but somehow it never took him to the shore.

'I get so scared sometimes that I'm going to forget – that Connor will forget – just how incredible she was.'

I shook my head vehemently. 'That won't ever happen. You won't forget. The kind of love you shared doesn't just die. It can't.' I wasn't sure which of us I was trying to convince, and it wasn't as if I was speaking from experience. As much as I'd felt for Tom, this kind of love was in an entirely different category.

What happened next was my fault, not Alex's. It was my suggestion, not his. That doesn't absolve either of us. But then I'd no idea my actions were going to need absolution.

'Would you… Would you like to listen to it?'

My voice was a church-like whisper, but it brought his head up sharply, as though responding to a gunshot. He didn't ask me to explain. He knew exactly what I meant.

He was several inches shorter than Mac but tall enough that he needed to bend low to accept my offer. My legs were trembling when I stood before him, hands at my sides, as with something approaching reverence Alex lowered his head until his cheek rested against the wall of my chest.

The fabric of my dress was thin, and Lisa's heart was obligingly thumping away with enough vigour to ensure he'd have no difficulty hearing it.

He gasped softly, his head pressing harder against me, as though he couldn't get close enough. My left breast became a pillow as he laid his head against the heart he hadn't heard beating for more than eight months.

To keep my balance, I'd moved my hands, resting them lightly on his shoulders, and at some point his hands had moved to either side of my waist. Did we stand like that for minutes or hours? I truly don't know. I only realised he was crying when I felt the dampness of his tears on my dress. Instinctively I moved one hand from his shoulder to soothingly stroke the back of his head – the last in a long list of things I should never have done.

One minute he was listening to Lisa's heart, and the next his lips were on mine, searching for something he was never going to find. God help me, but for just a moment I began to respond, before the good sense I'd so carelessly abandoned came rushing back.

My hands were on his shoulders again, only this time they were pushing him away.

'No, Alex. No.'

His eyes were glazed, and not just with tears as he backed away from me. If anything, he looked even more horrified than I did.

'Molly… I… I didn't mean…'

My arms were flapping like wings that were incapable of flight. I also took a step backwards, and then another until I felt the edge of the settee against my legs.

'It was completely my fault,' I said, which I think we both knew wasn't quite true.

'I didn't think it was… What I mean is… I knew it was you.'

We stared at each other for a very long moment, neither of us sure if his words had made things better or a great deal worse.

'I think you should leave now,' I said, and he nodded vigorously in agreement.

I followed him to the front door, where he paused, searching for yet another apology. He shook his head, tormented that he'd failed to find one.

'Goodnight, Alex,' I said, opening the door and praying he'd walk through it before I began to cry and this heart I'd been given broke in two.

He did so with only seconds to spare.

CHAPTER TWENTY-SEVEN

Alex

The previous evening kept coming back to Alex in snatched images, like random photographs shaken out of an album; disjointed scenes from a dream. Although ironically there'd been no dreams, because there'd been no sleep for him after he'd returned from Molly's house. Long before dawn had even thought about breaking, he'd thrown back the covers and swung himself out of bed.

By 6 a.m. he was in the sports centre car park, drinking his third coffee of the morning and waiting for the flicker of fluorescent lighting to confirm they were open for business. He'd never been the first person at the gym before, and there was an eerie quality to the rows of silent machines and the hollow acoustics of the changing room.

Alex pushed himself harder than usual, hoping that a vigorous workout might purge all memory of the previous evening from his system. Not the whole evening, just the parts of it when he'd behaved like an idiot. His face felt hot, which might have been due to the session on the rowing machine, or maybe it was the indelible stain of embarrassment on his cheeks.

He stood under the needle-sharp shower jets, slowly turning the dial from steam-inducing 'hot' to breath-stealing 'cold'. There were more people around by the time he stepped out of the cubicle, and the low hum of conversation in the locker room felt as noisy as a roaring crowd.

He dressed rapidly and considered his options. He wasn't due to pick up Connor from Todd's until ten o'clock, which was still two hours away. He toyed with the idea of going to the office and burying his emotions with work, as he'd done so many times since losing Lisa. But that would only delay the inevitable. Confession was good for the soul, or so they said, and there was only one place Alex's soul wanted to be.

He jogged to the car, his trainers creating small avalanches of gravel in their wake. The smell of Molly's perfume hit him as he opened the driver's door. Not strong, like Lisa's had been on his suit, but vague and lingering, as if trapped in the air-conditioning system. He had no idea if that was even possible. It was far more likely to be his guilt conjuring up the smell. An olfactory I-told-you-so, which he should have heeded. But how could he have known how tangled all this would become? *Perhaps you should have listened to your brother*, his conscience reminded him.

The throaty purr of the idling engine sounded like a cat, which immediately made Alex think of Barbara. His senses had become traitors, leapfrogging over logic and linking everything, however tenuously, to the people Lisa had saved.

He left the sports centre car park at speed, sending up further sprays of gravel as his hands gripped the steering wheel too tightly.

Part of him wanted the huge wrought-iron gates to be locked, because that would have given him a legitimate excuse to go no further. But that was a coward's way out, and Lisa deserved far better than that. Far better than him – but then he'd always known that. He lifted the latch and the gate creaked open. He almost laughed at the cliché, as though it had been dubbed in by an enthusiastic sound engineer. Even the knee-high ground mist he waded through looked like it had been pumped out by a special-effects department.

Not that Alex needed to see the path to know where it curved and turned. His feet had walked this route enough times to find their own way to the place where Lisa lay. He came to see her often, and always alone; this was no place for Connor, not until he was much older. It was a decision he knew Todd and Dee disagreed with, but on this he was unwavering.

The sky was almost light now, but darkness hung in this place in quiet pockets, perhaps out of respect for its inhabitants. Each time Alex saw the simple white headstone, the truth of it hit him all over again. Here there was no pretending Lisa was simply away on a holiday, or visiting friends, or even that they were going through a trial separation. Here the truth was bald, stark and unyielding, and etched into marble lest he forget it.

An odd liquefying sensation attacked the bones in his knees as he sank down onto the muddy grass. His fingertips felt cold as he brought them to his lips and then pressed them gently against her name.

'Hi, babe. It's me. I think I might have got myself into a bit of trouble…'

'What happened to you?' Dee asked, opening the door to him a few minutes before ten o'clock.

Alex glanced down at the mud-caked patches on the knees of his jeans. 'Oh, I tripped over on the verge,' he said. Dee was astute and an early-morning visit to Lisa's grave would immediately have set off alarm bells.

'Actually, I meant the panda look.' She stepped back to allow him access to their hallway.

Alex glanced at his reflection in the oak-framed mirror on the wall and wished he hadn't. 'I didn't sleep well last night,' he admitted.

A barefoot Connor had padded out of the kitchen at the sound of the front door, and Alex caught the fleeting look of relief in his son's eyes when he saw it was him. It broke his heart to think that in Connor's mind every single goodbye might be the very last one. The way it had been with his mum.

'Got time for a coffee?' Dee asked breezily, already heading towards the bright and welcoming kitchen. 'Todd might even have left you a Danish if you're lucky.'

Alex felt a lot of things that day, but in all honesty lucky wasn't one of them.

'Was everything all right when you drove Molly back home last night?'

Dee timed her question badly. Alex had a mouth full of apricots and pastry, which gave him some valuable thinking time as he pantomimed chewing away.

'What do you mean by that?'

Dee's eyes went to the two children, who were playing a board game beside the patio doors. They appeared totally disinterested in their parents' conversation.

'Oh. Nothing. It's just… a kind of weird situation, you know. You seem… You seem to like her.'

This time it was Alex's eyes that flew to the children. Had Connor heard his aunt's words? He had his back to Alex, so it was impossible to tell, but there was an odd stillness about his small frame, as though he was waiting for Alex's reply.

'I do like her. I like her in the same way that I like Barbara, Jamie and Mac.' The lie tasted bitter, contrasting with the sweetness of the apricot on his tongue.

Dee's eyes said she didn't believe him, but she shrugged, giving him the benefit of the doubt. Her voice was low, travelling no further than Alex's ears. 'Just promise me you'll be careful, Alex. I'm worried the lines are getting blurry here.'

'Not even for a moment,' Alex reassured her. The lies were piling up. Pretty soon there were going to be too many to count.

*

'Aren't we going home?'

'We're just taking a little detour to buy some flowers,' Alex explained, keeping half an eye on the road and the other on his son's face in the rear-view mirror.

'Are they for Molly?'

Alex crunched the gears noisily, like a learner on their first lesson. So Connor *had* heard what Dee had said, after all.

'Why would I give Molly flowers?'

Connor gave an eloquent shrug. 'I dunno. You used to give them to Mummy all the time.'

'That was different,' Alex said, swallowing down a tightness that ran from his throat to his chest. 'I loved Mummy, and it made her happy to get flowers, so that's why I gave them to her.'

'Don't you want Molly to be happy?'

Alex was seriously going to have to start limiting the time Connor spent with Dee, because he appeared to be picking up all her best interrogation techniques.

'Yes, I want everyone in the world to be happy,' Alex replied, aware he sounded an awful lot like a beauty pageant contestant.

'Molly's nice,' Connor said, lifting his eyes to the mirror to meet his dad's. 'She's like Mummy.'

Every book Alex had read, every internet article, every podcast on cellular memory had somehow been leading him to this point. But they had reached it too soon. Connor was trying to unlock a door that no one was ready to open yet.

'The flowers are for Barbara,' Alex said firmly. 'They're to say thank you for looking after you last night.'

'More flowers? Oh, Alex, you shouldn't have. But my, aren't they beautiful?'

'Connor picked them out,' he said, gently urging the little boy forward to surrender the bouquet.

Barbara took the flowers, setting them to one side as she held her arms open for Connor. In a move that surprised Alex, his son allowed himself to be momentarily buried against Barbara's not inconsiderable bosom. That was definitely something new. Even before what had happened with Lisa, Connor had always been reticent about showing affection with anyone outside of his immediate family.

'Well, I'm feeling doubly spoiled this morning – you're my second visitors of the day.'

'Oh, we definitely don't want to intrude,' began Alex when Barbara stood back to usher them into the hallway.

'Nonsense. Anyway, you know my other guest just as well as I do.'

Molly, thought Alex. She'd said something the night before about how lonely Barbara must be, and how she was going to try to pop round to see her more often. What were the odds of them both deciding to do so today?

Having delivered the flowers and received the hug, Connor was now hanging back, half hidden by Alex's legs. Years ago Lisa had patiently coaxed him out of this nervous habit, though lately it had made an unwelcome return. But a strange mewling sound coming from the lounge saw him emerge from behind Alex's hip. 'What was that?' he asked curiously.

Barbara's eyes twinkled, as though everything was going exactly the way she had intended. 'That's the kittens you can hear,' she said, bending down and holding out her hand in invitation. 'Would you like to see them?'

Connor disappeared down the hallway at speed, taking with him any hope Alex had of avoiding an awkward encounter with Molly.

'Are they Meg's kittens?' he asked, pleased with himself for remembering the cat's name.

It seemed to please Barbara too. She gave a nod as though Alex had passed a test he hadn't even known he was sitting.

'They are. Six little beauties. Come and meet them.'

Alex pasted what he hoped was an appropriate smile on his face and prepared to encounter the woman he'd left in tears twelve hours ago.

But the voice that greeted him wasn't that of the person whose lips he had briefly crushed beneath his own. It was Jamie's.

He was sitting cross-legged on the floor beside an array of polystyrene packing and several TV remote controls.

'Oh, you've got it working already. You're such a clever young man, Jamie.'

Jamie got fluidly to his feet, in a way Alex remembered his limbs had also once been capable of, back in his teens and twenties. 'Hi guys,' he said, holding his hand out not to Alex but to Connor.

Alex's eyes widened as the two performed a complicated fist-bumping, high-fiving, slapping routine.

'You remembered it,' cried Jamie, clearly delighted.

Connor was smiling as he turned away from his friend and dropped to his knees before a cage in the corner of the room. Barbara crouched down beside him, identifying each fluffy bundle to an entranced Connor.

Alex turned back to Jamie, who was gathering up the polystyrene scattered across the floor and bundling it into the box the television had come in. 'This was nice of you,' he said, hoping he didn't sound patronising.

Jamie didn't appear to take offence. 'She said she bought it weeks ago but had no one she could ask to set it up for her. That made me kind of sad.'

Both men looked across at Barbara, who was patiently explaining to Connor how the kittens needed to stay with their mother in their cage for now.

'So she can look after them,' Connor said solemnly.

'That's right, sweetie. When they're a little bit older they won't need her any more.'

Connor shook his head, his jaw stubbornly set. 'They're always going to need their Mummy,' he contradicted.

Barbara brought a wrinkled hand to her face and brushed a tear from her cheek. She wasn't the only one, Alex realised. Jamie quickly bent his head to study the TV instruction leaflet, even though he was done setting it up.

'Would you like to hold them, Connor?' Barbara asked, her voice gentle.

The little boy's eyes flew to Alex, as if already preparing to be disappointed. *It's what he expects from me*, Alex thought sadly.

'I don't know, Barbara. Connor's not used to handling pets and they're very young and delicate.'

'He'll be fine with them,' Barbara said, drawing back the catch on the cage before Alex had a chance to raise any further objection. She positioned Connor's hands to form a tiny cradle and then placed a pure white kitten within them.

She watched them for a while, before getting to her feet. 'I think a cup of tea is in order,' she announced, disappearing off to the kitchen.

'That'll be my fourth; I'll be peeing on the bus all the way home,' Jamie joked.

'Still not driving yet?'

For a few seconds Jamie looked totally confused, and then he remembered what he'd previously told them. Alex felt an unexpected surge of compassion for him. It must have been exhausting trying to stay on top of so many fabricated stories.

Alex and Connor ended up staying far longer than they'd intended, mainly because Connor looked happier than Alex had seen him in ages as he played with each of Meg's kittens in turn. He couldn't help noticing that he kept returning to the one that Barbara had first placed in his hands, the little white moggy.

'Looks like you'll be getting a new family member, mate,' Jamie teased quietly, watching as Connor crooned reassuringly to the kitten.

'No, I don't think so. We've got enough to cope with right now. We don't need to add to the things we have to worry about. Maybe when Connor is a few years older we'll think about getting a dog.'

Barbara said nothing, but Alex was very aware of her watching him carefully over the rim of her teacup.

When he announced it was time to leave, Connor's shoulders slumped dejectedly.

'I'm sure Barbara will let us come back and see the kittens again,' he said.

'Any time at all. You're always welcome. All of you,' Barbara said.

'Can I offer you a lift home, Jamie?'

For just a split second a look of panic flashed across Jamie's face. 'Erm, thanks, but I'm meeting some friends for a game of footie in the park in a while.'

Jamie didn't look as though he was dressed for a sporting afternoon, and he certainly didn't have a kit bag with him, but Alex had no intention of calling him out on it. 'Is football your sport?' he asked, gamely going along with the pretence.

'Well, that and swimming,' he said, getting to his feet and swiping the last two chocolate digestives off the plate. 'I was a lifeguard before I got sick. Saved two people from drowning, actually. Got a medal and everything.'

Connor was the only person in the lounge who looked as though he totally believed what they'd just been told. He was gazing at Jamie as if he was a Marvel superhero.

'Can you swim, little man?' asked Jamie.

Connor shook his head from side to side.

'Connor's always been a bit nervous around water. We were going to sign him up for lessons last summer…' Alex's voice trailed away. It was yet another of Lisa's plans he had failed to follow through on. *Next summer*, he silently promised himself.

CHAPTER TWENTY-EIGHT

Molly

'I hate to say this, but maybe Bertie should go on a diet.'

'Shhh,' said my mother, covering the terrier's ears with her hands. 'Please do not even think of using the F-word in front of him.' My mother's devotion to the feisty little terrier never ceased to surprise me. In her own way she was every bit as attached to her canine companion as Barbara was to her cats.

The house was fragrant with the aroma of roasting chicken, which Bertie's twitching nose had clearly clocked. Mum always went a little overboard when I visited, but I knew better than to tell her I'd be just as happy with a sandwich. When the oven timer pinged, Mum disappeared into the kitchen, firmly refusing my offer of help. 'You just sit down and take it easy,' she urged, unable to totally let go of the past, when I'd been largely incapable of assisting her.

'Let me spoil you, Molly,' she said softly. 'I'm so very thankful that I can get to do it.'

I couldn't really argue with a comment like that. If this was what it took to keep her happy, then I would willingly eat an entire poultry farm of chickens.

We'd spent a very relaxed morning looking through the photos from her cruise holiday, before she hesitantly confessed she was thinking of booking another one.

'I know it's a lot of money,' she said, sounding guilty, 'and that I said the last one would be a once-in-a-lifetime trip—'

'Honestly, Mum, I think it's a great idea, and you definitely don't have to justify it to me.'

She looked relieved, and her expression softened as she focused on something beyond my shoulder. I knew the topography of her lounge as well as my own, so I could tell she was looking at the bookcase where one of the last photos of my father was positioned.

'Daddy would have wanted you to explore the world and make new friends. He wouldn't have wanted you to spend your time alone, missing him.'

I should have realised that I had just strayed into an area where Mum would surely follow.

'Talking of new friends and people moving on…' she began. I sighed, knowing exactly where this conversation was heading. 'Are you still seeing the family of your donor and the other organ recipients?' It sounded alien to hear them referred to in that clinical way. To me they were now just Alex, Connor, Mac, Jamie and Barbara. But I knew Mum was confused by our ongoing relationship. 'Where is it all leading?' she said.

'Well, I don't think they're going to ask for any of the organs back,' I told her, mistakenly going for humour.

'This isn't a joking matter, Molly. You all seem to be so… involved with each other.'

Mum had never interfered before in my choice of friends, not even the couple of dubious boyfriend choices I'd made in my teens, so it sat a little uncomfortably with both of us that she was concerned about my relationship with Lisa's family and the other recipients.

But I honestly couldn't see the harm in everyone keeping in touch on WhatsApp, or occasionally meeting up – even if quite a few of those meetings had been unplanned. It was decidedly odd, in a city this size, how frequently our paths had crossed.

I'd bumped into Mac twice: once in the hospital corridor on my latest check-up, when we'd grabbed a quick coffee before our appointments, and then again just last week in the foyer of the multiplex cinema.

Kyra and I were there to see a cheesy romcom and were debating which excessively large popcorn to buy when I looked up and saw Mac leaning nonchalantly against a pillar. He appeared to be waiting for someone, and as he was standing near the Ladies, I suspected it might be Andi.

Our film was about to start, so it was a fleeting hello and goodbye. The house lights were already dimming as Kyra and I slid into our seats. Under cover of the opening credits, Kyra leant across and squeezed my forearm. 'I have just one word to say,' she said in a whisper that still managed to earn her a frown from the woman in front of us. 'Phwoar. Just phwoar.'

'That's three words,' I hissed back, smiling in the darkness. Kyra and Mac? I'd mentioned it to her once ages ago, but could that actually become a reality? The idea distracted me so much, I failed to enjoy the film.

The other random meetings had been more mundane. I'd seen Barbara in the supermarket and had given her a lift home, ignoring her protests that she could easily wait for a taxi. And I'd spotted Jamie and a slightly downtrodden older woman coming out of a shop in town. From their facial resemblance, she had to have been his mother, although she didn't fit the glamorous, coffee-morning-attending, horse-riding individual I'd pictured from his descriptions. She'd appeared quite distressed, and he was obviously comforting her. I was debating going over to say hi, when I noticed the shop they'd just left had three brass balls hanging over its entrance. Whatever they'd been doing in there, it had clearly upset them both and I didn't want to intrude. Like a spy in a movie, I'd ducked into a shop doorway, skulking in the shadows and hiding from sight until they were gone.

I was trying very hard not to give meaning to these random encounters, because I refused to face the glaring conclusion: that fate seemed determined to keep drawing us all together, like broken pieces of a magnet.

However, there was one person I hadn't seen recently, by either accident or design, and given what had happened at our last encounter, that was perfectly fine with me.

Mum called out something from the kitchen, and I must have answered appropriately, although I had no idea what I'd said, because my thoughts were tugging me back to the last time I'd seen Alex.

His first apology had come via a text that he must have pulled over to send on his way home. The second came on a card, nestled deep within the foliage of a bouquet that was waiting for me when I got home from work. Perhaps if I'd had the courage to respond to either of those, I could have avoided apology number three, which Alex had felt the need to deliver in person a short while later.

He was standing on my doorstep, the soft evening rain misting around him like spray from a waterfall. Even under the lights of my outside lamp I could tell that the dark circles beneath his eyes could have given mine a run for their money.

'Alex,' I said, trying to sound more surprised than shocked. I'd hoped for more time to sort out my confused feelings about what had happened between us. Although, in reality, had anything happened at all? It had been just one unguarded moment, a slip-up that was surely best forgotten.

'Come in,' I urged, shivering slightly in the cold night air.

He shook his head, raindrops spraying around him like discarded jewels. 'No. I don't think that's a good idea. This won't take long.'

Something plummeted deep within me. It felt horribly like an internal organ.

'I…' he began 'I wanted to see you. I wanted to say how sorry I was about—'

'That's fine. You don't need to say anything,' I interjected, hoping to shoot down his entire prepared speech before he even began it.

'But I do,' he said, his eyes full of anguish I had no idea how to ease. 'I care about you, Molly. You've been a good friend to me when I needed one, while I… Well, I don't think I can honestly say the same. And that kills me because you deserve better, especially after all that you've been through. You deserve someone who looks into your eyes and sees no one but you. I'm not sure that's something I can do right now.' He turned away, the confession too hard to deliver to my face. 'I'm not sure if it's something I'll ever be able to do.'

I was gripping the edge of the door frame so hard, it was actually hurting my hand, but it was good to have some tangible pain to focus on.

'Alex, there's no need to say anything else. We have something that ties us together so uniquely, it was almost inevitable that the strands were going to get tangled. What happened the other night was no one's fault. It was one of those things.'

I inwardly winced at the cliché. Because, of course, there were no 'things' that existed like this. We were in uncharted territory, and we'd taken a pretty serious wrong turn. My biggest fear now was that we'd veered so far off the pathway, we weren't going to be able to find our way back. Too late, the words of caution voiced by the transplant coordinators as to why donor families and recipients shouldn't ever meet came echoing back.

'I don't want to lose you as a friend, Molly, and I'm really worried that after the way I acted the other night that's going to happen.'

I swallowed audibly.

'And I know that's selfish of me, and if you decide you just want to keep your distance from now on, then obviously I'll respect that. But I'm praying that you won't, because I'm not the only one who needs you… Connor does too – maybe even more than me.'

The thought of never again seeing that wonderful little boy felt like a dagger sliding between my ribs, searching for my heart.

'How he is when he's with you,' continued Alex, 'the way you've been able to connect with him… well, it's something no one else has been able to do since…'

Please don't say it, I silently pleaded. *Don't say her name.* Perhaps Alex read the panic in my eyes, for he changed tack.

'Can we turn back the clock?' he asked. 'Can you trust me enough not to screw up again? Will you let me be your friend once more?'

It would have taken someone far colder than me to have refused him that.

'You never stopped being that, Alex. Not for a single moment.'

Beneath my ribcage the quickening beat of my heart slowly steadied.

CHAPTER TWENTY-NINE

Alex

Alex had never believed in signs or portents. Lisa had loved that kind of stuff, cheerfully admitting that she'd visited a medium shortly after meeting him. The medium had confirmed she'd recently met the man she was going to marry.

'Oh, really? Is it anyone I know?' he'd asked, drawing her into his arms and nibbling lightly on the side of her neck. She'd collapsed against him, her sigh of pleasure arousing him more than he'd wanted her to see. He'd needed no psychic to tell him that his days of searching were over. He'd found the person he was meant to spend the rest of his life with.

But now things were happening that weren't just shaking his belief system, they were razing it to the ground. The rational part of his mind had already taken a huge leap of faith by embracing the cellular memory theory. He took reassurance from the number of respected doctors and professionals who acknowledged that there were too many cited instances to ignore and that there was definitely something in it. But that wasn't all of it. It was as though Alex had opened a door – just a crack to begin with – and now all kinds of thoughts were finding their way through it.

It was after ten, and Alex was debating whether to start another episode of the thriller box set he'd been watching, admittedly with very little interest. He'd have been hard pushed to outline the dark and twisty plot or name a single character from the show. And yet these days the TV was seldom switched off. Because beneath a canopy of voices, Alex was able to pretend he wasn't spending yet another night alone.

The knock on the window startled him enough to set his heart racing. Why would someone pad through the flowerbeds to rap on the window rather than ring the front doorbell? Feeling foolish, Alex looked around for a weapon, should he need one, but could find nothing more deadly than the TV remote control. He strode to the window and gripped the curtains, yanking them apart. For one dreadful horror-movie moment, the face he saw staring into his lounge was his own. He gasped and the remote slipped from his fingers to bounce on the floor, scattering batteries as it fell. It took a few seconds for Alex to realise that he was seeing his own reflection in the glass, superimposed over a face that did indeed look very much like his.

'Todd! You scared the shit out of me,' Alex hissed.

His brother looked sheepish as he shrugged and pointed meaningfully towards the front door. By the time Alex had crossed the hallway, he'd calmed down. No more spooky box sets, he promised himself as he opened the door.

'What the hell were you doing creeping around in the under-growth like a burglar?'

'I didn't want to ring the bell and wake Connor.'

'I think he'd have woken up anyway as I bludgeoned what I thought was an intruder over the head,' Alex said, more rattled than he wanted to let on.

'Would that bludgeoning have been with the TV remote control?' Todd asked, grinning widely.

Alex gave a reluctant laugh. 'Oh, you saw that, did you?'

They'd crossed into the kitchen and Alex had gone automatically to the fridge, pulling out two bottles of beer. He waggled one at his brother and received a nod in confirmation. They didn't bother with glasses but drank straight from the ice-cold bottles, leaning up against the kitchen units.

'So did Dee kick you out?' Alex was joking, knowing perfectly well that his brother's marriage was every bit as strong as his own had been.

'No, I'm after a favour.'

Alex nodded encouragingly. After all they'd done for him since the accident, there was very little Todd could ask of him that he'd refuse.

Todd delved into the pocket of his trousers. 'I've got a dongle in here somewhere.'

'Don't we all, mate. But I'd just as soon not see it.'

Todd's laughter was far more likely to wake Connor than the doorbell, but he did nothing to stifle it. There was relief in his eyes, and tears too, but for once these were tears of laughter.

'I think that may be the first joke you've cracked in almost a year.'

Was that true? Alex had always been a natural joker, with a quick wit. Whenever he thought back on the days, weeks, months and years of his marriage, which he did a lot, there were two things that always struck him: the love, and the laughter. He'd lost both in one fell swoop.

Todd's searching fingers had finally found what he was looking for. 'There's an urgent report I need to print out for work, but our supposedly top-of-the-range printer has decided to stop working. Can I use yours?'

'Of course,' Alex said easily. 'You know where it is.'

His brother headed towards the stairs.

'Maybe you could ask Jamie to have a look at yours. Didn't he say something about being a whizz with IT stuff?'

Todd paused with one foot on the lower step and gave a wry smile. 'Was that before or after he was a roadie, an entrepreneur, a lifeguard and a rally driver?'

'Bloody lawyers,' Alex said good-naturedly. 'You're all so sceptical and suspicious.' Ironically, he was soon to find out just how accurate that jocular comment was.

Alex had finished his beer and had just decided against having a second one when Todd's voice carried down from the upstairs hallway.

'Have you got any more paper?' he said in an overloud stage whisper. 'Your printer's run out.'

'Top right-hand drawer of the desk,' Alex replied.

He'd emptied the kitchen bin and was halfway through doing the same with the dishwasher when his hand suddenly froze mid-task. He straightened up fast enough to hear several of his vertebrae crack in protest. *The desk. The top drawer.*

He raced into the hall, but Todd was already descending the stairs, with the evidence Alex had wanted to keep from him in his arms. His eyes met Todd's, and this time there was no humour in either brother's expression. Alex returned to the kitchen with heavy steps, pulled out a chair at the table and sat down with a look of resignation on his face.

Todd was going to do the whole lawyer thing, Alex realised, as he watched his brother set out the books on the table, making sure they were all facing Alex, just in case he might have forgotten what they were about. Eight books, each one of them on cellular memory. In his head, Alex could practically hear his brother intoning, *If it pleases the court, I'd like to present the following as evidence…*

'What the fuck are these?'

Alex toyed briefly with going for 'books', but one glance at his brother's concerned face killed the quip.

'I got them ages ago. I'd forgotten I even had them.' It was quite shocking how easily the lie fell from his lips.

'Then why is there a receipt from last week being used as a bookmark?' Todd shot back.

Alex gave a grudging nod of admiration. Todd was eminently suited to his chosen profession.

'There've been documented case histories that—'

Todd silenced his words with a single glare. 'Yes, they're right up there with the "I was abducted by aliens" accounts.' He sighed, sounding suddenly much older than his years, and swept his hand over the table. 'These aren't textbooks, Alex. They have no factual basis. Cellular memory isn't even a proven phenomenon – it's what they call a pseudoscience.'

Alex was secretly impressed that his brother even knew the phrase. It proved he too had studied the topic – although clearly they'd reached very different conclusions.

Wearily, Todd lowered himself onto the chair across from Alex. 'Okay,' he said, leaning forward and resting his elbows on the table. 'Let me have it. Tell me exactly what you believe is happening here.'

Alex shook his head. 'No. What's the point? You already think I'm crazy.'

Todd reached out, pushing the books aside to grasp his brother's hand, which felt weirdly symbolic. 'I don't think that. Not at all. I think you're in pain, and that you're confused, and that you've latched onto something that you think will help you. Whereas I'm afraid it's going to drag you even further under. But I still want to hear what you think.' He released Alex's hand and raised both of his in a gesture of surrender. 'I promise I won't interrupt or say anything until you're done.'

It wasn't the most comfortable twenty minutes of Alex's life. Even to his own ears, his theories sounded fantastical spoken out loud for the very first time. In his head they hadn't sounded nearly so crazy.

'So, let me get this right,' said Todd, speaking slowly as he mentally filed away everything his brother had told him. 'You believe that the love Lisa felt for you remained within the heart when it was transplanted into Molly. That when Lisa told you she'd love you for as long as her heart kept beating, this was a literal declaration rather than just something lovely to say?'

Alex dropped his eyes to study the whorls in the wooden table. It was easier than meeting his brother's gaze.

'And where does that leave Molly?' Todd questioned. 'Has she told you that she's unexpectedly discovered herself to be in love with you?'

In a blinding flashback, Alex saw the kiss in Molly's lounge, and how they'd both recoiled from it. He could almost feel her small hands again on his shoulders, pushing him away.

'There is something there – with Molly, I mean,' Alex insisted. 'I felt it even before we met. It was there in her letters to me.'

'It was gratitude, Alex. And yes, maybe that did quickly grow into a genuine friendship, but I honestly think these feelings you're experiencing have a far more logical explanation.'

Alex raised his head slowly.

'Molly's a lovely girl. And you might not be able to remember this, but she is also very much the type of girl you always used to be attracted to. Little and curvy. It was practically your girlfriend blueprint when you were younger. Lisa was the anomaly; she was something different.' There was genuine love for his late sister-in-law in Todd's eyes as he reached for Alex's hand once again. 'In every single way, she was different.' He sighed.

'I know you don't want to hear this. I know you're going to say it's too soon or that... hell, I don't know... that it will never happen, not ever. But if you ask me, I think you're attracted to Molly, sexually attracted, and because you can't bear the thought of betraying Lisa's memory, you've somehow convinced yourself that Lisa is alive within Molly. That Molly is nothing more than a vehicle to bring Lisa back to you.'

Todd reached for his beer bottle and drained the remains in a single swallow. 'And frankly that's a pretty shit deal for both Molly and Lisa.'

He began counting points off on his fingers, one at a time. 'Molly isn't Lisa; the heart is simply a pump that moves blood around the body; it has no emotions outside the realms of a Hallmark card; the recipients of Lisa's organs weren't brought into your life for some big hidden purpose; it was all just chance.'

He'd run out of fingers, but not of things to say. 'When Lisa said her love wouldn't die, she was right, it won't. But it didn't leapfrog into a host body. It will live on forever, but in your heart, not Molly's. You have to stop this now, mate, before you hurt someone. Before you do something stupid.'

The kiss was there again, front and centre stage in Alex's head.

'I think I might have already done that.'

CHAPTER THIRTY

Molly

I always liked to reserve the first day of the school holidays for doing absolutely nothing. But not today. Today, even though I'd completed my Christmas shopping several weeks earlier, I was heading into the centre of town, in the middle of a snowstorm, in order to make one more purchase – which wasn't even mine.

The odds of the white Christmas the weather forecasters had been predicting had been slashed dramatically overnight. When I'd opened my bedroom curtains in the morning, it was to find my unremarkable street transformed into a winter wonderland. The familiar grey colour palette was gone as road and pavements were hidden beneath the previous night's snowfall. Under their deep crust of snow, even the wheelie bins now looked magical.

The radio was warning drivers to stay off the roads, and I didn't need telling twice. I wrapped up cosily in boots, jeans and a chunky red jumper, tucked my hair up in a bobble hat, and wound a scarf so many times around my neck it was quite hard to turn my head.

He'd phoned me the day before, catching me mid-nap, and I'd been too slow and sleepy to think of an excuse to say no. Would I have given him one if I'd been more awake, I wondered.

'Hello,' I'd mumbled, swiping to answer the call without reading the screen first.

'Molly?' The caller seemed confused, and I could hardly blame them. I sounded like I had a mouth stuffed full of marshmallows.

'Uh huh,' I replied inarticulately.

'Did I wake you?' The voice was hesitant.

'Who *is* this?' I asked, wriggling to free myself from a fleecy throw I'd wrapped around my legs.

'It's Mac,' said the voice in my ear. 'I'm sorry, have I called at a bad time?'

It was dark beyond my lounge window, but at this time of year it was dark by the middle of the afternoon. I had no idea if I'd been asleep for hours or just minutes.

'I don't know. Maybe. What time is it?'

His soft laughter rumbled down the phone line. 'It's a little after eight. Were you in bed?' And then before I had a chance to reply, he added rapidly, 'Are you feeling okay?'

'I'm fine. I was just resting my eyes.' It was the euphemism my dad would use every time he was caught asleep in front of the TV, and the memory made my own eyes prickle uncomfortably. I missed him even more at this time of year.

'I was wondering if you were free tomorrow. I know it's terribly short notice, but I could do with a woman's input. I'll throw in lunch and mulled wine if you say yes,' he added enticingly.

'What exactly is it that we're going to be doing?'

'Shopping. For Andi's baby. I could really use your help.'

He'd had me at 'mulled wine' then almost lost me again at 'Andi', but what kind of friend would I have been to refuse his request?

The holiday season has always been my favourite time of year, and I'm hokey enough to love the way it makes total strangers forget to dislike each other and even go out of their way to share seasons' greetings. I'd exchanged four 'Happy Christmases' with fellow passengers before I was halfway to town. The bus was crowded and steamy, but if you ignored the smell of damp bodies, it was actually rather nice. I'd caught it by the skin of my teeth for my phone had rung just as I was about to leave the house.

'Kyra!' I exclaimed, glancing automatically at my watch. 'What are you doing calling me? Shouldn't you be at 36,000 feet right now, knocking back margaritas with your breakfast?' She laughed ruefully. 'Please don't say you missed your flight,' I continued. Kyra had practically been counting down the hours for her trip back to Australia for the holidays and would be devastated not to go.

'No. My plane is right here at the airport, and so, unfortunately, am I. Have you looked out the window yet this morning, Mol? It's like the bloody Arctic out there.'

Coming from an Australian state where winter necessitated nothing more than a slightly thicker jumper, Kyra still had issues with our British winters.

'Actually, I'm just about to head out in it, right now.'

'What?' she exclaimed, her voice rising above those of the frustrated travellers chattering around her. 'You've ruined my mental image. I thought you'd be curled up on the settee, watching *Love Actually* in your PJs while scoffing a box of Marks & Spencer mince pies.'

To be fair, that had been exactly what I'd planned to do before Mac's call. 'Later,' I promised. 'This morning I'm meeting someone in town for some last-minute shopping.'

'You're shopping without me? You traitor,' she teased, unable to keep the amusement from her voice. Her next comment got lost behind the boom of a tannoy announcement.

'Sorry. What did you say?'

'I asked who you were shopping with.'

I swallowed, and prayed for another flight announcement, but sadly the line was suddenly as clear as a bell.

'It's Alex, isn't it?' Kyra guessed incorrectly. I didn't need to see her face to imagine her smooth brow creased in disapproval, for it was right there in her voice. Stupidly I felt myself flushing, because Kyra still knew nothing about what had happened between Alex and me and how it had confirmed how wrong it would be to allow our friendship to develop into anything else. The version of events Kyra been given had been carefully edited and sanitised as though what occurred that night was a guilty secret, which in a way I suppose it was.

'No. It's not Alex. I'm helping Mac, actually.'

'That's just as bad.'

'How do you work that out?' I asked, aware that I was now fidgeting uncomfortably as though on a witness stand. 'Mac is a friend, nothing more.'

Kyra's response was a dismissive snort. 'A friend who I suspect would like to be a whole lot more.'

'No. You're one hundred per cent wrong,' I declared emphatically, as almost in wonder I lifted my fingers to my cheeks. They were red hot. The flush had turned into a fiery blush.

'I truly hope I am, because I'm worried that these friendships of yours are, at best, a little odd, and at worst... they're kind of incestuous.' It was a word she must have known would plant an ugly seed because she immediately lightened her tone 'Can't you just find a regular weirdo on a dating site, like the rest of us do?'

'I'll add it to my list of New Year's resolutions,' I promised, thankful we were now back to our usual banter. Kyra's concern came from a place of love, I knew that. But she didn't know – or understand – the connection I felt to both Mac and Alex. And yes, Mac was undeniably attractive, and in another time and place... well, things might have been different. But I was too sensible to indulge in pointless 'what ifs'. Because even if – hypothetically – I should find myself attracted to... someone, I came with the kind of baggage that no one in their right mind would choose to take on. I was a bad bet for a long-term future with anyone and no amount of argument was going to change that.

Fortunately another announcement in the background cut short our conversation.

'Finally,' Kyra declared. 'I've gotta go, Mols. We're boarding. Take care of yourself and remember that old Aussie saying, 'mates don't date'.

'You just made that up,' I said on a laugh. 'Fly safe and I'll see you soon.'

'I wasn't sure you'd still be able to make it,' Mac said, stepping out from beneath the canopy of the department store where we'd agreed to meet. He was in a dark pea coat that made his shoulders look broader than ever. Despite the awning, his hair and coat were peppered with snowflakes.

'You can't keep a good woman away from a shopping trip,' I said lightly, a little thrown when his hand reached out to cup my elbow. He kept hold of me as he steered us through the throng of oncoming shoppers, many of them wielding their carrier bags like weapons. The revolving doors separated us, and once inside, Mac made no move to take my arm again.

'So, where do you want to start?' I asked, already tugging at the scarf around my neck. The store felt as hot as a sauna, and I was in danger of swooning like a Victorian damsel if I didn't shed some layers fast. An image of the pair of us on the front cover of a trashy novel popped into my head, with Mac scooping me up in his arms and sweeping me up a winding staircase. Damn Kyra and her stupid theories.

'Sorry,' I said, my mind all over the place and my cheeks pink, 'what did you say?'

'I was just saying thank you in advance for giving up your day to help me shop.' He flashed me a boyish grin.

Would this take the whole day, I wondered. Surely he only had to pick out one little gift? 'We should probably head to the baby department, on the fifth floor,' I said.

Another grin, this one decidedly sheepish. 'That'd be a good place to start…' He left the rest of the sentence dangling, waiting for me to reach up and clasp hold of it.

'Mac, is there something you haven't mentioned yet?'

He gave a smiling wince, as though I'd just trodden on his toe. 'Such a clichéd guy thing, isn't it, waiting until the last moment to buy anything. There er… might be a couple of other Christmas gifts I still need to get.'

I summoned up my best teacherly 'spill-the-beans' face. Apparently it worked just as well on thirty-six-year-old architects as it did with six-year-olds. He cracked like a nut.

'Okay. Maybe more than just a couple of gifts.' He looked so contrite, it was almost comical. 'I'd like to get presents for the Stevens family, and for Barbara and Jamie too.' This was way more than just popping into the baby department and picking up a couple of cute little outfits, and yet even though he'd misled me, I couldn't think of a single way I'd rather spend my day.

I kept him in suspense for a few moments longer, just to prove I wasn't a total pushover, and then got my own back. 'You know that scene in *Pretty Woman* when Richard Gere gives Julia Roberts his credit card…'

If Mac imagined I was genetically better equipped to know what to buy for a baby, he was in for a shock. I stepped out of the lift and felt like I'd landed in another country. To our left were scores of prams, buggies and car seats, and to our right was a maze of cots, cribs and other equipment I couldn't even identify. Directly in front of us was the clothing section, with outfits ranging in size from 'how could any human be that small' to 'I bet I could almost fit into that'.

I gave a helpless shrug. 'I have no idea where we should even begin.'

To be fair, Mac looked slightly less nonplussed than me. 'Andi mentioned something about having a registry here?'

I glanced up at him with surprise. 'You do know that means you could have chosen whatever you wanted online? You didn't have to come and pick it out in person.'

'I know.' He looked embarrassed. 'But I like *seeing* things,' he said simply.

The penny dropped with a clang so loud, I was surprised nearby shoppers couldn't hear it. Mac was embracing the gift he'd been given. Just as I did whenever I chose to run rather walk up a flight of stairs or swim a further ten lengths of the pool. I did it because nothing stopped me now. I did it because I could.

Understanding and liking him even more than before, I linked my arm through his and pointed us towards the customer services desk. 'Come on then, let's get shopping.'

Once I'd got past how odd it was to be doing this, I actually had fun shopping for Andi's baby. It only felt uncomfortable when I paused to wonder again about Mac's connection to the infant.

'Can I help you?' asked an immaculately dressed woman in black as Mac and I wandered around the area where the cots were displayed. I had a printout of Andi's registry in my hand, but I was beginning to suspect Mac wanted to buy something more substantial than anything on the list.

'I see you're both looking at the cribs. Many couples like to go for the bedside ones if they're thinking about sleeping together.'

'Oh, we're not sleeping together,' I blurted out unthinkingly, waving my hand in Mac's direction. I'm not sure if it was the expression on the assistant's face or Mac's muffled laughter that immediately highlighted my gaffe. 'I mean, we're not sleeping together with the baby – or any other way, come to that.' I shook my head as I clumsily tried to extricate myself from the hole I'd just dug. The assistant had the air of a woman who was going to enjoy retelling this story a great many times.

Behind me, Mac was still chuckling. I threw him a look but ruined the effect when my own lips began to quiver. I drew in a deep breath and turned back to the assistant.

'We're buying the crib for a friend of ours,' I explained firmly.

'Ah, I see. Well, we have some lovely traditional ones over here,' she said, gesturing towards another section.

'We're buying a crib?' Mac whispered into my ear as we dutifully followed the assistant.

'Looks like it,' I whispered back.

The one we picked was gorgeous, and somewhere along the way I totally forgot I was choosing it for a small human I'd probably never meet. For just a moment I allowed myself to imagine I was picking out furniture with the man I loved for our own nursery, a room there was a very good chance I'd never have need of. Having a baby wasn't impossible following a heart transplant, but after seeing how losing Lisa had affected Connor, how could I ever risk doing that to a child of my own?

'This is the one I'd get,' I said decisively, caressing the hand-carved wood.

Mac was standing on the opposite side of the crib. Our eyes met over it, and just for a moment... I shook my head, reality hitting me like a douse of cold water.

'We'll take this one,' he said unexpectedly.

Only then did I think to examine the swinging price tag. 'Have you seen how much it costs?' I hissed as we followed a clearly delighted assistant to the till.

There was an odd look in his eyes as he dismissed my concerns. Mac was about to part with a considerable sum of money and I couldn't work out whether it was to please me or to please Andi. Or which of those two answers bothered me the most.

*

Two hours later, our shopping was almost complete. I'd picked out two gorgeous scarves: pale blue cashmere for Dee, and patterned silk for Barbara, and a doll with a cry like an air-raid siren for Maisie.

'Are you sure?' Mac queried, after I demonstrated its banshee howl.

'I have insider knowledge,' I said, patting my nose wisely. 'Half the girls in my class have it on their Christmas list.'

Mac shrugged good-humouredly. 'Clearly I've got a lot to learn about children. Today's lesson is that a great many of their toys should come with earplugs.'

I smiled, taking the glossy carrier bag from the shop assistant. 'Do you see yourself having any?' I asked, stepping straight over the boundary from polite conversation to inappropriate.

Mac came to an unexpected stop in the middle of the toy-department floor. It was hardly an appropriate location for such a question, with remote-control helicopters flying above our heads and shoppers jostling busily around us.

'I take it you mean kids rather than earplugs?'

He was more like me than I'd realised. In awkward moments I always reached for humour, and it seemed as though Mac did the same. But surprisingly he chose to answer me honestly.

'Yes. I hope one day I'll have a family. It had always been on the cards, until…' His hand reached up and unconsciously brushed the corner of his eye in a gesture that touched my heart. 'When I lost my sight, everything changed. It closed doors that I'd taken for granted would always be open to me.'

His story was also mine, and I suddenly felt much closer to him. It also made me remember what Andi had said about his ex-girlfriend. Carrie. My head was preoccupied with these thoughts when a football suddenly came flying straight at me, threatening to dislodge them. With lightning-fast reflexes, Mac caught the ball a split second before it made contact with my face.

'I'm so sorry, I told him not to touch them,' said a harried woman holding the arm of a surly-looking little boy. Amidst her profuse apologies, the moment with Mac was lost, and by the time the pair had disappeared back into the crowd, there was no picking up the dropped threads of our conversation.

'I was thinking of getting something techie for Jamie, maybe one of those activity trackers?' Mac said, studying a display of watch-like devices that could record everything from your rate of respiration to what you'd had for breakfast. 'He was talking about rebuilding his fitness, and I don't think I've ever seen him wear one of these – have you?'

The last time I'd seen Jamie, he was looking troubled as he walked out of a pawn shop. There was a good chance Mac's generous gift might end up there too, but that wasn't my secret to share.

'I'm sure he'd love one.'

The only gifts Mac didn't need my help with were the two expensive bottles of aged malt whisky he bought for Alex and Todd and the construction kit he picked out for Connor.

'I always loved this kind of thing when I was a kid,' he said, carrying the enormous box over to the counter. 'I guess I've always been into building things.'

By the time we made our way back onto the street, the weather had worsened. The sky was the colour of pewter and the snowflakes were so large and persistent that they were settling on even the moving vehicles.

'Perhaps we should cut the day short?' I suggested, ignoring my growling stomach.

'That would be a shame,' Mac said. 'I managed to get us a table for lunch at Edmonds.'

I tried and failed not to look impressed. Edmonds had a reputation for excellent food, great wine and a waiting list for reservations. Behind its eighteenth-century townhouse exterior was an intimate dining area with rustic tables that were always lit by candles, even in the middle of the day. Not surprisingly, it was a popular choice for romantic first dates and marriage proposals.

'I thought we'd just be grabbing a sandwich from Pret,' I said, looking down at my jeans and jumper apologetically. 'I'm not really dressed for anywhere fancy.'

I felt Mac's eyes run over me like a scorch. 'You look fine. More than fine,' he corrected. 'You look lovely.' And then before things teetered into awkward, he spun the mood around 180 on a conversational skidpad 'And I don't think a sandwich is a fitting way to thank you for helping me today.'

The restaurant was only a few streets away, and although Mac offered to hail a taxi, I assured him I was happy to walk in the snow. Between the pulled-down bobble hat and the pulled-up scarf there was hardly any exposed skin. And yet the wind still managed to drive tiny icy crystals into my face, no doubt ruining the make-up I'd applied so carefully that morning.

We were one street away from the restaurant when I spotted something that made me tug on Mac's arm, which I'd been unashamedly hanging onto. It was too late to regret my choice of footwear, but the heels on my boots had left me as sure-footed as Bambi on the cobbled side streets.

'Is there time before our reservation to pop in here?' I asked, inclining my head towards the three-storey Tudor building which housed one of the biggest bookshops in the city.

'Of course,' he replied equably. 'Are you looking for something specific?'

He was holding the shop door open for me while shaking the snow from his hair, which the elements had turned the colour of mahogany. A few persistent flakes had settled on his eyelashes and were sparkling like diamond chips. I had a disturbingly strong urge to reach up and wipe them free.

'I've been trying to track down a book I remember reading when I was a child,' I explained, already heading towards the impressive wooden staircase. 'It's about a little boy who stows away on a rocket to the moon, and when he gets there he meets his grandfather who passed away before he was born. I thought it would be a lovely gift—'

'—for Connor,' Mac completed, his voice full of affection.

Our eyes locked in understanding. The links that had been forged between us felt as strong as ever.

'The book's been out of print for years, and the only copies I've managed to find online were ridiculously expensive. So I've taken to looking in every second-hand bookshop I happen to go past. I feel like I'm meant to find this book and give it to him.'

We'd paused at a turn in the stairs and I heard my words as though a stranger had spoken them. 'That sounds way more crazy than I thought it was going to.' I laughed nervously.

In reply, Mac took hold of my hand, guiding me towards the next flight and following the signs to the pre-owned books section. 'It makes perfect sense to me,' he said quietly.

That was when I realised how badly I wanted to kiss him.

CHAPTER THIRTY-ONE

Molly

There's a smell to old books that someone really ought to bottle. It took me instantly back to my childhood and long school holidays spent in the dusty storeroom of the local library where Mum worked. It was the place where a sometimes lonely, shy little girl had found friends at a school for wizards and travelled back in time to drink ginger beer and solve mysteries with five imaginary pals.

It was no surprise that books went on to play a significant part in my chosen career. Storytime was, and always would be, my favourite part of the teaching day.

I left Mac browsing the section on historical architecture and promised that I wouldn't be long. I realised that might have been a tad over-optimistic when I discovered the pre-loved children's books weren't shelved in alphabetical order. There were so many titles from my childhood calling out to me that it was a genuine struggle to ignore them. Among them were plenty I'd have loved to read again, but none was the story I was looking for. Eventually I gave a resigned sigh; it was always going to be a long shot.

I zigzagged back to where I'd left Mac, checking the shelves as I passed. I was about four stacks away when I realised he was talking to someone. I couldn't make out his words at first, but there was something about the tone of his voice that stopped me in my tracks; it sounded taut, like an excessively tightened guitar string about to snap. I strained my ears to listen.

'I didn't know I was meant to,' I heard him say.

'It would have been nice if you'd asked me. After all, I was there the whole time you were designing it.'

'And then you weren't,' Mac added pointedly.

It didn't take a genius to work out the identity of the unseen woman. It had to be his ex-girlfriend, Carrie. And from the sounds of it, she seemed to think she should have been invited to his recent opening ceremony. I was truly indignant – and I didn't even know the woman.

'You made it perfectly clear, Carrie, that you wanted a clean break.' Mac's voice was cool and even.

There was a long silence and I was afraid they'd be able to hear me breathing. This was definitely the kind of conversation I shouldn't be overhearing. It was private and painful – maybe not for her, but I could hear it in Mac's voice.

'We were together for a very long time,' the woman reminded him, her voice low, like a purr.

'Things are different now,' Mac said, guillotining that line of conversation before it could be taken any further.

'You're looking good, Mac; really well.'

I heard the click of heels on the wooden floor and guessed she must have just closed the gap between them. Curiosity is a dreadful thing. It kills cats and makes otherwise sensible school teachers attempt to crane around the corner of what had appeared to be a sturdily stacked pile of books. They wobbled teasingly on the shelf before falling to the floor in a cacophony of thumps, sending up small puffs of dust as they landed.

There was nothing for it but to step out from behind the book stacks and pretend I hadn't just been blatantly eavesdropping on their very personal conversation.

Their heads were already turned my way when I emerged, their gazes pinioning me like a convict caught in a prison yard searchlight.

'Molly,' said Mac, his entire tone changing when he spoke my name.

I gave a 'who else?' comical shrug and an apologetic smile.

I tried really hard not to stare at the woman who had broken Mac's heart, but it was difficult. She was the kind of beautiful that could have made even Kyra look plain. Her hair was long, with a sheen I thought existed only in conditioner commercials. I clocked the huge almond-shaped eyes and the mouth painted with brilliant red lipstick before forcing myself to look only at Mac.

There was something in his eyes, a message he was trying to convey. I blinked dazedly. Was I reading this right? If not, I was about to make a huge fool of myself. I inhaled and decided to follow my instincts.

I allowed a huge smile to transform my face as I hurried towards him.

'Sorry, hon,' I said fondly, slipping my hand through the crook of his arm and looking up into his face. 'That took way longer than I thought. Have I made us late for lunch?'

For just a heartbeat I wondered if I'd got it wrong, but then the muscles in his arm tightened, pulling me even closer against his side.

'Not at all. We're fine,' he said, inclining his head towards mine. The smell of old books was drowned out by his aftershave. It was the one he'd been wearing on the night he drove me home from the planetarium. My subconscious had obviously decided to store the memory.

As though I'd only just noticed we weren't alone, I turned to the woman standing before us.

'Hello,' I said, making sure my voice was cheery and unconcerned.

Her eyes had narrowed slightly and were clearly begging for an explanation. I was happy to leave that one to Mac.

'Carrie, this is my girlfriend, Molly. Molly, this is Carrie.' No descriptor was added to her name, and I could tell she didn't like that.

If looks could have killed, I would have been a lost cause, but this new heart of mine was proving to be a great deal braver than my old one. I held out my hand. It took an awfully long time before she took it.

'Nice to meet you,' I lied.

She was unnerved; that much was obvious. Ignoring me, she turned to Mac. 'I didn't realise you were seeing someone.'

In response, Mac repositioned his arm, to loop it around my shoulders. His body felt warm against mine. One of us was trembling slightly, and I'm pretty sure it was me.

'Molly and I have been together for a while now,' he said.

Those huge tawny-coloured eyes swivelled towards me. 'How did you two meet?'

The arm around my shoulders tensed, telling me all I needed to know. Mac didn't want Carrie to learn about our connection with Lisa, or Alex. That was fine with me.

'Mac almost ran me over when I was collecting—'

'—conkers,' we said in unison, looking at each other and laughing, as though we really were a couple.

This seemed to rob Carrie of a response and Mac made good use of the moment. He glanced at his watch and made an apologetic face.

'We really ought to get going, babe, if we're going to make our reservation.'

His hand had fallen from my shoulder, but it immediately reached for my free one as we turned towards the stairs.

'Is that the time?' Carrie asked in that bizarre way people do when they've just looked at their watch. She'd made a big show of pulling back the sleeve of her jacket to reveal a very expensive timepiece. Mac's eyes flickered, and I knew with absolute certainty it had been a gift from him.

He led me towards the stairs and I went willingly, happy to leave Carrie standing by the balustrade. We were halfway down when she called out her parting shot.

'Give me a ring sometime, Mac, so we can catch up properly.'

I might only have been a temporary, pretend girlfriend, but that riled me more than I'd expected. *I am right here, woman. Right here.*

The snowstorm had intensified further, so I stopped to pull on my hat and scarf again. Mac's eyes flicked upwards, and I imagined his ex was still staring down at us. Which was why I made no protest when he reached across to fasten my scarf more securely around me and tuck away a few loose strands of hair that had escaped from my hat. His hands dropped to the two trailing scarf ends and taking hold of them he gently pulled me towards him. His lips were soft as they pressed a kiss on my forehead. I smiled up at him, playing my part the way I imagined he wanted me to. As he turned to hold open the door, I threw a quick backward glance over my shoulder up to the balcony. It was empty. Carrie was nowhere to be seen.

'I owe you a huge apology,' Mac said as soon as the waiter who'd shown us to our table disappeared with our coats.

I leant closer towards him, mindful of the flickering candle in its wax-encrusted bottle between us. Given my clumsiness on previous occasions, I could hardly blame him for shifting it out of my way. I smiled. Whatever Mac felt he had to apologise for, it certainly wasn't the venue he'd picked for our lunch. There was a Dickensian charm to the restaurant, with its scrubbed wooden floors, low-beamed ceiling and walls haphazardly crammed with vintage prints. Plus our table was surely the best in the restaurant, nestled in a cosy bay window that looked out onto the street. Outside, the storm raged on, but through the mullioned glass panes it was like peering into a vigorously shaken snow globe.

Conversation had been virtually impossible as we'd hurried through the cobbled streets from the bookstore. The wind would have whipped our words away like confetti in a hurricane. It was only now, in the warmth and seclusion of the restaurant, that what had happened in the bookshop could be discussed.

'I acted like a complete idiot. What I did was incredibly immature and disrespectful. I'm sorry for dragging you into it, Molly.'

He sounded truly mortified, as though having me pose as his faux girlfriend for a few minutes had crossed an unforgivable line. I rapidly replayed the scene in my head but could see nothing that warranted that level of remorse.

'That's okay. I was happy to play along.' *More than happy*, a voice in my head silently acknowledged.

'Well, you should never have had to.' Mac took a long swallow from his glass of water, as though something had left a bad taste in his mouth. 'You like to think you're past all the petty resentments and recriminations,' he continued, 'that you've grown and learnt something about yourself.' His small laugh was tinged with irony. 'And then you get caught on the hop and start acting like a teenager hell-bent on scoring points, and worse than that, you risk messing up a good friendship.'

'Really, Mac, it's not a big deal,' I assured him, wondering how inappropriate it would be if I reached for his hand and gave it a reassuring squeeze. I was extremely glad I'd done nothing of the sort as he continued with a regretful look in his eyes.

'There's a connection between the four of us that goes beyond anything I can explain. It's complex and unique. We're the legacy of a woman we never even met, and I'm not sure how appropriate it would be to allow things to get more complicated than that.'

I needed no further explanation. A door I'd only just realised I'd like to open was being slammed shut. Mac's words fell with the devastation of a bomb and there was only one way to defuse them.

'Well, I hope you intend to let Barbara down gently, because I'm pretty sure she's planning to either marry or adopt you.'

Mac's laugh was impossible to ignore. It drew eyes towards us, and expressions softened as people looked our way. They were reaching a thousand conclusions about us, and every single one of them was wrong.

Instinctively I knew that under different circumstances we could have been so much more. But fate had entrenched us so firmly in the Friend Zone, we might as well have been cemented there. Thoughts of kissing Mac, of how natural his hand had felt in mine, were dangerous and inappropriate, and I was going to have to work much harder at suppressing them. From now on they would be a guilty, middle-of-the-night secret that I'd share with no one but my conscience.

Three delicious courses and a glass of Baileys later – well, it was almost Christmas – Mac discreetly asked the waiter for the bill. He swiped it off the silver platter with the dexterity of a magician, shaking his head slightly when I determinedly reached for my purse.

'I promised you lunch,' he reminded me with a smile. I might have challenged him, but he totally threw me with a question I hadn't seen coming.

'Do you see much of your ex, Tom?'

I was amazed he'd remembered Tom's name. Perhaps though, after bumping into Carrie, it wasn't such an unexpected question.

'No. I wish him well, but we're different people now than when we first got together. In fact, a good friend of mine found his profile on a dating site not that long ago, so he's definitely moved on.'

Mac was studying me carefully, as though past hurts might have left their mark on my face. I held his gaze without flinching because it truly didn't upset me any more. And if I was honest, perhaps it never really had.

'Perhaps that's something I should think about. What happened with Carrie today is a timely reminder that I'm not going to trip over a new partner randomly.'

Like in a hospital car park, you mean? For a horrifying moment I thought I'd actually said those words out loud, but as Mac was still smiling easily in my direction, I guessed I hadn't.

'Maybe I'll join a dating site,' he said.

It was all I could do to swallow the Baileys down without choking in panic. I couldn't imagine anyone coming across Mac's profile and swiping left instead of right. It shouldn't have mattered to me this much – and yet it did.

CHAPTER THIRTY-TWO

Alex

It was always going to be shit, Alex knew that. He'd read enough about bereavement to know the first twelve months were one long succession of horrible firsts. The first Christmas without Lisa ran true to form and was every bit as horrendous as he'd imagined it would be.

As in previous years, he and Connor spent the day with Todd and Dee. But that empty place at their dining room table robbed him of his appetite. Beneath the Christmas tree in the lounge there was the usual mountain of presents for the children. Maisie tore through hers as though in training for an Olympic event, with scarcely time to see what she'd been given before reaching for the next gift. Connor was considerably slower, picking laboriously away at the Sellotape and ribbons and pretending to look delighted at his pile of toys, while fooling no one.

Alex sat on the settee watching his son, a mulled wine in his hands and sadness in his eyes. He'd spent more than they'd ever done before on Connor's presents, knowing all the while that the thing he wanted most was something he couldn't give him.

It was a truth that had been brought home to him just a week before. Connor had spent the day with Dee and Maisie, allowing Alex to devote some time to meetings at the office. Dee was busily chopping vegetables for their evening meal when Alex wandered into the kitchen to collect his son. She raised her head to greet him, her eyes as red as her hair.

'Onions?' he asked, swiping a carrot stick from the pile on the board, before noticing the onions were actually still waiting to be peeled and sliced.

Dee shook her head, wiping the back of one hand furiously over her cheek. There was a part of Alex that had already guessed why she was crying, even before she explained.

'I took the kids to the garden centre this afternoon. You know, the one across town that has the really great Father Christmas grotto?'

Alex nodded, realising where this story was going, and not liking it.

'Maisie typically took twice as long as all the other kids giving Santa her wish list.' Dee smiled, even though her eyes were again filling with tears. 'And then it was Connor's turn.'

Alex was leaning against the kitchen units. Though he was making a big effort to appear relaxed, the tension was thrumming within him, like power through a pylon. At his sides, his hands were balled tightly into fists.

'The queue had built up while Maisie was wittering on. I guess everyone was hoping Connor wasn't going to take as long as she had.'

Alex saw the scene in his head as clearly as if he'd been there. He almost told Dee she didn't need to finish her story – he already knew how it was going to end.

'Connor looked so serious when it was his turn. And when the guy asked him what he wanted for Christmas, he said… He said…' Dee was having trouble getting the words past the lump in her throat.

'That he wanted his mummy to come home,' Alex completed.

Dee nodded dumbly and reached for a handful of tissues from the box on the worktop. 'Santa just about held it together, but both of the elves were crying, as were half the mums waiting in the queue.' She blew her nose noisily. 'It was carnage in the grotto.'

Alex crossed the room in two quick strides and enveloped her in a huge hug, which was every bit as much for him as it was for her.

'He still thinks she's coming back for him,' Dee whispered sadly into his shirt front.

'I know,' Alex said into the ruffled mess of her hair. 'Lisa made a promise to him before she left the house on that last morning.'

'About taking him to the Astronomy Fair?'

'Yes. Until we get past that day, I don't think he's ever going to accept she's not coming back.'

It was two days after Christmas, in the wasteland period before New Year's Eve – another date on the calendar which Alex was already dreading. A compilation of previous celebrations kept running through his head, from boozy parties in the pre-Connor days to quiet nights beside the fireplace, sharing a bottle of wine and a lingering kiss as one year transitioned into the next. Alex closed his eyes, shutting out the brightly lit kitchen, and could almost feel the heat of Lisa's skin against his body once more; her breath mingling with his; her heart pounding in tandem with his own. *With every beat of my heart.* He groaned softly.

A knock on the front door was a very welcome interruption. Alex's footsteps quickened as he walked the length of the hallway and saw a slight figure through the frosted glass panel. He'd been trying very hard to banish all thoughts of Molly over the last few weeks, but it was startling how quickly she'd leapfrogged straight into his head. She was still very much on his mind as he opened the door, and it threw him that she wasn't the caller waiting on his doorstep. It took him a moment to swiftly rearrange his features into a more appropriate expression.

'Barbara, this is a lovely surprise,' he exclaimed, bending down and kissing her soft, powdered cheek. Her trademark smell of lily of the valley filled his senses as she hugged him.

'Come in out of the cold,' he urged, stepping back to usher her into his home. But she seemed oddly reluctant. 'Is something wrong?' he asked, his heart skipping a beat in panic. 'Are you feeling well? Is there a problem?'

The four lives Lisa had changed were immediately in his thoughts. He caught a fleeting glimpse of his future and knew he was always going to worry about them. Not just because Lisa lived on through them, but because he'd come to genuinely care about each of them.

'Not wrong, exactly,' Barbara said, looking decidedly uncomfortable. 'Although I am a little worried about how you're going to react. I have a feeling you might not be very happy with me.'

Alex gave a small laugh. It was impossible to imagine this sweet old lady doing anything he'd disapprove of. 'What have you done – robbed a bank?' he teased.

Barbara was giving him only half her attention; the rest was focused on something she'd positioned just out of sight beside his door. 'If only it was that simple,' she said mysteriously, nervously biting on her lower lip.

Alex was starting to get concerned now. 'Barbara, whatever it is, I'm here for you. You know that. If there's a problem, if something's bothering you, we can figure it out together.'

His words of reassurance brought a smile to her worried face. 'Oh good. I really hope you remember saying that, Alex, my dear, because I've brought you a little something.'

She bent down to retrieve the little something, but before she'd moved it across his threshold, a small mewling cry told him all he needed to know.

'Oh no,' he said, looking down at the cardboard pet carrier Barbara had placed on his mat.

From within the box came a determined scratching sound. The container vibrated on the coconut mat, making the huge red rosette tied to its handle jiggle up and down.

'No, Barbara,' Alex repeated, trying not to sound like the very worst version of Scrooge as he shook his head from side to side. 'We do not need or want a kitten in this house.'

He'd always thought her eyes were soft, the colour of bluebells in spring, but right now they'd taken on the steely glint of gunmetal as she lifted them to his.

'This isn't for you, Alex. It's for Connor,' she said pointedly.

He glanced back over his shoulder, making sure Connor was nowhere around. Thankfully, he was obviously still upstairs, playing in his bedroom. Alex opened his mouth to speak, every objection already lined up and waiting to be fired. But Barbara cleverly shot him down in flames before he could voice them.

'Do you think I might come in after all, Alex dear? It's a bit cold for my old bones standing out here.'

Alex was being played. He knew that, but there was no way he was going to let Barbara win this one. His life felt as though it was in permanent disarray, and looking after Connor and himself took up all of his energy; he simply didn't have the mental capacity to take responsibility for another living being.

Barbara slipped off her coat and handed it to him. She had him wrong-footed and she knew it. He hung her coat up, realising she'd probably been planning this little surprise for quite a while. He cast one last glance up the staircase before saying quietly, 'Let's go into the kitchen to talk.'

She followed him meekly enough. *Oh yeah, like butter wouldn't melt in her mouth*, he thought, bending to reposition the pet carrier in a far less prominent position beneath the coat rack.

Barbara was sitting at his kitchen table waiting for him. He opened his mouth to speak, but she raised her hand in objection, silencing him.

'I am not a dotty old lady.'

Alex was about to protest that he'd never said she was, but she powered ahead before he could interrupt.

'I am a responsible pet owner and have cared for enough unwanted strays in my life to never foist an animal on a home where it wasn't wanted – or needed.'

'Well, there you are then,' interjected Alex, as quick as a missile as she drew in a breath. 'Thank you for thinking of us, Barbara, but I'm afraid this cat would be very much *un*wanted.'

'Cats are not toys; they are not something you should casually give away like a box of chocolates or a bunch of flowers. They have feelings and need love, care and attention.'

Alex was on the point of saying his well of those particular commodities had pretty much run dry, but she was talking again, this time with a noticeable quaver in her voice.

'But sometimes, Alex, we need things in our lives without even realising it. Connor needs this cat. He needs it to help him out of the terrible dark place he's in right now because of losing his mummy. He's a very confused little boy, Alex.'

Embarrassingly, Alex could feel his eyes beginning to smart with tears. He could hear the emotion in his voice as he whispered hoarsely, 'I know that. Of course I do.'

'I know this is going to sound a little batty, but there is something inside me, something I simply can't explain, that is telling me that this is absolutely the right thing to do to help Connor. I trust this feeling, this voice, and I'm hoping and praying you will too.'

She'd made a compelling case, but Alex wasn't even close to wavering.

'I just don't think that now is the right time for us to—'

He broke off suddenly as the kitchen door opened and Connor walked into the room, a snow-white bundle of fur cradled in his arms. Alex recognised it as the kitten Connor had bonded with when they'd visited Barbara's house.

'Whose kitten is this?' Connor breathed, his voice full of something Alex hadn't heard there for a very long time. Hope.

It wasn't Barbara's compelling and heartfelt speech, or even the impossible situation she'd put him in. It was the expression on Connor's face as he lifted his eyes and looked with desperate longing at his father.

Alex's voice sounded thick as he crossed the room and laid his hand gently on his son's shoulder.

'It's yours, Connor. The kitten is yours.'

Forty-five minutes later, after the world's fastest crash course in feline husbandry, Barbara was preparing to leave. In the middle of Alex's kitchen floor was a pile of supplies that he'd helped Barbara retrieve from the boot of her neighbour's car.

'It was so kind of Terry to drive me over today,' Barbara said chirpily as they walked back into the house carrying a pet bed, a litter tray and a selection of kitten food between them.

'Are you sure he wouldn't like to come in?' Alex asked worriedly as he cast a backward glance at the car.

'Oh, no. He said he'd rather listen to the sport programme on the radio.' She dropped her voice as though revealing a rather unsavoury character flaw. 'I don't think Terry likes cats very much.'

Alex nearly said he quite sympathised with the man, but Barbara was looking so ridiculously pleased with how events had panned out, he didn't want to burst her bubble. And then there was Connor, kneeling on the kitchen floor, waggling a feather-tipped toy at the cat with the kind of delight on his face that none of Alex's expensive Christmas gifts had been able to put there.

'Have you decided what you're going to call her?' Barbara asked Connor, bending down to his level and watching with approval as he played with the new arrival with infinite gentleness.

Connor looked up, turning not to Barbara but to Alex for approval. 'I'm going to call her Lunar, because she's white like the moon, and because I think Mummy would have liked that name.'

It was the first time Alex had heard Connor speak about Lisa in the past tense and it got to him in a way that made his voice sound oddly gruff. 'I think she would have liked it very much. Lunar it is, then.'

Barbara left soon after, reaching up to give Alex a long hard hug as he stood beside her at the front door.

'You've done a wonderful thing today, Alex. I am very proud of you.'

He hugged her back just as warmly, suddenly not wanting her to go. This had nothing to do with not knowing how to care for their newest family member. He was touched by her words and a little bit proud of himself as well. But more importantly, he felt sure that Lisa would have been proud of him too.

CHAPTER THIRTY-THREE

Molly

New Year's Eve. A time for celebration, I reminded myself, as I wandered the aisles of my local supermarket, which looked as though locusts had recently descended. The shelves were as depleted as the ones in my own fridge, which was precisely why I was on a shopping excursion while the rest of the city was getting ready to party.

Twelve months ago I'd seriously thought I might never get to sing another chorus of 'Auld Lang Syne', so part of me was determined to celebrate that I was still here, and healthy once again. So what did it matter if I didn't have anyone to see the New Year in with? That's why they put Jools Holland and his *Hootenanny* on the telly. The old Scottish word for 'party' made me smile, and oddly also conjured up an image of Mac in my head. I unravelled the connection as I remembered him confessing that Scotland was his favourite place to celebrate Hogmanay. Had he travelled to Edinburgh to spend the holiday with Andi, I wondered. A shiver danced down the length of my spine, and not just because I was standing beside the chiller cabinet.

Well, I was celebrating too, I acknowledged with a determined nod of my head as I reached for a packet of party food and threw it into my basket alongside the bottle of champagne and the box of chocolates already in there.

I'd fleetingly considered asking Alex what he was doing later, but good sense had kicked in before I'd made the call. Alex's thoughts would naturally be focused on Lisa tonight, and the last thing he'd want would be to spend the evening with someone who was only here because the woman he loved was not.

The tray of party food was on the worktop, waiting for the oven to heat up, and the champagne was nestled on a rack in my fridge. As I waited for my kitchen appliances to do their job, I ran a deep sudsy bath and slipped into the perfumed water, telling myself I was perfectly happy to spend the last five hours of the year alone.

There were friends who I could have called, I acknowledged as I sank into the bubbles, though I hadn't seen much of the old crowd over the last year or so. When Tom and I separated, I was surprised to discover that our friends fell into 'his' and 'hers' categories. Like the toaster, the lava lamp neither of us liked, and the crazily expensive wine rack, our mutual friends were divvied up when we went our different ways. I was a little hurt that more had gone with him than had stayed with me. *But at least I kept the lamp*, I reminded myself as I slid beneath the suds to rinse my hair. *And my sense of humour*, I added with a smile, wiping the bubbles from my ears.

The bathwater was beginning to cool and my fingertips were turning wrinkly as I stepped from the tub, my limbs slippery from the suds. I reached for my towelling robe, pausing before cinching it around me. A few bubbles lingered on my chest, effectively hiding my scar. I watched in the mirror as I wiped them away, revealing the line that bisected my breasts. I ran one finger thoughtfully along it, as though it was a raised relief-map charting the journey I'd been on.

New Year's Eve is a night of resolutions, and although I was five hours early, one came to me then. From now on I would no longer allow myself to feel embarrassed about the blemishes on my body. I'd spent so much time and energy trying to hide my scar, I'd been blind to the fact that it was the mark of a miracle. It was also a reminder that a woman I'd never met had given me the greatest gift I'd ever receive.

With determination I strode into the bedroom and reached for the floral make-up bag filled with the collection of concealers I used each day to hide something I should have been displaying proudly. *No more*, I promised myself as I upended the bag. As the cosmetics clattered noisily into the bin, they sounded like the breaking links of a chain.

The euphoric smile remained on my face as I combed and dried my hair, which typically went perfectly, the way it only did when I wasn't going anywhere.

It was only when I went to slip my mobile into my pocket that I discovered I'd missed two calls. Both were from Mac. *He's probably just phoning to wish me Happy New Year before his evening gets too messy and he forgets*, I told myself. Although the idea of Mac being anything other than in full control was too big a stretch for my imagination. I sat down on the edge of the bed and stared at his name on my phone's screen as though if I looked at it long enough, I'd be able to intuit what he'd wanted.

I was still deliberating whether to call him back when the phone vibrated in my palm. Surprise made me clumsy and the mobile slipped from my fingers. *Three calls in an hour?* Was something wrong? Concern robbed my voice of its usual friendliness as I retrieved the phone and jabbed at the tick icon to answer his call.

'Yes?'

'Oh, hello, Molly. It's Mac.'

I strained my ears for the sound of a party in the background but could hear nothing.

'Is something wrong? I just saw that I'd missed a couple of calls from you.'

There was an unfamiliar note in his voice, and it took me a moment or two to place it. Embarrassment. It was hidden ineffectively beneath an unsure laugh.

'No. Everything's fine. I… I just had something I wanted to ask you…' He paused, and the strain of waiting for him to finish his sentence felt like torture. 'Only I'm sure it's a totally ludicrous question. And the more I think about it, the more certain I am that your answer will be "No".'

'What is it you want to ask?' Looking down, I saw I'd unconsciously crossed my fingers. How stupid was I going to feel if Mac's question wasn't the one I was hoping to hear? But, unbelievably, it was.

'I was just wondering if you'd made plans for tonight. Which now that I hear it out loud, is just ridiculous. Of course you'll have something planned. Why wouldn't you?' It was so unusual to hear him sounding anything less than composed, I took far too long to reply. 'I'm sorry, it was silly to expect you'd be free tonight.'

'No,' I said, a little breathlessly.

'No, you're not free?'

'No, I don't have any plans for tonight,' I said, making no attempt to play it cool. 'I was actually planning on spending the evening alone with the TV.'

He was smiling now. I could hear it in his voice. 'Is that an idea you're prepared to reconsider? Because if it is, I'd really like to see out the old year with a new friend.'

Okay, I thought with a rueful smile. I heard the message hidden not so subtly within the invitation, but it did nothing to slow my pulse rate. Presumably Mac's original plans for the evening had fallen through, and inviting me was Plan B. I was probably only one call higher up the list than Barbara or Jamie. But I didn't care.

As I stood before my open wardrobe trying to decide what to wear, I realised how little appeal there'd been in having to spend the evening alone. Even though I knew this would be a

totally platonic date, excitement trilled through me. My hand
skimmed over the row of hangers on the rail, considering and
rejecting every outfit until it settled on a dress hidden beneath a
plastic cover. I'd bought it over a year earlier but had never had
an occasion to wear it; more recently, I'd not had the confidence
either. The fabric was soft, the type that found my curves and
clung determinedly to them. The dress was a shade of red that
turned heads for all the right reasons, with long, tight sleeves
and an off-the-shoulder neckline that dipped into a plunging V.
I slipped it on and then surveyed my reflection critically. There
did seem to be an awful lot of creamy skin on display, and for a
second I glanced longingly at the jumble of concealers in my bin.
I shook my head. I hadn't imagined my new resolution would
be tested quite this soon, but I was determined not to break it
before midnight even came around.

A quick brush of smoky grey on my eyelids and a slick of scarlet
gloss – the same shade as the dress – on my lips, and I was done.
The girl in the mirror was someone I hadn't bumped into in quite
a long time, and to be honest it was rather nice to see her again.

The Uber driver kept up a constant stream of chatter on the
drive to Mac's apartment, which thankfully left me no time to
reflect on the evening ahead. When the car pulled up at the kerb
beside an impressive modern development, my jaw dropped in a
very uncool way. Dense, floodlit shrubbery flanked a porticoed
entrance, where the name of the building was carved into a black
granite block.

I climbed from the car, cradling the chilled champagne I'd
plucked from my fridge as my eyes travelled up the building.
Each apartment had a large wraparound balcony, and my gaze
settled on the one on the top floor. From within Mac's flat, yellow
lights glowed invitingly. With a heart that was beating a little too

fast, I crossed the pavement and pressed the button beside the plate-glass doors.

My heels clipped out a staccato rhythm as I crossed the polished stone of the entrance foyer, and four nervous Mollys then stared back at me from the walls of the lift; all of them looked startled to find Mac waiting for me in the top-floor corridor. Was there any chance at all that he hadn't seen me practising my 'relaxed' smile of greeting as the doors slid apart? From the tell-tale twitch of his lips, I doubted it.

He bent to graze my cheek with a friendly peck, and the hand he placed amiably on my shoulder made a mockery of the fledgling fantasies I'd been indulging in on the ride over.

Mac's home could have been lifted straight out of the pages of a glossy magazine – the aspirational kind I only ever read in the dentist's waiting room. I could tell at a glance that the Swedish retail warehouse where I'd furnished most of my rooms had played very little part in Mac's decor. That cream leather sofa alone had probably cost more than I made in six months, and the rich patina of the walnut floor was definitely not a laminate. And yet for all the luxury and elegance, the flat was still welcoming, in a masculine way. If Carrie had had any input in its design, Mac must have removed all evidence after their break-up. *Good*, I thought somewhat childishly.

'Can I take your coat?'

Although 'no' wasn't really an acceptable answer, it was definitely the one I wanted to give. The dress I'd chosen screamed 'date' rather than a casual evening with a friend, and my gaffe was going to be obvious the minute I slipped off my coat. Mac's own black jeans and soft grey marl T-shirt were far more suitable, although the way the fabric emphasised his biceps whenever he moved was an unexpectedly disturbing distraction.

He was waiting patiently, one hand extended, and short of telling him I was feeling chilly and would like to keep my coat on, I had no option but to remove it. My fingers trembled as they forced reluctant buttons through holes that seemed to have shrunk since I left home. My attention was fixed on Mac's face as I slipped the coat from my shoulders. His eyes flickered, but it was impossible to tell if that was due to the expanse of cleavage on show or the scar that ran through it. I forced myself to stand taller and own that this was me now.

'You look lovely,' he said, and for a moment there was an expression of admiration on his face I don't think I was meant to see. It was so fleeting there was no time to process it before he hid it away behind a neutral smile.

'Thank you.'

He'd taken my bottle of modest supermarket champagne with delight, as if I'd brought along vintage Dom Pérignon. 'Shall we save this for midnight?' he asked, turning towards a modern kitchen with glossy cupboard doors and sliding it into the fridge.

I nodded as my eyes took a 360-degree journey around the place he called home.

The open-plan layout was spacious enough that even the baby grand piano in the corner didn't make it look cramped. A wall of sliding glass doors led out onto the balcony, and it was easy to imagine city sunsets on warm summer evenings, with a glass of wine in hand. The only thing wrong with that image was the lingering spectre of Carrie, which I couldn't seem to erase.

'You have an incredible view from up here,' I said, mesmerised by the lights of the city twinkling below us like a laser show.

'That was the main reason I bought this place,' Mac said, a small laugh chasing his words. 'Although, ironically, for half the time I've lived here I couldn't actually see it. A view like this was wasted on a guy slowly losing his sight.'

Mac rarely spoke about the period when his failing eyesight had gradually stolen his life away, one piece at a time, taking his job, his independence and finally his girlfriend from him. Even now, when it was all in the past, I could hear the emotion in his voice.

Never had I wanted to hug someone more than I did Mac right then. In case the impulse proved too hard to resist, I crossed the room to stand before a modern gas fire with extremely realistic-looking flames. Mac must have moved to join me with the stealth of a cat burglar, because I had no idea he was standing right behind me when I stepped back and somehow managed to tread on his foot with one very pointed stiletto heel.

'Oh God, Mac, I'm so sorry,' I said as he gave a muffled sound containing a very earthy Anglo Saxon exclamation. 'Are you okay? Did I hurt you?'

I instinctively dropped to my knees to examine his injury, as though he were one of my pupils who'd fallen in the playground. Thankfully I could see no blood staining his pale grey sock, but that didn't mean I hadn't punctured his skin with my weapons-grade heel.

'I'm fine,' he said, holding out his hand to me. 'It's nothing, honestly.'

I took the hand and allowed him to pull me back up to my feet. The manoeuvre brought us so close, I could feel the warmth of his body through his T-shirt. Like a guilty trespasser, I quickly retreated out of his personal space.

'I've no idea why I'm like this around you,' I said with an embarrassed laugh. 'Believe it or not, I'm not usually clumsy.'

'Perhaps I make you nervous?'

I swallowed a gulp. 'No, I don't think that's it.'

He gave an easy shrug and changed the topic, although the one he opted for was almost as uncomfortable.

'Well, notwithstanding my broken foot, I just want to say how glad I am that you could come this evening. It's been quite a year, and I can't think of anyone I'd rather kiss it goodbye with.'

My cheeks flushed, and with an honesty I'd probably regret later, I spoke from the heart.

'Nor me.'

He bit his lip as though trying to stop his next comment from escaping, but it found a way. 'I felt sure Alex would have beaten me to it.'

His comment was like a casually thrown grenade, and my mouth opened and closed like a goldfish as I sought for and rejected several replies. I was still no closer to picking one when the trilling of Mac's phone offered me a reprieve.

He glanced down at the screen and gave an apologetic smile. 'I'm sorry, Molly. Do you mind if I take this?'

I shook my head, more than glad of the interruption.

'Andi,' he exclaimed, his voice so warm I could practically feel the temperature in the room shoot up a few degrees. Not wanting him to think I was eavesdropping, I wandered towards the windows and tried to distract myself with the view.

Mac's comment about Alex was troubling on many levels. Did everyone think the same thing? It was getting harder and harder to dismiss the suspicion that Alex continued to look for his wife in me. I shivered, despite the heat of the room. If that was really what was happening, surely the kindest thing I could do for everyone was to walk away? But doing that would mean I'd lose all contact with not just Alex but also Connor. The thought of never seeing either of them again filled me with an irrational dread. I rested my head against the cool glass of Mac's windows, as though in need of a compress to ward off a migraine.

'Are you okay?' Mac called across the room.

I found a smile and pasted it in place before turning to face him. 'I'm fine.'

'Andi said hi,' he said easily.

'That was nice of her.' And then as though I'd lost all ability to filter my thoughts before they popped out of my mouth: 'Actually, I imagined you'd be spending New Year's Eve with her.'

Mac looked genuinely puzzled. 'Really? I think that would probably be the last thing they'd want and playing third wheel doesn't really appeal to me.'

'Third wheel?'

'Her fiancé Scott is home for the holidays and until his assignment in Japan is over, we all know better than to intrude on their time together.'

'Oh,' I said, only just managing to hide my grin.

'And besides,' added Mac, 'I already said *you* were the person I'd like to see the year out with.' There was absolutely no way of hiding the grin this time, so I didn't even try.

'Fancy helping me prepare our dinner?' he asked, picking up a very large chopping knife and then pretending to look worried. 'How safe are we if we put this in your hands?'

It was just the antidote I needed. I answered with a beam and crossed the room to the kitchen area. 'Let's chance it,' I said. 'Put me to work.'

It had been a long time since I'd shared a kitchen, and I'd forgotten how companionable it was to prepare a meal with someone. The kitchen was well laid out but compact, and we moved around each other with smooth, effortless choreography, as though we'd done this many times before.

Twenty minutes later Mac carried our two steaming plates of pasta to the table, while I followed him with the wine and glasses.

'This looks wonderful,' I declared. I felt a bit like a *MasterChef* judge as he watched me spear a mouthful of his signature dish, spaghetti carbonara, onto my fork, waiting for my verdict. I didn't normally have any trouble swallowing, but it was surprisingly hard to do so with his eyes fixed on my mouth.

I reached for my glass of wine and lifted it to him in a salute. 'Delicious.'

'Next time I'll make you my stroganoff,' he said, looking ridiculously pleased.

Next time. The words hung in the air between us; they felt like a promise, but not one I could imagine ever coming to pass.

Mac was as good a host as he was a cook, and as we passed from pasta to pavlova to coffee, the conversation flowed with ease. The stories of his student escapades were particularly hilarious, although it was hard to equate the responsible man I knew with the wild rule-breaker he'd apparently been fifteen years earlier. It also made me feel I'd frittered away too many of my own uni days in study halls and the library.

'I think that's actually what you're meant to do,' Mac said, his eyes twinkling with amusement as he got to his feet and began gathering up our plates.

'It just makes me sound so boring,' I said.

He was halfway to the kitchen, his arms stacked high with dishes, but he stopped to look back at me over his shoulder.

'You are many things, Molly Kendall, but boring is definitely not one of them.'

'Why don't you pick out some music for us to listen to?' Mac suggested as he began loading the dishwasher. With a glass of wine in hand, I headed for the impressive sound system, but a detour past his baby grand piano gave me a better idea.

'Would you play something for us instead?'

'Sibelius?' he asked with a crooked smile as he straightened up from his task. 'He's not known for his party tunes.'

I glanced at the sheet music on the stand. 'Maybe something a little livelier?'

His grin was my answer. 'There are some music books in the cabinet beside the piano. You should find a few jazz ones in there, with the kind of songs your dad would probably have enjoyed.'

My nose prickled and my eyes felt suddenly scratchy. Mac had remembered my dad's passion for jazz. It was such a small detail and it shouldn't have felt significant – but it did.

I dropped to my knees before the cupboard and began flicking through the eclectic music books in Mac's collection. My fingers had fastened on a volume with the word 'Jazz' on the cover when I saw something wedged in beside it. Something that looked out of place.

The clang of saucepans and clatter of cutlery meant Mac was still busy in the kitchen, but that was not an excuse for me to pluck the sketchpad from the cabinet. It was clearly not a musical score and none of my business. And yet the Pandora pull to look inside it was impossible to resist. I set down my wine glass and drew the book onto my lap.

Put it back. It's private, the Jiminy Cricket voice of my conscience whispered in my head. But something was stopping me, something that went way beyond normal nosiness.

From the turn of that first page, I was hooked. I'd assumed that, as an architect, Mac would be skilled at drawing, but I'd never imagined he'd be so good that the breath would catch in my throat as I gazed down at the first sketch.

It was as detailed and accurate as a photograph – no, it went even deeper than that. No amount of pixels could have captured the look in Connor's eyes in the way Mac's pencil had. The little boy was looking at something or someone in the distance with a fledgling smile on his lips. It was so realistic, I quickly flicked the page as though this was a cartoon sequence and his smile would hatch in the next drawing.

But the following page was different, depicting a collage of faces. Jamie and Barbara featured most prominently, but Dee and Todd were there too, and even Maisie. I knew without asking that none of the subjects had posed for these portraits. They were drawn from memory, and the level of detail was scarily accurate. Mac had an incredibly keen eye – or at least he did now.

I was breathing a little faster as I turned the page once again. There was no smile on the lips of this portrait, but Mac had captured Alex in deft strokes, rendering with heart-twisting poignancy the haunted expression Alex didn't realise others could see. Of their own volition, my fingers gently traced the contours of his face, as though in a caress.

I was unaware that the cacophony of clanging pots and pans had ceased. I had no idea Mac had left the kitchen and was standing directly behind me until his shadow fell across the page with Alex's face staring back at me. I jerked my hand away from the drawing as though I'd been burnt.

'I'd forgotten that was in there.' Mac's voice sounded strange – tight, in a way it hadn't done before. Was he embarrassed that I'd found the sketchpad?

'These are really good.'

Mac shrugged and his eyes were oddly shuttered.

'Are there more?' I asked, already turning the page before he could reply. I sensed he'd like nothing more than to pull the pad from my hands, if only he could find a way of doing so.

I had no idea why I was so shocked. Shouldn't I have been expecting this? Especially as every other member of our group had been drawn.

He'd made me beautiful in a way the mirror confirmed I'd never actually achieve. Unlike with the others, Mac had drawn me in a variety of mediums. I seemed most wistful in the charcoal ones. The pencil sketches were more accurate, so detailed that in the one where my eyes were closed beneath the sun's rays I could see the individual lashes on my cheeks. I looked truly at peace.

Drawings of me outnumbered the others by about five to one, and yet I was embarrassingly slow to realise how peculiar that was.

'How come there are so many of me?' I asked artlessly, and it wasn't until I saw his jaw clench that I realised it was the wrong question.

'You have a great face for portraits. The angles and lines of your bone structure are...' Mac looked as though he wanted to be somewhere else right then, very badly. 'You're easy to draw,' he concluded. There was something in his eyes that warned me not to press him further, and so I didn't.

My fingers were clumsy as I went to return the pad to the cabinet. It slipped from my hold, falling open on the final page at the back. Mac made a sound, not quite a laugh, but there was wry amusement in it. This drawing wasn't of a person, but that didn't make it any less dramatic. It depicted a storm-lashed pier.

'Where's this?' I asked.

Mac gave a twisted smile. 'Strangely, I don't know the name of the place, even though I've ended up there many times.'

I bent to study the sketch more closely. To one side of the pier I could make out a small amusement park. He'd even drawn the sleeper tracks of a miniature railway and one solitary carriage. But the main focus of Mac's picture was the long jetty engulfed in the kind of waves that swept away everything in their path.

'That's quite a wild storm you've drawn,' I observed, flicking back through the book and noting that he'd drawn this same scene several times over. In each version the dark grey sky was split by jagged shards of lightning.

'The weird thing is that the weather was always warm and balmy whenever I was there. This was the place I kept ending up on my middle-of-the-night drives when I went through that period of insomnia last summer.' He reached for the sketchpad and this time I offered no resistance. 'But I never saw the pier look like this, not in real life. I've no idea why I kept drawing it in a storm.'

I'd never been the type of girl who dated the guitar player in school. My teenage boyfriends were more likely to have joined the maths club than a rock band. Even Tom, who'd loved nothing better than to sing lustily in the shower, missed every other note he tried to hit. I'd never had anyone play to me before – just to me. I had no idea it would feel so intimate and intense.

'Serenade' is a word that had never entered my vocabulary before, but I could think of no other to describe the experience of having Mac play to me as the clock inched us closer to midnight. When he settled himself at the piano keyboard, I moved to the comfort of the settee and kicked off my shoes. The couch was as soft as chamois leather, and I curled up on it, tucking my legs beneath me like a contented cat.

The great thing about live music is that, by necessity, it halts all conversation, which after the awkward moments with the sketchpad was just what we needed to get the evening back on course. Even so, I found my thoughts returning to those drawings of me as the room filled with lilting jazz melodies. They were hard to dismiss. Was I reading too much into them? Perhaps it really was that I was easier to draw than the others?

Somewhere between the songs my father had loved and the ones Mac introduced me to that night, I began to relax again. Mac played every song in the book, moving seamlessly from one to the next as though doing a set in a club. I didn't speak or interrupt until the final notes of the last song were fading away, and then – cheesy as it was – I began to clap.

He smiled and shook his head in an it-was-nothing kind of way, but I could see my enthusiastic response had pleased him. His impromptu recital had taken us close to twelve o'clock, and I couldn't believe our night together was almost over.

'I want to shout "Encore!",' I told him, unfurling my legs and getting to my feet, 'but I think that's just being selfish. You must be tired of playing by now.'

'I could probably manage a few more,' he said with a smile, his fingers moving effortlessly back over the keys. He was playing from memory now, not following a score, and segued from classics to pop songs that spanned the decades. I leant against the piano, and while he never once looked at his hands, I was mesmerised by them.

'Thank you so much for playing for me,' I said when eventually he paused. 'I can't think of a lovelier way to end a year that hasn't been the easiest to get through.' As understatements go, that one was pretty huge.

'It *has* had its ups and downs,' Mac agreed. His fingers were absently picking out a melody, but his eyes were on me. 'But I wouldn't change anything. Although…' He hesitated. 'Although, there are times I wish I'd never met you—'

My mouth dropped open. That was definitely not what I'd expected him to say.

'—this way,' he added quickly. 'I wish I hadn't met you the way we did. I think, in other circumstances, things could have been very different.'

To ask how would have been disingenuous. It felt as though tonight was a chance to speak of things that might never be said again. I'd always found Mac's eyes compelling, but though I'd looked into them many times, he'd never before allowed me to glimpse in them what might have been. But I saw that now – saw everything that would never be, and it overwhelmed me.

I smiled shakily and moved away from the piano.

'I'm just going to use your bathroom, if that's okay?'

There's nothing more likely to kill a moment than telling someone you need the loo. Except that I didn't. But I did need the sanctuary of the neat white-tiled room to collect my racing thoughts. The large illuminated mirror above the basin showed my cheeks were stained with a becoming flush. The wine hadn't done that – Mac had. For the first time I allowed myself to admit just how much I liked him. My eyes glittered back at me as I slowly shook my head. Mac had drawn an indelible line of friendship in the sand and wasn't going to let us cross it.

I glanced at my watch. There were only ten minutes left until midnight. Mac had promised we'd get the best view of the city's fireworks display from his balcony. But if I lingered any longer in his bathroom I was going to miss them.

He was still tinkering at the piano when I returned. He looked up at the sound of my footsteps, his fingers instantly abandoning whatever he'd been playing. It had sounded vaguely familiar, but I'd only caught a few notes before he'd stopped. That one had been for him, not me. It was only as he slid open the balcony doors and ushered me out into the cool night air that I placed the tune. 'The Lady in Red'.

He'd brought my champagne out with us and popped the cork in preparation, pouring out two glasses. From the street below, the sound of revellers floated through the air towards us.

'I didn't mean to make you feel uncomfortable with what I said just now.'

I turned to face him. 'You didn't.'

'I just wanted you to know that if things had been different, if there weren't people who'd be hurt by my actions…'

I nodded. I understood. I truly did.

'Will this make things awkward between us?' Mac asked softly.

I smiled, wanting to erase that worried expression from his face. 'Nah. What happens on the balcony stays on the balcony.'

He smiled down at me, so tenderly that the cold December air seemed to stop nipping at my bare shoulders.

'Well, in that case,' he replied, his voice husky, 'I'm going to say something I probably shouldn't.'

The voices from the street were growing more and more excitable.

'I want to kiss you, Molly. I don't think I've ever wanted to kiss anyone more in my whole life. But it's not fair. And I don't even know if it's what you want.' He glanced at his watch. 'It's almost the countdown. So if this is something you don't want me to do, tell me now before the clock chimes.'

The seconds were ticking away and yet strangely time seemed to be standing still. From the pavement and the balconies below us, a chorus of voices began to chant. 'Ten, nine, eight…'

They got to 'seven' and I could bear it no longer. With a passion that shocked me, I reached up and pulled his head down towards mine.

I never saw the fireworks, not the ones that arced across the midnight sky. But the ones soaring within my new heart would have eclipsed them anyway.

CHAPTER THIRTY-FOUR

Alex

'I believe this is yours.'

Alex instinctively held out his hand, expecting his elderly neighbour to pass him a piece of incorrectly delivered post or a parcel he'd taken in. He hesitated when he saw the small plastic bag dangling from the end of Gordon Grafton's arthritic finger.

'Erm, I don't think that's mine, Gordon,' Alex said with a kindly smile.

In reply, Gordon took a step forward, his foot now across the threshold of Alex's open front door.

'I think you'll find that it is.'

Humouring him, Alex bent a little lower to study the bag. 'No, that's definitely not mine. What is it, anyway?'

The permanent scowl that had been on his neighbour's face for the last two years seemed to deepen.

'It's faeces, young man. Excrement, poo, cra—'

'Okay,' Alex interrupted, holding up a hand to stop him, while casting an anxious glance over his shoulder. He was all for broadening Connor's vocabulary – but not like this. He eyed the swinging bag with considerably more distaste now that he knew what it contained. 'And why exactly do you think it has anything to do with us?'

'You have a cat, don't you? A new one?'

Alex shook his head in amused disbelief. *Be kind*, he imagined he could hear Lisa intoning. *He's a lonely old man who hasn't been the same since Elsie passed away.* He took a steadying breath. Lisa had always been far more tolerant of their curmudgeonly neighbour than him. And yet in a way he understood Gordon much better now they were in the same boat. Almost. Although the glittering fury in Gordon's rheumy eyes told Alex this was clearly not going to be a bonding moment.

'It's true we've recently got a kitten—' he confirmed, wondering if Gordon's Neighbourhood Watch enthusiasm ran to spying on his neighbours with a long-range telescope.

'There you are then,' Gordon interrupted triumphantly, dropping the bag onto the coconut doormat beside Alex's bare feet.

Alex could hear the sound of the kitchen door opening, meaning Connor was about to join him. It tempered his response by quite some measure.

'Although we do have a kitten, Gordon, I'm afraid the contents of this delightful bag are not hers. She's too young to be allowed outside yet and uses a litter tray in our porch.'

Gordon's nostrils flared, so much so that he looked in danger of adding to the multitude of broken capillaries that surrounded them.

'Says you. But you do keep your windows open, don't you, even in winter?'

The old guy really needed to take up whist or bowls, or something, Alex thought; he clearly had way too much time on his hands, with nothing better to do than stake out his neighbours. He was in full flow now.

'It seems obvious that your animal escaped from a window, crossed the road and defecated on my cyclamen, and then jumped back in again.'

'Lunar wouldn't do that,' a small voice beside Alex's thigh quietly insisted. 'She'd be too scared of the road.'

Alex's hand settled on Conor's shoulder and pulled him a little closer to his side. His son was trembling.

'I really do think it must have been another cat, Gordon,' Alex said, still trying to be amiable and neighbourly, in the way he knew Lisa would have wanted. He bent to pick up the bag from the mat. 'But I will happily dispose of this in my dustbin for you.'

Gordon Grafton made a dissatisfied harrumphing sound. 'It *is* your cat. No one else in the street has one.'

Alex could see little use in pointing out that cats liked to wander. The Phantom Pooper could, in fact, live many streets away. 'Did you actually see Lunar in your garden?' he asked reasonably.

Gordon made an angry bulldog growl, which Alex took to be a 'no'. 'I suppose I'm just going to have to prove it to you,' he said with irritation. 'I will be setting up a recording device to catch your animal befouling my flowerbeds. In the meantime, kindly keep it under control.'

The fraying strands of Alex's patience were about to snap. 'Gordon, you must do what you have to do,' he said with a smile that couldn't have looked more forced. He took a step back and firmly closed his front door.

'Why is Mr Grafton being so mean to Lunar? She didn't do anything.'

Alex dropped down onto his haunches and was dismayed to see fearful tears had flooded Connor's eyes. His son was clearly terrified that their grumpy neighbour was going to do something to his beloved pet. *Over my dead body*, Alex thought fiercely, suddenly the most ardent pet owner in the world.

'I know she didn't, champ. Mr Gordon is just…' *A miserable old bastard?* He bit his lip on the uncharitable thought. 'He's just confused and sad. He misses his wife. You remember Elsie, don't you? She used to make you those delicious brownies you liked so much.'

Connor nodded solemnly.

'Well, Gordon is sad that Elsie passed away. Missing his wife makes him unhappy and a little bit angry.' They were tiptoeing on the edge of a subject he normally avoided. Alex held his breath as he waited for Connor to say something about Lisa.

'Lunar only poops in the litter tray,' Connor said stubbornly.

Alex straightened and ruffled his son's hair, aware that an important opportunity might just have been lost. He was wondering if he could turn the conversation around when the doorbell rang once again. He sighed, preparing himself for a second verbal assault from his neighbour, who'd probably remembered something else to complain about.

'Yes, Gordon?' he asked as he opened the front door, only to find it wasn't Gordon on their doorstep this time, it was the postman. Alex reorganised his features into a more genuine smile.

'Got one here that's too big for your letterbox,' the postman announced cheerily, passing him a bundle of mail.

'Thank you,' Alex said, taking it with more enthusiasm than he had the last delivery.

He stood on the doormat flicking through the post. Most of it was bills or junk mail, with the exception of the item at the bottom of the pile. *One minute you're getting on with your life, picking up the pieces and making progress,* he thought, *and then a single, dumb, computer-generated mailshot has you sliding right back down into the well of grief again.*

How many years would it be, he wondered, before the sight of mail addressed to Lisa didn't feel like a knife wound to his stomach? And this wasn't just any old piece of junk mail. Did no one at the organisation know what had happened? Surely someone must have informed them of the tragedy that had befallen one of their key speakers when she was on her way to that same event last year?

He was staring down miserably at the colourful flier, unaware that Connor was looking at it with interest.

'What's that?' he asked Alex, his eyes fixed on the eye-catching image of an eclipse, which the organisers were using this year to advertise their event.

'Nothing,' Alex said, wincing as he looked down at the card inviting his dead wife to this year's Astronomy Fair. 'It's just junk,' he said, crumpling the piece of card in one hand and dropping it into the wastepaper basket in the hall.

In hindsight, he really ought to have known better than to do that.

CHAPTER THIRTY-FIVE

Molly

His hand felt so natural in mine. Although his grip was admittedly a little tight, as if he was anxious about losing me. That would never happen, I vowed.

'Are you having fun?'

Connor's smile was tentative; he was unsure if that was even allowed, let alone something he should admit to. 'I think so,' he said cautiously.

That was good enough for now.

'What would you like to do next?'

His eyes darted left and right, skimming past the dodgem cars, which I was pretty certain every child in my class would have chosen, and the ornate carousel with the enticing calliope music.

'I don't know.'

Despite the crisp threat of snow in the air, the fair was surprisingly busy. It was a popular destination during the February half-term holidays, although not one I had planned on attending.

The wind bit sharply, and even with my thick coat and chunky woollen scarf, I was shivering. The paracetamols I'd taken that morning were wearing off, and the aches and pains they'd been keeping at bay were returning with a vengeance. It was just my luck to have picked up a bug on my week off.

Ordinarily, I would have said 'no' to today, knowing that Alex would not appreciate me potentially passing on this cold or flu to either him or Connor. But he'd sounded so desperate when he called yesterday, I hadn't even thought about refusing.

'It would only be for a few hours,' he'd promised on the phone. 'Four at the most.'

'It's fine, don't worry about it. I didn't have anything planned for tomorrow anyway.' *Except curling up on the couch with my duvet and a supply of Day Nurse*, I silently added.

'You're a life saver, Molly. With Todd and Dee away on holiday, I couldn't think of anyone else I'd trust enough to ask. I can't thank you enough.'

He was still thanking me when I turned up at his home earlier today with a bag full of books and games I thought Connor might enjoy. It was obvious within minutes that none of those would be needed. As soon as the front door had closed behind me, Connor was tugging urgently at my hand, desperate to introduce me to the bundle of white fluff curled up in her bed in the corner of the kitchen. The tiny kitten was miraculously managing to do what no one else had been able to achieve: she was making Connor happy again. For the first time ever, as he crouched on the floor gently stroking the cat, I saw a normal little boy and not a tortured soul with the weight of the world on his shoulders. I sent up a silent thank you to Barbara for being possibly the wisest woman I'd ever met.

'Oh, I see you've met our new family member then,' Alex said, walking into the kitchen with his overcoat draped over one arm. He looked very different in a business suit. *Handsome. He looks handsome*, I told myself. *It's okay, you're allowed to think it.*

'You look very… dapper,' I substituted at the last moment, and then inwardly cringed. *Dapper?* I sounded like I'd wandered straight out of a Jane Austen novel. Alex must have thought so too, from the twinkle in his eye. It was the first time we'd seen each other in almost eight weeks, and despite everything I felt for Mac, there was still a jolt of… magnetism, that hit me when I saw Alex in his dark grey suit and tie. Were these feelings even mine, I wondered as my heart skittered weirdly and a powerful sensation of déjà vu rocked me to my core. I'd seen Alex like this before, in this very kitchen, my unreliable memory informed me, even though I knew I hadn't.

'This is potentially a really big day for our company. I've been chasing this client for months, and they've suddenly agreed to meet with me, but only if I can see them today.'

'It's fine, Alex.' I looked down at Connor and dropped him a wink. 'Actually, I'm glad you asked me because Barbara told me all about Lunar ages ago, and I've been itching to meet her.'

'You should have said. You know you're always welcome to come over.'

Above Connor's bent head our eyes met and held, silently acknowledging that wasn't entirely true. For weeks we'd both been tentatively trying to heal the breach in our friendship, without once referring to the indiscretion that had caused it. The *kiss-that-never-was* felt like a lifetime ago, and yet it continued to cast an uncomfortable shadow. It should have been forgotten, eclipsed in my head by the very real kiss I'd shared with Mac on New Year's Eve. Illicit kisses – brief moments of madness that threatened friendships and yet were impossible to forget.

Would I still have kissed Mac as one year chimed into the next if I'd known then that it wouldn't change anything? If I'd known without a shadow of a doubt that however strong the attraction was, his reasons for keeping us purely platonic were stronger?

'*Perhaps he doesn't want to risk getting involved with someone who might not grow old with him?*' I'd suggested to Kyra.

'*If he's that shallow then you don't want him anyway,*' she'd shot back, all fire and indignation.

Except I did. I really did.

I'd been one number away from calling him more times than I cared to admit. I no longer even knew what was holding me back. It wasn't pride, because I'd have happily sacrificed that in a heartbeat. No, it was more a fear that if I pushed Mac too hard for an answer he'd pull away completely, not just from me, but from Alex and the others too. I couldn't be the one responsible for breaking our connection, not when I knew how much it meant to everyone.

But at least, finally, Alex and I seemed to be back where we were before we'd almost ruined everything. It was so good to see him and Connor again, it made me even more determined to never let anything jeopardise our relationship again. It was that resolve that had led me to say an immediate 'yes' when he'd asked me to look after Connor today, despite feeling under the weather.

'We *were* going to go to the funfair today,' Connor murmured, directing his comment to the cat, who truthfully didn't look as though she cared one way or the other.

When it comes to guilt-tripping, no one does it better than a seven-year-old.

'I know I promised that we would,' said Alex, sounding wretched, 'but I don't think I'm going to get back in time.'

'Maybe you could go another day?' I suggested chirpily.

Withering looks are something else little children are particularly good at.

'Today is the last day of the fair.'

'Well… I've an idea: why don't you and I go together, and then maybe your dad could meet us there when his meeting is finished?'

Father and son swivelled their heads towards me with such perfect synchronicity it was almost funny.

Had I overstepped the mark? Perhaps I ought to have spoken to Alex first before rearranging his day as though I had a perfect right to do so.

'I couldn't ask you to do that, Molly.' Alex had to be an excellent poker player, because I had absolutely no idea if he thought my suggestion was a great idea or a terrible one. His face gave nothing away.

'You didn't ask; I volunteered,' I reminded him. 'It's been years since I've been to a fair. It will be fun.'

And it was. Or at least it had been until I started to feel unwell again. I learnt several things that day at the fair. I discovered it was way harder than it looked to knock a coconut off a wooden pole. Did they superglue them on, or something? I learnt it didn't matter how many tickets you bought for the lucky dip, you were always going to come up with a cheap plastic toy as your prize. But the most important thing I learnt was how different it felt being in charge of one little boy rather than a whole class of them.

I wasn't sure when it happened. It might have been when I watched him nibbling on a cloud of pink candyfloss, or when I realised the yank on my arm was because he was actually skipping beside me or when he unwrapped the last lucky-dip gift and gave it to me with a shy smile. Out of all the moments I would remember that day, it was when he slipped the cheap plastic flower bracelet onto my wrist that I finally acknowledged I had fallen in love. And it wasn't with Alex or even with Mac – it was with Connor. What I felt for him was so strong, it seemed as though it had always been there, lying dormant deep within me, waiting to be set free.

The realisation was as troubling as it was wonderful. This child wasn't mine, even though my heart was achingly disputing that fact. My place could only ever be on the periphery of his life, and suddenly that wasn't enough. Not even close.

I stood beside a miniature carousel, on which Connor was happily journeying to nowhere in slow circles, and felt a chill that had nothing to do with the plummeting barometer. I was undistinguishable among the parents. I waved when they waved, and smiled and cheered as our small charges came into view, but I was nothing more than an imposter, walking in shoes that weren't mine and were too big to fill.

'Hold on tight,' urged a mother standing beside me, every time her young son passed by. She gave a nervous laugh as though I might be judging her. 'You never stop worrying about them, do you?' she said, assuming quite naturally we were members of the same club.

It didn't even occur to me to correct her. 'No, you don't.'

Connor came back into sight, his small hands fisted into a unicorn's bright blue mane. He was laughing, and the sound was so unfamiliar, I wanted to instantly bottle it.

'How old is yours?' asked the stranger at my elbow.

My chest felt tight, and not in a good way. Lying had never sat comfortably with me. 'He's seven. Connor is seven.'

'Oh, that's a lovely name. It's Irish, isn't it?'

I nodded, turning slightly away from the woman who seemed determined to make a pathological liar out of me. The ride was taking an extraordinarily long time to come to an end.

'Molly,' cried Connor, slithering off the back of his mythical creature and running towards me. I opened my arms to catch him, as he cried my name again. Distorted by the wind, the cries of the other riders and the amplified music, it almost sounded like 'Mummy'.

I bought us hot dogs from a stand but could manage only a single bite before the greasy onions made my stomach flip in protest. Connor didn't even notice when I discreetly binned the rest.

'Would you like to go and look at the ice rink?' I asked as he polished off his lunch in three enormous bites.

His nod was hesitant.

'It's okay. We don't have to skate if you don't want to; we can just watch.'

The rink was a surprise. Far bigger than I expected, and already busy with skaters whose skills ranged from those who looked one wobble away from disaster to the ones who fancied themselves as the next big Olympic hope. In my teenage years I'd been a regular at my local rink, although admittedly I hadn't set foot on the ice in over fifteen years. It was surprising how much the swish of blades scoring the ice made me want to join them.

Connor sipped on the hot chocolate I'd bought him while he watched with rapt attention as children far younger than him were led around the ice by their parents. I could see he was seriously tempted.

I pulled my phone from my pocket and reread the message Alex had sent about ten minutes earlier.

Still in meeting. Really sorry. Should be with you in about an hour. Hope that's okay? A

Part of me knew I shouldn't even be thinking about taking Connor onto the ice without getting Alex's permission first. But did he really want to be bothered during an important business meeting with a question he'd surely say 'yes' to? Wouldn't he just be pleased to know that Connor was interested in trying something a little more adventurous?

I made up my mind quickly, to avoid overthinking it. I slid my mobile back into my jeans, the message I'd mentally composed never quite making it to my phone's keypad.

'Do you fancy having a go?' I asked, nodding in the direction of the rink.

Connor's eyes widened in surprise, but there was no fear in them, just trust. My heart gave a small lurch.

'You won't let go of me, will you?'

'Never,' I promised. 'Cross my heart.' I drew an invisible X across my chest with a finger.

I should have noticed the way he paled at that, but I was already turning away to hire our skates.

It began so well. With Connor's gloved hands firmly clamped in mine, I led him onto the ice. Muscle memory took over the minute my blades connected with the surface. My knees bent automatically, and my back straightened as I slowly glided away from the edge. Connor was a quick learner, with more natural ability than I'd been expecting. It took only a couple of circuits of the rink before he relaxed his death-grip on me, and a further few before he was holding onto me with just one hand.

The rink was clearly a popular draw at the fair and was growing increasingly crowded.

'Just one more circuit, okay?' I said, glancing around with concern when a large gang of noisy teenagers barrelled onto the rink. I heard several 'tsks' of disapproval from nearby adults as the group swept recklessly through the skaters, weaving and slaloming at speeds they could scarcely control. I tightened my grip on Connor's hand and increased our own speed, my eyes focused on the nearest exit.

The music pumping through the speakers was loud. Perhaps that was why the teenagers didn't heed the chorus of warning whistles being blown by the ice marshals. 'Slow down,' screamed a male voice from somewhere behind me.

I pulled Connor closer to my side. We were just a few yards from the nearest exit when a figure in black came hurtling towards us. My brain slowed down even as my legs speeded up. But there was no way to get out of his path, and the teenager was clearly incapable of stopping. He was almost upon us, as relentless as a charging rhino. I acted purely on instinct, grabbing Connor's shoulders and pushing him roughly out of the way. Less than a second later, my legs were knocked out from under me by the out-of-control skater.

I hit the ice hard, my shoulder and hip taking most of the impact. I immediately tried to scramble back to my feet, forgetting every lesson I'd learnt about how to stand up following a tumble. I fell again, once more landing on my hip. Tears of pain blurred my vision, but I swiped them away as I swivelled on the ice to find Connor. For a heart-stopping moment I couldn't spot him, but then I saw he'd already been helped up by a couple of skaters and was being led off the ice.

My pounding heart, which had conjured up images of cracked skulls or broken spines, slowed down from its racing panic. Aside from being white-faced with shock, Connor appeared to be unscathed. Ignoring the pain from my hip, which I imagined was now an interesting shade of purple, I finally remembered how to get up from the ice. I went from two knees to one and then onto my feet. The youth who'd caused the collision was being severely chastised by the rink marshals, and as much as I'd have loved to have joined in, my priorities were elsewhere.

'Are you okay?' asked a female marshal who'd sped to my side. She laid a hand on my arm, but I shook it off.

'I'm fine. It was just a tumble,' I said, trying to move past her.

Annoyingly, she was still blocking my path. 'We've got a first-aid station set up. You really should get checked out. You hit the ice pretty hard.'

'I'm all right,' I insisted, my voice now several degrees cooler than the surface we were standing on.

'Yes. But it's in our insurance that if—'

I tried to push past her in a way that was so out of character, it startled me. 'I'm not about to sue you, the fair or anyone else. It's nothing worse than a bruise or two.'

She remained unconvinced and the last shreds of my patience finally pinged like a piece of elastic. My voice rose to a level it rarely achieved. 'Will you please just get out of my way. I need to get to my son.'

We both looked shocked. She by my reaction; me by what I'd just said.

She gave an eloquent shrug and skated out of my way. I could hear her disgruntled mutterings behind me, but I was focused on only one thing.

'Are you okay, Connor? Were you hurt when you fell over?'

The kindly couple who'd picked him up stepped back, and Connor shot towards me like a rocket. He threw one arm tightly around me, squeezing with all his strength against my painfully injured hip. I scarcely felt it.

'I thought you were dead,' he cried, his voice hitching on a heart-breaking sob.

The rescuing couple both laughed, but the sound died in their throats when they noticed I wasn't joining in. I saw the bemused glance they exchanged, but my attention was only on Connor.

'It was just a little fall,' I said, deliberately trivialising the worst tumble I'd ever taken on the ice. 'It happens all the time when people go skating. You just have to pick yourself up and not let it worry you. Otherwise you'd never go back on the ice again.'

'We don't have to go back on again, do we?' Connor asked fearfully.

This time I did laugh. 'No, we don't. We're done for today, kiddo.'

I remembered to thank the couple for helping Connor, and they continued their role as Good Samaritans by returning our skates for us and bringing back our shoes. The effort of bending down to zip up my boots almost defeated me, and by the time they were both fastened, I was drenched in sweat and feeling decidedly wobbly again. I thought longingly of the packet of paracetamols locked out of reach in the glovebox of my car.

I straightened slowly, wincing from my injuries, and was surprised to see that although Connor had slipped his feet into his trainers, he hadn't tied the laces.

'Can you do it for me?'

I frowned and crouched down before him. Did he not know how to do this? Most children of his age would have long since mastered the motor skills required. Shrugging it off, I tied the laces securely, having to stop halfway through to wipe a sticky film of sweat from my brow. I was burning up.

'Why don't we go back to the car and wait there for your daddy?' I suggested.

Connor's white, pinched face made it clear he'd had enough of the fair for one day. That made two of us.

The fair was much busier now. As the families with younger children began to leave, they were quickly replaced by groups of teenagers. I held on tightly to Connor's hand and pulled him in close, flinching as he inadvertently bumped against my bruised hip with every stride. I pulled us to a stop and switched places so I could have him on my other side, but as I reached for his other hand, he squealed in pain.

'What is it? What's wrong?' I asked, my voice squeaky with panic.

'My wrist hurts,' he confessed.

I moved us out of the fast-moving flow of pedestrians and stretched out my hand, palm side up.

'Can I see it?'

I knew even before he slowly lifted the arm that something was broken. I tried to keep the shock from my face, but I think he saw it anyway.

'Oh Connor, why didn't you say something?'

'I'm sorry,' he said, his voice quavering with tears. 'I didn't want you to be cross with me. I didn't want you to say we couldn't go out together again.'

I shook my head, momentarily robbed of coherent speech. Was he really so scared of losing someone else from his life that he'd suffer a broken bone in silence rather than run the risk? What agonies had this wonderful little boy had to endure to bring him to this point?

He looked so scared, and now that I knew the reason, the white face made much more sense. I crouched down before him and the only reason I didn't enfold him tightly in a hug was for fear of hurting his damaged arm.

I reached out and very gently wiped the tears from his cheeks. 'Firstly, there's nothing you could ever do or say that would make you lose me. I will always be here; I will always be your friend, for as long as you want me to be.' Some of the anxiety clouding his eyes lifted at that. 'And secondly, you *have* to tell grown-ups when something is hurting you. Whether it is here...' I pointed to his wrist. 'Or here...' I lightly touched his forehead. 'Or in here,' I finished, pointing my finger at his heart.

His slow nod was filled with a misery no child should know.

'I'm sorry,' he said again.

'Never mind, sweetheart. But we have to get you to a hospital so they can make your wrist better.'

Somehow, an already ghostly white Connor blanched and turned even paler. His head was shaking vigorously from side to side, and it took me far longer than it should have done to realise it was the word 'hospital' that had caused his distress. All Connor knew about hospitals was that his mother had gone into one and had never come out again.

Mindful of his injury and ignoring the protests from mine, I bent down and scooped him up. He clung to me like a baby primate, his legs locking around my waist, his one good arm encircling my neck. He was heavier than he looked, but my knees would have had to buckle and send me crashing to the ground before I'd ever have let go of him. Slowly, digging deep for reserves I didn't know I had, I began to trot and then run towards the car park.

It had filled up since we'd arrived, several hours earlier. Dusk was rapidly falling and all I could see was a sea of vehicles. As I scanned the rows of cars, with no memory of where I'd parked, the first flames of panic began to take hold. Connor was whimpering softly against the side of my neck, his tears puddling on my collarbone.

I'd always thought of myself as being good in a crisis, but delayed shock was rendering me sloppy and useless. I realised I shouldn't be taking Connor anywhere without first letting Alex know what had happened.

Careful not to cause him any more pain, I readjusted my hold on the boy in my arms and reached into the back pocket of my jeans for my phone. My moan of disbelief momentarily silenced Connor's sobs. The screen wasn't just cracked, it was destroyed. It looked as though it had been ground underfoot by a belligerent giant. Turning it on was futile, but I tried to anyway. Nothing. Although there was a calming voice in my head, telling me not to panic, I appeared to be doing a pretty effective job of ignoring it.

'What's wrong?' Connor cried, catching my despair as though it was a virus.

'Nothing, sweetie. We're just going to have to wait until we get to the hospital before we can call your daddy. Don't worry,' I added, as I set off again at a breath-stealing jog in the hunt for my car.

We hurried up and down the rows of parked vehicles to the low background drone of Connor's whimpers. There was a stitch in my side that felt like a burning stab wound, and hot salty tears of frustration were starting to blur my vision. Where the hell was my car? And then, two rows away, I finally saw a blink of headlights in response to the summons from my key fob. Unthinkingly, I ran towards it and was suddenly dazzled by another set of headlights. I froze in their twin beams like a terrified rabbit as the shriek of hastily applied brakes filled the car park. I was trembling so violently from the near miss, I was slow to realise the driver had leapt out of their car and was racing towards us.

'Molly! What's wrong? What's happened?'

Alex's voice was taut with concern. And I could hardly blame him for that. He'd entrusted his precious child into my care and just a few hours later he'd found me with his injured little boy in my arms, running wildly around a car park like a crazy person. I shouldn't have been left in charge of a goldfish, much less someone's child.

'Molly?' Alex urged again, already shepherding us towards his car.

I quickly explained what had happened on the rink and braced myself for the censure I deserved.

'Get in the car,' was all he said, his tone tense but controlled.

I climbed into the rear seat carefully, Connor still attached as though he'd been welded to me. Somehow Alex managed to secure a seatbelt around both of us; although he was careful, Connor's yelp of pain was inevitable. Too late, I remembered my first-aid training about not moving a casualty.

'Should we call an ambulance?' I asked worriedly.

Alex's face was a mask, allowing no glimpse of his emotions. 'No. I can get him to the hospital faster.' He jumped back into the car with the dexterity of a getaway driver and was already gunning the engine as he slammed shut the door. 'Just hold onto him tightly for me. Keep him safe.'

I nodded, my own face a white, tear-stained reflection in the rear-view mirror. I didn't need to be told twice.

CHAPTER THIRTY-SIX

Molly

I never intended to deliberately mislead the hospital staff. But like an actor who keeps missing their cue, I failed to seize each opportunity to correct the hospital's mistaken assumption that I was Connor's mum.

I should have mentioned it to the woman on reception, who looked surprised when I failed to answer almost every question about Connor's medical history. 'His dad will know the answer to that one,' started to wear thin after the fifth time of repeating it.

I should definitely have mentioned it to the doctor in Triage, who comfortingly told me, 'It's always much worse for the parents than it is for the children.' But as Alex still hadn't joined us in A & E at that point, I was afraid they wouldn't examine Connor's arm without a parent present. *Is it lying if you simply don't say anything?* I wondered. If it was, then I could live with my deception.

We were asked to return to the waiting area until they called us up to Radiology for X-rays. Connor looked like a wounded soldier beside me, with his arm now dressed in a temporary sling. My gaze kept flashing from him to the doors of the department. Where was Alex? How could it possibly be taking this long to park his car? I reached for my phone, before remembering my fall had turned it into a useless piece of junk.

I was used to hospitals and had been in and out of them more times than I could count since becoming ill. But I truly didn't think I had ever been inside one this hot before. Despite pulling off my coat, I felt as though I was quietly cooking as we sat waiting on the uncomfortable plastic chairs. Perspiration was trickling down my back faster than raindrops on a window pane, and it was impossible to know if the shivers juddering through me were from nerves or a fever.

'Connor Stevens?' called out a woman, referring to a file in her hands.

I got to my feet a little too quickly and felt the head rush of an incipient faint. *Don't you dare*, I warned my treacherous body.

'Here,' I replied to the woman wearing a tunic with *Radiology* printed across it.

We followed her to the bank of lifts, after the receptionist had assured me she would send my 'husband' up as soon as he arrived. I glanced down nervously at Connor, who must surely have heard every single occasion when I'd failed to correct the mistake. His eyes looked troubled, and he reached out for me with his uninjured arm as we stepped into the lift.

'Your mummy will be able to come into the room with you when we take a picture of your poorly arm,' the woman from Radiology told him kindly.

Connor's eyes darted between me and the woman. I held my breath, waiting for him to correct her, but he said nothing.

Another set of chairs in another hospital corridor. This one seemed, impossibly, even hotter than the one we'd just left. The door in front of us opened, and a radiographer emerged carrying a lead-lined apron, which I presumed was for me. I could see Connor craning past the man and catching his first glimpse of the machinery within the room. Fear was coming off him in palpable waves. My arm tightened automatically around his small shoulders, and it was a shock to discover he was trembling even more violently than me.

'Do you think we could just have a minute to—' I began, before the ping of the lift cut me off.

Alex ran through the opening doors like he was on his way to put out a fire.

'Thank God,' I breathed in relief. 'What took you so long?' Even to my own ears, I sounded like an angry spouse.

'Some idiot drove straight into my car in the multi-storey,' he said.

Connor's eyes widened in terror.

'I'm okay,' he reassured him, looking down with a worried expression at the sling protecting Connor's arm.

'I'm afraid only one parent can accompany the patient,' said the radiographer, extending the protective apron in our direction. 'Who would you like with you, young man? Your daddy or your mummy?'

It was all too much for Connor. And who could blame him. With an anguished wail, he looked from me to Alex and then said the words that sliced into me like a knife.

'She's not my mummy. I don't know where my mummy has gone.'

It took a good ten minutes before our combined efforts managed to calm Connor down enough so they could take the X-ray. Alex obviously accompanied him because, as Connor had so accurately pointed out, I had no place being there. As they stood to go in, I managed to catch the radiographer's attention to quietly ask, 'Is there a water fountain somewhere nearby?' The stress of the last few minutes had done nothing to reduce what felt like my sky-high temperature.

'There's one just down the corridor.'

I waited until Alex and Connor had disappeared before getting to my feet. The room swirled around me like a centrifuge before eventually coming to a standstill. I trailed one hand against the wall for support as I slowly negotiated my way along the corridor. Beneath my feet the linoleum felt as if it was buckling and rippling, as though in an earthquake.

The water I splashed on my face helped a little, and I drank greedily from a conical paper cup. From what felt like miles away, I could hear Connor crying. I turned too quickly, aware that he and Alex had now emerged from the X-ray room, but they were fuzzy and indistinct, as though lost in fog. I took two faltering steps and the fog rolled towards me, swallowing me up.

For the second time that day I fell to the floor. But this time I didn't get up again.

CHAPTER THIRTY-SEVEN

Alex

The order in which he made the phone calls was telling. It was as though his subconscious knew – even before he did – that the final call would be the most important and the hardest to make. Jamie had been shocked, Barbara had been thrown into a state of panic. But Mac… Mac had been… Alex could only think back to that dreadful day the previous year in a different hospital. Mac, Alex realised, had reacted just as he himself had done on learning what had happened to Lisa.

The phone rang long enough for Alex to be convinced it was about to go to voicemail. He closed his eyes and replayed again that awful moment when he'd seen Molly collapse. Even though he'd known there was no chance of reaching her in time, he'd sprinted down the hospital corridor towards her. She was unconscious before he got there. Two doctors who happened to be walking in the opposite direction were already crouched down beside her.

He'd stepped back shakily, giving them space but unable to take his eyes off Molly's terrifyingly pale face. The doctors fired questions up at him, but all he could see was the concern in their eyes as they tried to find a pulse. For one dreadful moment he didn't think there was one. His knees felt like buckling as the two doctors exchanged worried glances.

'Got it! It's weak and thready, but at least it's there.'

There was already an orderly running down the corridor pushing a stretcher, and Alex flattened himself against the wall to get out of their way.

'Is there anything else you can tell us?' one of the doctors asked.

'Her name is Molly Kendall, she's thirty-two years old, and in April of last year she had a heart transplant.'

'Hi, Alex. What's up?' Mac's voice jolted him straight back into the present.

'I… I'm calling from the hospital.' Alex thought he heard a sharply indrawn breath at the other end of the phone line. Had he got this right? He was trusting his intuition here – something Lisa would have found hilariously funny.

'What's wrong?' Mac shot back, and the fear was already there in his voice. Alex knew from personal experience what it took to put it there. It took caring about someone you simply couldn't imagine living without.

'It's Molly,' Alex said.

'Which hospital?'

To Alex's ears it sounded as though Mac was already running. He gave the details as coherently as he could. 'They've taken her into ICU. I'll meet you there.'

They both hung up without saying goodbye, unwilling to squander a single second.

It was impossible for Alex not to travel back in time as he paced the corridor outside the Intensive Care ward. The last time he'd been in a place like this, when the life of someone he loved was hanging in the balance, it had ended in his worst nightmare. Was history about to repeat itself?

He collapsed onto a nearby plastic chair, his head dropping into his hands. It was different this time. What he felt for Molly was a kind of love – but not the type he and Lisa had shared.

How had it taken him this long to finally recognise that although the heart of the woman he loved continued to beat, that woman wasn't Lisa, and never could be? And that the heart which had once loved him now belonged to another man. A man who Alex imagined was at this very moment breaking every speed limit to reach Molly's side.

For so long, Alex had believed Lisa's heart had come back to him, but he knew better now. He finally realised it lived on to find love again. He groaned softly, because all he'd done was get in the way of allowing that to happen. He'd seen the attraction between Molly and Mac. He'd seen the way Mac looked at her, noted how his voice subtly changed whenever he casually asked Alex about Molly. The signs had all been there, painted in letters ten foot high, and yet he'd refused to acknowledge them. Something was keeping the two of them apart, and Alex had been far too slow to realise that 'something' was very probably him.

He glanced worriedly at his watch. The kindly woman from Radiography who'd volunteered to keep Connor with her for a while should probably be relieved of that responsibility now. It had allowed him to accompany Molly to the ICU, but Alex had other responsibilities he had to consider and prioritise.

Five more minutes, he promised himself. *If Mac isn't here by then, I'm sorry, Molly, but I'm going to have to leave you.* Was she even aware he was there, he wondered – pacing the corridor outside the ward, jumping up hopefully every time a doctor emerged, only to slump back down again at the lack of news?

He heard Mac before he saw him. The pounding of feet racing along the corridor, the deep rumble of a hastily asked question, and then suddenly the buzz of the doors opening as the man who cared about Molly more than perhaps even *he* knew, raced towards him.

Neither of the men were natural huggers, and yet they embraced like brothers. When they broke apart it wasn't at all clear who had been supporting who.

'Tell me everything,' Mac implored, his head nodding as Alex shared the limited information he had.

'She assumed she was coming down with a bug,' Alex explained, feeling more than a little stupid as Mac's expression turned grave. He clearly knew far more about organ rejection than Alex did.

'Fever and chills are classic symptoms of rejection. Molly should have known that.'

Alex wondered if what Mac really meant was that *he* should have known that. If so, he was right. He'd brought these four people into his life and made friends of each of them, but he'd never moved past the way they'd met. If he cared about them the way he claimed, he ought to have been looking out for them, the way Lisa always looked out for her friends. He'd failed them, all of them, and by association that meant he'd failed Lisa too.

'Have they said what they're doing for her?' Mac asked, his eyes flicking towards the closed doors of the unit.

Alex shook his head.

'They can reverse it,' Mac said. 'If they've caught it early enough, they can reverse the rejection.'

Alex's smile was too weak to sustain for more than a few seconds. From the look of Molly when they'd rushed her here, that window of opportunity might have been and gone.

'It's my fault,' Connor said miserably, his cornflower-blue eyes flooding with tears. 'I shouted at Molly that she wasn't my mummy, and that made her so sad, she fell down on the floor.'

Alex swallowed the golf ball lodged in his throat. 'No, sweetheart. It's nothing to do with anything you said or did. Molly got sick, that's why she fell down. But now the doctors are giving her some super-strong medicine that'll make her better again.' He was lying to Connor, and the consequences of doing so weren't lost on him.

'Can we go and see her?' Connor begged. 'I want to tell her I'm sorry.'

Alex pulled Connor against his chest, mindful of the wrist that was now dressed in a splint. 'I'm sorry, champ, they've got strict rules about children visiting the patients where Molly is.'

And even if they didn't, there was no way he was going to allow Connor to see what *he'd* seen when he'd left the ICU. The thirty seconds he'd been allowed at Molly's bedside had reminded him all too vividly of his first visit to Lisa after the train crash. He would never put his son through that.

'Besides, we need to get home to check on Lunar. She's never been on her own for this long before.'

There was no victory to be had in playing the one ace in his hand, Alex thought miserably. But he wanted Connor back home and as far away as possible from this place where lives were sometimes miraculously saved and sometimes tragically lost.

Alex eyed the tray of cremated chicken goujons and tried to decide if any could be salvaged. He was halfway to the kitchen bin when the doorbell rang.

At first glance Barbara appeared to be perfectly composed and coping well. But as she bustled into his kitchen, Alex noticed the buttons of her cardigan were incorrectly fastened, and she was wearing mismatched shoes.

'I do hope you haven't already eaten,' she said, setting down the tea-towel-covered dish she'd brought with her in the taxi.

Alex glanced ruefully at the charred remains on the grill tray. 'Not yet.'

'Good, because for some strange reason I made a simply enormous shepherd's pie this afternoon. Far too big for just me.' She reached over and gently squeezed Alex's forearm. 'It's almost like I knew,' she added softly.

He smiled back. 'Thank you for coming at such short notice. It's really good of you.'

Barbara waved her hand, flapping away his nonsense. 'Where else would I possibly be at a time like this?'

Alex's throat tightened as he turned towards the bin. He spent far longer than was necessary dispatching the ruined chicken goujons to its depths, before eventually swivelling round.

'I thought Mac might appreciate some company at the hospital. Or maybe we could take it in shifts to sit with Molly.'

Barbara nodded, and without bothering to ask, switched on his oven and slid her dish inside.

'Did anyone reach Molly's mother yet? How do you even get a message to someone on a cruise ship, anyway?'

Alex shook his head worriedly. 'Molly will have to give us the details when she wakes up.' His eyes locked with Barbara's, knowing both of them had mentally substituted an 'if' into that sentence.

Alex reached for his car keys on the kitchen counter, only to discover Barbara was both faster and stronger than he'd imagined a woman of her age to be.

'And where do you think you're dashing off to?' she challenged.

For a moment Alex was concerned she might not be up to the task of looking after Connor. Had she forgotten they'd just this minute been talking about him going to the hospital?

Barbara was wagging her finger in castigation. 'You're not going anywhere, young man, without a good hot meal inside you first.'

Alex, who currently felt closer to Barbara's age than his own, still managed to muster up a smile at being called 'young man'. For a woman who'd never been a mother or a grandmother, Barbara had taken to both roles as though they'd always been hers.

Alex's attention was fixed on the oven, as if by staring at the shepherd's pie he might somehow help it heat faster. As much as he hated hospitals, he was anxious to get back.

In the meantime Barbara had made herself at home, busily setting the table for their meal before joining Alex. She laid a hand gently on his forearm. 'I'm sure Molly will be fine. She's a fighter, that girl, and she has Mac with her now.'

Alex blinked, wondering if he was the one who'd been blind instead of the man who was now at Molly's bedside. 'I was quite surprised how badly shaken up Mac was when he arrived at the hospital,' he said carefully.

'Were you?' Two words, so gently spoken, yet they pierced through Alex's armour. He turned his head slowly towards Barbara.

'Have I misjudged him? Have I read Mac wrong?'

'Only you know that, Alex my dear,' Barbara said with the kind of wisdom Alex doubted he'd ever achieve. 'Mac is a quiet one, not a heart on his sleeve person, like you,' Barbara said.

'It's just he always seemed to be holding back and I never really understood why.' Barbara's blue eyes were fixed on his, as she waited for him to join up his own dots. 'I think I might have been wrong... not just about Mac, but about a great many things.'

Barbara reached for Alex's hand and squeezed it warmly. 'Don't be so hard on yourself, Alex. You've been through a lot.'

The guilt felt like a boulder someone had placed in the middle of his chest.

'We all have,' he said sadly.

The bed was empty. Alex rocked on his feet, the rubber of his soles squeaking on the linoleum floor. He glanced around, trying not to let panic fill the gaps. This was definitely the right unit, wasn't it? Yes, he remembered that cork noticeboard filled with photographs of patients and thank you cards. This was the right place, but the bed Molly had occupied only three hours earlier was now stripped of its covers. Did it mean...? Had she...? It was an impossible thought to finish.

The swish of the door opening made him turn so fast, he felt dizzy.

'Excuse me, the young woman who was in this bed – Molly Kendall – can you tell me where she is?'

The nurse seemed momentarily fazed, and when Alex caught sight of his reflection in the mirror above the basin in the corner, he understood why. He looked like a crazy person. He deliberately slowed his speech and his breathing. The racing heart remained totally outside of his control.

'Earlier today Molly Kendall was in this bed – and now it's empty. Do you know where she is?'

The nurse looked apologetic. 'I'm sorry, I've only just come on duty. Let me find out for you. Please wait here.'

Alex knew exactly why he'd been told to remain in the now empty room. That's what they did in places like this, when bad news was about to be delivered. He gave an involuntary shiver. He was right to have spent his whole life hating hospitals, because nothing good ever happened in them.

The nurse's face was maddeningly unreadable when she returned.

'Molly Kendall has been moved to another room on the unit.'

'Why?'

The nurse finally smiled. 'Because she's showing signs of improvement. She came round a little while ago and although she's still very weak, the doctors are encouraged by her initial response to the medication. I can take you to her if you like?'

He followed her down the corridor, his smile so impossibly wide, he probably looked completely unbalanced.

'It's the door at the end,' the nurse informed him, turning away with an apology when summoned by a colleague.

From within the room, Alex could hear the soft rumble of a voice he recognised as Mac's. He paused by the entrance, hidden from view by the open door. His hand was fisted to knock on the frame, but before it connected, he froze. Although he couldn't hear what Mac was saying, he could hear the tone. It was intimate; it was confessional; and it was… nothing to do with him.

Through the gap between the door and the jamb he saw the two people Lisa had unwittingly brought together. Mac was pulled up as close as he could get to Molly's bed. His voice was hoarse, barely recognisable, and it was obvious he was fighting back the tears. As Alex watched, a pale white hand, with a cannula and tubes attached, came into view. Very slowly the hand reached up to rest against Mac's cheek.

Alex paused for a long moment, imagining that in some distant place Lisa was smiling gently in approval. Silently he turned around and walked away.

CHAPTER THIRTY-EIGHT

Alex

Connor's cry was loud enough to carry to every room in the house. The box of cat biscuits Alex had been tipping into a bowl, slipped from his fingers. Tiny triangles of kitty kibble rained like hailstones onto the checkerboard tiles.

'Connor, what's wrong?' cried Alex, already crunching cat food beneath his feet as he ran into the hallway. The answer was a second wail of anguish.

Alex thundered up the stairs to Connor's bedroom, already fearing the worst. Had he fallen and hurt his arm? They'd had an appointment at the Fracture Clinic that afternoon and the doctors had assured him that Connor's injury was healing well. But that didn't stop Alex from worrying about the long list of complications he'd been foolish enough to look up online.

It was early evening and the upstairs hall was in darkness, but Alex didn't pause to turn on the lights. For one crazy moment he thought there'd been a break-in. Connor's room was in disarray. Books had been thrown from the shelves and were scattered across the carpet as if flung by a poltergeist. Alex quickly stepped over them to reach Connor who was standing sorrowfully beside the window. His sobs were now at the breath-hitching, inarticulate stage.

'What is it? What's wrong?' Alex asked, his eyes darting inexpertly over his son's body for signs of injury. There was none to be seen. 'It's okay. I'm here now,' Alex said. 'Calm down and tell me what's wrong.'

He crouched down before Connor, the way he'd seen Lisa do a thousand times before. He could imagine his son falling willingly into her outstretched arms, but in Alex's embrace he felt like a tiny, sad mannequin. Connor's face was wet with tears and Alex fruitlessly searched his pockets for a tissue that he didn't expect to locate.

'I can't find it,' Connor said between hiccupping sobs. 'I've looked and looked but I can't find it anywhere.'

Alex's panic began to drop like mercury in a barometer. 'What is it you've lost?' he asked scanning the room as though it was a crime scene. 'Tell me what it is, and we'll look for it together. I'm good at finding things.' That was a blatant lie, and one that would doubtless have amused Lisa who'd been the household retriever of all things that had gone astray.

'The red star. The one with the funny name. Mummy used to show me how to find it, but I can't remember how to do it on my own.'

Alex's stomach plummeted. 'It's okay. Don't get upset. *I'll* help you find it,' he said with a confidence he was far from feeling.

'But you don't know about the stars like Mummy does.'

Alex throat tightened uncomfortably. 'I know this was something you and Mummy did together, but I can help you. I really can. Mummy taught me lots over the years.'

Connor's eyes were full of doubt as Alex pushed aside the curtains and threw open the bedroom window. It was a clear and cloudless night, which Alex knew was good for stargazing. Which was about all he did know, if truth be told. He surveyed the world Lisa had so comfortably inhabited and felt so far from her that the distance could be measured in light years.

'Do we need Mummy's telescope to see this red star?' Alex asked, already panicking that he was halfway to failure before he'd even begun.

'No. Mummy just showed me where to find it in the sky. But I don't know where to look for it without her. I don't know *anything* without Mummy.'

This was so much more than Alex's ability to locate some weirdly named star, he realised, as he helplessly scanned the night skies. This was about not letting Connor down. Again.

He tried innumerable Google searches, and even flipped through the astronomy books Connor had thrown on the floor in frustration. 'It's got to be here somewhere,' he muttered more to himself than Connor. 'Are you sure you can't remember what it was called?'

Connor, who had wordlessly retreated into a corner of the room with Lunar in his arms, shook his head sorrowfully. Alex disappeared into the upstairs office he'd shared with Lisa and returned with an armful of her astronomy textbooks, but they were pitched at a level so far above his head, they were almost as unreachable as the stars themselves. Doggedly Alex ploughed through them, dashing at intervals to the window with an open book or internet page in hand for reference. Each time Connor would glance up hopefully, only to turn away with a dejected look when Alex once again failed to locate the mysterious star with the 'funny' name.

'I'll find it, Connor, I will,' he promised, his voice sounded oddly scratchy, as though his throat was lined with barbed wire. It took the drip of a single tear falling onto the page he was trying to decipher for him to realise he was crying.

From the corner of the room Connor yawned noisily and when Alex glanced at his watch he was shocked to discover it was almost Connor's bedtime and he hadn't yet prepared their dinner. He was failing on so many levels as a parent, it was getting hard to keep count.

'I'm really sorry, champ,' he said, his knees cracking in protest as he got up from the bedroom floor. 'This might take me a little longer than I first thought. But I *will* find it.'

Connor rose fluidly from his cross-legged position in the corner. 'Mummy will know,' he said, sounding forlorn. 'I'll get her to show me again when she comes back. It doesn't matter.'

Except to Alex it did. It mattered a lot.

It mattered as he threw together a hasty meal of pasta and something tomatoey from a jar for their dinner. It mattered as he ran Connor's bath, and tucked him up in bed with yet another apology. It mattered so much that halfway through a TV car show, a programme he usually enjoyed, he switched off the set and climbed determinedly back up the stairs.

He looked in briefly on Connor who was sleeping soundly beneath a spiralling projection of stars from the night light he couldn't bear to put away. Alex stared at the galaxy on the ceiling and then returned to Lisa's textbooks which he'd piled back on her desk.

He found what he'd been searching for in the pages of well-thumbed book Lisa must have had since her university days. His pulse had quickened at the sight of her handwriting on the inside cover. He'd run his fingers over the faded ink of the name she'd had before she'd taken his, and as he glanced at the book's index a single word seemed to leap off the page at him.

'Betelgeuse,' he said, his voice caught somewhere between a laugh and a sob. 'The star with the funny name.'

He flipped to the page, which didn't show *Beetlejuice* the poltergeist from the Hollywood film, but instead a fiery red star which was apparently a thousand times larger than the sun. He scanned the paragraph as relief thumped heavily in his chest.

It took a while for his untrained eyes to search the night sky and locate Venus, which was his first reference point. But as though she was still there, still helping him, Alex remembered asking Lisa how to locate the planet named after the goddess of love on one of their first dates. She'd laughed and teased him for being corny, and he had simply shrugged and kissed her, falling more in love with her with every passing second.

Connor was too soundly asleep for him to disturb with his discovery. It could wait. Alex cast a solitary shadow as he stood at the open window, a smile gently curving his lips as he successfully located the glowing red dot in the sky. A cool breeze ruffled Alex's hair and for a just a moment it didn't feel as though he was standing there alone.

CHAPTER THIRTY-NINE

Molly

'Do you think it's more of a nice dress thing, or a pair of jeans and shirt kind of thing?' I asked, turning from my wardrobe with a hanger in each hand.

His smile was slow. 'You might be asking the wrong person here. My vote would probably go for what you're wearing right now.'

The bedroom mirror caught my smile, as well as my current outfit. The pink lacy bra and matching briefs were sheer, sexy, and made no pretence at being practical. My relationship with Mac was still very much at the Victoria's Secret rather than the Bridget Jones undies stage.

'In fact,' he added, rising from the bed and coming up behind me to circle his arms around my waist, 'if anything, I think you might be a little *over*dressed.' He glanced at the clock on my bedside table. 'Do you think we have time to do anything about that?'

Desire was a low, lazy serpent that slowly uncoiled inside me at his suggestion. I too glanced at the clock, and shook my head.

Mac's sigh echoed my own disappointment. 'Later then,' he whispered into my ear, gently pulling away from me.

I resisted the temptation to wriggle back against the firm contours of his body.

'I'm going to have a shower,' he said, heading towards the doorway and stopping only to add with a grin, 'A cold one, I think.'

I was smiling as I sat down at my dressing table to fix my hair and make-up. It was only seven weeks since that day in the hospital when everything changed between us. I'd spent most of that time in a state of amazement at how something so new could already feel so settled, and so right.

His was the first face I saw when I came round at the hospital, and as sappy as it was to admit, I knew in that moment it was the face I wanted to see every single time I opened my eyes to start a new day.

'Don't ever scare me like that again,' he said, and I was shocked to see tears shining brightly in his eyes.

'Right now the only thing I want you to concentrate on is getting better again. But I want you to know this isn't going away – *I'm* not going away.'

And he'd been true to his word. He was at every visiting session throughout my five-day stay in hospital. He was the first one through the doors when they opened, and the last to be evicted at the end of every evening.

On the second day, when I was starting to feel more like me again, he took my hand, now free of its drip, and held it gently between his.

'That old song is wrong, you know. A kiss isn't just a kiss; sometimes it's a wake-up call to something you've been too scared to admit.' He lifted my hand to his lips, grazing the knuckles with the gentlest of kisses. 'Ever since New Year's Eve, I've been trying to keep my distance, trying to give you some space.'

'I know,' I said sadly. 'I assumed it was because you regretted what happened on the balcony.'

He shook his head slowly, but I still needed to hear the actual words.

'I tried to convince myself there was nothing between us, but I knew all along I was lying to myself,' he said.

'I thought you saw me as just a friend,' I admitted, too hesitant to be the first to jump off the diving board.

'Friends don't feel the way I feel about you,' he replied, his remarkable blue eyes staring deeply into mine. 'For far too long, I've spent my days rationalising away what I feel, telling myself I should stand aside because of Alex. I've been going to sleep at night with it all squared away in my mind, but in the morning…' His voice trailed away, and I suddenly found it much harder to breathe. 'But in the morning I always wake up loving you again.'

'You… You love me?' I asked incredulously.

Mac shifted position to perch on the edge of the bed, leaning close enough to probably send every monitor I was attached to into overdrive. Any minute now someone was likely to come racing into the room pushing a crash cart.

'I'm falling in love with you, Molly Kendall. I have been falling in love with you from the first day I met you, and I know I'm going to keep on doing that every single day of my life. What I feel for you is so strong, I can't imagine a time when it will ever stop growing.'

He looked at me and everything he'd just said was there on his face. And yet I still couldn't take it in.

'It's okay if you don't feel the same – or even if you never feel this way.' He gave a rueful smile. 'Although I really hope that one day you will.'

He paused, his heart and soul open to me.

Very slowly, I smiled and nodded. 'I already do,' I whispered. 'Have we got to the bit where you kiss me yet?'

'We have,' he said, leaning in.

And just like that, everything changed for the better.

*

'Very nice,' Mac said approvingly as I came down the stairs forty minutes later in a pair of indigo jeans and a tailored white shirt. I'd left the top three buttons undone, revealing the scar I no longer felt the need to hide. Now whenever I saw it, I remembered only Mac's tender gaze the first time I'd laid naked in his arms. His head had bent to the long red line and he'd kissed it, almost reverently. 'Without this, there would be no you,' he'd said huskily. 'It's a constant reminder of how lucky I am.'

It had been the moment to finally voice my fears. 'You do know that the doctors can't tell me how much time this new heart has given me. If I'm lucky then it might be as much as twenty-five years—'

'I believe the record is actually thirty-four,' Mac interrupted. He'd done his research. 'I understand there are risks, Molly. But there are risks *everywhere*.' His smile was sad. 'Even something as innocent as getting on a train can be dangerous.' His hands gently cupped my face. 'The one thing all of this has taught me is that none of us can predict the future. But there is one thing I know for certain; I would rather have twenty-five years with you, than fifty or more with anyone else. If you'll have me, that is.'

There had never been a question so easy to answer. My heart was pounding, as though in approval, as I pulled him closer and kissed him.

That same heart gave its customary little jolt as I saw him waiting patiently for me in the hallway, my jacket already in his hand.

'You're definitely going to need this,' he said, holding it out for me.

I opened the front door and saw instantly what he meant. It had been raining hard all morning, the kind of rain where you turned on every light in the house and it still felt gloomy. This was the storm the weather forecasters had been predicting all week, and it looked as though it might be even more ferocious than they'd expected.

We ran to Mac's car at the kerb as though dodging artillery in the trenches. The black fabric of his shirt was plastered to his back and shoulders by the time he jumped into the driver's seat. I tried not to let the Colin Firth effect distract me as I turned my attention to the rain lashing the windscreen.

'Do you think it's okay to drive in this?' I asked, very glad we'd decided to take his car rather than mine. As we watched, a neighbour's dustbin left their front garden and scooted down onto the pavement as though swept along by a giant invisible hand.

'Yes,' Mac said reassuringly. 'But I'm going to take it slow. If we're late, we're late. Alex will understand.'

I was silent for most of the drive, allowing Mac to concentrate on the treacherous road conditions. Not surprisingly, my thoughts turned to the mysterious event we were going to.

'I want to mark the fact it's been a year now since... since everything happened,' Alex had said when he'd called to invite me to this gathering of Lisa's organ recipients. Although we were in regular contact with each other, this would be the first time we'd all been together since the night of the bonfire party. 'I've something I want – no, *need* – to say to all of you.' I tried pressing him for a clue, but he was deliberately cagey. 'I'll tell you all next week,' was all I could get out of him.

'Do you think you might be seeing Mac sometime before then to pass on the invitation?' he added, his voice suddenly uncertain.

As Mac was at that moment submerged in the jasmine-scented water of my bathtub, it was an easy assurance to give.

'Why do you think Alex wants to see all of us together?' I'd immediately asked Mac as I slipped back into the fragrant water to join him.

'I don't know. I guess we'll find out next week,' Mac replied evenly, confirming my suspicion that a lack of curiosity might actually be a male chromosome deficiency.

CHAPTER FORTY

Alex

'So, the quiche goes in first, then the sausage rolls, and then ten minutes later you can put in the tray of onion bhajis.'

'Got it,' Alex said, with the unearned confidence of a man who'd never burnt a single thing in his life.

'You think I'm crazy, don't you?' he added.

'No. Lots of people still serve quiche when they have guests coming round. It's retro.'

There were many things Alex felt he didn't understand in the world, but why his brother had fallen in love with Dee wasn't one of them.

'You think the *party* is a bad idea,' he pressed. 'You think I'm just going to make everyone feel uncomfortable.'

'It could happen,' Dee said, suddenly sounding serious. 'The potential is there for maximum awkwardness. I guess it's a risk you have to be willing to run.'

'I just feel it's time now. It's like everything has been on pause – even grieving properly,' he admitted sadly. 'All this time I've been waiting for something to happen – some big sign, or revelation, something that will finally make sense of the shitshow of the last twelve months.'

'There was never going to be an easy way to get through this first year,' Dee said.

Or the rest of my life, Alex silently added. But something had shifted inside him as he'd sat on the damp grass beside Lisa's grave on the anniversary of her death. The way he'd been behaving wasn't helping either Connor or him to move forward. He saw the truth of that now, with a clarity he'd not had before.

The love of his life had died in a tragic and senseless accident. The people her death had saved weren't 'chosen' to come into his and Connor's life for some higher mystical purpose. They weren't 'selected' – except randomly, by virtue of having reached the right point on the NHS lists. They were right-place, right-time individuals, every bit as much as Lisa was wrong place, wrong time.

He needed to apologise to all of them.

'You do understand why I didn't ask you and Todd to come today?' he said worriedly.

'Absolutely. Neither of us can stand quiche.'

He hung up laughing, which was exactly what his sister-in-law had intended.

CHAPTER FORTY-ONE

Molly

Barbara and Jamie had diametrically opposite styles of greeting. Barbara rose from Alex's couch with her lips and arms stretched wide. She enveloped first me and then Mac in the kind of hug that made breathing a challenge.

Jamie was decidedly more laid-back and cool, setting aside his phone to lift one arm in greeting, as though hailing me from a distance far greater than just the width of the lounge.

'Yo, Mols,' he called out.

I smiled, unsure of the appropriate response but certain I was at least a decade too old to pull off a 'yo' in reply.

'You're looking way better than you did in the hospital – far less like a zombie now.'

'Thanks,' I said, taking the backhanded compliment at face value.

'I think you look beautiful,' Barbara said, slipping her arm through mine and squeezing it gently. 'Practically glowing, I'd say.' Her eyes twinkled as they darted mischievously between Mac and me.

I inwardly groaned. We'd only been here a matter of minutes, and our intention to keep the focus swivelled firmly away from our relationship was already in danger of failing. Luckily Alex was too busy hanging up our coats and getting us a drink to have overheard.

He looked anxious and on edge as he passed me the soft drink I'd requested and Mac a bottle of beer. His own glass contained an amber-coloured liquid that he downed in one nervous gulp. He crossed the room to stand in front of the fireplace, his hand fingering his now empty glass. It felt like a scene from an Agatha Christie film, where the detective (Alex) was about to confront the room full of suspects (us). I swirled the cola in my glass, suddenly regretting I hadn't gone for something stronger.

'I… er wasn't going to do this straight off. I thought I'd leave what I had to say until later, after we'd eaten.' He lifted his glass to his lips and seemed truly surprised to find it empty. 'But as Connor is tucked away upstairs playing with Lunar' – Barbara gave a Cheshire-cat smile – 'it seems like a good time to get this off my chest.'

His words triggered a worried glance that travelled the room like a virus.

Alex cleared his throat. 'I don't think I've been this nervous since the speech I gave at our wedding.' His eyes went to a beautiful silver-framed photo of him and Lisa on that day. The image seemed to calm him.

'I wrote out what I wanted to say today – it ran to six pages.'

All four of us tried to hide our dismay, with varying degrees of success.

Alex laughed. 'Don't worry. I tore it up before you all got here. Because what I have to say can be condensed into just a few sentences.'

I was rather proud that no one actually sighed out loud in relief.

'I want to start by apologising. I've not been a good enough friend to any of you. In fact, I've been downright disingenuous.'

A chorus of denials filled the room.

Alex shook his head sadly. 'It's true. I brought you into our lives – Connor's and mine – but my motives have been… questionable, at best.'

He shuffled uncomfortably, taking a sudden interest in his tan-coloured loafers. 'I haven't been as honest with you as I should have been. I was looking for Lisa; searching for her in every single one of you.'

His words were directed to all four of us, but his eyes were on me. For a long moment it seemed as though we'd all stopped breathing. The house was that silent.

'I've watched too closely, without ever seeing you properly. I've listened too acutely, without hearing what you were saying.'

'No, no, Alex dear,' protested Barbara, looking genuinely upset. 'You've given us all so much – and that has nothing to do with giving your consent to the transplants. I think each of our lives is better now than the one we had before. I know mine is. This kidney…' – she gestured vaguely to her body – 'I could have got it from anyone. But this family, that I now feel I'm a part of…' She reached into the pocket of her cardigan and withdrew an embroidered handkerchief to delicately dab at her eyes. 'This family is something only you could have given to me.'

'Yeah, man. Don't beat yourself up about it. Okay, so you've acted a bit freaky at times' – I swallowed a gulp and saw Mac do the same – 'but we understood. We got it. And we're all cool with it, right?' Jamie, our new self-appointed spokesman, turned to the people Lisa had helped, and all three of us nodded.

There was no mistaking the glint of tears in Alex's eyes now. 'Thank you. All of you. You're being kinder than I deserve. Even though I now accept the way we were brought together was entirely random, without any agenda, reason or purpose, I really hope we'll stay in each other's lives for a very long time to come.'

'I sounded like a right dick, didn't I?'

I grinned even while I was shaking my head. The timely interruption of the pinging oven had sent Alex hurrying to the kitchen, and I'd followed a moment or two later to see if he needed any help.

'You sounded like a man who was healing and starting to move on. There's absolutely nothing stupid about that.'

Alex pulled a tray of food from the oven, and without waiting to be asked I went straight to a cupboard and got out a serving platter. Despite everything he'd just finished saying, Alex's eyes widened in surprise.

'I remembered it was there from when I made the gingerbread men,' I explained.

He gave an embarrassed laugh. 'It's going to take a while to stop looking for signs where they clearly don't exist,' he admitted ruefully.

'Hi. Sorry to interrupt.'

We both turned to see a disembodied head peering round the door.

'Is it okay if I go upstairs and see Connor? I downloaded a game for him on my phone that he's going to love.'

'Sure,' Alex said. 'You know the way.'

He must have seen my surprised expression as Jamie left the room and thundered up the stairs.

'Did Jamie not tell you he's been doing some work for me?'

This time it was my eyes that widened. 'You needed a roadie, or a lifeguard?'

Alex laughed quietly, remembering some of the more colourful claims Jamie had made in the past. 'No. Actually he's been helping out with some IT stuff for the office move. He's spent quite a bit of time here over the last couple of weeks. Connor absolutely hero worships him.'

There was a lot to be read between the lines of what Alex had said.

'It was nice of you to give him a job.'

We shared a look of understanding.

'I had to be careful how I phrased it. I didn't want to offend him. I told him I realised he didn't need the money, but I had to pay him a wage for insurance purposes.'

For just a moment I thought how much easier it would have been if Lisa's heart had fallen in love with this man all over again. But then I thought about Mac, who was waiting patiently for me in the other room and realised everything had worked out exactly the way it was supposed to.

Jamie's tread was even heavier on the stairs when he raced back down them a minute later. He burst into the kitchen with enough force that the door was still swinging on its hinges as he declared, 'Connor's not there.'

Alex was halfway through transferring a large quiche onto a serving plate. He paused and looked up, his brow furrowing. 'You looked in the right room?'

The question earned him a truly withering look from Jamie.

'He's probably in the bathroom,' Alex said, although I noticed the quiche remained frozen in mid-air on its way to the dish.

'That's what I thought. "He'll just be taking a whizz," I reckoned. But I checked the bathroom and it's empty. And when I called his name, he didn't answer.'

The quiche fell onto the platter with a squelching plop as Alex stopped trying to pretend he wasn't concerned. He strode into the hall and long before he'd reached the foot of the stairs he'd called Connor's name three times, loud enough for him to have heard wherever he was in the house. Through the open door of the lounge Mac looked up, a question clearly visible on his face. *Is anything wrong?* I gave a small shake of my head, because that was what I wanted to believe, despite the twisting in my gut that was playing origami with my internal organs.

Alex took the stairs like a hurdler, his feet only connecting with every third tread. 'Connor!' he cried, dashing straight into his room.

Jamie and I, only a few steps behind him, shared a worried look.

Like a whirlwind, Alex spun around, pushing past us as he left his son's empty room and began flinging open every other bedroom door.

'Connor, come out now! This isn't funny.'

Somehow I already knew this was more serious than an innocent game of hide-and-seek taken one step too far.

Alex emerged from the last of the upstairs rooms, twin sparks of panic blazing in his eyes.

'Slow down. Let's look again properly,' I urged, laying my hand on his forearm. It was like placing my palm on a generator; his whole body was pulsating with tension.

'I'll go and check downstairs,' Jamie said, already heading in that direction. 'Maybe he snuck past us and we never noticed.'

Mac was already waiting at the bottom of the stairs with a look on his face that said he'd grasped the seriousness of the situation. 'I'll check the garden,' he announced.

I stepped back into Connor's room, dropped to my knees beside his bed as though in prayer, and slid onto my stomach. Beneath the bed I found several pieces of Lego, a rogue sock and half a dozen crayons, but no sign of a boy who'd taken a prank a little too far.

Alex was at that stage of panic where you start looking in totally improbable places. Having checked all the wardrobes, he was now pulling open drawers as though his son might have learnt circus-level contortionist skills without telling anyone. I followed in his wake, searching each room more methodically in case Alex had missed the kneehole in Lisa's old desk or the space behind the bathroom door. Both were empty.

Alex must have run up and down the stairs three or four times, unable to believe Jamie when he reported that there was no sign of Connor on the ground floor either.

'I checked outside, front and back, and looked inside the shed and in your car, but I can't see him anywhere,' Mac said, his shirt once again plastered to his body.

I glanced worriedly through the window. The rain was still hitting the ground with the ferocity of a pressure washer. Surely Connor wouldn't have ventured outside to play in weather like this? *He didn't; he's not that sort of boy*, confirmed a voice in my head that oddly didn't sound like me at all.

As I stood in the doorway of Connor's empty bedroom, I was aware that my movements were being followed by a pair of baleful, emerald eyes. I turned slowly to look at Connor's beloved pet, who was curled up in a ball in the middle of his bed.

'Where's he gone, Lunar? Can't you help us find him?'

In a *Lassie* film, that request would probably have resulted in us being led to the nearest mineshaft. But this wasn't a film, and cats don't operate in the same way. And yet would Connor really have gone somewhere and abandoned Lunar? Didn't Alex say he practically never left the cat's side?

Down on the ground floor, I could hear Alex still calling for his son. There was also the deep rumble of a voice I'd come to love, which appeared to be asking the kind of level-headed questions that we should all have been posing.

'Let's look at this calmly,' said Mac. 'He's clearly not in the house, so where is he likely to have gone on his own?'

'Nowhere. We never let him go out without one of us being with him.' In his anxiety, Alex was referring to Lisa in the present tense again.

'How about Todd and Dee's? Do you think he might have tried to get himself there?'

'It's too far. He wouldn't know how.'

With infinite patience, Mac kept asking all the right questions. 'Okay. Well let's think about closer to home, then. Is there a neighbour he likes? Or a schoolfriend who lives nearby? How about a park or a playground you take him to?'

'No. He just wouldn't do that,' Alex shot back, panic indistinguishable from anger in his voice.

From behind me the cat gave a long, plaintive miaow as though tired of the commotion that was disrupting her sleep. I was about to leave the bedroom when I glimpsed something out of the corner of my eye that stopped me. I could feel myself holding my breath as I retraced my steps to the bed, my heart beating far too fast and erratically, as though trying to tell me something. There was definitely something on the bed; I could see the tiniest glimpse of it protruding from beneath Lunar's coiled body. Very gently I nudged the cat to one side, to retrieve whatever it was she'd chosen to curl up on.

I swallowed noisily as I read and then reread the note in my hand. I was shaking so much, the large, childish script was hard to decipher.

'Alex, come here! I've found something,' I yelled.

Seconds later, the note was in Alex's hand, which if anything was trembling even more than mine.

'Shit,' he cried, his fingers raking through his hair, giving him a manic look that matched the expression in his eyes.

'What does it say?' asked Barbara, who along with Mac and Jamie had followed Alex up the stairs on hearing my cry.

Alex was staring at the sheet in his hands as though it was a ransom request. His eyes were darting over the crayoned words as though searching them for a hidden meaning.

'Gone to see Mummy,' I read out loud, my voice unnaturally high.

'What does that mean?' asked Barbara, as bewildered as the rest of us. All except Alex.

He pushed past us and ran back down the stairs. We followed in his wake like rats trailing a piper.

'Where are my fucking keys?' he yelled, racing from kitchen to lounge as though one of us had deliberately hidden them. 'Where the hell are my car keys?'

While the others started to look for them, I made a grab for Alex's wrists. In the state he was in, the last thing he should have been doing was getting behind the wheel of a car.

'Molly, please let go of me,' he snapped, pulling away roughly enough to break one of my nails. I didn't even feel it.

'Not until you tell me where you're going.'

There was a terror on his face that was going to haunt my nightmares for a long time to come.

'Isn't it obvious? I know where Connor has gone.' Everyone froze in their search for the missing keys and turned towards him. 'It's bloody obvious, isn't it? He said he's "gone to see Mummy". He finally got tired of waiting for me to take him there.'

'Where?' asked Barbara.

'The cemetery. To Lisa's grave. It's the one place I've never let him go.'

His words took the wind out of our collective sails, and in the ensuing doldrums Alex finally spotted the missing car keys in a small ceramic bowl, which I suspected was where they always lived.

'Alex, please take a moment to think this through,' I implored, trying to grasp the back of his shirt to slow him down. The fabric slipped through my fingers, but at least he paused on the threshold of the open front door. It was hard to hear him through the thundering rain and with the wind shrieking in the background, urging him to hurry.

'Does Connor even know where the cemetery is?' I asked.

'We've driven past it. He probably thinks he knows how to get there.'

'But isn't it miles from here?' said Jamie, clearly as upset as the rest of us.

'It is,' cried Alex, his voice cracking with emotion. 'So the sooner I set off to find him, the less likely he is to step out into a busy road or get picked up by some goddam pervert.'

His words stunned us into the silence he needed to run from his own front door. He stopped just once before hurling himself into the car. 'Stay here, all of you, in case he comes back. I'll call you as soon as I find him.'

The squeal of his tyres on the slick tarmac sounded like the wail of a banshee. It curdled my blood and left me standing in the rain long after Alex's tail lights had disappeared into the storm.

An arm slipped around my waist and gently pulled me away from the open door, shutting it firmly behind me. 'Jamie and I are going to search the nearby streets. Connor might have gone outside and then taken shelter from the rain somewhere.' It was a reasonable suggestion, but I could tell from Mac's eyes that he didn't put much store in it.

'If Alex phones to say he's found him somewhere en route, just give me a call.'

'He won't be phoning,' said Jamie from somewhere behind us. We turned around to see him emerge from the kitchen with something slim and metallic in his hand. 'Alex left in such a hurry he didn't pick up his phone. He can't get in touch with us, and we can't reach him either.'

I stared mindlessly at Alex's forgotten phone, as though this was one problem too many for me to cope with. Fortunately, the man I'd fallen in love with was made of sterner stuff.

'Okay. That doesn't alter things. Alex is still going to drive to the cemetery to look for Connor, and we're still going to search much closer to home.'

'Shouldn't we… Shouldn't we call the police?' I asked, hating that this would turn Connor from a temporarily lost child into one who was 'missing'.

'One step at a time. We could find him sheltering in someone's garden a few houses away,' Mac said. He pulled me towards him, pressing a hard and urgent kiss upon my lips. 'You stay here with Barbara in case he comes back on his own.'

CHAPTER FORTY-TWO

Molly

'I'll make us some tea,' said Barbara, her voice brittle with concern as she disappeared in the direction of the kitchen. It was the panacea of her generation, and if keeping busy helped her, I was happy to drink gallons of the stuff.

'Okay. I'm just going to take another quick look in Connor's room,' I said, unable to shake the feeling that I was somehow missing something.

I surveyed his bedroom once more, but all it revealed was that he loved astronomy, the moon – and his mum. There were framed photographs of the two of them on either side of his bed. They were laughing in both pictures: one in the snow; the other on a beach, eyes crinkled against the sun as they faced the camera. I liked how Alex had made sure Lisa's face was still the first thing Connor saw each day.

She lived on in other vital ways than simply the organs she'd donated. She was certainly here in the shelves housing Connor's favourite possessions, I realised, as my hand travelled along a unit where books, models, and toys relating to space were crammed tightly together. I paused when I reached a gap where two tell-tale shapes were visible in a light film of dust; one round, one cylindrical. What had sat there, I wondered.

Convinced there were no answers to be found in this room, I headed for the door, pausing to pick up the photo of Lisa and Connor on the beach. 'Can't you help me?' I asked the smiling woman in the frame. 'I'm trying to find him for you.'

From the ground floor I could hear Barbara calling my name, presumably telling me the tea was now ready. I bent to replace the photograph on the bedside cabinet, but it wouldn't stand up straight. I frowned, turned it over and saw the problem. A small square of paper had been forced into the back of the frame, which I'd dislodged. It fell to the carpet.

My fingers were trembling as I bent to retrieve it, as though I already knew it was significant. I unfolded it carefully, noting the creases that revealed it had once been crumpled into a ball. To my shame, I didn't stop to consider whether this was prying or invading Connor's privacy. All that concerned me was that somewhere out there, in the worst storm we'd had in years, a young boy was lost, and there was nothing I wouldn't do to find him. Nothing.

Despite the creases, the image of the eclipse was still striking. I could see why Connor had wanted to keep it. But the reason he'd wanted to hide it was on the reverse side of the flier. A soft gasp escaped my lips as I realised I was holding an invitation for Lisa to attend this year's Astronomy Fair, and then a much louder gasp followed when I read the date of the event. Today. The Astronomy Fair was happening today. Was that where Connor had gone?

Above the sound of the wind rattling the window frame, I heard an echo of a conversation I'd had with Alex months before: *It was the last thing Lisa said to Connor on the day she died. She promised they'd go on the train to the Astronomy Fair next year. I think that's why he won't accept she isn't coming back for him – because she promised, and she never broke her word to him.*

I was not one to believe in signs, portents or omens, but I did believe there was a reason why I'd been drawn back to Connor's room. And I was pretty sure I was holding that reason in my hand right then.

I ran down the stairs far quicker than I should, and almost cannoned into Barbara, who was about to climb them in search of me.

'I know how we can find out which direction Connor took when he left the house,' she said excitedly.

Her revelation trumped mine by a country mile.

'How?'

'Gordon should be able to tell us,' she said, pulling down both of our coats from the rack in the hall.

'Great. Erm… who exactly is Gordon?' I asked, already shoving my arms into my sleeves.

'He's a curmudgeonly grump of a man with an unfortunate dislike of cats. Thank goodness,' she added mysteriously.

I followed her out of the house and into the storm, although mentally I was lagging several pages behind. She had to raise her voice to be heard above the drumming of the rain as we briskly crossed the road, dodging a minefield of deep puddles.

'Alex's neighbour complained about Connor's cat, so I paid him a visit to give him a piece of my mind,' Barbara said, looking embarrassed. 'He's not such a bad old stick; he's just lonely, I think.' Her smile revealed she might like Alex's neighbour a little more than she was admitting to. 'Not that I could get him to change his mind, though, which obviously is a blessing, as it turns out.' She paused at the foot of a neatly tended front garden on the corner of the street.

'Change his mind about what?' I asked, hurrying after her as she sped up the path and knocked smartly on the front door.

'That,' Barbara said succinctly, pointing to a device fixed to the roof of the porch; a device I recognised; a device that was pointing not only at the flowerbeds edging the front garden but also at the crossroads beyond it.

*

'It's probably not going to be of any help. That's not what it was installed for. It's not even that sharp a picture. I couldn't afford the fancy models.'

Gordon Grafton had grumbled and moaned from the moment he'd answered the front door. He was like a human version of A. A. Milne's Eeyore, all gloom and despondency. And yet I'd seen the glimmer that had briefly lit up his eyes when he recognised the woman standing on his doorstep. The fondness I suspected Barbara felt for Alex's elderly neighbour appeared to be reciprocated.

'There!' I said, my finger jabbing excitedly at the grainy image on the ancient laptop. All three of us craned towards the screen, where a small figure wearing a bright yellow raincoat had just appeared. Barbara and I groaned in unison as a large dark van swept onto the screen, obscuring Connor and the opposite side of the road from view.

I was perched, quite literally, on the edge of my seat as we waited for the van to execute a right-hand turn and get out of the way. By the time it did, Connor was almost out of camera range.

'Can you zoom in or sharpen up the image?' I asked.

Gordon's wiry grey eyebrows rose like a pair of levitating gerbils. 'This isn't bloody *CSI*, you know,' he replied testily, but he nevertheless prodded at several keys before finally finding the one to freeze the recording.

'What's that he's holding?' asked Barbara, peering so closely at the screen, her nose was practically grazing it.

'Looks like a bat and a football to me. Perhaps the lad was heading for the park?' suggested Gordon.

I shook my head, my mind returning to the imprints on the shelf in Connor's bedroom. I now knew which objects were missing.

'He's carrying a telescope and a papier-mâché model of the moon,' I said softly. It confirmed what I'd already suspected to be true. Connor was trying to make his own way to the Astronomy Fair. He'd gone to find his mummy.

To say that Mac and Jamie were saturated was an understatement. Their clothes were stuck to their bodies, their hair flat against their heads as though they'd just been dunked in a pool. I found a stack of towels from the airing cupboard, while Barbara brewed up some more tea.

'But if Connor *is* trying to get to the train station,' Jamie said, rubbing at his hair with a towel until it stood porcupine straight on his head, 'isn't he heading in the wrong direction? If what you saw on that old geezer's video is right?'

I frowned because he made an excellent point. Connor *had* been seen heading in the opposite direction of both the station and the cemetery.

'I think it's safe to say that Connor probably didn't have a clue which way he should be heading,' Mac said, accepting the mug of tea Barbara passed him with a grateful smile. 'The only thing it does tell us is that Alex is highly unlikely to come across him on his journey to the cemetery.'

'Then we should go after him ourselves,' I said, leaping to my feet. 'If we follow the road we saw Connor heading down, we're much more likely to find him than Alex is.'

'Agreed,' said Mac. 'And if—' He broke off as the ringing of a mobile phone interrupted him. We looked from one person to the next, but no one jumped up to answer it.

'It's not mine,' said Jamie.

'Nor mine,' said Barbara.

Mac and I exchanged glances; the ringtone was neither of ours either.

'It's Alex's!' cried Jamie, jumping up and scoping the room. 'Where the hell did I put his phone?' He hurried towards the hallway, but the ringing had stopped before he'd even left the kitchen.

He returned a few moments later with Alex's phone in his hand. I was so busy looking at the mobile, I was slow to notice his healthy colour had drained to a sickly pallor.

'What is it? What's wrong?' Bad news was beginning to feel like a stack of dominoes just waiting to tumble our way.

In reply, Jamie gingerly set the phone down on Alex's kitchen table so we could all see the message on the home screen.

Missed call. Lisa

There was a long silence as we absorbed the impossibility of what we were seeing.

'You don't think that she… that she found a way to…' began Jamie, sounding genuinely spooked.

Thankfully, Mac was more pragmatic. 'There's a logical explanation to this,' he said firmly. 'This isn't anything supernatural.'

I reached hesitantly for the phone. 'There is an explanation, although it still doesn't make sense.' Three pairs of eyes swivelled in my direction. 'Alex gave Connor Lisa's old mobile phone. He uses it to speak to her – pretend conversations,' I added hastily, noticing Jamie's wide-eyed stare. 'But Alex said the phone hadn't been charged since Lisa died. The battery would have gone flat long ago.'

The colour flooded back into Jamie's cheeks. 'Erm… that's not strictly true. I kind of gave it a quick charge last week, so he could play a game on it.'

There was a brief time-lag as we registered this information, and then four pairs of hands simultaneously pounced on the phone as though playing a high-stakes game of Snap. Mac got to it first and quickly pressed the button to return the last incoming call.

'Pick up, pick up,' I murmured under my breath. 'Please, Connor, pick up the phone.'

Mac shook his head as he set the phone back down on the table. 'It's either switched off or flat again,' he said with a disappointed sigh.

'But it just rang,' I cried, closer to tears of frustration than I wanted to admit. 'He was trying to reach us.'

'Hang on a minute,' said Jamie, peering at the phone. 'I think he left a message.'

I wasn't sure how much more of this rollercoaster of emotions my new heart could withstand. It felt as though we were hurtling from despair to hope every twenty seconds.

After listening to the message for the fourth time, I had to concur with Jamie's assessment.

'Bum dial,' he said gloomily as we once again listened to its jumble of random, indistinct sounds.

Barbara looked confused as she considered something that sounded anatomically impossible.

'It means it was an accidental call,' I explained. 'Connor must have leant against the phone without realising it, and it rang the last number that had been dialled. He probably didn't even realise the call had connected.'

Mac downed the remainder of his tea and got to his feet. 'We should go. We can cover more ground in the car than on foot, and three pairs of eyes are better than two.' He laid one hand gently on Barbara's shoulder. 'Are you okay holding the fort here alone in case Alex gets in touch or returns?'

'Or Connor comes back,' she added hopefully.

Mac's smile might have convinced her, but I saw the doubt behind it. 'Absolutely.'

Barbara nodded solemnly.

'Okay then, guys. Let's go.'

CHAPTER FORTY-THREE

Molly

Two beers and no lunch meant it was safer for me to drive than Mac. He threw his keys to me across the bonnet and I caught them in one hand. Jamie climbed into the back. Despite switching the wipers to maximum speed, they struggled to clear the windscreen of the fast-falling rain. Even with three pairs of eyes looking for him, it was going to be tricky to spot one small lost boy in these conditions.

I paused before pulling away from the junction where Connor was last caught on camera. Were we making a huge mistake in not alerting the police that he was missing? What if Alex's worst fears were realised and someone had offered him a lift? Was he old enough to know not to accept? I shook my head as my imagination conjured up the kind of headlines that would strike terror into any parent's heart. *Except you're not a parent*, a voice in my head took pains to remind me. I ignored it.

'Jamie, why don't you take the right-hand side of the road and I'll do the left?' suggested Mac, who was proving to be far better in a crisis than the rest of us.

'I'll look straight ahead,' I volunteered, and then proceeded to instantly fail at that when the bus in front of us pulled away from its stop and I almost drove Mac's car right into it. For a dreadful moment I thought the brakes weren't going to find purchase on the rain-slicked tarmac, but with a squeal of protest they brought us to a halt just inches from the back of the bus. I hadn't thought it was possible for my anxiety levels to soar any higher off the chart, but somehow they managed it.

'I'm so sorry,' I apologised shakily to my two passengers.

Mac laid a comforting hand over mine on the wheel. 'He pulled out without looking or indicating. It wasn't you, Molly.' His voice was remarkably calm for a man who'd almost seen his very expensive car written off.

I turned towards him with a less than steady smile. 'Are you sure you want me to drive?'

'I'm probably over the limit, and Jamie doesn't have a licence, so you remain our designated driver.'

I pulled back into the flow of traffic, mindful now that it was clearly a busy bus route. I crawled along at a good ten miles below the speed limit, partly because of the storm but more to make it easier for Mac and Jamie to spot Connor. My tortoise-like progress earned a cacophony of protests from car horns and a few colourful comments delivered through rolled-down windows. Jamie took particular delight in responding to those, with hand gestures you definitely don't find in the Highway Code.

Five miles down the road there was still no sight of a small boy dressed in a canary-yellow raincoat.

'Shouldn't we have spotted him by now?' I asked. 'How far could a seven-year-old have walked anyway?'

'Apparently just under three miles an hour – I googled it,' Jamie said. 'But as we don't know when he set off, that doesn't tell us how far he's walked.'

I felt rather than saw Mac stiffen in the passenger seat beside me. 'Pull over,' he said urgently.

'Have you spotted him?' I cried, almost stalling the car in my haste to do as he'd asked.

Mac shook his head as I drew up beside the kerb. 'Turn off the engine,' he said.

I could see in the rear-view mirror that Jamie was just as perplexed as I was.

'And the wipers too,' Mac added. 'I need it to be as quiet as possible.'

I bit my tongue and did what he said.

With an unreadable expression on his face, Mac reached for Alex's phone, which we'd brought with us in the car. 'Just don't say anything for a moment,' he requested.

He scrolled through the icons on the phone until he found the one to replay the message Connor had inadvertently left on his father's mobile. Even the tick of the dashboard clock sounded too loud as I watched Mac replay the message half a dozen times, not on speaker phone this time but with the mobile pressed tightly against his ear.

After the last repetition he set the phone back down on the centre console. There was a small, satisfied look on his face that gave me a glimmer of hope.

'I don't think we're going to find Connor walking down this road,' he began.

'But this is definitely where—'

He cut me off. 'This is the right road, but I don't think he's walking any more.'

Those terrifying headlines filled my head again, making it hard to concentrate on his next words.

'I think he's on a bus – or at least he was.'

'Huh? How do you work that out?'

'Listen,' Mac urged, setting up the message to play again and holding the phone to my ear.

As hard as I tried, I could decipher nothing from the jumble of sounds to confirm Mac's suspicion. Even Jamie, who, being younger, presumably had better hearing, failed to discern what Mac could.

'It's not just a myth that blind people can hear more acutely than sighted people,' he explained. 'When I lost my vision, I noticed a difference. Every sound became sharper, more defined – sometimes even magnified. And that hasn't left me, even after the cornea transplants. I think I can hear the faint sound of a ringing bell on the recording. The kind you press when you want a bus to make a stop.'

Jamie and I each took another turn with the phone, but even with knowing what we were listening out for, we still couldn't hear it.

'I think I can also make out the vague sound of birds cawing in the distance. I think they're gulls.'

'So Connor is on a bus?' said Jamie, already sounding as though our mission had failed. 'Then we're never going to find him.'

'He was on a bus,' Mac corrected. 'But I think the sounds on the recording are of him getting off.'

'Even assuming he managed to catch a bus by himself, had money for his fare, and didn't get challenged by the driver, where on earth did he think he was going? If he'd asked to go to the train station, he'd have been told he was heading the wrong way.'

Mac sighed heavily. 'I don't know. But something tells me he thinks he's heading in the right direction. My gut instinct is to keep going down this road and hope we get lucky and spot him.'

It wasn't much of a plan, but it was the only one we had. I reached for the key and turned the engine back on. No one said much for the next twenty minutes, and my grip on the wheel tightened with every mile we travelled. Surely Connor wouldn't have ventured this far from his home? I was on the point of suggesting we turn around and return, when Mac jolted upright in the seat beside me as though he'd been electrocuted.

'Turn left here,' he directed suddenly.

It was almost too late to make the turn, and I must have left a fair bit of rubber on the road as I swung the wheel sharply to the left. The car bucked and swerved, and I waited until it was back under my control before glancing at Mac. He was craned forward as far as his seatbelt would allow, both hands resting on the dashboard as he attempted to peer through the storm.

'I think there's a roundabout a couple of hundred yards down this road. If there is, take the right-hand exit.'

'You know this area?'

'Not really. Well, yes and no.'

His answer told me precisely nothing, but before I could question him further, through the torrential rain the roundabout appeared, just as he'd predicted. I flicked the indicator and made the right-hand turn.

'This road is on a steep incline, so keep your speed low,' he advised. 'At the bottom there's a T-junction with a church on the left. Turn right there.'

Like the roundabout, the church and junction duly materialised.

'I don't get it,' said Jamie, his head appearing in the gap between the two front seats. 'If you don't know this area, what's with all the directions?'

Mac gave a troubled sigh. Something was happening here that he was clearly grappling to make sense of.

'The road splits up ahead. Keep to the left,' he said, shaking his head as though even he couldn't believe what he was about to say. 'I've never been here in daylight,' he added. 'But last summer, after my transplant, I went through a period of insomnia that I tried to cure by driving around in the middle of the night.'

I inhaled sharply, suddenly remembering the conversation we'd had. 'You told me you kept ending up at the same place. It was by a pier, wasn't it?'

Mac looked like a man who could no longer trust everything he knew to be true.

'Those drawings in your flat – the ones of the pier in the middle of a raging storm,' I said quietly, my eyes going to the rolling grey clouds above us and the lightning forking across the sky, 'they were of today, weren't they?'

In reply, Mac simply shook his head, not in denial but in disbelief.

'Mac!' I gasped as the road curved around, because although I'd definitely never been there before, I recognised where we were from Mac's sketches. 'This is it. This is the place you drew.'

'I am officially freaked out of my fuckin' mind,' said Jamie. 'What the hell is going on here?'

Mac shook his head. It appeared to be his default reflex. 'I think this might be where Connor was heading,' he admitted. 'Although how I knew that nine months ago, I have no idea.'

There was a small designated parking area that I pulled into, leaving the car skewed at an angle across two bays. Not that it mattered, because no one else was there. It wasn't exactly a walking-along-the-seafront sort of day.

We jumped out and set off briskly in the direction of the pier. It was probably a bustling tourist spot during the summer months, and we passed a sign for a small amusement park, which was obviously closed for the season. The pathway leading to the pier was also cordoned off with a length of yellow and black tape. Tacked onto an adjacent post was a local authority notice, just in case the tape hadn't made it clear enough.

Danger. Pier Closed due to weather conditions.

We paused and exchanged a three-way worried glance. With perfect synchronicity we all ducked beneath the tape and continued down the path. A little further ahead, the amusement park came into view. I paused, clutching at Mac's arm as I remembered an important detail from his drawing.

'Over there,' I cried, having to raise my voice to be heard above the howling wind, which kept trying to hurl my words from me. 'Wasn't there a miniature railway on the pier?'

The penny dropped for all three of us at exactly the same moment. Could that be where Connor was heading?

'Perhaps he'd been here before with Lisa and thought this was the train she was talking about?'

It made a horrible kind of sense. Without saying a word, we switched direction and hurried towards the railway. This time the barricade was more formidable, with a steel gate and a sturdy padlock.

'He couldn't have got past this, could he?' asked Jamie, testing the gate with his shoulder. It didn't budge.

Where is he? I silently asked whichever deity was in charge of lost little boys who were desperately trying to find their mum. *If Connor found the railway closed, where would he have gone?* I tried putting myself inside the head of a child his age and came up with an answer that turned the blood in my veins to ice.

'You don't think he'd have gone onto the jetty, do you?'

Another fork of lightning flashed across the sky, and no one paused long enough to reply. As though a starting pistol had been fired, we headed towards the jetty; within seconds, we were all jogging.

Built in Victorian times, the jetty was a long timber boardwalk, constructed to allow small boats to dock. There was nothing on it today, and if there had been, there was a good chance the sea would have swept them away. Wave after wave crashed and broke against its pillars, sending up enormous flumes of spray.

'What's that?' shouted Mac above the shriek of the wind.

I squinted into the rain, desperately hoping he was mistaken. But his restored vision had spotted something I hadn't noticed: something small and yellow at the very end of the jetty.

'Connor!' For the first time in my life I screamed, but it was all for nothing. He was too far away to hear me. Mac and Jamie added their voices to mine, but the small figure in yellow still didn't turn our way.

He appeared to be walking along the far edge of the jetty. It was hard to run and shout at the same time, but I kept trying. There was a stitch in my side as painful as a knife wound, but I ignored it as I kept on racing towards him. And then my warning shouts turned into a cry of horror as an epic wave crashed against the jetty, engulfing it in water. When the wave washed away, the jetty was empty. Connor was gone.

I ran faster than I'd ever done in my life, vaguely aware of a fast-moving blur on my right. Jamie sprinted past me, his legs pounding like pistons as he overtook Mac, who was already a considerable distance up ahead. I was totally winded, but Jamie still had enough air in his lungs – Lisa's lungs – to keep calling Connor's name as he ran. Without even breaking stride, he shrugged off his jacket, leaving it discarded on the boards. His trainers came next, kicked off impressively as he ran. He teetered to a stop at the very edge of the jetty, fighting against his own momentum to steady himself. He took a moment to glance down into the swirling sea and then bent his knees and jumped cleanly into the water.

Mac and I reached the end of the jetty within seconds of each other. I clung onto his arm, not just for balance but in terror as I stared down into the roiling depths. I could see neither Connor nor Jamie. Mac was already pulling off his own jacket, his intention clear. As terrified as I was for his safety, I knew I would only be seconds behind him if he went in.

And then, through the foam and waves, I saw a head, dark and sleek as a seal. It was Jamie. The water was so turbulent, it seemed impossible that he could even remain afloat, and yet he was managing to tread water without too much difficulty. He executed a 360-degree turn and then took an enormous breath and disappeared beneath the water again.

'I'm going in,' Mac yelled, his shoes already discarded.

'Wait!' I screamed, my voice hoarse with panic. 'I think I can see something. Look!' I'd glimpsed a yellow object bobbing up like a cork among the waves. It was gone just as quickly, only to reappear seconds later. Even from this distance I could read the grim determination on Jamie's face as he surfaced with one arm hooked firmly around Connor's waist. Fighting against the battering waves, he began to swim towards the jetty.

'He's got him!' I cried, dropping to my knees in relief as tears mingled with the rain pouring down my face. But as I followed Jamie's slow progress through the water, I realised the figure in his arms wasn't moving. No! This couldn't be happening. We couldn't have been led to this place only to arrive too late to save him.

Mac was no longer beside me, having swung over the edge of the jetty to climb down the ladder that led to the water. With an arm looped around the jetty's pillar, he leant out at a terrifying angle to narrow the distance between Jamie and dry land. The sea pounded both men, as though determined to claim a life that day, but with superhuman effort Jamie kicked towards the ladder and Mac reached far enough out to pluck Connor from the water.

Mac climbed back up the ladder like a fireman, with an unconscious Connor over his shoulder. There was a horrible boneless quality to Connor as Mac set him gently down on the wooden boards.

'Is he okay? Is he breathing?' cried Jamie, appearing at the top of the ladder and then promptly throwing up an impossible amount of seawater.

I scrabbled on my knees to Connor's side, fighting my raging panic. I knew first aid, it was a requirement of my job, but there was a world of difference between doing mouth-to-mouth on a plastic dummy and resuscitating a real-life child. And this was Connor; a child I loved.

Connor's skin had an inhuman hue, like an alabaster statue, and when I bent my head to his blue-tinged lips I couldn't feel even a whisper of breath against my face. My worst nightmare was coming true.

But then suddenly, from deep within his throat, there came an alien gurgling. 'That's it, Connor,' I urged. 'Breathe. You can do it. Breathe for me, baby.'

Jamie was still coughing up copious amounts of saltwater, and Mac was speaking urgently into his phone, summoning the emergency services.

The wind and the storm seemed to fade away as I leant over Connor's inert form, pleading with him to come back to me. And then, like a miracle, he did.

A raw spasm of coughs racked his little body and I turned his head to one side as he ejected litres of grimy seawater. When he was done, I bundled his shivering frame into my arms.

It was only then that I began to sob. When I looked up, I saw that both Mac and Jamie were also unashamedly crying.

'Mummy?' Connor cried, struggling against me.

'No, sweetheart. It's Molly.'

He twisted in my embrace, straining to look beyond me, back towards the sea. 'Where's Mummy gone? She was in the water with me. She kept pushing me back up.'

I tightened my hold on him. 'No, sweetie, it was Jamie who was in the water with you. He rescued you.'

I turned to face Jamie, overcome with awe and admiration. 'You were amazing, Jamie. A real hero.'

'Said I used to be a lifeguard, didn't I?' he muttered with a nonchalance quite at odds with his violent trembling.

'The ambulance is on its way,' announced Mac, dropping down beside me onto the deck and wrapping his jacket around me and Connor. It was already so wet, it didn't provide much protection, but I appreciated the gesture.

The wind was shrieking so loudly, I wondered if we'd even hear the approaching sirens. It whipped around us, sounding like a voice crying out in despair. It took a moment for me to realise that actually there was a voice, and one I knew. Although I'd never heard such anguish in it before.

'Connor! Connor! Connor!'

I looked up to see Alex racing down the boardwalk towards us.

'I messaged Barbara from the car earlier,' explained Jamie. 'I told her we were heading for the pier.'

'Daddy!' cried Connor against me, and for a tiny moment I hesitated before releasing him into his father's arms.

Alex's words were an indecipherable mumble of shocked relief and a prayer of thanks as he held Connor against his chest. When the boy's spindly arms came up and fastened around his father's back, I sat back on my heels and prepared to stand. Mac's hand was there outstretched to help me, the way I already knew it always would be, through the years ahead of us.

'I'm sorry, Daddy. Are you very angry with me?' whispered Connor.

The sob that came out of Alex sounded as though it had been ripped from him. 'No, no, no,' he cried, rocking his son in his arms, the way I imagined he'd done when Connor was a baby. 'Never. It's me I'm angry with. This is all my fault.'

'I just wanted to see Mummy again. And I did. She said she'd be here today, and she was.'

Alex glanced up with an incredulous expression on his face.

'He thought he saw her when he was in the sea,' I mouthed silently.

Alex nodded grimly, and then stiffened when Connor added, 'But she's gone now. I can't see her any more. Daddy, I think she might have died.' He was crying now – and he wasn't the only one.

'Your mummy *has* gone, Connor. But that doesn't mean she will ever stop loving you. And even though she isn't here with us any more, we still have each other. I'm here, son. I will always be here.'

In the distance the two-tone strains of a siren could finally be heard.

'I love you, Connor,' continued Alex. 'And I'm so sorry I haven't been able to show you how much recently. But I promise I'm going to do better from now on.'

'I love you too, Daddy,' Connor said, his eyes going one last time to the tumultuous sea. 'To the moon and back.'

CHAPTER FORTY-FOUR

Alex

Five months later

'Bride or groom?'

'Erm… both?' Alex replied with a confused shrug.

'No problem,' assured the usher in his thick Scottish accent. 'Just sit wherever you like.' He passed Alex a thick vellum order of service from the stack he was holding and turned to greet the next guests.

Two steps down the aisle a small tug on his sleeve brought Alex to a halt.

'Do you have to tell them which one you like best? Because my favourite's Molly.'

Alex did his best to suppress his smile. Bending low, he whispered confidentially into Connor's ear, 'Me too.' He ran a hand affectionately over Connor's hair, absently noticing there was far less to ruffle these days. His mission to be a better parent had included quite a few things Connor probably wished had remained overlooked, including trips to the dentist and the barber.

'Can we sit here?' asked Connor, pointing to a pew at the very back of the church. It wouldn't give them the best view of the ceremony, but Alex could see the attraction. Sunlight was streaming through an elaborate stained-glass window, bathing the pew in a psychedelic palette of greens and blues.

'Wherever you like,' he said.

Connor slid happily onto the seat, positioning himself beneath the arc of light. A woman Alex didn't know turned around in her pew to watch his son's childish delight. Her smile faltered slightly when she heard Connor observe, 'It's like the aurora borealis, isn't it?'

Alex laughed softly, knowing how much Lisa would have enjoyed that comment and the look on the stranger's face. Connor was still very much his mother's son.

The church Mac and Molly had chosen was old and quint-essentially English. Everything about it was perfect, from its flagstoned aisle, worn smooth from centuries of worshippers' feet, to the garlands of flowers hanging in swags along the pews. Alex breathed in their scent and his senses tripped, spiralling him back in time to a different church, where the flowers hadn't been gathered into garlands but woven into wreaths.

In his head he heard an echo of Todd voicing his concern. 'Are you sure you're up to it?' his brother had asked, looking down at the silver-edged invitation Alex had received.

'Sooner or later I'm going to have to set foot inside a church again,' Alex had said.

'Actually, I meant are you going to be okay seeing Molly getting married to someone else? I know you had... feelings for her.'

'They weren't real,' Alex replied. 'I see that now. I just got confused for a while, but Molly's heart found its own way home. She and Mac make a great couple.'

There was a big fat 'I told you so' on his brother's face. 'Well, thank God you finally came to your senses and dropped all that *Twilight Zone* rubbish.'

Alex had nodded, knowing that was what it would take to stop Todd worrying about him. But that wasn't how Alex really felt – or had done since the day of the storm.

He dreamt about it less now. But it was still there, buried deep in the darkest, most fearful corner of his mind. On the nights it came back, he would wake with a gasp, the bedsheets tangled around his thrashing legs. In the nightmares he was always running but never quite managed to get to the end of the jetty in time. He was forever too late to reach Connor's side. You didn't need to be a psychoanalyst to interpret the meaning of those dreams.

'Oh look, there's Barbara,' Connor exclaimed, snapping Alex back to the present. His son climbed onto a hassock and began waving wildly at their friend, as though signalling a plane to land. It might not have been church-appropriate behaviour, but it was wonderfully normal for a seven-year-old boy. Alex took advantage of their location and offered up a silent prayer of thanks.

Barbara had snagged a pew near the altar, and even though she was some distance away, her fuchsia-pink ensemble dazzled in the shadowy church. She'd dressed for the occasion, and her hat was truly an Ascot-worthy creation of feathers and flowers, and quite likely to take out the eye of whoever was sitting beside her. Who was that sitting next to her, Alex wondered, as Barbara tapped her companion's arm and directed his attention towards Alex and Connor.

His mouth dropped in an O of surprise as he recognised his neighbour. Graham Grafton gave a military-style salute in greeting, and ridiculously Alex saluted back – though his was more Boy Scout than army. *Well, well, well*, he thought, allowing himself a small grin.

The church was starting to fill up now, and over the heads of a great many strangers Alex spotted another face he recognised, although admittedly Jamie was almost unrecognisable today in a smart suit and tie. He waved at Connor and Alex and then returned to his task of setting up a tripod and what appeared to be a very professional digital camera. Was wedding photographer yet another of Jamie's former professions? After what had happened on the jetty, Alex would never doubt him again.

As his gaze continued to travel along the rows of guests, Alex was unprepared for the stomach-lurching shock when Connor excitedly cried out, 'Look, it's Mummy.'

To his embarrassment, Alex looked first towards the doors of the church before realising that Connor was actually staring at the back page of the order of service. Feeling disorientated and more than a little foolish, he gently took the pamphlet from Connor's fingers. The back page held two black and white photographs. The first was of an elderly man Alex didn't recognise, and the second was a photograph Dee had taken of Lisa on their last family Christmas together. At the top of the page, in large, looping script, were the words: *Loved ones who couldn't be with us today.* Beneath the first picture was the caption: *Henry – father of the bride.* Below the second it said: *Lisa – the friend who brought us together.*

It was a lovely touch, and Alex stared at the photograph for a very long time. This was always going to be an unusual wedding. Mac's 'best person' was his old university friend Andi, who'd organised a stag do that had likely caused permanent liver damage in all who had attended. Rather than having traditional hymns for the ceremony, Molly and Mac had opted for jazz classics instead. It was a charming homage to Molly's dad, and even though Alex hadn't seen the front pew, he knew Molly had arranged for an order of service to be placed on the seat her dad would have occupied, along with his old reading glasses, 'because he never could see a thing without them'.

Perhaps that's how it should be, Alex thought. *We should always include the people we've lost in our everyday lives.* It was what he'd been trying to do for the last five months. He and Connor now took turns wearing Lisa's old apron when cooking their dinner.

They listened to her favourite music all the time, and Alex mentioned her as often as possible in their conversations. These days Connor shared his love of astronomy with his dad, and together they sat in the garden, looking through the lens of Lisa's precious telescope. 'That's where Mummy is now,' Connor had told him on more than one occasion. 'She's looking down on us from the stars.' Alex agreed. And it made it a little easier when he finally took Connor to the place where Lisa lay.

'Hi, Mummy. It's me,' Connor had whispered, his finger tracing the inscription on the carved marble headstone. *Wife and Mummy.*

'Sorry it took me so long, babe,' Alex had apologised when Connor had scampered off to pick wild daisies for her plot. 'You know me – I don't always get it right first time.' He watched with a smile as Connor ran back with an armful of what he suspected were colourful weeds. 'But I'm doing better now – we both are. You can relax. I think I've got this.'

He'd come a long way since the day he'd shakily signed the organ-donation forms. He'd wasted so much time looking for answers in places they were never going to be found. And yet as hard as he'd looked, he'd never worked out the real reason why it was these four individuals who Lisa had saved. It was like a piece of abstract art. He'd been standing too close to it to make out what it was meant to be. It was only when he stepped back, when he looked at it from a distance, that he'd finally understood.

It had all been about the day of the storm, the day when they'd nearly lost Connor.

If Barbara had never received her kidney transplant, their paths would never have crossed. She wouldn't have bought Connor the kitten, a kitten that so incensed their neighbour, he set up a surveillance device. A device that had been of vital assistance in the search for Connor.

If Mac hadn't received Lisa's corneas, he wouldn't have been in the car that day, deciphering the sounds on a recording that no one else could make out. Nor would he have spotted Connor at the end of the jetty.

And if Lisa's lungs had gone to someone else, then a young man with a tendency to exaggerate, but who occasionally told the truth, wouldn't have been able to race along the jetty and jump into the sea to save Connor from drowning.

'In a way, they all rescued him,' Dee had said, overcome with emotion at how close they'd come to losing another member of their small family.

'Great theory,' Todd had countered, 'but it's flawed. What's Molly's role in all this? Who does she save?'

Alex said nothing, because in his heart he knew Dee was only partly right. It wasn't the group who'd rescued his son, it was the woman whose death had allowed them to do so. The person who'd really saved Connor was Lisa, his mum.

The final strains of 'Feeling Good' faded away, and the church fell silent. All eyes were turned towards the closed vestibule doors, waiting for the moment when Molly would walk up the aisle with her mother, who'd be giving her daughter away.

'Bloody hell, that was close,' said an out-of-breath voice beside him.

Alex spun around, momentarily blinded by the light from the stained-glass window. Through a rainbow of colours, he saw a tall, blond-haired, young woman standing at the end of their pew. She was beautiful, and backlit by the light from the window appeared almost ethereal, as though not quite of this world.

Something indefinable kicked within him.

'That was scarily tight. I had to peg it all the way from the car park. Molly would have absolutely slayed me if I'd missed her wedding.'

'You're just in time,' Alex whispered, and strangely it felt as though he wasn't only talking about the ceremony.

'Do you mind if I squeeze in here on the end?' she asked, already doing so.

Truthfully, Alex didn't mind. Not at all. He inched up and she slid in beside him.

A buzz of excitement filled the church and from the bustle of activity by the doors, Alex guessed that Molly was about to make her big entrance. Every head was turned towards the back of the church, but Alex found it impossible to look away from the woman beside him. Her smile was dazzling, and deep within him a tiny spark flickered into existence.

'I should probably introduce myself,' the woman said, as the song Molly had chosen to accompany her passage down the aisle began to play.

She held out a slim-fingered, tanned hand.

The doors swung open as Etta James's unmistakable voice filled the church, singing the haunting opening lines of her greatest hit. 'At last…'

'I'm Kyra,' the woman whispered.

'Alex,' he replied.

A LETTER FROM DANI

I want to begin by saying a huge thank you for choosing to read *Gone Too Soon*. Books are like your children – you're not supposed to have favourites – but I don't mind admitting this one really stole my heart.

If you enjoyed it and want to keep up to date with all my latest releases, just sign up at the following link. Your email address will never be shared and you can unsubscribe at any time.

www.bookouture.com/dani-atkins

At its heart *Gone Too Soon* is a love story, which might sound strange for it opens with a devastating tragedy that tears a young family apart. When we first meet Lisa, Alex, and their son Connor it's the morning of the last day they will ever spend together. And while *Gone Too Soon* is a book about rebuilding your life and finding a way through the grief of losing someone you love, it's also about discovering that sometimes the love you had isn't lost at all. Sometimes it finds its way back to you.

I wanted to write a story about heroes – not the kind who run into burning buildings, but the kind who save thousands of lives across the world every single year. These heroes are the people who carry an organ donor card, and their brave families who at their very darkest hour find the courage to help others.

Gone Too Soon brings together an eclectic group of people who find unexpected friendships, new families, and love, in a way they'd never imagined. I loved meeting these people and seeing how one selfless heroic act could change so many lives for the better, and how the universe has a strange way of repaying every good deed.

2020 felt like the right year to write this book, as the law surrounding organ donation in the UK has now changed. This isn't the first time I've written about this topic, as it has popped up in several of my books. Perhaps unknowingly I've been mapping out the lives of Alex, Lisa, and Connor and the four incredible strangers they meet for a very long time.

I hope you enjoy the book, that you laugh and cry with the characters, and fall a little bit in love with them, as I did when writing it.

I love hearing from my readers. You can get in touch on my Facebook page or on Twitter. Thank you!

Stay safe and stay well.

Warmest best wishes to you and yours,
Dani xx

DaniAtkinsAuthor

@AtkinsDani

ACKNOWLEDGEMENTS

Writing acknowledgements is hard. First there's the fear of leaving someone out. But even worse is knowing the time has come to say a final goodbye to the people who have been living in your head for a very long time.

So somewhat unusually I'm going to start by thanking Alex, Lisa, Connor, Molly, Mac, Barbara and Jamie for the hours we've shared; for the sleep you've made me lose; and for the tears and the laughter. I might not always have been sure where we were going on our journey, but I'm very pleased with where we ended up. I'm going to miss you.

This felt like an important year to write a book that featured organ donation. In May of 2020 the law on organ donation in England changed to an opt-out system in order to help save and improve more lives. Full details can be found on the NHS Blood and Transplant website. This has been my go-to reference for research and to read the many inspiring stories of both recipients and donor families. I would like to use this space to thank every single family who bravely gave their consent for a loved one's organs to be donated. The donors and their families are true heroes.

2020 has been a very strange year for us all. When things seemed bleak and almost unbelievable, thank goodness there were books around to help us to escape the madness. I'm sure I am not alone in saying I've read more this year than ever before. And to its immense credit the publishing industry hasn't skipped a beat. So I'd like to thank every single publishing house – not just mine – for keeping the books coming and giving us a virtual passport to escape.

Head of Zeus, my UK publishing home, have been of tremendous support and this book would not be what it is today without the invaluable guidance of my editor Laura Palmer and her incredible team. Thanks too to everyone in publicity, marketing, sales and a special thank you to Debbie Clement for designing what I believe is a truly gorgeous cover.

Thanks too to Kathryn Taussig and the team at Bookouture for their enthusiasm and support for *A Million Dreams*. I'm very happy to have been welcomed so warmly into the Bookouture family.

Kate Burke at Blake Friedmann has been my agent from the very beginning of my writing career and the idea of doing any of this without her is simply unthinkable. You're stuck with me for a very long time, Kate.

I have made many wonderful friends in the publishing world – almost too many to name here – but there is a small group that no acknowledgements would be complete without. Thank you Kate Thompson, Fiona Ford, Sasha Wagstaff, and Faith Bleasdale. I have really missed our 'office' outings and although Zoom is great, I can't wait until normal service is resumed.

There are so many authors I have missed seeing this year that when all of this is finally over I doubt any of us will have time to write books – we'll be too busy catching up. Paige Toon, Kate Riordan, Holly Hepburn, Catherine Isaac, Heidi Swain, Milly Johnson, Alice Peterson, Kate Furnivall, Juliet Ashton, Penny Parkes, Anstey Harris, Iona Grey, Isabelle Broom, Gill Paul, I really hope to see you all again, very soon.

Thanks have to go to two of my best friends Hazel Davies and Debbie Keyworth for being the first readers of this book (and, fair warning, for all the others I've yet to write).

To all my friends, who have been with me on this journey, thank you for your love and support, with a special shout out to Sheila, Kim, Christine and Barb.

Thanks also goes to the mum of my good friend, Bev. Having read all my books, Bev confided that her mum would love it if I named a character in my next one after her. So here you go, Barbara, thank you for lending me your name. I hope you love your namesake in this book as much I do.

Thank you to everyone who has read one of my books and taken the time to leave a review or to message me to say how much you enjoyed it. You make me want to write the next one.

On a very personal note I would like to use this page to offer a special message of gratitude to our incredible NHS. Just weeks after completing this book I had a health emergency. Life felt very much as though it was imitating art to find myself blue-lighted to hospital and ending up in a cardiac unit. Thanks to the magnificent care I received I was soon back home again. And even though this incident might never find its way into any of my books, it will stay with me for a very long time. Thank you, NHS.

And lastly, to the three people who are my sun, stars and entire universe. Ralph, Kimberley and Luke… I couldn't do any of this without you.

Dani Atkins
October 2020